Alembical 2

a distillation of three novellas

I hope you enjoy
these stories,
J. Kathleen Cheney

Alembical 2

a distillation of three novellas

edited by
Arthur Dorrance and Lawrence M. Schoen

Alembical 2© 2010 by Paper Golem LLC
    Introduction © 2010 by Walter H. Hunt
    The Paragon Lure© 2010 by Tony Pi
    Second Chance © 2010 by David D. Levine
    Iron Shoes © 2010 by J. Kathleen Cheney

Tubes—a photograph by Rebecca Sennett—is used here with her permission.

Published by Paper Golem LLC
1049 Union Meeting Road
Blue Bell, PA 19422 USA

http://www.papergolem.com

Cover Art by Rebecca Sennett
Book Design by Lawrence M. Schoen

ISBN   Hard Cover   978-0-9795349-7-3   0-9795349-7-6
           Soft Cover   978-0-9795349-8-0   0-9795349-8-4

Paper Golem

for Jay,
who inspires

INTRODUCTION

Lawrence has invited me to write an introduction to this excellent collection of novellas, an honor which I greatly appreciate, and for which I trust I am adequately prepared. What did he want? Oh, nothing complicated: "general thoughts on the art of the novella (perhaps some of your own insights gained from trying to write to that length after a career as a novelist), hints at common threads that you feel tie the three disparate novellas together, and maybe some musings on the rising state of the small press as meeting the needs of a previously under-served niche." As usual, the good Doctor asks much, but expects much of those whom he respects.

So, to business. I would like to dispose of the last item first - musings on the rising state of the small press. We live in a tremendous age in the publishing industry; there was a time not too long ago where an effort of the sort you hold in your hands would have been impractical, perhaps impossible, but technical advances and improvements in distribution, including the advent of the World Wide Web (some *advent*: it's been around long enough to vote in most states, though not long enough to drink—but that's a discussion for another time) have allowed entrepreneurs to bring works such as *Alembical* to market. I hope to write something for it in the future.

And that leads me back to the first and second items. I am a novelist; I came to the art without the normal intermediate step of shorter fiction, plunging instead into the deeper pool of the novel from the beginning of my professional career. I am more of a reader of novels than of shorter fiction as well, though I have numerous well-thumbed books on my shelf from such stellar authors as Zelazny, Bradbury, and Clarke that show beyond doubt how much you can accomplish in a relatively small number of words. As a reader I can only wonder; as a writer I feel daunted. Even the more expansive form of the novella is challenging; there's a need to *get right to it* and *not be distracted* and to avoid unnecessary *woolgathering*, or whatever an editor of novellas might say to a prospective author (like me!) when the finish line is at 20,000 words instead of 100,000 or more. Reading the three stories in this volume in preparation to assay this introduction reminded me again of the skills that will be required for a work of my own to some day fit within its covers.

The three stories—Tony Pi's *The Paragon Lure*, J. Kathleen Cheney's *Iron Shoes*, and David D. Levine's *Second Chance*—seem at the outset to be quite different. In *Paragon*, we are dropped into the world of antiques and auctions, but like Ian MacShane's *Lovejoy*, it's a good deal more complicated: indeed, in the modern-day London setting, there is a considerable aspect of the supernatural which feels… natural. In *Iron Shoes*, we are in early twentieth-century Saratoga Springs, where the author gives us an entirely novel turn on the widow/mortgage/high-stakes horse race trope, with excellent results. Finally, *Second Chance* takes us to the near future and an expedition to Tau Ceti, where the setting provides dramatic backdrop to a set of social interactions.

What do they have in common? I thought about this for a while, and it finally occurred to me—these stories are all about *time*. In *Paragon*, the long-lived rivals and friends harken back to an earlier period: Shakespeare's England, where we catch a look at the mighty Queen Elizabeth. *Iron Shoes* reminds us that in an era when automobiles were beginning to replace horse-drawn buggies, there might still be some of the Fair Folk around; it's best to placate them, and to listen to those who can weave charms and possess the Second Sight. *Second Chance* lacks the supernatural that appears in the earlier two stories, but it, too, is about time—the lapse of years since the probe was launched, the time in the past at which transmissions ceased from Earth, the youth of the crew of *Cassiopeia* compared to the older people they had been before the mission. Time, in this case, must heal all wounds.

This conclusion also resonated with my earlier thoughts about the form of the novella. Any novella must grapple with time: how much can the author cover between beginning and end? How much can be devoted to plot, to character, to exposition? In each story in this volume, the writer is necessarily required to provide some background information—Felix Lea's background motivations in *Paragon*, Imogen Hawkes' ancestry in *Iron Shoes*, the characters' previous history in *Second Chance*. The reader is not presumed to know anything about the auction business and Elizabeth's England, or horse racing and turn-of-the-century New York, or stellar exploration and spaceship technology. All of this framework, like the sets for a stage play, must be artfully arranged and set in place by the author. And he, or she, has to do this convincingly, entertainingly, and—most important—*quickly*: because there just isn't enough *time*.

I read the stories with care (and with interest), but it still took me only a few hours to get through them. I feel that any of those three worlds are places I'd gladly visit again, but the story told within each one is complete and satisfying. And in the end I'm still not completely sure *how they did it* in the small amount of time.

I hope that your experience with the work and worlds of these three fine writers is as enjoyable as mine has been. Lawrence has found three fine stories that will captivate and entertain you, and make their time yours while you dwell within. There is no greater challenge for a writer, and no greater pleasure to see it fulfilled.

Walter H. Hunt
Bellingham, MA
January 2010

The Paragon Lure
Tony Pi

i.

Even master thieves needed time off, and for me it was Tuesday nights, when I'd push aside blueprints and guard rotations to play darts down at the Three Squires Pub. Thomas Thickett, my partner-in-crime, knew well enough not to interrupt my evening except in a true emergency. So when he burst through the doors, waving a white booklet to catch my attention, I took a breather from my dart game and beckoned him to a quiet corner of the pub.

"You said to tell you straight away if I ever came across something on your list, Guv," Thicks said, huffing. "You'll want to see Lots Seven, Eleven, and Thirteen. I earmarked them for you."

"Thanks." I didn't mind Thicks calling me *Guv*, a relic of his cabbie days. Usually used to address a fare, the word might seem impersonal at first, but I often had to take an alias on the spur of the moment, and a term like *Guv* lessened the chances of him calling me by the wrong name at the wrong time.

I took the booklet from Thicks, an auction catalogue from Winters Auction House for a collection called *The Romance of Myths and Jewels*. The cover photo showed the silhouette of a woman wearing a golden earring set with an exquisite half-pearl. My breath caught in my throat. Could it be the other half of Cleopatra's Pearl?

I held the catalogue under better light and flipped it open to Lot Seven, smoothing out the page's folded corner. There was a close-up of the earring on the cover.

LOT 7
14K GOLD AND PEARL PENDANT-EARRING, 'CLEOPATRA'S PEARL', circa 1st century BC
40,000–50,000 GBP
DESCRIPTION
    A single drop-shaped white half-pearl measuring approximately 37 by 22 mm, set in 14K gold.
CATALOGUE NOTE
    Cleopatra once possessed two of the largest pearls in the ancient world. Pliny the Elder tells of the tale that she wagered Mark Antony

that she could spend ten million *sesterces* on a meal, and dissolved one of her pearl earrings in a cup of wine vinegar. The other, split in two, had been made into earrings for the statue of Venus at the Parthenon in Rome. This earring may be one of the two lost halves of Cleopatra's Pearl.

Accompanied by SSEF report no. 101007 stating that the pearl was found to be natural.

The earring in the photograph could well be sister to the one I stole four hundred years ago from Bee.

The man I had been playing darts with, a bespectacled middle-aged gent with a mischievous grin, joined us. "What about our game, Felix? Ready to forfeit?"

"Hardly." Hell, I *invented* darts in the fourteenth century. I designed the hand-eye coordination in this body to be damn near flawless: hitting the mark and winning the game would be mere reflex. "Hal, meet Thomas Thickett, a business associate of mine. Thicks, this is Doctor Hal Russell, Head Curator of the Ancient Egypt and Sudan Department at the British Museum."

"Call me Thicks, Doc," said Thickett as they shook hands. If Hal had known what Thicks did for a living these days, he might have reconsidered it. Every good thief needed a trustworthy fence, and Thicks was mine. But to simply label Thicks a fence was like calling a surgeon a butcher. A London cabbie in his younger days, he stumbled into the fencing business and found a talent for it. Now in his early fifties, Thicks was one of the top 'fixers' in Europe. With countless contacts in both legitimate and black-market trades, he could arrange to buy, sell, smuggle or forge anything with an impressive turn-around time.

Hal, on the other hand, was a mark turned friend. I had befriended him to discover flaws in current BM security, and to Hal I was Felix Lea, art dealer and proprietor of the Arlequim Gallery in Mayfair. But as I got to know Hal over the past few months, he impressed me with his charity, his passion for his job, and his unparalleled memory for obscure historical trivia. Now, I no longer had the heart to rob him.

"My word, a new catalogue from Winters London!" Hal glanced at the page. "Cleopatra's Pearl? Absurd. There's no way to confirm the authenticity of such an earring. That's why Winters will never be another Sotheby's or Christie's. Only fools fall for their outrageous claims."

Fools or immortals, I added silently, though sometimes it was hard to tell them apart.

"Oh, I don't know," said Thicks, returning from the bar with a pint of Guinness. "Who doesn't love a good story to go with their toys?"

Hal shrugged. "You're a hopeless romantic. Go ahead, pay an exorbitant sum for a provenance that can't be proven. Fools and their money are soon parted."

"People want to believe in myths and legends," I said. "Let them. It does no harm."

Thicks reached over and flipped the page to Lot Eleven. "Here's another."

It was a familiar gold funereal mask, another treasure I thought had been lost with Bee's death.

"Now *that* could be authentic," said Hal, straightening his glasses for a closer look. "New Kingdom period, I'd say. Heavens, they claim it's solid gold. Where on Earth did they dig this up?"

"That's what I would like to know." Two pieces from Bee's infamous hoard had somehow found their way to auction. Could the Paragon of Elsinore be among them?

I turned the page to Lot Thirteen.

LOT 13
PLATINUM, DIAMOND AND PEARL PENDANT, 'THE PARAGON OF ELSINORE', circa 1897
50,000–60,000 GBP
DESCRIPTION

Decorated at the centre with a white pearl measuring approximately 34 mm within a stylised platinum spiral conch design set with cushion-shaped, single-cut and rose diamonds on a later chain, length: 445 mm approximately.
CATALOGUE NOTE

The spectacular spiral shell is attributed to Philip Wolfers (1858-1929), Belgian jeweller and son of Louis Wolfers of Wolfers Frères, Court Jewellers. The pendant, marked with his monogram and the stamp 'ex unique', bears his signature touch of the Art Nouveau theme of metamorphosis.

The flawless pearl nestling untouched in the platinum spiral has a legend of its own. There is a story in theatrical circles that Shakespeare's company, the Lord Chamberlain's Men, performed *Hamlet* on the request of Elizabeth the First near the end of her days. So moved by their performance, the Queen rewarded Shakespeare with a perfect white pearl to secretly replace the stage prop used in the final Act. The Queen's secret pearl—the Paragon of Elsinore— circulated in the theatrical circles until the nineteenth century, when it was lost during a performance of *Hamlet* at Drury Lane by the great tragedian Edmund Kean. At last, the Paragon has finally returned to the world's stage.

Accompanied by SSEF report no. 101008 stating that the pearl was found to be natural.

Hal jabbed his finger at the catalogue note. "There, another preposterous claim with no basis in historical fact. The last Shakespearean play Queen Elizabeth the First would have seen before her death was *A Midsummer Night's Dream*, not *Hamlet!*"

While Hal was usually right about such trivia, he was wrong this time. I had been there on stage in 1603, playing the role of First Gravedigger before Gloriana, the Virgin Queen, and knew too well the secret of the pearl. I didn't correct him, speeding through the rest of the catalogue instead. A few more pieces from Bee's collection appeared in the pages, along with objects connected with one ancient myth or another, such as a bronze minotaur figurine and a bust of Medusa.

"Look here, Guv." Thicks pointed out a notice for a gala this Friday night to showcase the treasures. Items would be available for viewing from Friday to Sunday, but the actual auction would take place Monday evening. "Should we go?"

Assuming these *objets-d'art* were not forgeries, then someone had found Bee's cache and put them on the auction block. Whoever did so might know how alluring the Paragon of Elsinore was to me. Could this be a lure to draw me out of hiding?

"I'm tempted," I admitted.

Hal pulled out a well-worn notebook and jotted down the dates.

"You're going, Hal?" I asked. "I thought you didn't believe the claims they made."

"For the most part, but that funereal mask is another matter. If it happens to be authentic, acquiring it for the Museum would be a coup," Hal said. "I'd have to see it first, of course, and hope the funds in my acquisitions budget are sufficient. Granted, I'd need a miracle to obtain the board's approval by Monday, but no harm in looking, is there?"

"True enough." I would need to make my own verifications that the jewels were genuine. "I'm afraid Thicks and I have a few urgent business details to discuss, Hal. Thanks for the game. See you Friday at Winters, then?"

"Certainly, but what about our dart game?" Hal asked.

I had forgotten completely about it. In my distraction, I had slipped my last dart into my pocket.

In one smooth motion, I drew the dart and whipped it past a couple of startled barflies, nailing the bull's-eye.

Hal stared at the board in disbelief. "You jammy beggar!" he muttered.

"The next round's on Hal!" I shouted to the bartender, and escaped into the night with Thicks.

ii.

After exiting the Three Squires, Thicks asked about the claims in the catalogue. "Was Doctor Russell right about those stories being made up? I mean, I'd love for them to be true."

We headed east down Formosa Street towards my flat on Warrington Crescent, taking in the June evening air as we talked. "My dear Thicks, I wouldn't have put them on my watch-list if I didn't believe the stories were real," I said. "The question is, are these forgeries, or are they truly from Bee's collection?"

"I don't think you've mentioned Bee before, Guv," Thicks said. "Another shape-shifter like you?"

"An old enemy." I recited the list of her infamous historical identities for Thickett's benefit. "She was once Cleopatra, self-styled goddess and pharaoh, schemer and poisoner. As Empress Messalina, she sent those who spurned her to death, and conspired to kill her husband Claudius. Medea, Lucrezia Borgia, Catherine de Médicis. Many I have loved and protected died at her hands."

"Not a woman to cross, then," Thicks said, nudging me with an elbow. "So it really could be Cleopatra's Pearl?"

"There's one way to find out," I replied. "I stole the matching earring four hundred years ago, and still have it." Thicks nodded, but cast a nervous glance over his shoulder.

I turned and looked down the street. Nothing seemed out of the ordinary. "Something wrong?"

Thicks loosened his collar. "Just nerves."

We turned onto Warrington Crescent, where the white stucco façades marked the transition from Maida Vale to Little Venice. Admittedly, I chose this neighbourhood because of the name, in honour of the fond memories I had of the real Venice. It was also close enough for me to walk to my gallery in Mayfair if I chose. An entire row of homes— dubbed Hathersage Mews as a tribute to my birthplace—belonged to me under different aliases.

I unlocked the door to my flat, disengaged the alarm, and preceded Thicks to the den, the nerve-centre of our operations. I opened the safe behind the painting of Sherwood Forest and retrieved my half of Cleopatra's Pearl from a small jewel box in the back.

I joined Thicks by the desk lamp and compared the earring with the one in the catalogue.

Thickett's eyes widened. "They're two of a kind."

"On the surface, yes. But to be absolutely certain, I need to compare the cut side." I held the half-pearl with its inside exposed. "Every pearl's unique. The layers of nacre deposited around the nucleus are as individual as a fingerprint or the age-ring cross-section of a tree. If they are halves of the same pearl, a simple comparison of the growth rings will prove it."

"I see. But why's it so important to know if they're a match?" Thicks asked.

"For one thing, both halves of Cleopatra's Pearl belong together," I said. "For another, if these are from Bee's cache, then I want to know who has the rest. There's more to her treasures than the ones being auctioned off. Her da Vinci painting, for one, her gold and diamonds for another. If I could lay my hands on those, I intend to return the art to the public and donate all moneys to charity. That's the only way to wash the blood off those spoils."

"Wouldn't she still have it?" Thicks asked.

"She's long dead," I replied. "During the Second World War, she had been a secret advisor to Hitler on matters of the occult. In 1943, I watched her die the death she deserved." I gazed at the lustre of the earring in my hand and remembered the flames and her screams.

"If there's anything I learned from you, Guv, is not to trust my eyes," Thicks replied.

"There's a sliver of a chance she survived," I admitted. "If Bee had access to a piece of amber, she might have used the healing power of Lightning within to escape death." I left unsaid the obvious truth: if Bee lived, she would surely thirst for revenge. The auction could be a trap to catch or kill me.

"What about this Polygon of Elsinore?" Thicks asked. "How will you know that's the real thing?"

I held back a chuckle at his error and corrected him. "*Paragon*. It's a double-entendre: a paragon is someone or something that's the best example of its kind, but it also means a grand pearl that's a perfect sphere. I'll know it by its Lightning."

My explanation confused Thicks. "Wait, Guv. Lightning's what you lot use to change shapes, right?" he asked. "I thought you used only amber and silk."

"You're right, amber and silk are the two primary sources of Lightning trusted by the Elect," I said. I paused, wondering how to explain pearls, or even honey. "Ultimately, Lightning comes from insects. Amber preserves and amplifies the Lightning from a dead insect over millennia, whereas silk comes from the cocoons after the silkworms inside are killed by boiling water, the heat from an oven, or a needle. But some pearls also have an insectoid origin."

Thicks scratched his head. "I thought pearls come from grains of sand."

"Few actually grow around sand," I explained. "A pearl is formed when an oyster has an irritant inside its shell. The mollusk would deposit layers of nacre around the irritant, which is sometimes a parasite like a trematode or water mite. Thus, some pearls are in fact tiny sarcophagi for an insect, much like some ambers are."

"So why do you only ever ask for amber and silk?" he asked.

"Because no one among the Elect has figured out how to tap the Lightning inside a pearl yet, or cares to share the knowledge publicly. An Elect can sense pearl Lightning but can't do anything with it. Every such pearl has its own spirit, as it were." I flipped the catalogue open to Lot Thirteen again, remembering the feel of the perfect pearl. "To touch the Paragon of Elsinore is to know the fire and glory of Elizabeth the Virgin Queen. She was a paragon of womanhood, you might say."

"So I've heard. How did you get to meet Q. E. One, Guv?" he asked. "What was she like?"

"Elizabeth was a shrewd and matchless queen, even in her twilight years." I put down the earring and the catalogue and poured two snifters of brandy from the liquor cabinet, offering one to Thicks. Have a seat, my friend, and I'll tell you of my last audience with Good Queen Bess, and why I must know the fate of the Paragon of Elsinore."

"Cheers," Thicks said, sipping from his glass and taking residence on the den's settee.

I settled into my own chair behind the desk, dug deep into my memories, and began my tale.

iii.

During the reign of Queen Elizabeth the First, I had served her initially as Sir Richard Walsingham's best spy, performing missions of dubious morality in the name of England. After the spymaster's death, I decided to remain in England to shadow the actor Robert Armin. Quick-witted and kind, Robert had great sympathy for outcasts like madmen and 'naturals', those who were simple of mind yet wise in their words. His compassion for them burned as bright as Robin of Sherwood's for the poor, and spoke well of his readiness to hear and even accept what sounded mad to a thinking man's ear. And so I revealed to Robert what I was: a thief of shapes who would pay him well to share his face and name.

It took three days to persuade him my words were more than a fool's jest, seven more to convince him he had not gone mad, and twelve to prove I was not the Devil come to hound him. In the end, Robert came to trust that I only had his best interest at heart, and allowed me to take his shape and share his life.

Shadowing Robert Armin turned out to be a mutually beneficial arrangement for the both of us. I saw the world anew through Robert's eyes, and he taught me much about the stage. After all, the better I learned to act, the better a shape-thief I would become. I continued to shadow Robert's rise in the theatre, learning his roles as well as he. In his stead, I joined the Lord Chamberlain's Men as a shareholder in 1599, replacing Will Kemp as Shakespeare's leading comic actor. On occasion, I still took on missions in service to the Queen.

My addition to the troupe did not find favour with another sharer, William Sly. Had it been merely one actor's pride matched against another's, it would have been a fleeting rivalry. But in truth, Sly was also Elect, going by the name Cricket amongst our kind, and we competed for Shakespeare's attention. As Sly, Cricket fancied himself a great stage actor, claiming such roles as Hotspur in *Henry the IV, Part I* and Horatio in *Hamlet* as his own. My study of the licenced fool, on the other hand, inspired Shakespeare to write such parts as Touchstone in *As You Like It*, Feste in *Twelfth Night*, and the Fool in *King Lear*.

My final audience with Queen Elizabeth came on New Year's Day, 1603, in the last days of her reign.

What led to the impromptu performance of *Hamlet* had been Elizabeth's will. The Master of Revels, Edmund Tilney, had engaged the Lord Chamberlain's Men to perform *A Midsummer Night's Dream* before the Queen, at Hampton Court Palace on New Year's Day, 1603. The *Dream* had always been a favourite of mine, abundant with the theme of metamorphosis. Wearing the body of a forty-year-old man, I was too long in the tooth to play the roguish Puck, but the part of Nick Bottom suited me well with its singing parts and the comic transformation into a man with the head of an ass.

While Oberon instructed Puck to undo the mischiefs of the summer's night, I observed Elizabeth from the shadows off-stage. Now in her sixty-ninth year of life and the forty-fourth year of her reign, the Queen showed a certain lethargy I had not seen in her before. Even the ceruse make-up could not hide the wrinkles on her face as well as the painters of the day, who concealed her true age in their portraits.

I pulled aside a young maid assisting with the costumes and asked her about the Queen. "How long has Her Majesty been in this deep melancholy?"

"Since the autumn," she replied with a tinge of sadness mixed with fear in her voice. "She's been oddly silent of late, but none of the fools or courtiers could cheer her."

I thanked her and hastened back to the stage for the beginning of Act Four, knowing my Elizabeth grew sullen at the loss of old friends and the nearness of death. I gave my all to my performance as Bottom, hoping that the play's humour would ease her unspoken sorrow.

At the end of the *Dream*, the courtiers gave thunderous applause, but Elizabeth gave no sign that the play gave her any cheer. All the players bowed before Her Majesty and awaited her words.

"Master Shakespeare, we commend thee and thy players on a performance to remember," said Elizabeth. "But we are in the mood for another. Our courtiers sometimes speak of the play *Hamlet*, and say thou payest tribute to the memory of our fool, Richard Tarlton, in Yorick. Is it true?"

I glanced at William Shakespeare, wondering how he would respond. Will *had* based Yorick on Tarlton, but the homage went no further than a skull and a soliloquy by Hamlet. I, in the role of First Gravedigger, would need speak ill of the old jester, calling him 'a whoreson of a mad fellow' and wishing 'a pestilence on him for a mad rogue'. Furthermore, he saw the Queen's sullen mood as plain as any other, and *Hamlet* was among the darkest of his tragedies. If we performed it, it might send Her Majesty deeper into depression.

Still, only Tarlton in life could draw the Queen from such melancholy. Perhaps Elizabeth needed her licenced fool now, to speak plain to her as he once did.

"It is as you say, Your Majesty. I meant Yorick to be Tarlton," Will replied. "It would be an honour for our company to perform *Hamlet* for your enjoyment. Of course, I must ask the Master of Revels if he has the costumes we need for the play."

It was a shrewd move on Will's part, deferring the final decision to the Master of Revels. The Revels Office demanded only the finest costumes and scenery for the royal performances, and used large quantities of silk of all varieties, from velvet to damask, sarsenet to taffeta and caffa. I borrowed garments often and freely from his wardrobes.

Tilney glared at Will before responding. "Your Grace, the wardrobes and stage props at the palace are best fit for comedies, not for a play such as *Hamlet*. If I might suggest instead *The Merry Wives of Windsor* or *Twelfth Night*—"

"It will be *Hamlet* tonight, Master Tilney," said the Queen. For a moment, her old brisk nature shone like a ray of sunlight through her gloom. "Lush costumes might please the eye, but actors carry the tale. Only a lazy mind needs such embellishments to tell the players apart."

Tilney bowed. "As you will, Your Majesty."

"As for props, Master Shakespeare, what wouldst thou need aside from what thou hast already?" asked the Queen.

"Three foils, two cups, a dagger and a pearl, Your Majesty," answered Will.

"Master Tilney, see to it that the players have what they require, but we shall provide the pearl," said Elizabeth. She summoned the Lord Great Chamberlain to her side. "There is a small jewel-box in our bedchamber, its lid inlaid with a Tudor rose. Fetch it for us."

I nudged Will. "Remember the skulls."

Will turned white as a ghost. "Pray pardon, Your Grace, but we will also need two skulls."

"We are not in the habit of keeping skulls in Hampton Court Palace, Master Shakespeare," said the Queen.

"If I may, Your Majesty, two knight's helms may work in their stead, and engage the court's imagination further," I said.

"A sensible suggestion, Master Armin," agreed the Queen. "Add the helms to the props, Master Tilney."

When the Lord Great Chamberlain returned, Elizabeth plucked a great pearl from her jewel box for all the court to admire. The pearl, perfectly round and lustrous, captivated me. I had never seen its equal.

"A gift from Sir Thomas Gresham," said Elizabeth. "We are glad he chose not to crush this paragon and drink it to our health as he once did with another. Will it do, Master Shakespeare?"

"Verily, Your Grace," said Will, his eyes widening. "You are too kind."

Thus, by royal edict, our company staged *The Tragicall Historie of Hamlet, Prince of Denmarke* that evening of January first 1603, the last play Queen Elizabeth would ever see.

A few players despaired that they had not enough time to prepare for the Danish play. The lines from the earlier performance of *Dream* lingered on their tongues, they moaned, and they would have only three scant hours to fill their stomachs and rehearse their roles in *Hamlet*.

Will Shakespeare chastised them. "Come! Thou art a Lord Chamberlain's Man, each and every one. Let us prove to our beloved Queen that we do not fear dwindling Time, nor falter when our bodies tire. Her Majesty demands it of us, and we will obey."

He left unsaid that our performance might be our last before the ailing Queen, but every man heard what he did not say. Will's speech roused the company's spirits, and we vowed to give the Queen our best.

The longest of Shakespeare's plays, *Hamlet* challenged the company's endurance as the night wore on.

Off-stage, I could not resist a close look at the Queen's pearl. Taking the pearl from the cup on the props table, I marveled at its beauty. My fingertips sensed the ebb and flow of Lightning within, subtle tides in the cloud-white orb.

Will Shakespeare caught sight of me, pinched the pearl from my grasp and ushered me towards the curtain. "Act Five will begin anon, my flap-ear'd Clown. To stage, to stage!"

And so I took to the stage as First Gravedigger, bantering with the Second Gravedigger as we dug imaginary graves. It pained me to sing the lyrics about old age before the Queen, but I kept true to the words.

"But age, with his stealing steps,
Hath claw'd me in his clutch,
And hath shipped me intil the land,
As if I had never been such."

I threw a knight's helm out of the stage-grave, and played through the scene with Richard Burbage as Hamlet and William Sly as Horatio.

The pearl made its debut in the final scene, when King Claudius put the poisoned pearl in Hamlet's victory cup, intending to murder the prince. Instead, tragedy struck when Queen Gertrude drank from the goblet, sealing her own fate. I caught Elizabeth in a moment of rare weakness, wiping away a tear from the corner of her eye.

The death of Hamlet and the arrival of Fortinbras ended the play, casting a cloud of deep gloom over the audience.

Behind the stage, the Master of Revels fretted beside me. "If this ill-conceived play upsets Her Majesty further, the lords will have my head," he muttered.

"Did you not hear Hamlet's soliloquy, Tilney?" I said. "Burbage's performance tonight crowned him as the premiere actor of his generation, and only the deaf would dare call the play tonight anything other than a triumph."

We presented ourselves before the Queen once more, bowing before her. Will Shakespeare knelt before her and held the pearl in his cupped hands. "Your Majesty, the pearl."

Elizabeth gestured for an attendant to take the pearl and return it to her. "The play pleases us, Master Shakespeare," said the Queen. I could hear the sighs of relief from her courtiers. "*Hamlet* is truly a masterpiece. And thou, Master Burbage, thy portrayal of the Prince of Denmark will make thee immortal, of that we have no doubt."

My fellow actors thanked the Queen for her kind words.

"We shall retire for the evening," the Queen announced, and stood. The Court and players bowed again as she left the Great Hall with her attendants.

After her departure, as we prepared to change out of our costumes, a servant approached me. "Master Armin, the Queen wishes a word in private in the Chapel Royal."

"As she commands," I said, giving a slight bow.

Taking me to the Royal Pew of the Chapel Royal, in the section reserved for the monarch, the servant announced me to Elizabeth.

I bowed.

The Queen, standing by the large bay window looking down at the Chapel proper, turned and acknowledged my arrival. In the glow of the candlelight, Elizabeth's white hair seemed to regain a touch of the vibrant red of her youth. In her hands she held a small silk bundle. She thanked her attendant and dismissed him.

"I am at your service, Your Majesty," I said.

"Robert Armin, Sir Flea. For thy years of faithful service and thy masterful portrayals of the wise fool on stage, I grant thee the licence to speak free as Richard Tarlton did so long ago. Thou hast earned it. For tonight, be my jester, and chastise me as a Queen's fool should," she said.

Elizabeth had not used the Royal we, which surprised but convinced me that I had truly been given fool's licence. "As you wish, Your Majesty," I answered.

"Good. Then tell me plain whether my mood today befits me."

"Methinks Your Majesty knows," I said. "The Court worries that you have fallen into a troubling depression, and brought the Lord Chamberlain's Men to cheer you with *A Midsummer Night's Dream*. Instead you demand a play where monarchs and princes die, digging a grave deeper into your melancholy. I daresay you took more delight in worrying the lords and ladies than the play itself. Not that I find fault in that, my good queen. Given the chance, I'd flaunt my authority and put them in the same gloom!"

She contemplated my words. "What thou sayest is I cannot bear this melancholy alone, and so I sought to lessen my own burden by burdening my Court?"

"When pain or hunger ails a newborn, she has no words to speak her needs. By instinct, she mews instead to her mother and distresses all who hear her cry. Yet when instinct must yield to intelligence, the child learns words to speak her woes."

"Thou darest compare me to a child?" asked Elizabeth, anger in her voice.

I recognised her challenge as a test. Did I have the strength of will to admonish a Queen as an all-licenced fool should? "My apologies, my queen. I cannot hear you over that mewling."

Elizabeth calmed. "Thou speakest with Tarlton's voice and reason, Sir Flea. I shall endeavour to learn the words."

"What ails you, Your Majesty?" I asked.

"Time," she answered. "Time steals away my joy. I have lost a great many friends of late, and I hear it calling for me. That is why I have summoned thee, Sir Flea. Before his death, Walsingham told me his suspicions about thy true nature and thy true name. Art thou immortal, John Little of Hathersage?"

The Queen's spymaster had known more about me than I thought. Francis Walsingham died almost thirteen years ago. Had Elizabeth kept my secret for so long, choosing at last to confront me in the twilight of her years?

"What else did Walsingham tell you, my queen?" I asked.

"That thou art more than a thief of precious things. He had seen thee steal the face and flesh of other men, even his own visage, and on occasion change into a giant of a man. He sought out the legends of a changing man loyal to the Crown. In an old manuscript, he found a mention of a man with the power of Proteus in the service of Richard the Lionheart, and it named thee John Little the Flea. Do not worry, Sir Flea. *Video et taceo*. I see and keep silent."

I thought I had destroyed all copies of that scroll long ago. I wondered whether I should admit the truth to the Queen or deny it. Some among my kind would kill to keep our shape-shifting powers hidden, but I was not one of them. I believed Elizabeth, a woman I greatly admired and trusted, would keep her word and take my secret to her grave.

"Indeed, I am John Little of Hathersage, from whence the nickname Flea came," I admitted. "I am a thief of shapes, over four hundred years of age."

I studied her reaction. Elizabeth was a woman of extraordinary intelligence, and had had twelve years to consider Walsingham's suspicions. Would she brand me as a warlock or devil, or accept the impossible? I realised why she met me in the Chapel Royal: a devil would not dare set foot in a holy place.

"So Walsingham had guessed the truth," Elizabeth said.

"Aye, Your Majesty," I said. "We can only live so long in one identity before questions of age and death draw suspicion to us. Among my people, shadowing a man is one way to shed the past and experience life anew. I am Armin's shadow, learning the ways of his mind and world in borrowed flesh, just as I once shadowed Walsingham. In return, I protect and guide them."

A few preferred to roam rather than change shapes, like Locust. Others, like Midge, created novel bodies and invented pasts for them, but such sculpted origins made them eternal outsiders. Some, like Cricket, would find a life tragically cut short and step into their shoes, none the wiser. Most reviled were the shifters who did not hesitate to take a life by force, like Scorpion.

"I would see this marvelous power of yours," she said.

"My Queen, transformation is not a simple matter of will," I explained. "The magic which we call Lightning comes not from within, but from silk and amber."

As though she knew how I would respond, Elizabeth held out the silk bundle in her palm and unfolded it, revealing the pearl from the play and a piece of amber.

"Thou wouldst ask for an amber from Walsingham on each mission, and now I understand why," she said. "I had wondered why thou would always request an imperfect gem, Sir Flea, until I considered your name. The bug within empowers thee, does it not?"

"You are wise, Majesty. Insects are so vital to us that each Elect takes the name of one. Flea, Cricket, Midge."

"The Elect? As in the Chosen?" she asked.

"Yes. The word has acquired that meaning, though originally the name came from the Greek word *elektron*, which means 'amber'," I explained.

"How does it work, this Lightning?"

"Bugs have the natural gift of metamorphosis, like a caterpillar binds itself in silk to become a butterfly. An insect trapped in the amber gives that magic to the gem. When they kill a silkworm for its silk, that same power bleeds into the threads."

"Show me how thou wouldst steal a shape, like mine," she said.

I shook my head. "Alas, Your Grace, I cannot take a woman's shape." There was a rare exception where a man might become a woman, but I decided against mentioning it. "May I?" I asked, indicating the amber in her hand.

She nodded. "Proceed."

I gently took the gem from her, my finger grazing the silk. Even that brief touch told me that the silk held her image in its weave. I held the amber up. A small wasp lay preserved in the midst of bubbles of air.

The power in the amber would allow me to make permanent changes to my whole body, but there was only so much Lightning within each gem. I decided to alter but one significant detail of my appearance, as it would serve the purpose of convincing the Queen.

"A moment, Your Majesty." I closed my eyes and conjured an image of myself with the first finger of my right hand missing up to the knuckle. I had borne that very injury long ago but had regrown the lost digit. Willing the pattern onto the amber, I held my hand for Elizabeth to see. Then, I drew Lightning through the pattern and deleted the finger, suffering through the painful shift.

Elizabeth gasped.

Though the finger was gone, it felt as though I had it still, bone, skin and all, a phantom grafted onto the clean knuckle.

"I'faith! I pray my senses do not deceive me! If this be a mid-winter's dream, then let me not wake," said Elizabeth. A glimmer of hope shone in her eyes.

I realised what the Queen desired. She sought to escape death.

I took a step back. "Your Majesty, do not ask this of me. I cannot teach you the art."

"Dost thou deem me unworthy of immortality?" she asked.

I tried to explain. "My Queen, the power is fickle in whom it chooses. It is not a legacy from father to son or mother to daughter. Neither is it a skill any man or woman could learn. The power comes unbidden to those who would use the gift for good and those who would abuse it."

"And which of those art thou, Flea?" she asked.

"Sometimes both, oft times neither. But I like to believe I am a good man at heart." As I had been summoned to play the Queen's licenced fool, I had an obligation to be stern with Elizabeth as no other man in England dared. "Your Majesty, it is no weakness to fear the spectre of death."

"I do not fear to die."

"Then you are more fool than I," I said. "Every living thing has its end."

She clenched the pearl and silk in a fist. "Even thee? Time waits at my gate, not thine."

"Even I," I admitted. "I might shape away the advancing years, but other deaths await at the tip of an unseen blade, on the edge of an executioner's axe, or a fall from a precipice. Best say the Elect are long-lived than immortal, my good Queen. Even we fear the end."

"Thou sayest the gift is fickle, but there remains a chance I might possess this power?"

"All men aspire to become king, but the crown fits a paltry few," I cautioned.

"Nevertheless, one cannot know failure until one tries," she said. "Teach me, Sir Flea."

As I feared, in telling the Queen, I had given her the hope of eternal life. If I could have given Elizabeth a measure of my powers, I would; she would wield the power well. Only odds were, she would find failure. It had happened before, allies who sought the same chance to escape death, only to fail and accuse me of hoarding the secret. Had Elizabeth the wisdom to understand that some dreams must die?

I sighed. "As you command, Your Grace." I closed my eyes and concentrated on the shape of Robert Armin once again, but whole. Once I had restored my finger, I bowed and presented her with the amber. She took it from me and held it in her right hand, keeping the silk and pearl in her left.

"To open the path to the power, one must sense the Lightning within the amber," I said. "What do you feel when you touch the gem, Your Grace?"

"The amber is warm," she said.

"Hold the amber to the candlelight and gaze at the wasp at its heart," I said. "Though the creature is long dead, will it back to life."

Elizabeth did as I asked and held the gem a-tremble before her. For a long time she stood before the candle-flame regarding the wasp. Her steely meditation upon the amber made beads of sweat rolled down her whitened cheeks.

It was not enough.

"Your Majesty," I said softly. "Pray put the gem down."

"I shall not concede defeat!" she said.

"You must."

"Sir Flea, 'must' is not a word to be uttered in my presence!"

"Then I shall shout it in every hall of the palace, my queen, and hope the echoes of that word reach your ears! If the gift had chosen you, Your Grace, by now the power would have blackened the tips of your fingers with its fire. May I?" I opened my hand for the gem.

The amber tumbled from Elizabeth's hand to the carpeted floor. Her fingers did not bear the telltale signs of Lightning's burn.

"I should have thee whipped for thine insolence, fool," she said.

"Fool as you made me, my queen," I reminded her.

"So my life would ebb to nothing, and the world forget me when I am dust," she whispered. "Would all I have wrought for England be undone?"

I knelt before her. "Never, Your Majesty. Your reign already immortalises the name Elizabeth. So long as I breathe, I will cry your glory from the four corners of the world."

Silence hung between us.

"Had anyone but thee spoken those words, Sir Flea, I would call it a mere boast," she said at last.

"I speak the truth. As I have kept Robin of Sherwood's memory alive, I will do the same for my Queen and Empire," I pledged.

"I believe you," Elizabeth said. She opened her left hand and held forth the pearl and the silk. "I will give thee another legend to recount for eternity, my errant knight. Return this pearl to Master Shakespeare with my blessings. May the Paragon of Elsinore bless his play in my name."

"But Your Majesty, this pearl is too valuable to leave in the hands of players!" I protested.

"Then impress upon Shakespeare that the Paragon must pass from hand to trusted hand *sub rosa*, else doom befalls them," Elizabeth replied.

"A curse? But it is merely a pearl."

"Thou art the hand of my will, Sir Flea." The curl of a smile graced her face for the first time since I came to Court. "I trust thee to make mischief when circumstance warrants."

I understood. "As you wish, Majesty." I received the pearl and the silk from her. As I did, I could not resist a glimpse at the image of her caught in the silk. While I could not take her shape, I could read her pattern. Though I shied from imagining Elizabeth in the nude, I explored the state of her illness through the copy of her flesh in the silk. Alas, the frailty of her silk-ghost told me my Gloriana had but months to live, a revelation that only confirmed what I dreaded.

What startled me was the change in the Paragon of Elsinore. The power within had waxed, echoing the indomitable strength and temper of the Queen. I marveled at the new magic sealed within, tantalizing me with its power and yet denying me. Had Elizabeth, in her attempt to draw Lightning from amber, somehow imbued the Paragon with her essence?

I did not tell her what I sensed in the pearl. I hardly understood it myself.

"I tire," said Elizabeth, her voice weak. "Rise, Sir Flea, and go to thy tasks, my fool."

"As you command." I bowed, holding back a tear of loss. "By your leave, Your Grace."

It was the last time I saw my Elizabeth. She died March twenty-fourth, 1603.

But to this day, I keep her legacy alive.

iv.

At the end of my reminiscence, I leaned back in my chair and thought of Elizabeth.

"Shakespeare and the Queen!" Thicks said. "Brilliant story, Guv. That pearl must mean a lot to you."

I gave a nod. "It does. I do not know how or why, but the Paragon of Elsinore claimed Elizabeth as its mistress that day, preserving her spirit in its lustre. There never will be another like it. I did as she asked and gave the pearl to Will Shakespeare, telling him of the Queen's wishes. And, as Elizabeth commanded, I made the curse real. Once, a young apprentice tried to flee with the pearl, having learned its true worth. I gave him the fright of his life, and made the Paragon mysteriously reappear among Shakespeare's possessions. After two other similar incidents, no one doubted the pearl's curse, and it became a secret legend of the stage, as Elizabeth intended."

"I only know the curse of *Macbeth*," Thicks said. "That your doing, too?"

"No, I had no hand in the curse of the Scottish play," I said. Saying the name of the play in a theatre brought bad luck to the production and everyone in it, except as lines in the play. Deaths on stage and off, falling stage weights, muggings and even actors turning mute had been attributed to the curse. "That, my dear Thicks, remains something even I cannot explain. As for the Paragon of Elsinore, it passed from company to company, protected by the legend of the curse, until Bee stole it from Drury Lane to spite me. If that pearl is the genuine Paragon of Elsinore, I intend to restore its legend, enforcing its curse if need be. I owe it to Elizabeth."

"Sounds fun. I assume you'll steal these pearls?" Thicks asked.

"Steal or buy, I haven't decided yet," I admitted. "Assuming they're genuine, the artifacts would be steals at the listed prices."

Thicks held up a thumb drive. "In any case, I've got the specs on the Winters Auction House and their operations. Looks like an easy mission."

I smiled. Again, Thicks anticipated my needs, even before I knew what they were myself. "Thank you."

I opened a secret panel in my desk, connected the flash drive to a data-port and flicked the concealed switch. The wide mirror on the wall opposite the desk shimmered and transformed into a screen, displaying the files on Winters London. I called up the blueprints for the auction house and a picture of the owner, Kay Winters. Freckled with thinning ginger hair, the fortyish Winters seemed like a kindly English gentleman.

"Unfortunately, there remains one further complication. Kirk Winters is no stranger to me, but a thespian rival of old," I explained. "Meet Cricket, once known as William Sly."

"Him?" Thicks slipped on his reading glasses.

"When I set up the Arlequim Gallery, I familiarised myself with the local art and auction scene, and in the process discovered Cricket," I said. "He intentionally built Winters Auction House on Curtain Road, on the site of the Elizabethan playhouse we knew and loved. As a homage, the new building's design incorporates elements of the old Curtain. I bet Cricket wrote the historical descriptions in the Winters Catalogue."

"So, if an Elect set a trap to lure you out..."

"...then Cricket could be either the mastermind or an unwitting pawn," I said, finishing his thought. "Trust Bee's cache to resurface at an Elect auction house."

"Why does that make my hair stand on end?" Thicks muttered.

"It troubles me as well. Someone among the Elect wants me to play their game." I thought I had left all that behind. The Elect often feuded and engaged each other in intrigues, and I myself had indulged in a few plots of my own. I had a few theories on why we did it. One, it whittled away the boredom of the years. Two, old hatreds died hard. Three, for power. Bee had taken the lives of many I cared for, the last time in 1943 when she had drawn me into another of her games. A woman I loved died because of it. After that final, fateful clash with Bee that ended with her death, I decided to retreat from Elect society, needing time away from my immortal brethren. I had cut all contact with the Elect thereafter, using my abilities to infiltrate and sabotage the German war effort from within. Post World War Two, I lost myself in espionage games.

In the early seventies, anticipating the role that computers would one day play in society, I crafted a new identity, Rafael Sali, a young Italian-American student at the Department of Electrical Engineering and Computer Sciences at the University of Berkeley. Over the following decades, I established myself in Silicon Valley with my company, Magister Security, pioneering the development of such security technologies as integrated alarm and monitor systems, biometrics, intranet and internet security. Even when masquerading as Rafe Sali, I treated myself to the occasional heist. It was on one such caper in the mid-nineties that I first met and befriended Thomas Thickett, and we had worked together ever since. I trusted him enough to let him help me fake Sali's death a couple years ago and craft my new identity as Felix Lea.

"What will you do?" Thicks asked.

Was I ready to come out of hiding? Perhaps, but it reminded me of Robin and the Golden Arrow all over again, when the Sheriff of Nottingham had tried to draw us from the greenwood with an archery contest. Or, Hamlet and *The Mousetrap* to catch the conscience of a king.

I sighed. "Trap or not, I will learn nothing about the current state of Elect affairs if I don't re-establish contact. I think it's time to renew my acquaintance with Cricket and find out all I can about this auction. By hook or by crook, I will have the Paragon of Elsinore."

"I'll arrange a getaway car, then, and restock your arsenal of tricks. By the way, I took the liberty of securing this for the gala on Friday," Thicks said, reaching into a pocket and producing an invitation printed on handmade paper.

"What would I do without you, Thicks? Thank you."

He shrugged. "Just part of my job. G'night, Guv."

"Good night, my friend."

After he left, I resumed my study of Cricket's new face. I sang the Gravedigger's song from *Hamlet* softly to myself to stir up memories of our time together centuries ago. Memory was a funny thing, and for an Elect, even more so. When you lived as long as we did, so many memories competed for attention that the mind often glorified certain details or tucked them away in the subconscious. Just as a song, a scent, or a taste often triggered an old memory in ordinary people, it worked much the same for my kind, but the key difference lay in our affinity for objects.

When the Elect used amber or silk, in addition to drawing Lightning through touch, we also read the psychic patterns imposed on those tools through the same sense. That ability had a mnemonic application as well, as touching an old object linked to a past event sharpened our recollection of that time. Psychics used to call the skill psychometry, but nowadays, to distinguish it from the use of the word in psychology for something else, the ability became known as token-object reading. The Elect often kept such mementos to remind them of times gone by. For instance, Bee's Egyptian funereal mask might have been a token from an old incarnation of hers. I myself kept small mementos, such as the golden arrowhead that remind me of my greenwood days, and the half of Cleopatra's Pearl still in my possession.

Immortals often laid claim to certain talents and disciplines, proclaiming themselves as the best among us. For Cricket and I, the Elizabethan stage had been our battlefield. As rivals, we competed for Shakespeare's best lines. I held the crown as Shakespeare's comic relief, a victory of sorts. Cricket as

Sly could never compete with Richard Burbage for lead roles like Hamlet or Richard the Third, and had to settle for important but secondary characters like Hotspur and Horatio. I suspected he resented me for my greater fame, such as it was. Yet we kept ourselves in each other's good graces, knowing that only one immortal could understand another. Our relationship, marked by an undercurrent of tension, never developed beyond professional courtesy. He faked his own death in 1608, moving to Paris to participate the neo-classical French drama scene. I lost track of Cricket in the seventeen-hundreds, and his current guise as Kirk Winters came as a surprise to me, as his past interests always revolved around theatre. Still, pursuing a single calling for centuries wore on the soul. After all, I could hardly criticise Cricket for trying a new career. Beyond thievery, I myself once dabbled in medicine, espionage, and computer technology. Variety was the spice of lives.

Could Cricket have set the Paragon lure to trap me? Maybe.

It did not escape me that crickets made excellent live bait.

v.

The following morning, I put on a business suit over a silk shirt and tie in preparation for my visit to Winters Auction House. I had not visited Winters in person thus far, to avoid running into Cricket by accident. Usually, I sent Mel Sweeney, my assistant at the Arlequim Gallery, to bid on items on my behalf when a piece at Winters took my fancy. However, the Paragon of Elsinore demanded my personal attention. As a precaution, I slipped two pieces of amber into my trouser pocket, in case I needed to perform an unexpected change. I re-armed the alarm and left Hathersage Mews to take the Tube at Warwick Station.

En route, as I was changing from the Circle Line to the Northern Line at King's Cross Station, I became certain I was being followed.

A not-unattractive woman in her late twenties with straight, dark brown hair, sporting glasses and a taupe suit, had been tailing me since Warwick Station, perhaps earlier. So well-trained in the art she was, I might not have spotted her on an ordinary day. However, my usual caution compounded with the suspicious circumstances of the auction made me acutely aware of the young lady. Scenarios ran rampant in my head. Was she an agent of Bee's, or Bee herself? Perhaps another ancient foe, like Mantis? A student of Cricket's or a new player in the Elect games altogether?

I calmed myself. Like the insect she patterned herself after, Bee was not the kind of woman to do the dirty work herself. She cleaved to the role of the queen, sending agents she named Drones to do her dirty work.

Of course, I could be overreacting. By choosing to return to the world of the Elect, I began thinking like one again, and paranoia was the norm when you were dealing with shape-shifters.

Another thought occurred to me. Could Thickett's strange behaviour after we left the Three Squires be due to the same woman tailing me?

I decided to keep an eye on my mysterious shadow. Changing faces would fail to shake her at this stage. A good tail observed more than the face but also clothes. Adopting a different size might confuse her, but the alteration would render my clothes an uncomfortable fit. Losing the woman in the crowd would change little in the equation, as anyone trying to draw me out of hiding with Bee's cache would expect me to head for Winters London anyway.

Acting oblivious to my tail, I boarded the train on the North Line towards Morden, getting off at Old Street. Strolling down the street, I made a quick call on my cell.

A cheery woman's voice answered the phone. "Arlequim Gallery. Good afternoon."

"Mel, Felix here. Listen, I'm on the trail of a few choice pieces for the gallery, and you know what that means," I said. I cast a backward glance, glimpsing of the woman shadowing me on the other side of the street a block behind.

"Ah, off globe-trotting again, Mister Lea?" she replied.

"Naturally. Once again, I'm not sure when I'll be back. Could you mind the gallery in my absence?" I asked. If I did get drawn into an Elect plot, I might need to leave for locations unknown at a moment's notice.

"Don't you worry, sir," she said. "I have everything under control. Enjoy your trip."

After a brisk walk, I arrived at Winters Auction House on Curtain Road, amid a spate of trendy restaurants and wine bars. At the corner where Curtain Road met Rivington, Winters London occupied a white four-storey building that bore a token resemblance to the architecture of the original playhouse. Cricket had also purchased and annexed several properties adjacent to the main building for storage and transport. According to the schematics, Cricket's renovations several years ago had completely gutted the inside of the original buildings and redesigned them to his specifications.

I took note of the sign for the afternoon's auction, a collection of fine and rare wines. The doorman greeted me and opened the great oaken door for me. Aware that the woman still observed me from down the street, I entered the foyer and wondered if she would follow me in.

I approved of what I saw. A tasteful mix of the modern and the classical, great glass panels stood in stone bases on either side of the main walk, etched with phantasmagorical mythological figures. Two original life-sized marble statues, one of William Shakespeare and one of Christopher Marlowe, stood at either side of the doors into the main auction hall. Cricket spared no expense in the decor, not that he needed to worry about financing it. A careful immortal was also a wealthy immortal. While Winters could not compete with Sotheby's or Christie's in fame or volume of transactions, its elegance and reputation for unique artifacts appealed to a certain subset of the idle rich.

"Good afternoon. I'd like to see Mister Winters, please." I said to the receptionist. "My name is Felix Lea, proprietor of the Arlequim Gallery."

"Oh, the charming one in Mayfair?" asked the woman. "You had that lovely exhibit of Japanese prints last autumn, didn't you? My husband and I simply adored it."

I gave her my card. "That's us."

"Just a moment, Mister Lea." She made a call and spoke to someone, and flashed a smile. "Mister Winters says to send you up. Go down the hallway to your right and take either the lift or the stairs. Fourth floor, end of the hall."

"Thank you." I followed her directions and headed up the stairway. At the top, Cricket waited in the doorway to his office, his face beaming.

"That really you, Flea?" His question boomed throughout the corridor.

I strode the distance and extended my hand. "Alive and well, Crick. Long time no see."

He smirked and pumped my hand. "*Thou flea, thou nit—*"

"*—thou winter-cricket thou!*" I finished the quote. Our favourite line from *The Taming of the Shrew*, the only phrase in Shakespeare's works with both our Elect names, was a fitting way to renew our acquaintance.

"Come in, come in!" He ushered me into his office. Not unexpectedly furnished with antiques, a Victorian-style desk made of cherrywood dominated Cricket's office while books on art and theatre lined the bookshelves. Velvet curtains framed the windows, and the distinctive scents of mint and mango filled the air in this room. Hung on the wall behind the desk was a collection of beautiful masks: a pair of familiar Greek comedy and tragedy faces, a toothed African Dan mask, the white face and blooded lips of a Yorimasa Noh piece, and a pale Venetian plague doctor's mask with its beak-like nose.

"Couldn't resist the allusion to the winter-cricket in your alias, could you?" I asked.

"You're one to talk," he shot back. "Felix Lea? *F. Lea?*"

I shrugged and smiled.

He closed the door and grabbed a chair, pushing it in front of his cluttered desk. "Please, have a seat. My word, Flea, everyone thought you had died! Well, everyone except Mantis. She insists that you've stolen some of the best pieces in her collection over the past few decades."

"Maybe I did take a couple of her things for old time's sake," I admitted.

My oldest living enemy, Mantis had once plagued Robin and me in the greenwood days in the guise of the Sheriff of Nottingham. Back then, of course, she had been a man. When we Elect switched shapes, biological sex remained one variable we could not voluntarily change. However, once in a blue moon, a change would go inexplicably wrong, turning Elect men permanently into women. Since ancient times, our kind named this irreversible metamorphosis the Widowing, as it meant the death of a man's life and the beginning of new life for the woman he had become. Why the opposite change from woman to man failed to happen remained a point of heated philosophical debate amongst the Elect, as well as a source of frustration for those who had been so Widowed. Mantis Widowed in the early years of the twentieth century.

Cricket sank into his black leather chair behind his desk. The masks behind him peered at me over his shoulders. "You disappeared off the face of the Earth. The rumours of your death even made some of the Grubs consider taking your name for their own, but the Imagines cautioned them against it," Cricket said. Insect terminology played a large role in Elect jargon. If you survived a year as a Grub, you became a Nymph. Stay alive for the next hundred years and you earned the title of Imago, joining the ranks of the Imagines. "What brand of mischief have you been indulging in for the past few decades, Flea?"

"Besides tormenting Mantis, you mean? Oh, a little Cold War espionage and the occasional heist," I said, teasing him with slivers of truth, but unwilling to part with all my secrets. I invested many years in the identity Rafe Sali guiding the development of security technology, and consequently had the upper hand in bypassing those systems. Revealing that past would strip me of that advantage.

"Fine, keep the delicious details to yourself," he said. "Lord knows I have my share of secrets. Are you back in the game for good?"

"With a vengeance," I replied. "You know why I've come."

"Bee's cache," Cricket guessed. "I knew when I saw the items up for bid that you'd come for the Paragon, if you were still alive. I suspect many of the Elect thought the same. Whether you'd come to steal or bid for it, however, cost me many nights of sleep."

"Depends," I said. "Who's selling?"

"Ah, there's the rub. I'm not altogether sure," he replied. "Whoever the consignor is, he or she is operating through an agent by the name of Gage Singleton. Singleton's an American with a reputation for ensuring the privacy of his clients, making a good commission on the sales he brokers. Needless to say, some deals fall slightly on the shady side."

I made a mental note to ask Thicks about Singleton, as he had contacts within those circles. "So you know nothing about the seller?"

"Besides an obsessive concern over security, not much," Cricket said. "Singleton's client made some unusual requests regarding the viewing and the auction, insisting on the presence of his personal security team at both. Maybe he knew you'd come after the pearls? In any case, the items up for bid won't arrive until shortly before the viewing, so you can forget about breaking in."

"Can you confirm the authenticity of the Paragon of Elsinore?" I asked.

"Beyond doubt," Cricket answered. "Singleton brought the key pieces for my personal examination. The Paragon might be part of a pendant now, but it's pristine. When I touched it, it still burned with the memories of Elizabeth's Golden Age."

So it might be authentic, after all! "Planning to bid on it yourself?"

Cricket shook his head. "I leave it to you. The only item I want from Bee's cache is the lost da Vinci painting, which was not among the items in the consignment."

I filed the information away. "I find it curious that the owner of Bee's cache is using an American intermediate but choosing Winters London to sell the items," I said. "Why not Sotheby's New York? Why you?" I had my suspicions, but I wanted to hear Cricket's speculations.

"My connection to the Elect, perhaps," he said. "After all, who but the Elect could appreciate the magnificence of the Paragon, or the history of Cleopatra's Pearl? Then again, my usual clientele have a taste for eclectic myths and legends of the past, and money to waste on their indulgences. It might be merely that."

I nodded. "I've been away for too long. Have the power dynamics changed much?"

"Some. The biggest change came with the death of Bee," Cricket said. "The major hives of activity remain Venice, New York City, Cairo and Tokyo, and I doubt that will change for another century or two. Antlion still holds sway over Venice, although he has also extended his reach to Las Vegas. Scarab controls the Middle East with an iron fist, while Mantis retains her domination of worldwide amber mining industries through Adamantis Mining. Moth remains mistress of silk in the East, while Spider continues to play den mother to Grubs and Nymphs. In recent years, only one youngling, Waterstrider, has made a name for himself after turning Imago."

"What's Waterstrider's current instar?" I asked. An instar was the scientific term for an insect's stage of life, an intermediate form between moults in the developmental stage. A recent addition to Elect jargon, we used the word to describe a stable body shape sculpted from amber Lightning, an identity that we intended to live for a significant period of time. Ages ago, instars were called moults.

"Barun Gupta, owner of Grand Orient Pearls, the largest cultured pearl supplier in India. Although he's based out of Hyderabad, he visits London often and has attended auctions at this establishment on several occasions," Cricket said. "He has an interest in both cultured and natural pearls, so you can bet he'll make an appearance at the showing. Know him?"

I shook my head. My path seldom crossed those in the East. "Who else can I expect?"

"Hard to say. Any number of Elect might attend incognito, or none," said Cricket. "Most merely send an agent to represent their interests. You can bet Scarab will have someone present to bid on the Egyptian relics. As for Mantis and Antlion, I doubt they'd come personally."

I shrugged. "They might, if they set the lure for me in the first place."

Cricket sighed. "Flea, there's that ego of yours at work again. Does it always have to be about you? Couldn't a lucky treasure hunter have simply stumbled across Bee's cache?"

"My instincts tell me no. There's one Elect you neglected to mention. Bee."

"You think she's still alive, then?" Cricket asked. "I thought Antlion said she died at your hands."

"He would say that." I looked into the eyes of the plague doctor's mask behind Cricket, but did not elaborate.

Cricket continued to pry. "How did she die? Antlion never went into details."

"Neither will I." Some experiences you lived through but never told another living soul, and Antlion and I came to a mutual agreement regarding that infamous day.

"So be it," Cricket said. "You think Singleton's her Drone?"

I shrugged and stood. "She does prefer to work through agents." Alone among the Elect, Bee knew of a secret honey concoction that could imbue a non-Elect with the power to temporarily change shape, though the formula had its flaws and dangers. She would often tempt loyal servants with such power and name them Drones, making them carry out her plots and assassinations. "Thank you for the chat. Oh, and one more favour, Crick. Keep mum about my return."

"Why should I?" Cricket asked, all smiles. "Mantis alone would pay handsomely to know you're still alive, and where to find you."

"True," I said. "But suppose you sell my identity now, and my enemies hunt me down before your auction. The consignor might have no further need for a trap and pull the items up for bid. Not the best business practice for your auction house, is it?"

My words were enough to give Cricket pause.

He picked up the phone. "Then let's make sure my secretary sends you an invitation to the gala."

With practiced sleight-of-hand, I produced the invitation Thicks gave me. "Way ahead of you, Crick. See you then."

vi.

Stepping out of Cricket's office, I spied two security guards about to enter the lift, and an idea came to mind. If I stole the appearance of one of the men, I could surprise and confront the woman tailing me. The bald guard with the thick black beard had only an inch on my height, having a better shape to steal given my present clothes than his taller, barrel-chested partner.

I called to them to hold the door, hurried in and stood between the two. "Thank you," I said. As I put my hands in my pocket, I grazed the hand of my intended mark with the cuff of my silk shirt. The touch of his skin against the silk sufficed to snatch his shape, though it took concentration to ensure my own pattern did not overwrite the guard's.

The guards exited the lift two levels down, while I continued to the ground floor. Moments before the lift doors opened, I drew Lightning from the silk through the stolen imprint, adopting the face and body of the bald guard. My suit felt tighter, but not unmanageable. I took off my jacket and slung it over my arm before strolling through the foyer and exiting the building.

I glanced around for the mystery woman, and glimpsed her sitting at a table in the window of Café Matisse across the street, watching the entrance to Winters.

I crossed the road and entered the café. The Café Matisse paid tribute to its painter namesake, adopting the same colours and designs as found in Matisse's masterpiece, *The Dessert: Harmony in Red*. The designers did an admirable job of translating the painting into décor, from the wicker-seat chairs to the scarlet tablecloths and wallpaper. Centrepieces of wax fruit and the glass gooseneck bottles of oil and balsamic vinegar reinforced the illusion that we were inside Matisse's painting.

My mystery woman barely acknowledged my entrance, even though I had on the same shoes and trousers. Either she excelled at surveillance and was playing dumb, or she never considered that I could change my appearance. If the latter, then who could she be?

I headed for the gents' room, identified by Henri Matisse's self-portrait on the door. Once out of sight, I dropped the face and donned my jacket again, then returned to the bar and ordered a latté from the barista. As I was waiting, I noticed that the paper serviettes had a Matisse painting on them: *Annelies, White Tulips and Anemones*. I smiled, appreciating their efforts to teach art by stealth.

With cup in hand, I quietly approached the woman's table, but winced when I saw her idly doodling over the art on her serviette with a ballpoint pen.

"Devil-horns and cat-whiskers for Annelies? Have you no respect for art?" I asked.

She turned at the sound of my voice, a look of surprise flashing across her face, but almost as swiftly adopted a professional demeanour and scrunched up the defiled serviette. "It's hardly the real thing."

"Appreciate beauty wherever it's found. I do," I said. "Mind if I sit?"

"Not at all, Lea," she replied. "I've been meaning to speak to you." She had an angelic glow to her face, and the corners of her lips curled in the hint of a fiery smile despite herself. Fit, not dainty, she would likely hold her own if it came to a fight. In another time, another place, I might have flirted with her, despite her being a touch stalker-ish. Still, I couldn't shake the feeling that I already knew her from somewhere.

I settled in the chair across from her. "I'm afraid you have the advantage of me, Miss...?"

"Detective Sergeant Olivia Hughes, Metropolitan Police," she said, flashing her badge.

A plain clothes detective from Criminal Investigations Department? A list of recent thefts flashed through my mind—jobs in Milan, Singapore, and Chicago—but none had fallen within the jurisdiction of Scotland Yard. "Am I in trouble, Detective Hughes?"

"Officially, no, but I'm not here on official business, Lea."

I sipped from my cup. "Then why did you follow me?"

"I wanted to warn you to stay away from my father."

It suddenly hit me where I had seen a picture of her before. Thicks always carried a photograph of his daughter in his wallet, and spoke fondly of his Livie. Olivia. She had been much younger in the photo. I banished all thoughts of seducing the detective from my mind. "Thicks is your father?"

At my use of the nickname, Olivia winced. "Don't call him that. It makes him sound...dim."

"We both know that's far from the truth. I mean no disrespect when I call him by that name, and he knows it," I said. "Seems like it's you who has the problem with the name Thickett, Detective Hughes. Why the name change?"

"After my parents' divorce, I took my mother's maiden name," Olivia said. "It doesn't mean I love my father any less."

"Your father never mentioned you were a detective," I said, though I could see why he would hide the fact. I never had much patience for the law.

"Didn't think he would, given the circles he travels in," Olivia said. "He promised he'd keep out of trouble, but I know he's gone back to his old ways."

Usually at my behest, but I didn't dare tell her that, nor how brilliant Thicks did his job. "Your father has a good heart, Olivia," I said instead.

"How do you know? He's broken the law more than once. He may hide his tracks well, but a good daughter knows when her father's telling porkies. He even got away with murder," Olivia said, watching my reaction.

"Murder? Surely you're exaggerating." I couldn't conceive of her father killing anyone.

"I love my father, but I also serve the law," Olivia replied. "I warn you now, Lea, stay away from him. If I catch you encouraging him to do anything illegal, I *will* arrest you and bury you in the prison system."

So that was why she'd been tailing me, to see if I was responsible for her father's dealings with the criminal underworld. Alas, I was. Olivia was only trying to protect her father, but Thicks had an outlaw's soul like mine, and would never consider going straight. I suspected Olivia would not accept our Robin Hood philosophy as justification for our benevolent crimes.

"Olivia, I don't abandon my friends, and neither does your father. But I promise you I will keep your father safe at the cost of my own life," I said. "I will do no less, given how many times your father has done the same for me."

"I'll hold you to that, Lea," Olivia said. She finished her coffee and stood. "I'll be keeping an eye on you. I may be conflicted about turning my own father in, but I have no such qualms about arresting his associates. Don't go looking for trouble."

I rose as well out of politeness. "Trouble usually finds *me*."

After Olivia had gone, I picked up the serviette she had scrunched up and smoothed it out, wondering what she had written. There was little notes to herself—*water geraniums* and *buy more peach chutney*—but also my name and the words *smug* and *poncy* underneath it.

Poncy? I frowned and examined my clothes, wondering what gave her that impression. Certainly I was impeccably dressed, but *poncy*? How did I come across as snobbish or shallow? The question lingered in my mind, ruining my enjoyment of the latté.

I dialed Thicks on my cell phone. "It's me. I had a most intriguing conversation with a Detective Olivia Hughes just now, mate."

"Wha—*Livie*?" Thicks sounded positively ill. "Sorry, Guv, I never meant to hide it from you! When you and I first started, my l'il girl was still in school, see? All she cared about then was lacrosse. I thought she'd go into journalism or sports medicine. She never showed any interest in joining the Police Cadets, so how was I supposed to know she'd join the bloody Met?"

"No need to apologize, Thicks, what's done is done," I said. "But I'm curious. Why does she think you murdered someone? Is there something else you're not telling me?"

"Oh, that." He cleared his throat. "Remember when we faked your death in Belize, when you were changing identities? Well, a couple months ago, Livie came to my flat for a visit. She snooped around and found receipts tying me to diving equipment and boat rentals in Belize, as well as my picture of you as Sali. She put two and two together and thinks she got four, and accused me of murdering you. Of course I couldn't tell her the truth."

"Ah." Thickett's loyalty to me shone through once more. He never told his own daughter of my secret life as a shape-shifter, even though it would have saved him from becoming a murder suspect in Olivia's eyes. Then again, would she have believed him? Either a murder suspect or raving mad; not an easy choice. "Sorry I stirred up trouble between you and your daughter, Thicks. If it's any comfort, her action proves she still loves you. Let me see if I can do anything to prove your innocence in my 'death'."

"That's kind of you, Guv, but it'll take some doing to convince my Livie." He changed the subject. "By the by, will you need any special equipment for the gala Friday?"

"Yes, I will," I said. "For starters, earbuds for communication and a dinner jacket with hidden pockets for gear. Also, the weather forecast predicts rain Friday night, and I think a custom-made brolly would be just the thing...."

vii.

On Thursday afternoon in the comfort of my den, I started combing through the files on Singleton, Waterstrider, and Winters London.

Waterstrider, or Barun Gupta in his current guise, took the shape of a fit Indian man in his mid-thirties. As Cricket said, Waterstrider owned Grand Orient Pearls, though he had other controlling interests in companies throughout India that included shipping, textile manufacturing, and business process outsourcing. To his credit, he had a sterling reputation for being a fair but determined negotiator. However, given my withdrawal from the Elect circles, I knew nothing about his true motives or history of instars. The only thing certain was that he had spent at least a hundred years as Elect, to join the ranks of the Imagines.

I opened the file on Gage Singleton. His photograph showed a tall, gaunt Caucasian male in his early fifties, bald and beardless. Small round glasses perched on the bridge of his nose. According to the intelligence we had on him, he was indeed a notorious middleman with a solid record, renowned for protecting the privacy of his clients. He had served a stint in the U.S. Army in his twenties before settling into his present civilian occupation. About five years ago, he was the lone survivor in a car accident that took the lives of his wife and his only son, but seemed to have escaped serious injury himself. He had never been charged with a crime, and had traveled to countless countries on behalf of his clients.

Although I had fully intended to memorise the blueprints next, my curiosity about Olivia Hughes got the better of me. Thomas Thickett was a man I considered to be my closest friend today, and I had thought I knew every little thing there was to know about him: his secret fear of vomiting, his addiction to *Antiques Roadshow*, even how he superstitiously bets only on horses whose names start with *T*—and yet I was drawing a blank on his relationship with his daughter. I knew why he avoided telling me about her: burglars and coppers oughtn't mix. But this sudden revelation about Olivia rocked my faith in Thicks. I wouldn't be able to put her out of my mind unless I knew who she truly was. So it was that I initiated a runaround subroutine and hacked into the Metropolitan Police Service systems as I had on many occasions before.

Olivia's service record flashed onto the screen. She served two years as a uniformed Police Constable out of Fulham before transferring to the Criminal Investigation Department. She excelled during her one-year training to become a Detective Constable, exhibiting an uncanny instinct about fraudsters. She made Detective Sergeant within two years, thanks to the diligent work she did to catch a serial killer last fall.

I read with interest about the only blemish on her record, early in her career—the time she let an exhibition Lamborghini Murcielago LP640 at a London autoshow be nicked by a brash car thief from under her nose. I remembered reading about that incident in *The Independent*, so I dug up the article online to refresh my memory. Apparently, the thief's joyride in the stolen Lamborghini ended abruptly in the window of a fish and chips shop in Notting Hill. The photo showed the Murcielago draped in the red fallen chip shop canopy. To the right of the vehicle, a distressed female constable was trying to calm the angry owner. Although her face was half-hidden and she wore her hair shorter then, it was a younger Olivia Hughes.

There was a clatter and crash at the door to my den. "*Guv!*" Thicks shouted. He had dropped the tea service and was staring aghast at the screen.

I hurriedly closed my browser window, feeling guilty, but it only made things worse when Olivia's service records popped up instead. "My apologies, Thicks," I stammered. "I was curious about your daughter." I tapped a key and initiated the subroutine to erase the data trail.

"She'll never live that down, will she?" Thicks knelt to pick up the fallen tray, defending his daughter all the while. "That was her one and only mistake, you know, end of her first year probation. She came to me afterward in tears, and it took my world-famous sticky toffee pudding to cheer her up."

I helped him with the mess. "You mean that goopy death-by-sugar you call dessert?"

"Well, under the circumstances, I couldn't treat her to a deep-fried Mars Bar, could I? In any case, it did the trick. She swore she'd never muck up such an important assignment again, and she's kept that promise to this very day," Thicks said. "In any case, you'll see Livie's more than her police work, if you take the time to get to know her."

Thicks had a point. The way to understand another person was to spend some time in their company, not nosing around in their personnel files. I squeezed Thickett's shoulder. "You're right, mate. After we deal with this auction business, the three of us should have dinner together and sort things out."

"As long as we don't go for fish," Thicks said.

"No fish!" I promised. "Anyway, let's get back to work. The gala tomorrow might be murder."

viii.

As the weatherman predicted, Friday was wet and windy. I sat in the back of a black stretch limo, going over final preparations for the gala while Thicks played chauffeur. After straightening my black silk bowtie in a mirror,

I checked my supply of amber and silk. Two ambers rested in hidden but easily accessible pockets, one in my dinner jacket, the other in my trousers. My white shirt was silk, as were the handmade cummerbund and the braided strangle-cord hidden in my sleeve.

"Great workmanship on the umbrella, by the way." Upon first glance, it appeared no different from a standard Brigg umbrella with a lion-headed handle. However, the custom modifications to the umbrella made it a sturdy bludgeoning weapon, and the handle hid a broadband signal jammer.

"Don't thank me, thank Rhys," Thicks said. "I'll pass it along next time I see him."

"Please do. How do I activate the jammer?" I asked.

"See the metal band at the base of the handle? It spins. Turn it clockwise once and it'll jam all radio transmissions in a five-block radius, including our own. Use with care." Thicks handed me a small metal box.

"Brilliant." I opened the box and took out the earpiece and the miniature microphone. As small as a flea, the earpiece glued easily into my left ear, while I clipped the microphone-transmitter wafer under my shirt collar and activated it. "Testing. Testing."

"Read you loud and clear, Guv," Thicks said. He raised the soundproof glass between the driver's seat and the back of the limousine, then tapped a button on his transceiver.

"How's this?" said his voice over the earpiece.

"Perfect," I said.

He lowered the glass plate again. "You expecting trouble tonight?"

"Best case scenario, I confirm the authenticity of the Paragon and Cleopatra's Pearl, leave without incident, and return Monday to bid on both."

"And worst case?"

"I walk into Bee's trap and never come out," I said. "Don't stray too far after you drop me off. I may need the cavalry."

"Thought you might," Thicks said. "You can count on me, Guv. I've loaded extra gadgets in the boot, and there's a crossbow in the compartment under the seat."

"Excellent." I punched in a code on my mobile and called up a digital photo of my half of Cleopatra's Pearl and its pattern of rings. If I found the opportunity, I could compare the photograph with the earring on auction to confirm its authenticity. I relocked the file and slipped the phone back in its holster.

The limousine pulled up behind two others on Curtain Road, forcing us to wait for their chauffeurs to finish assisting their patrons out of the rain. I took the brief moment we had to tell Thicks something that had been on my mind since my conversation with his daughter.

"Thicks, we've worked together for a long time, haven't we?"

"Yeah. Why?"

"So far, it's been great planning and executing the heists with you, but the game's about to change. Now that I'm reintroducing myself to the Elect, the level of danger will double," I explained. "People around me tend to get hurt."

"So? What's the problem?" Thicks asked.

"After tonight, if you want to quit my employ, I would understand."

"You're letting me go, Guv?" Thicks turned around to look me in the eye. "Livie got to you, didn't she?"

"I'm giving you the option to bow out. You've family to think of."

"Beg your pardon, Guv, but you're as much my family as Liv," Thicks said. "Like it or not, you need me. I'm not going anywhere."

I nodded, admiring his loyalty. "Then you need to take better care of yourself. Now that I'm not the only shape-shifter around, we'll need a password system to confirm we are who we say we are, because voices are easily copied. Whenever I contact you, I'll identify myself with the next code phrase on a pre-established list. For example, the first three passwords might be *Iago*, *Puck*, and *Mercutio*. We can work out a fuller list after the party."

"Sure, Guv. Sounds like a lot of memory work, but I guess it can't be helped." A space freed up and Thicks drove ahead to fill the spot. "Have a great time."

"Thanks." I glanced at my watch. Quarter to eight. Putting on a raincoat and opening the door, I raised my umbrella against the steady fall of rain. Dashing the few meters from the curb and entering the foyer, I stopped to shake the water off my umbrella. Two hulking security guards, dressed in dark blue uniforms, stood inside the doors. I didn't recognise them from the Winters security personnel files, which put me on edge. Why weren't Winters personnel manning the doors? I had thought Singleton's men would support the existing Winters force, not replace them entirely.

"Invitation, please," said the ginger-headed one.

I showed mine. I memorised his face and dubbed him Rosencrantz, for lack of a better name.

"Do you have a mobile phone, sir?" the blond guard asked. I labeled him Guildenstern.

"Yes. Why?"

"Mobiles and cameras are prohibited from tonight's private viewing, sir," Guildenstern said. "Please deposit all such items at the coat check along with your umbrella."

"I see." Though they wore no visible weapons, I suspected they carried pistols inside their jackets.

I gave my raincoat, umbrella and mobile to the woman at the coat check to the right of the lobby entrance. Soft classical music came through the open doors of the main auction hall. A handful of richly-dressed art patrons chatted by the entrance to the hall. I recognized three of them: Lord and Lady Aird and the insufferable art critic, Basil Hamilton-Tharp. Another blue-suited security guard herded them inside. Older than the first two guards, the middle-aged man bore a scar on his chin. Judging from his physique, I would guess an ex-marine. Labeling him Fortinbras, I smiled as I passed, walking between the statues of Will Shakespeare and Kit Marlowe into the main hall.

I couldn't help but admire the beauty of the auction hall. As I knew from the blueprints, Cricket had styled the hall after the Curtain Theatre, but he had deviated from an exact replica of the former structure, incorporating modern touches and modifications more suitable for an auction hall. Resembling an octagonal amphitheatre with a large open central space, the stage projected into the pit, normally serving as the auctioneer's platform or a catwalk for item or model display. Three tiers of galleries overlooked the central room, but instead of serving as additional seating, paintings and photographs hung on the gallery walls. However, the stairs leading to the galleries had been cordoned off for the gala. The flooring and walls looked nothing like the cheap material that comprised the Curtain of old, giving Cricket's interpretation a classy and expensive look. The Herculean pillars were real marble, not merely painted, and the *frons scenae*—the stage wall— bore classical Greek and Roman images.

The chairs that normally filled the auction hall had been removed to accommodate the guests at the gala. A cursory glance gave a count of thirty or so guests in attendance, with slightly more men than women. Six waiters offered hors d'oeuvres and champagne to the guests while a string quartet played on stage. Glass display cases featuring the items on auction crowded around the base of the stage, a pair of Singleton's men standing watch over the collection. Continuing my *Hamlet* naming scheme, I dubbed them Polonius and Reynaldo. Two other guards watched from the galleries, one on the floor above us, the other in the topmost gallery. They became Horatio and Osric, respectively.

The last visible guard, a muscular bearded man—call him Laertes—

stood behind the most beautiful woman in the room. A svelte Indian woman in a red satin dress modeled Cleopatra's Pearl in her left ear, and the Paragon of Elsinore in its pendant setting around her neck. Beaming as bright as the morning star, she basked in the attention of a group of ladies in elegant eveningwear.

Though I ached to inspect the jewels up close, I decided to bide my time. If I showed undue attention to the pearls, I might reveal myself too soon. Assuming, of course, that Cricket had not already betrayed my identity to the enemy. I took a glass of champagne from a passing waiter and surveyed the room. Theoretically, any woman here could be Bee in disguise, just as any guest could be secretly Elect. The old sense of paranoia that went hand-in-hand with Elect intrigue bedeviled me again. I shook it off and searched for four specific men in the crowd: Cricket, my friend Hal Russell, Waterstrider and Gage Singleton.

I couldn't locate Cricket, but found Hal in front of the glass display case of the funereal mask, chatting up a young ingénue. "The Curtain Theatre gave Curtain Road its name, of course," he told her. "The theatre itself, however, had nothing to do with a theatre curtain. Rather, it got its name from a nearby plot of land called Curtain Close. The grand theatrical curtains you know only came into use after—"

"Hal Russell, I'm sure the young lady would prefer a closer look at Cleo's Pearl to listening to minutiae of dramatic history," I said, smiling, giving the girl a chance to slink away.

"Come, Felix, nobody ever died from learning about the past," Hal said, crossing his arms.

"Nevertheless, remember why you came. What do you think of the mask? Is it the genuine article?"

"I'm leaning towards yes. I'd love to examine it closer, but Mister Singleton there won't permit it yet." Hal cocked his head towards a corner of the hall. "He said perhaps after the official welcome at eight."

I looked where he indicated and saw Gage Singleton in the flesh for the first time. Standing alone at the foot of a gallery stairway like a lamppost dressed in black-tie, Singleton sipped champagne and watched the crowd with a hawkish eye. The thin man carried a stainless steel briefcase with him and wore a headset like his guards. Given the irregularities in security I had already observed, I had no doubt he intended more than a festive gala this evening.

"Have you had a chance to see the jewels yet, Hal?" I asked.

Hal shook his head. "Even if that's the real Cleopatra's Pearl, I doubt I can convince the board to release adequate funds. But I'll tag along."

We pushed through the crowd and joined the potential bidders around the woman in red, who turned in place so that everyone could admire the earring and pendant. She knew grace in every move, coaxing the light to enhance the lustre of her pearl jewellery and shadows to accentuate her curves. Her bodyguard, Laertes, glowered behind her. Though I couldn't compare the earring she wore with the photo stuck in my mobile, I could easily see the pearl set within the silver conch pendant. It seemed the right size, shape and lustre for the Paragon of Elsinore. While a simple touch would confirm its authenticity, Laertes would likely crush my hand before my fingers got anywhere near the pearl.

"Good evening, ladies and gentlemen. My name is Patra," the model said. "You may look and admire, but please do not touch the jewellery."

Hal groaned. "As in Cleopatra?"

"Actually, Patra is a common Hindi surname," said an Indian gentleman who had joined us. "It also means 'the flyer' in Sanskrit."

Waterstrider. I wondered if he was a pawn, an innocent bystander, or a major player in this pearl affair?

Patra smiled. "Very good, Mister...?"

He bowed. "Barun Gupta, at your service. Only a woman as lovely as you could do these magnificent pearls justice, Patra."

The model blushed.

I peered at the pendant resting against the silk fabric of her dress, doing my best not to appear lecherous. "You own Grand Orient Pearls, do you not, Mister Gupta? Surely your company could produce pearls to rival these?" I asked.

"Through artificial means, yes. However, natural pearls are far more valuable than cultured ones, and these are among the most famous pearls in history," said Gupta. "I plan to add them to my collection."

"Not if I outbid you, sir." I extended my hand. "Felix Lea. I run the Arlequim Gallery in Mayfair. This is my friend from the British Museum, Doctor Hal Russell."

He gave my hand a vigorous shake, then Hal's. "Pleased to meet you, Mister Lea, Doctor Russell. May the richest man win."

I smiled. "Or the most daring." We exchanged business cards.

As Hal chatted with Waterstrider, I continued to search for Cricket, but still could not find him in the crowd. Cricket adored the spotlight, and ought to be drinking in the attention at his own gala. Why wasn't he?

"Pardon me, Miss Patra, gentlemen," I said, deciding to find our missing host. "Back in a flash." I left them, setting my champagne glass on a side table before re-entering the foyer. I headed for the lift in the right corridor. I hit the up button and the doors opened, but I had no sooner entered the lift when the guard I called Fortinbras stepped in the way and held it open. "Sir, the upper levels are off-limits to all but Winters personnel. Mister Singleton's official welcome will begin in five minutes. Kindly stay in the main room until then."

Singleton's welcome, not Winters'? Cricket would never give up the chance to take the stage to welcome his own guests. It confirmed for me that Cricket had landed himself in serious trouble, and Singleton the source of his woes.

I glanced behind Fortinbras. Neither Rosencrantz nor Guildenstern could see the lift from where they stood guard. Good. In my current shape, Fortinbras out-muscled me...but that was easily fixed.

I stepped up close to Fortinbras, staring up into his eyes. "How dare you! Don't you know who I am?" I said, raising my hand as though to slap him. He grabbed my wrist reflexively, touching my silk sleeve as I hoped. I pulled Lightning through the imprint he left in the silk and reshaped myself, bursting into his full size and tearing my suit. Surprised by my shifting into his virtual twin, Fortinbras never had a chance to react before I gave him a solid Glaswegian kiss, better known (albeit less poetically) as a headbutt. He yielded easily to the blow, crumpling to the floor of the lift unconscious. The impact ripped the shape I had stolen, restoring me to my Felix Lea form.

I dragged Fortinbras further into the lift so the doors could close. As the lift proceeded to the top floor, I put on his headset and searched him for weapons. A SIG P228 with twelve Luger 9mm rounds lay snug in a holster under his jacket. Although I rarely carried firearms on my heists, the situation tonight could turn ugly fast. I took the gun and holster from the guard and waited for the doors to open on the top floor before pressing emergency stop.

Should I take on Fortinbras' form for a while? Though a silk snapshot of his body would duplicate his bruised forehead and deliver a headache to match, a bit of subterfuge would be useful. I stripped the man and trussed him up with my cummerbund, and traded my clothes for his. Laying my hands on the silk bindings, I braced for pain and stole his shape once more. Pain exploded in my head like an elephant stepping on a landmine, but I suffered through the agony. Finally, I strapped on my own watch and checked the time. Three minutes of eight, not much time till Singleton's welcome. I hastily re-clipped my microphone-transmitter and stuffed my bowtie, lockpicks, ambers and other belongings into sundry pockets. The strangle-cord, I wrapped around my wrist.

I peeked down the corridor. No one was guarding Cricket's office. Walking past the door to the auction gallery as softly as I could, I listened at

Cricket's office door. I heard only quiet breathing. Trying the knob, I found it locked. Retrieving my lockpicks, I set to work. Thirty seconds later, I eased the door open, ready for anything.

ix.

Tied to his chair behind the desk, Cricket groaned through the gag over his mouth. I slipped inside and closed the door, making sure no one saw or heard me enter. "Cricket, can you hear me?" I asked, ungagging him and patting him on the cheek. "Crick!"

His eyelids fluttered, revealing glazed eyes. "No...stop..." he mumbled.

"Crick, it's Flea. Do you know where you are?"

"Flea..." A wild look flashed upon his face. "*Do you not remember a' saw a flea stick upon Bardolph's nose, and a' said it was a black soul burning in hell-fire?*" he said, pronouncing the words as though he still lived in Elizabethan times.

A line from *Henry the Fifth*. "A black soul, am I? Lovely. Forget where you are, do you know *when* you are? What do they want?"

"Flee, Flea!" he cried, or something like it. "Singleton...want...auction...."

"The auction items?" It didn't make any sense. They brought the items in the first place, so why would they want to steal it back? "How many men are there?"

"'Leven, mebbe twelve...such lovely weeds you have for hair!" Cricket's eyes closed again, but he continued to mutter non-sequiturs.

As I feared, Singleton hadn't tranquilised Cricket, but dosed him with a hallucinogenic compound. I stood a fifty-fifty chance of rousing an unconscious Cricket with amber Lightning, but giving him access to the power while he was experiencing hallucinations could result in freakish and deadly changes. A surgeon had better chances of performing a heart transplant dead-drunk. Somehow, Singleton knew exactly how to cripple one of us. Either someone taught him the trick, or he was Elect himself. I liked neither option.

Crick would be useless until he shook off the effects of the drug on his own. I picked up the phone on his desk. The line was dead. I couldn't find any mobile phones or wireless handhelds among Cricket's belongings, which reminded me of the guards' request to deposit all cells at the coat-check. Singleton wanted to cut the guests off from the outside world. Hardly reassuring.

I activated the microphone-transmitter and contacted Thicks. "Things have gone a bit pear-shaped, Thicks old boy."

"Guv?" came his voice over the earpiece.

"Cricket's been drugged and tied up in his office, while Singleton's replaced all the Winters security personnel with his own. Something big's about to happen."

Thicks muttered a curse under his breath. "What do you think they'll do?"

"Given their actions thus far, I suspect the guards will try to contain the crowd, taking them hostages. Then they'll try to identify me."

"How would they know it's you, Guv?" Thicks asked.

I pushed my hand into my pocket and held up a piece of amber. "We Elect rarely go anywhere without a source of Lightning. They'll be looking for ambers." Waterstrider might run into unexpected trouble down in the auction room, as would any other Elect among the guests.

"You getting out, then?"

I supposed I could easily escape through the window, but I had a duty to protect the party guests from Singleton. "Hal's in there, along with a lot of innocent people. The guards aren't wearing masks, which means one of two things. Either someone's promised them new faces and identities, or they will massacre the lot before they go. I can't gamble on Singleton sparing their lives. Thicks, I need you to swing around back to check Winters' loading bay for getaway cars."

"Right, Guv. I'll—" A tapping sound interrupted Thickett's reply. "Aw, bugger," he said, and the transmission cut off suddenly.

"Thicks?" No reply. "Thicks!" Worried, I glanced out the window, but couldn't catch sight of the limousine through the rain. Had they found him?

I had promised Olivia that I'd keep her father safe, but now I faced a dilemma. Should I leave and rescue Thicks from whatever danger he faced, or deal with the threat inside? The answer seemed clear. The people at the gala had little ability to escape Singleton's trap, while Thicks sat in a bulletproof limo with a host of tricks in its arsenal. I would have to trust Thicks to handle himself this time round.

In any case, I had a second problem to deal with. An American's voice came over the headset, deep and calm. "Commence Phase Two. Seal off the building and load the truck."

Phase One must have been the compromise of Winters security. If Cricket's count of their forces had not been psychedelic rantings, then I had twelve or more people to neutralize. I did a quick count of heads: Rosencrantz and Guildenstern controlled the major point of access, the main entrance, with Fortinbras perhaps assigned to patrol the building before I incapacitated him. That made three. Suppose two more men had been assigned to move goods out of Cricket's vault, with another driving the lorry. There might also be another man monitoring the close-circuit cameras in the basement security office. That left the largest group controlling the crowd in the main hall. Laertes watched the model. Polonius and Reynaldo on stage. Osric, the guard in the gallery on this level. Horatio in the gallery two floors down. And the big man himself, Gage Singleton, made an unlucky thirteen.

I might seem woefully outnumbered, but I had faced worse in countless wars. Though Cricket and Thicks couldn't help, I had the advantage of surprise, and would make the best of it. The mercenaries' timeline hinged on what transpired in the auction hall, and I needed to spy on the activities therein.

"Sorry, Cricket, I must leave you here," I said.

Stealing down the hall to the upper gallery door, I pressed my ear to the glass. The live music performance had come to an end, and polite applause echoed through the hall. Hoping the noise would conceal any sounds I made, I eased the door open and slipped in, my braided silk garrote at the ready.

The guard Osric watched the auction pit intently, never noticing my trespass into the gallery. A submachine gun lay at his foot, out of sight of anyone below. A Heckler & Koch MP5SD, by the looks of it, with an integrated silencer. Osric's build was comparable to the stolen form I currently wore. Good.

Gage Singleton's voice, the same as I'd heard on the headset, addressed the guests. "Ladies and gentlemen, welcome to the gala viewing for *The Romance of Myths and Jewels*. I hope you've enjoyed the evening's entertainment thus far. I'm afraid Mister Winters couldn't greet you himself, so I will be hosting tonight's festivities."

As Singleton spoke, I stepped behind Osric, slipped the strangle-cord around his neck and pulled him from the balustrade out of sight. As the guard struggled, I quickly dropped Fortinbras's shape and took his, using the image captured through the silk garrote. Osric fought for breath, but to no avail.

"Alas, I have good news and bad," Singleton continued. "The auction will not proceed as advertised on Monday, as my client has no intention of parting with these treasures. Instead, we offer you the auction of a lifetime, this very night. Guards!"

Shrieks and cries of surprise rose from the auction floor. When Osric lost consciousness, I loosened the garrote and lowered him to the floor, not wishing to take a life if given the choice. Grabbing the submachine gun, I returned to take the spot where he had been standing, dropping the stolen shape so I could use the newly-captured image in the garrote to impersonate him. The form took, but my copied neck burned where the strangle-cord had tightened.

Singleton's men corralled the frightened guests at gunpoint to the side of the auction floor opposite me. No sign of the waiters or musicians, likely dismissed prior to the hostage-taking. Horatio, the guard on the second level, covered the gala guests from with his submachine gun. He glanced up at me, and I nodded, copying his actions.

Singleton climbed onto the stage. "Try to escape, and you will die. Try to fight us, and you will die," he shouted to the crowd, not a trace of emotion in his words. "Most of your lives are already forfeit, but some of you will live. Cling to that hope. As many of you here are wealthy, or represent clients who are, we offer you the chance to bid on your lives in a silent auction. The twelve highest bidders will be spared. The rest will not leave the building alive."

Panic struck the crowd. Some women began to weep, while Basil Hamilton-Thorp fell to his knees, pleading. "P-please, I'm just an art critic! I can't possibly afford—"

"I've long believed death is a long-maligned art," Singleton said, drawing a gun from his jacket. "Congratulations. You're my next installation." I watched in horror as Singleton shot the critic in the chest. Mouth agape, Hamilton-Thorp crumpled to the floor.

"Anyone else eager to announce their financial straits?" Singleton asked. "No?"

I itched to fire a bullet at Singleton in retribution for the cold-blooded execution, but with so many gunmen in the auditorium, even a crack shot like me couldn't possibly disable them all without more people getting hurt or killed. To save them all, I had to bide my time.

Singleton placed his briefcase on the auctioneer's podium and opened it, revealing a custom-built laptop. "One by one, you will come up to the stage. First, you will be frisked for weapons. Next, transfer funds from you or your client's financial institution to the indicated account. I suggest you try your best to remember your account information. If you wish, you may pay for a companion. When all the transfers have been completed, the winners of the auction will be announced and released. Ask yourself how much you would pay to save your life, then look at the men and women next to you. What's life worth to them?"

I had heard enough. It was an audacious if ill-conceived plan, holding the patrons of Winters for their own ransom. Most of them would be too panicked to remember their bank information, but a shrewd man like Singleton likely anticipated that. I was willing to bet their real aim was to identify members of the Elect. By frisking the patrons one by one, they could search for hidden pieces of amber. Had I been caught in that crowd, they would have found me that way. I suspected the money and the items in Cricket's vaults were only secondary objectives.

Singleton's life-and-death auction would take some time, giving me the chance to slip away to eliminate his men one by one. How much lead time I had depended on when they would discover Osric or Fortinbras. I stepped back from the balustrade and vanished through the door.

x.

Back in the corridor, I tried to raise Thicks on the transmitter again. "Thicks, *please* come in."

"Guv?"

At the sound of Thickett's voice, I breathed a sigh of relief. "What happened?"

"Uh, we have a slight problem," he said.

Another voice came over the transmission. "Give it here, Dad. I want a word with him. Lea, what have you gotten my father into?"

I swore under my breath. "Detective Olivia." She must have staked out Winters London, or followed her father again. What should I tell the fair detective? As soon as I mentioned that armed men had taken hostages, she would call in CO19, the Specialist Firearms Command. Further escalation of the situation would only result in the deaths of all the hostages. On the other hand, I needed backup.

"You're not Lea," she said. "Who are you?"

I'd forgotten my voice had changed. "No time to explain, Olivia, but I am the same man you met at the café, and one of the good guys, no matter what you think. Ask your father later. Listen carefully, Detective. The lives of thirty hostages hang in the balance inside. While I'm outnumbered ten to one, I intend to do all I can to save them. Our only hope is to defuse the situation through subterfuge from within, so if you call for backup, things will turn bloody ugly, bloody quick."

"Hostages? Why?" she asked.

"Greed, vengeance, the usual," I said. I entered Cricket's office. He was still rambling incoherently. "Regardless, I need your father's help to save these people, and yours as well. Put him back on, please."

"Like hell! He's going to explain this arsenal first—"

"Livie, give that here!" said Thicks. "What do you need, Guv?"

I opened the window. "The advantage of darkness. First, deliver a set of night vision goggles to Winters' office on the top floor. Second, see if there's a way to cut power to the building on my signal. Third, if you could swing 'round back to the loading bay and check for getaway vehicles, I'd appreciate it."

"No problem, on my way," Thicks replied.

Olivia's voice cut in. "Lea! If this turns out to be a heist—"

"Then arrest me anytime, Detective. You know where I live." I looked down at the road, waiting for the limousine. After a minute, Thicks parked the limo across the street, rolled down his window, and waved.

I stepped away from the open window and waited. A red dot appeared on the bookcase, marking a leather-bound copy of *Les Misérables* by Victor Hugo. Moments later, a short harpoon bearing a small cylinder struck the mark, completing the delivery. I opened the cylinder and extracted the night-vision goggles and straps. Weighing only two pounds, the device was integrated with an infrared illuminator and could magnify light by a factor of 35,000x. Though a bit bulky, I clipped the goggles to my belt.

"Parcel received," I said over the microphone. "Thanks, Thicks. Talk to you soon."

"Take care, Guv."

I wrapped the silk garrote around my left wrist. Though I had spent all of the silk's Lightning impersonating Osric earlier, the material retained its ability to capture the next person's shape, allowing me to probe an enemy's weaknesses.

The looters might prove easiest to pick off one by one. From my memory of the floor plans, the nearest fire stairs should take me down to the ground level storage facilities behind the main auction room, but I would need an electronic key to get through the security door.

I searched Cricket's pockets and desk drawers, but no keys. Singleton must have them. But would Cricket keep a spare set somewhere, and if so, where might he hide it?

My gaze locked on the masks behind Cricket. Of course.

I looked behind each mask, finding a hidden panel behind the tragicomedy masks. I slid it open, finding keys and a proximity key card hanging on a hook within the recess.

I left the office and swiped the key card over the sensor at the fire door, disabling the alarm. I headed down the stairs to ground level and bypassed another door, slipping into the storage facilities. This warehouse-like part of the auction house consisted of three sections: the staging area directly behind the main hall, the loading bay, and the vault, small compared to the major auction houses but more than adequate to hold temporarily paintings, statues, jewellery and other merchandise in climate-controlled environments.

Entering the staging area, I quickly assessed the situation. The soundproof doors leading to the back of the auction room were shut, but the vault door had been keyed open. Past the forklifts, wooden crates and half-packed works of art, a lorry waited beyond a scrolled-up loading bay door. No sign of the guards I expected. Were they in the vault?

If I could reach the vault door fast enough, I could trap them inside.

I sprinted across the staging area towards the vault, but I could not reach it in time. A man and a woman—call them Claudius and Gertrude—emerged halfway from the vault, carrying a masterwork Impressionist painting between them. It was a Le Sidaner, worth a minimum of three hundred grand. Blast.

Their hands full, the pair froze when they saw me charging them. Gertrude, second to emerge from the vault, freed her right hand and reached for her pistol, but I pounced on her, knocking her away from the painting and into the wall. Alas, the impact broke the silken spell, turning me back to Felix Lea, tangled awkwardly in a suit too large for my frame.

Meanwhile, Claudius struggled with the Le Sidaner on his own, not sure whether to let go of the painting.

I wrestled with Gertrude, rolling with her into the doorway of the vault. An unexpectedly ferocious fighter, she choked me with an iron grip. As I struggled for breath, I brushed my garrote against her skin. The pattern in the silk revealed she had a bad left kidney. Previous injury? It would serve. I reached behind her, mustering as much strength as I could, delivering a kidney punch. She howled and released me. Springing to my feet, I shoved the stunned woman into the vault and slammed the door, which locked automatically.

I turned in time to see the oil painting fall towards me. I reflexively caught the masterpiece, the thief and connoisseur in me hating to see brilliant art ruined.

It was a mistake.

Claudius had drawn his gun, aiming it between my eyes. "Move and die."

I stood defiant, meeting his eyes with calm.

He activated his headset and spoke into the microphone with a Bostonian accent. "Kappa reporting. We have an intruder. Lambda's down. Request back-up at the vault!"

I heard the reply over my own headset. "Beta, check it out." Singleton's voice. He paused. "Beta?"

No reply. Beta must have been Fortinbras.

"Delta, go help Kappa," Singleton commanded. "Zeta, find Beta. And where the hell's Epsilon?"

"I can tell him exactly where I left his missing Greek letters," I said, helpfully.

"Shut up," said my captor, snarling. "Permission to kill, sir?"

"No, he's worth twenty million alive," said Singleton. "Maim."

A sadistic smile curled on Claudius' lips. "With pleasure." He lowered his gun and aimed at my right shoulder.

Before he could pull the trigger, something hit his head from behind. His eyes rolled up and he fell forward, crashing through the Le Sidaner painting.

Detective Olivia Hughes stood three meters behind the fallen mercenary, holding the remnants of a sixteenth century Russian panel painting that she had used to club Claudius.

I let the ruined Le Sidaner fall on top of the unconscious man. "Two paintings with one blow. Have you *any* idea how much they were worth, Detective?" I asked, fuming.

"Get over it. It's just pretentious art," she said.

"They're irreplaceable!" I said.

"So are lives."

"True, but—"

The doors to the auction floor slammed open. Time to go.

"Come on!" I said, racing back towards the fire door. Olivia followed close behind. I swiped the card and pushed the door open for Olivia, then tumbled into the stairwell behind her. Seconds after I slammed the door shut, the sound of bullets hitting the other side confirmed the gunman had opened fire.

"Up!" I shouted.

Olivia reached the floor above first, and I tossed the card key to her. She keyed the door open and we hurried through. I stepped right and plastered myself against the wall, while Olivia did the same on the left. I wrapped my silk bowtie in my left hand, my last piece of silk with a dose of Lightning.

The door opened and the man stepped through, gun leading the way. Olivia grabbed his arm and pulled him forward off-balance, while I slapped the tie in my left hand against the back of his neck, forcing him to the ground. Before he could fight back, Olivia jolted him with a stun gun and sent him into convulsions. It took little on our part thereafter to render him unconscious.

"Where'd you get that?" I asked.

"Dear old Dad, who shouldn't even own one," Olivia said.

"We make an excellent team, Olivia," I said.

"Don't expect a medal, Lea," she said, keeping her voice low. She cuffed the unconscious guard to the fire door.

I recognized the man as the one I called Reynaldo. I tested the handcuffs. Quite sturdy. "Another loan from your father?" I asked.

She said nothing, but took the man's pistol.

"You complain about me putting your father in danger, yet here you are," I said, stripping the headset off the guard and handing it to Olivia.

"I might be off-duty, but I'm still an officer of the Met. I don't trust the fate of thirty hostages in your hands, no matter how much praise my father heaps upon you," she said.

Did she envy my friendship with Thicks? Her father never talked about her, but I could well imagine him bragging about me. "He exaggerates," I said. "Five down, seven or eight to go."

"Make that six down," she said. "I took out the driver in the getaway."

"Did you? Many thanks," I said. "That leaves two in the foyer, four in the auction hall, and maybe one in the security office."

"What are they after?" she asked.

"Me," I said. "Apparently, I'm worth twenty million alive."

"You? You mean, if you only handed yourself to them, and it would resolve this entire mess?"

"Not that simple," I said. "I may be their primary objective, but as secondaries, they're looting the vault and making the hostages pay their own ransom. Singleton already shot a hostage, and he won't hesitate to kill the rest. Do this my way, and we will save more lives. Trust me."

"If Dad hadn't vouched for you, I would have the police surrounding this place already, or called my partner," Olivia said. She glanced at her watch. "In any case, Lea, Dad bought you some time. I made him promise to call the police in ten minutes, whether you manage to defuse the situation or not."

"Can he cut the power?"

"Just give the word, he said. What's your plan?" she asked.

"I'm taking out Rosencrantz and Guildenstern in the foyer."

"Who?"

"The two guards stationed there. You're staying put."

"Like hell I am!"

"Stubbornness is hereditary, I see." I mulled over a potential strategy. "All right. My umbrella's in the cloak room. We'll need it."

Olivia raised an eyebrow. "Hardly the time to worry about the rain, Lea."

"There's a broad-band signal jammer inside the umbrella head. I intended to use it to scramble Winters security communications, but it'll serve to jam Singleton's laptop signal and his team's communications," I explained.

"What about the guards in the foyer?" she asked.

"I have an idea, but I need a new face," I said. I touched the bowtie in my hand to Reynaldo at our feet, using the Lightning to take on his physical appearance.

Olivia stared as I changed shape, instinctively raising her gun and pointing it at me. "*How*?!"

I straightened my clothes, now that I filled the oversized suit better with my stolen frame. "We can waste time debating shape-shifting mechanics now, Detective, or save some hostages," I replied in the guard's voice.

"I thought Dad was pulling my leg," she said, lowering her weapon.

"He didn't exaggerate about this." I unstrapped my night-vision goggles and gave them to her. "I'll lure Rosencrantz and Guildenstern away from the foyer. After I tell your father to kill the lights, use these to find the umbrella. The emergency lights will go on, so you might still be seen, but there should be enough darkness to hide you."

"What does this umbrella look like? How do I activate it?" she asked.

"Lion's head handle. Look for the one with the greatest heft. When you find it, wait for my codeword, 'Yorick', through the headset. Find the activation ring at the base of the handle and turn it one revolution."

"Got it," she said.

At the corner, I peered around it towards the stairs. The coast was clear, for the moment.

"These stairs are closest to the cloak room. I'll take the stairs on the other side and lure the guards away. Will you be all right on your own?"

Olivia shot me a disdainful look.

"Right then. Good luck," I said.

I headed down the hall, passing the stairs. As I reached the lounge above the foyer, at the juncture of the two corridors, Guildenstern emerged from the stairway I passed and Rosencrantz from the stairs I was heading for, guns drawn.

Damn, I thought they would stay at their posts.

Seeing me, Rosencrantz nodded in greeting. I gave a nod in return and raised a finger to my mouth, signaling silence before pointing into the lounge, acting as though I had seen something there. He tensed and approached quietly. I turned and gave the same signals to Guildenstern, before raising the submachine gun slung over my shoulder and pointing it towards the lounge bar.

The pair entered the lounge, each at a distance of five paces away on either side of me, looking for the hidden foe. I pointed at the bar and indicated that Rosencrantz and I take the near side, while Guildenstern should sneak around to the far end.

I edged closer to Rosencrantz while Guildenstern crouched and scurried deeper into the lounge, his back to us. When my so-called partner moved slightly ahead of me, I let go of the submachine gun and grabbed him from behind, muffling his mouth and smashing his pistol hand against the bar. The impact knocked the gun from Rosencrantz's hand, but the noise startled Guildenstern, who spun around and aimed his gun at us. However, as I was holding Rosencrantz as a living shield, Guildenstern hesitated.

"Ackland! Have you gone mad?" Guildenstern shouted at me.

Rosencrantz struggled fiercely as I wrestled him to the ground behind the bar, out of sight. But when he bit down on my hand, the injury tore my disguise, returning me to my former self and stripping me of the greater strength I had while impersonating the guard. Rosencrantz broke free and grabbed me by the hair, smashing my head against the base of the liquor cabinet. Though the blow dazed me, I thrust my hands into my pockets and grabbed two things: the transmitter and an amber.

As he yanked my head back by the hair for another smash, I tapped Lightning from the amber, forcing my hair to shed by the roots. Surprised by my hair coming free in his hand, Rosencrantz lost his balance. I grabbed a handy champagne bottle and smashed it over his head. He slumped to the floor.

I barely had time to push him aside when Guildenstern appeared at the other end of the bar, gun firing. I leapt and rolled into the lounge, barely dodging the shots that plugged the liquor cabinet. I tumbled behind a couch and whipped out the transmitter. "Thicks, now!" I cried.

Guildenstern stepped out from behind the bar, hunting me.

Then the lights in the building—indeed, the whole neighbourhood—winked out.

The emergency lights flared to life, illuminating the lounge with minimal light. His silhouette in the bay window gave me my target. I wasted no time, darting closer to Guildenstern.

A message came through the headset. "Sit-rep, now!" Singleton shouted.

"Alpha, Zeta requesting backup—"

Before he could finish his sentence, I pounced from the shadows and threw my entire weight against him, pushing him through the window.

He screamed and fell. I caught myself before I tumbled into the street as well.

"Zeta? Zeta!" Singleton's voice sounded angry. "All units, report!"

I looked through the broken window at the pavement below. Zeta lay on the ground amid shattered glass, breathing but in no shape to move. The rain began to wash away the blood from his lacerations.

Stepping back, I hit the transmit button on the headset. "I'm afraid Zeta's stepped out for a smoke, Singleton," I said. "From here on out, you're dealing with me."

I hooked my microphone-transmitter to the headset and activated it, so Thicks could listen in on the conversation.

"Ah, our mysterious intruder," Singleton said. "So, the pearls did lure you here, Mister Flea. I had hoped to find you among the hostages."

"Sorry to disappoint you, Singleton, but the tables have turned. I've dispatched most of your little fraternity of Greek letters," I said, brushing newly fallen hair from my shoulders. The bald look seemed as good as any, so I left it as it was for now. I took out the backup amber, used its Lightning to heal my cuts, and stuffed it back into my pocket. "Might as well save yourself the trouble and surrender now."

Singleton laughed. "I don't think so. They said you'd be as hard to catch as a flea."

"Did they? Who put the bounty on my head?" I asked.

"They pay me well for my silence," answered Singleton.

"Well, don't count on collecting the twenty million," I said. "By the way, what am I worth dead?"

"A measly two million U.S.," he said. "Still, the ransoms will more than make up for it. I'll collect either way, whether I deliver you dead or alive."

"I'll take that under advisement. You should know, though, that Zeta made such a spectacular exit that I suspect the police will soon arrive, especially with the power outage and all."

Singleton grunted. "Changes nothing."

"Really? How soon will your hostages realise that four armed men couldn't possibly stop a mob of thirty?" I asked. "I'm giving you this one chance to bail out while you can, Singleton. Let the hostages go."

"No deal unless you surrender first," he said.

"I think not. I like my freedom, thank you." I headed for the stairs, but not to go down as I originally intended. I needed to see the auction room from a vantage point and figure out a strategy against Singleton.

"Then I'll kill the hostages one by one," Singleton threatened.

"That only works if I care more about their lives than mine," I lied. I was playing a dangerous game. I did want all of the hostages to live, but my affection for them was a weakness I couldn't let Singleton exploit. He had to believe that I had a heart of stone.

"I've read your file, Flea. You won't let all these innocents die."

I paused at the landing, holding my voice calm. "Maybe long ago, Singleton, but priorities change. Your file should also tell you that I am first and foremost a thief. I came for the Paragon of Elsinore and Cleopatra's Pearl, not to mingle with mortals."

"We'll see about that. Shall I shoot one as a test?" Singleton threatened.

I forced a laugh to make my lie more convincing. "Do what you will with the hostages. I'll be long gone before Firearms Command surrounds the place. After all, I'll have an easier time stealing the goods from the police than wasting my time in a gunfight with you."

"We'll see about that." I heard a muffled shot through the headset, followed by screams. I winced, knowing I had another death on my hands. "One hostage down, Mister Flea. Shall I kill another, or will you come to your senses and surrender?"

"Not tonight," I said. It all hinged on him believing every word I said. "Thank you for the lovely dance, Mister Singleton, but I must go. If you happen to escape with the pearls, then perhaps we will meet again."

An arc of electricity struck the back of my neck and sent me into painful convulsions. I collapsed on the floor, catching sight of Olivia in night-vision goggles emerging from the shadows, wielding the umbrella in one hand and wielding her stun gun in the other. I had been so focused on the conversation that I had not heard her behind me. Olivia must have thought I meant to let the hostages die.

"Bastard," she said, and jolted me again before I could form another word.

I screamed. If only I could reach an amber and stabilise myself with Lightning! But before I could stick my hand down my pocket, Olivia clubbed me in the head with the umbrella, hard, sending me reeling again. Everything started to spin.

Olivia activated her headset microphone and spoke. "I'm willing to negotiate a trade, Singleton, even if he isn't. One thief's life isn't worth thirty innocents'."

"Well, well, a new player in the game. And who might you be?" Singleton asked.

"Metropolitan Police," she said. "I have your Flea."

"Detective...don't...." I managed.

She ignored me. "If you want this selfish ponce, Singleton, you can have him in exchange for the hostages. Listen carefully..."

It was the last thing I heard before everything went black.

xi.

I dreamt an incredible dream.

My surroundings shimmered like mother-of-pearl, fading into iridescent white. Subtle flickers of pale rose tint caught my eye. When colours bled back into the world, I found myself lying paralyzed in a flowerbed blooming with roses and pansies, staring at the blue of the sky framed by the swaying flowers. Sunlight coalesced into webbings of golden silk, clinging to me where they touched my skin. The nameless despair in my heart seemed to lessen as I lay there unmoving, content to be far from the troubles of the world.

A spirit coalesced next to me, taking on a familiar shape. I recognized the bearded man as one I had borrowed centuries ago: Robert Armin. Was he the man I impersonated, or an aspect of me?

"So thou wouldst hide instead of fight?" Armin bent over me and scrutinized my face. "This will not do, Flea."

Of all the faces I had worn, why Armin's? I found my voice. "Leave me alone."

Armin brushed away the webs on me. "Where is thy courage of old? Do not let a single betrayal bury thee. Rouse and face thy foes."

His mention of a betrayal brought the memory of Olivia shooting me into sharp focus. I growled. "She should have trusted me as her father does."

"Let it go," he said. "Thou art not the only one in danger."

I tried to move again, but couldn't. My body would not respond. "There's no hope," I cried.

Armin sighed. "Thy body hath the power to overcome thine impediment, and only thy mind resists. It matters not whether a damsel or thy flesh betrays thee; only forgiveness shall move them to serve thee anew. If I cannot convince thee of this truth, perhaps *she* can." He backed out of sight.

A voice I thought I would never hear again, spoke to me from a distance.

"Wouldst thou lie there, Sir Flea, or greet thine Majesty as is required of thee?"

My heart pounded, and I forced myself to sit up, dusting the cobwebs off my body. My surroundings were the exact image of Fountain Court at Hampton Court Palace, as it had been in the age of Elizabeth. The courtyard once again hosted the original trick fountain and immaculate lawns, and I was in one of the flowerbeds. Sapphire dragonflies darted in the light mid-summer breeze. Gone were the later architectural additions by Sir Christopher Wren in the late seventeenth century and William Kent in the eighteenth, giving me the unsettling feeling of having traveled back in time four hundred years.

A lustrous quality tinged everything in sunlight, and all things in shadow possessed a touch of the fey. But if it was a mirage, why did it feel so real?

I turned to see the source of the words, a woman with long, red-gold hair and an aquiline nose, skin as smooth and pale as porcelain. Dressed in a regal white gown studded with diamonds, she stepped from the shadows with the delicate grace of a doe.

Elizabeth.

Not Elizabeth as I knew her in her golden years, but the Queen in her mask of youth, Gloriana the Faerie Queene as Spenser imagined her in his poem. Behind her came waifish handmaidens and silent courtiers in refined crimson silk; true to the image of the queen of fairies, Elizabeth had chosen courtiers who possess qualities of the otherworld, gliding over the ground as if afloat. Robert Armin joined them.

I hastened into proper kneeling posture. "Your Majesty!"

"Rise, Sir Flea," she said. "It has been far too long, my errant knight. Welcome to my Elsinore."

"Yes, and a sweet dream it is," I said.

"This is no dream, Flea. Thou art within the Paragon of Elsinore."

I frowned. "Pardon my ignorance, Your Majesty, but what do you mean?"

"Remember our conversation about immortality, in the Chapel Royal? The world gained its strange lustre when I gave thee that pearl. Thou didst vanish like a spirit, as did all others in my service. Hampton Court became a silent palace of eerie light and resplendent shadows, and I walked its halls alone. The only comfort had been the abatement of my pains. I did not hunger, though I felt the cold of the snows and stayed inside, where the hearthfires seemed to burn without end.

"Then one night, I felt and suffered through the moment of my death, the spectres of my woman-servants and the Archbishop of Canterbury on their knees surrounding me. I knew then Death had taken me, and fell into deep meditation on the nature of the afterlife. Why did I haunt the palace alone? I did not know.

"One day thereafter, I heard voices in the Great Hall, and found ghostly players had come to entertain me. Master Shakespeare, Richard Burbage, and thee, and the rest of the Lord Chamberlain's Men, performing *Hamlet* to free me from my solitude. I would have called it a memory of that performance that New Year's Day, save that the costumes had changed. The Paragon of Elsinore appeared in the play, as I had commanded, and I knew thou didst do as I asked."

I nodded. "I followed your instructions and gave the curse its bite, Your Majesty."

"Thou hast served me well, Sir Flea, as I knew thou wouldst," Elizabeth replied. Gone were her rot-black teeth, replaced by pearly whites. "Watching the play gave me strength. As time passed, the ghostly players returned again, oft-times with the same actors, other times with new faces and voices. I would always speak to thee, but my words never reached thine ears. I came to understand that the Paragon of Elsinore had become my Purgatory, and I was doomed to watch the performances of *Hamlet* for eternity. A punishment worthy of Tantalus, that."

"But Your Majesty, it seems you have found companionship and the secret of youth," I said, glancing at Robert Armin and her fey courtiers.

"Walk with me, Sir Flea," Elizabeth said. I obeyed and followed her to a flowerbed blooming with golden pansies. She lifted a hand adorned with jeweled rings before her, and whispered a word. A dragonfly came to her call, alighting on her finger.

"It had not always been thus. I remained on my own for years, even after thou abandoned the role of the Gravedigger in *Hamlet*. New actors came and went, both good and bad. The only constant remained the Paragon, always the same in the re-enactment of the play. I became aware that I could change small things with my will. Little by little, I dismissed winter and summoned spring. My youth returned to me, and I called the fey maidens out of the shadows to keep my company. They lessen my solitude, for the most part."

I thought over the implications. Whenever I touched the Paragon of Elsinore in ages past, I had felt the spirit of Elizabeth, this very woman before me, the willful Queen and all her strength caught within the jewel. Much like the Elect put their imprints onto amber, Elizabeth had done the same with the pearl, except this shard of her soul—for lack of a better word—lived on within her prison of pearl. In a way, she had achieved immortality in a way I never imagined possible.

"Much has changed since your reign, Your Majesty," I said.

"That I have learned," she said. "The way men dressed. The pronunciations of words. Women on stage. But all of it ended when the Paragon was stolen."

"You know of the theft?" I asked.

She nodded. "A time of darkness descended upon my lustrous world. A woman who called herself Bee came into the world of the pearl, fascinated by what I had wrought. I knew not that one of thy kind could enter my sanctuary, Sir Flea, and yet she found a way, seeking the secrets of the Paragon. She told me that she stole the pearl to spite thee. Her strength of will was formidable. Her creatures of shadow ravaged the palace, slaying and torturing my new subjects, all in search of how I came to dwell here. I had to master the elements of my world to thwart her."

She passed her hand over a patch of pansies, inking them violet as though it was the most natural thing in the world. Perhaps it was, here within her pearl.

"Did Bee harm you, Your Majesty?" I asked.

She shook her head. "She tried, but I learned to summon a champion to protect me. It was he who bore the wounds that would have been mine." She gestured, and Robert Armin stepped forward and bowed.

I bowed in kind.

"His wit comes from my fond memories of thee, and his power what I imagine thou wouldst wield," Elizabeth explained. "If not for Sir Robert Armin, my Arms, we would not have repelled Bee's incursions. I and my subjects returned to our idyllic lives, such as it is, and we owe much to my knight and fool."

"You said I was within the Paragon. How?" I asked.

"My mastery of the Paragon reveals to me those who touch it in the outside world," Elizabeth said. "The pearl had called forth an apparition of the dark-skinned woman who wore it, and I felt thy presence and jeopardy. She cradles now thy head in her lap, and touches an amber to thine skin, Sir Flea. Such knowledge is the only aid I may grant thee."

Lightning from the amber could rouse me from unconsciousness. "My Queen, I am in your debt—and thine, Sir Robert," I said, and bowed. "Thank you." The power of the pearl was greater than I imagined, and I understood now why Bee desired it. But had she solved the Paragon's mystery before her death? "Did Bee find the power she sought?"

"That, I know not," Elizabeth confessed. "But go with my blessings. They have need of thee."

I searched for the tickle of Lightning, and found it somewhere behind my ear. To tap that power from within a normal dream would have been calamitous, but Elizabeth's world allowed me to focus on my true appearance without my subconscious twisting my self-identity. I channeled the Lightning and willed it to heal me—

—and I awakened.

xii.

The haze clouding my mind began to lift. The prickle of Lightning was indeed behind my ear, from a piece of amber pressed to my skin. My aching head was cradled in a soft, satin lap. I punched through the pain and read the pattern captured in the satin weave, calling forth the image of Patra, the model who had worn the pearls at the gala. Everything Elizabeth said was true.

They must have drugged me, even after Olivia knocked me cold. I drew upon more Lightning to counter the effects of the tranquilizers in my system. I could not free my hands, finding them cuffed behind my back and pressed under my body. The floor shook beneath us, and the smell of petrol aggravated my nausea. Were we in a moving vehicle? My back and face felt bruised, and I wondered what abuses had been wrought on my body. I cracked my eyes open, gauging the situation. By the looks of it, I had been tossed into the back of their lorry. In the absence of an interior light source, I could only glimpse faces and shapes at intervals when streetlight filtered through the rear windows. The absence of light from the front suggested that the lorry model had a separate cab from the trailer.

Patra looked down at me in worry. The Paragon of Elsinore swung mere centimeters above my nose, tantalizing me. Taking advantage of the bumps in the road to make the shifting of my head seem natural, I took in more of my surroundings. Impressionist paintings secured for transport lined the lorry walls. Next to us, a man sat amidst a pair of unmoving bodies. Fallen guards, or was one of them Olivia? More threatening were the two figures standing by the rear doors, Laertes and Polonius, undoubtedly armed. I saw no sign of Singleton, who likely rode or drove in the cab.

Had Olivia succeeded in trading my life for the hostages? Or had Singleton overpowered her and killed everyone, except for the bargaining chips in the lorry? I didn't know. All I knew was that she had been dense enough to believe the lies meant only for Singleton's ears, and helped him capture me. Whichever deal Olivia made with Singleton, successful or not, it left Patra and Hal in danger. Patra, still wearing the bait jewellery, made sense as a hostage in their escape, though I did not know why Hal had been taken. Was he additional insurance, or did they discover his connection to me? I supposed Singleton could have seen us together at the gala. Either way, both he and Patra remained in jeopardy because of me. I did not intend to fail them.

One thing puzzled me. Where did Patra get the amber, and how did she know that I would need it? Could she be Elect? Or perhaps Waterstrider overheard Singleton call me Flea, realised what I would require to survive, and gave an amber secretly to Patra. Given the rapport and flirting between the pair earlier, Waterstrider could well have told her what to do. Regardless, I was in her debt.

My current *instar* had been designed with thievery and acrobatics in mind. I had taken the option of being double-jointed, to better squeeze into small spaces and escape from straitjackets and fetters. Working out of sight, I slipped out of the cuffs as Houdini once taught me. Fortunately, these weren't the speedcuffs used by Scotland Yard, but an older metallic design where the rotating part could make a full revolution to re-lock. That was the beauty of these kinds of handcuffs: after you had slipped them, you could slap them onto new wrists, giving me a much-needed weapon.

I curled my other hand and tapped Patra's leg. She sensed my signal but said nothing. Quietly, Patra removed the amber from my neck and slipped it in my open palm. I balled my hand, cocooning the amber in my fist, and waited for the perfect moment to strike.

"Guv, you there?" came Thickett's voice over the earpiece.

Good old Thicks! If he was close enough to transmit, he must have followed the lorry from the auction house. It was a mixed blessing. He could help us escape, but the limousine was hard to miss. They must know he was tailing them.

"Felix, I hope you can hear me, even if you can't answer. The lorry's heading down Clapham Road through Lambeth. I've almost caught up. I don't know if I can stop them, let's give it a go. Brace for impact in five, four, three—"

I knew I could count on Thicks. I readied my attack to coincide with the collision.

The lorry shook as the limousine smashed against the bumper from behind, and one of the hastily-secured paintings came free, sliding about the cabin. The mercenary Polonius fell forward, while Laertes caught himself and glanced out the back window. While Hal and Patra lost their balance as well, knowing when the impact was coming gave me a decided edge.

Recovering before the fallen Polonius, I whipped my legs around, striking him square in the chest. It knocked the wind out of him, long enough for me to right myself and confront Laertes.

The lorry driver sped up and wove through traffic, tossing all the occupants of the trailer like rag dolls from one side to the other. I grabbed a strap on the trailer wall with two fingers of my left hand, keeping the amber in my grasp while I steadied myself. Laertes, on the other hand, grabbed a door handle and raised his gun.

Before he could get a bead on me, I let go of the strap, snaking forth

with the handcuffs in my right hand and slapping one end around the wrist
of his gun hand. Laertes managed to squeeze off a shot, but I tugged his
cuffed hand, ruining his aim. The bullet ricocheted off the side of the trailer
instead. Laertes let go of the door and balled his free hand, swinging at my
jaw and connecting hard. It hurt like hell.

Polonius had shaken off his stupor, but had dropped his gun when he fell.
As he reached for it, the weaving of the lorry made the weapon slide towards
Hal. Hal fought Polonius for control of the weapon, while Patra grabbed the
fallen painting and smashed it against the mercenary, with little effect.

Still struggling with Laertes, I couldn't free myself to help Hal or Patra.
With a burst of strength, I forced Laerte's cuffed hand against his hand
holding the door, slapping the other cuff on. With his wrists chained together,
Laertes had to let go of the door to aim his gun. He tried to pistol-whip me,
swinging his bound hands at me, but I anticipated his move. Ducking his
swing, I grabbed him by the waist and pushed him against the lorry door,
lifting the latch.

The door swung open behind Laertes, and the sound of car horns and
distant sirens flooded the trailer. Mere meters behind the lorry was Thicks in
the limo, the front end smashed up.

Teetering on the brink, Laertes dropped his gun and tried to hang on to
something, anything.

Even me.

Laertes grabbed my shirt with his cuffed hands, on the brink of pulling
me with him into traffic. I managed to catch the door handle with my left
hand before he fell, hanging on for dear life. Pulled down by his weight on
my shirt, I almost dislocated my shoulder as the careening vehicle dragged
him mercilessly down the street.

The limo fell back, perhaps Thicks worrying that we would both fall out
of the lorry under his wheels.

The seconds seemed like hours until Laertes lost his grip, rolling into the
rain-soaked road.

Behind the wheel of the limo, Thicks barely avoided Laertes body, but the
limo hydroplaned sharply to my left, nearly colliding with an oncoming cab. Thicks
recovered and closed the distance again, grinning and waving at me through the
rain. "You're a sight for sore eyes, Guv!" he shouted over the transmitter.

I gave him a thumbs up.

Suddenly, Thicks cried, "Behind you!"

In my distraction, I had forgotten about Polonius, the guard who had
been struggling with Hal over the gun.

I had no time to turn around. I leapt onto the bonnet of the limousine, almost sliding off the slick surface. I let go of the amber so I could lock my fingers into the grooves that housed the windshield wiper. My source of Lightning flew out of sight, but I managed to hang on when Thicks swerved, saving me from a bullet in the back. The shot glanced off the bulletproof windshield.

Thicks floored the pedal and brought me out of the line of fire of the gunman, driving parallel to the lorry. Flicking a switch, he opened the sunroof. I fought the rushing winds and pelting rain on my face, crawling along the slippery roof.

The sirens grew louder. The high-speed chase down Clapham Road had attracted the attention of the police, probably for the best.

I almost made it to the sunroof when the getaway driver rammed the lorry against the side of the limousine. I slid but caught the edge of the sunroof, wasting more time pulling myself back up and safely into the limo.

"What now, Guv?" asked Thicks, trying to put more distance between our vehicle and theirs.

"I can't leave Hal and Patra with that gunman," I said, flipping open the seat before me. As Thicks promised, a crossbow and twelve bolts awaited within. "Pull back."

Thicks hit the brakes, pulling behind the lorry again.

Polonius was trying to close the lorry doors, but with the vehicle weaving dangerously through traffic, only now had he caught one of the handles.

I stood and fired a crossbow bolt into his right shoulder. He cried out, dropping the gun in his right hand and clutching at the wound with his other hand. With nothing to hold on to, when the lorry veered left onto Clapham High Street, Polonius fell out of the lorry and bounced off the limo's bonnet, out of sight.

That left only Singleton and whoever else rode in the cab, but how would we stop the lorry safely? I could shoot the tires or the driver, but at this high speed, the resulting crash on the rain-slicked street could kill everyone on board, including Hal and Patra.

I dropped back down into the limo. "Thicks, isn't Clapham Common's ahead?" The Common was a large acre of parkland with two ponds.

"It's coming up on our right," he said.

"Think you can force them onto grass?" I asked. The soggy ground might slow the lorry down.

"You mean, across oncoming traffic and up the sidewalk? This tin can against that monstrosity?" Thicks asked.

"This thing's armored, isn't it?"

"Against bullets, maybe," he said. "Well, you're the boss."

"Never call me boss," I reminded him, preferring to think of us as partners-in-crime. "You won't be doing it alone. Pull up alongside their left. I'm jumping it."

"Good luck, Felix," Thicks said.

I stuffed an amber from reserves into my pocket, loaded another bolt into the crossbow, and rose. This one was for Singleton.

As I instructed, Thicks pulled the limo to the lorry's left, and I caught Singleton's silhouette in the cab's passenger seat. He had seen us in the sideview mirror, drew his gun and fired at me. I ducked down, hearing the bullets thump against the roof of the limo like hail. I wouldn't get a chance to fire my crossbow, let alone jump the truck.

We were approaching the park fast. I had little time left, but if I could blind the driver....

I hunted through the portable arsenal Thicks assembled and found the smoke grenade. It had a three second delay. "Closer, Thicks!" I shouted.

The limousine charged forward.

I pulled the tab and poked my head out of the sunroof.

Singleton fired, his bullet grazing my cheek. It stung, but I ignored it. I stood and hurled the smoke grenade into the cab.

Choking white smoke burst forth, streaming from the cab's open window. Blinded by the smoke, the lorry veered into the lane of oncoming traffic, narrowly avoiding a disastrous collision.

The smoke obscured Singleton and likely blinded him and the driver. While they dealt with the smoke, I climbed out of the sunroof while Thicks pulled the limousine a hand's width next to the lorry. Reaching out, I grabbed hold of a handle and leapt the short distance, squeezing myself between the cab and the trailer, heading for the driver's side.

I cleared the narrow space a second before the whole vehicle shook. Thicks had forced the limousine against the side of the lorry, trying to push it up the sidewalk and into the park. Though it was a valiant attempt, ultimately it failed to budge the lorry from its path. It was all up to me.

The driver had rolled down the window to let the smoke escape. The smoke stung my eyes and made it hard to see, but I knew where to plant my fist. My knuckles smashed into his jaw. He reached through the window, trying to grab me, but I dodged his grasp and reached in, turning the steering wheel hard to the right.

With the limo's force and the sudden tug on the steering wheel, the lorry jumped the curb and steamrolled into the park. Thicks veered off in the limousine. The ground, though wet, proved not enough to impede the lorry's forward momentum. The entire vehicle plowed forward through the Common, heading for Long Pond directly ahead.

The lorry sailed off the edge of Long Pond and crashed into the shallow water. I lost my grip and fell into the pond, drenched but escaping major injuries. Slowed by the water, the lorry rolled to a halt a distance away.

I struggled to my feet and trudged through the water towards the vehicle. Pausing at the open rear doors, I glanced inside for Patra and Hal. "You OK in there?" I asked.

"No," Patra shouted. "That guard shot Doctor Russell in the stomach. He needs a hospital!"

I swore. "We'll get him one. What about the other prisoners?"

"They let them go when they traded for you," she said. "Hurry!"

I heard a door open at the front of the lorry. Singleton or the driver must have recovered from the impact already. "Damn. Singleton's still a threat, so stay put. Help will be here soon!"

I peeked around the lorry's left side where Singleton rode. The cab door seemed closed, but I did not see him or hear him wade through the water. Taking a few quick steps to survey the right side, I still could not spot him. Had he remained in the cab, or climbed on top of the lorry?

I took careful steps towards the cab. Although the smoke from the grenade had thinned, it still obscured vision. When I reached the driver's side window, the door kicked open suddenly, knocking me backwards into the pond. I inhaled and choked on some water, but before I could pull my head above the surface, Singleton leapt on top of me. He forced me down, straddling me and wrapping his hands around my throat, trying to drown me.

His mistake was leaving my arms free. I struck him with balled fists in the stomach, causing him to loosen his hold for a moment. I broke free of his hands and raised my head out of the water to catch my breath.

Singleton drew a knife, gripped it with both hands and drove it towards my heart. I barely caught his wrists in time, blocking the killing stroke. He did not relent, pressing the blade downward with all his strength while I fought back. Though he had the build of a scarecrow, adrenalin must have boosted the force of his assault. It proved difficult to keep my head above water while holding his knife at bay. Sooner or later, I would either choke under more water or take a hit from Singleton's knife.

"You're a hard bug to squash, Flea," he said.

"That's what they tell me." If only I could reach the amber in my pocket!

I took a gulp of air and sunk beneath the surface, gambling that I could stave the weapon off with my right hand while I grabbed for the amber with my left.

The strength of one hand could not stop Singleton's attack. The knife tip pierced my skin and drew blood. I abandoned the amber idea and refocused my effort on stopping the knife from sinking into my chest, but the struggle made it hard to hold my breath.

Though my head was underwater, I heard two muted pops. Singleton arched his back, gasped and loosened his grip. He fell sideways into the water.

I untangled myself from Singleton and broke the surface, gasping for fresh air.

A drenched Patra knelt in the water beside the trailer, a gun quivering in her hand. "B-bastard," she cried.

I pulled Singleton's head out of the water, but he was beyond help. Shot twice in the back, one of the bullets pierced his heart. I slipped my hand into his trouser pocket. He carried only a tube-shaped vial filled with a viscous liquid. I unstoppered it and smelled the contents: honey-sweet. He was a Drone, all right. I no longer had any doubt that Bee had engineered this trap.

I tucked the vial away and approached Patra. "Thank you, Patra," I said softly. "You can put the gun down now."

Still trembling, Patra dropped the pistol.

"How did you know about the amber?" I asked.

"Barun," she said.

I nodded. "Then I am in your debt, and his. Come on, let's check on Hal." I helped her wade through the water into the trailer, and hurried to Hal's side. "Hal. Can you hear me?"

"Loud and clear, Felix," he said, wincing.

I checked his wound. It was a through-and-through, and bad. He needed surgery straight away.

"Hang in there, Hal," I said. "You want that rematch, don't you?"

He managed a chuckle, a good sign.

"How did you end up here?" I asked, trying to distract him from his pain. There must be something I could do!

"They let half the people go before that lady detective told them where to collect you," he said, his voice weak. "They needed someone to help carry a prisoner. I volunteered."

"Good man." I opened the vial I took from Singleton, a final dose of Bee's shape-changing elixir. "Drink this, Hal."

"What...?"

"A special concoction of honey and royal jelly that'll help you heal. Drink and imagine yourself at the peak of health," I said. "Hell, think ten years younger. Mind-over-body."

He raised an eyebrow, but swallowed it as I instructed. I pocketed the empty vial and checked his wound. The bleeding was subsiding. "Good, keep it up." The doctors would call it a miracle at the hospital.

At last, the sirens and flashing blue lights in the distance signaled the imminent arrival of the Metropolitan Police.

I called Patra over. "Please, stay with him. Talk to him and keep him awake until the paramedics arrive."

"You're leaving?" she asked.

"The police will have questions that I'd rather not answer," I said. "Stay brave, Patra. Tell the police you shot Singleton in self-defense, and the rest of the hostages will confirm that he terrorized you all."

"But what if they ask about you?"

"Just say I was a nameless, faceless gentleman thief, in the wrong place at the right time. One last thing—the pearls you wear will be safer with me."

She seemed hesitant. "Isn't that stealing?"

"They were stolen in the first place," I assured her. It was more or less the truth, if not the whole truth.

"Take them, then. They've brought me nothing but bad luck." Patra removed the pendant and earring, handing them to me.

"Thank you." I put them in my pocket and stood. Police cars and an ambulance had arrived on scene, and it was time to disappear.

xiii.

In case my Lea identity had been compromised, I spent the night in Thickett's guest room, and after breakfast I examined the Paragon of Elsinore at leisure. I held the pendant up to eye-level, drew a deep breath and touched the pearl's lustrous surface through its platinum wire-frame shell.

Lightning pulsed through the jewel. The soul of Elizabeth the First in all her glory still reigned over the Paragon, as I knew it would. The Lightning bottled within personified that Golden Age, stronger than ever.

I let the power of the pearl pull me back into Elizabeth's world. Beyond the lustre, Elizabeth welcomed me.

I knelt. "Your Majesty, I am in your debt. Thank you for helping me wake. If there is a way to return Your Majesty to the living world, then I shall find it for you."

"I once asked thee for the gift of immortality, Sir Flea, and I have it. It is not what I had imagined, but the centuries of solitude have given me time to contemplate my fate," the Queen said. "If I am meant to exist within this pearl, then so shall it be. Only return my *Hamlet* to me."

"I shall see it done, Your Majesty," I promised. "The Paragon of Elsinore shall return to the stage, along with its curse."

She nodded. "Go with my blessings, Sir Flea, and I await thy next visitation," she said, lifting the dragonfly perched on her finger and letting it fly. As I watched the blue insect soar into the sky, the pearl lustre leeched colour from Elizabeth's world, and returned me to mine.

I came to, only to face a glowering Olivia in front of me. "Aw, bloody hell!"

"Hello, Lea. Might I have a word?" Olivia said.

"Sorry, Guv, she barged in," Thicks apologised.

Despite my irritation at seeing her, I took care to put the Paragon of Elsinore down gently. "Come to arrest me? Or to take a hammer to the jewellery?"

"Guv! Give her a chance to talk, would you? They're calling Livie a hero. My darling girl's going to make Detective Inspector for sure!"

"You must lie well, Detective."

"Dad explained that what you said to Singleton had been part of an act," Olivia said.

"Yes, it was a bluff. I was committed to freeing those people, but the mercenaries had to believe otherwise," I said. "I had the situation well in hand."

"Like hell. I act on facts, Lea, and what you said branded you as a heartless, self-centered bastard," Olivia said. "I had to take control of the situation. I don't regret what I did."

"And if I hadn't recovered in time, two more hostages would have died!" I said, thinking of Hal and Patra.

"I gambled that you'd worm your way out of any trouble, and I was right, wasn't I?" she shot back. "It seemed you cared only about the art—"

"Liv! Felix!" Thicks pushed between us. "What's past is past. You're both heroes and that's all that matters, innit? At least thank for Livie keeping our names out of the papers."

Olivia shrugged. "I did it for you, Dad. Besides, no one would believe what really happened. The mercs had wild enough stories without me complicating things with a man who changes shapes. But what are you, Felix Lea? And why did Singleton call you Flea?"

"I can give you some answers, Detective, but I doubt they will satisfy you," I replied. "What I tell you must be kept secret for your own safety, your father's, and mine. Is that clear?"

"She'll keep mum, Felix. Won't you, Livie?" Thicks said.

Olivia frowned but nodded.

I would have to trust that her word was as good as her father's. "Very well. I am a shape-shifter, but hardly the only one in the world," I then framed the basics of Elect society for Olivia.

Olivia digested what I said. "So this was fallout from a mob war between immortals?"

"Not a bad way of putting it," I said. "I need to find Bee. What did you find out from the mercenaries?"

"All are Americans, ex-military," Olivia said. "Singleton hired them for the job, but didn't tell them why. He promised them new identities and two hundred thousand U.S. plus commission for a successful mission. After looting the auction house, they were to take a private jet from Farnsborough to Frankfurt, where Singleton would reveal the next part of their plan."

"Except Singleton's dead," I said. "Blast. I will have to find Bee the hard way."

"Then I'm going with you, Guv," Thicks said.

"Dad!" Olivia protested.

"Life with me's about to get far more harrowing, Thicks," I warned him. "The news will spread that I'm alive, which means we may be entertaining my old friends and enemies soon."

"Listen to you two! There are risks, I know, but I've a knack for getting myself out of trouble." Thicks winked. "Trust me."

I did.

Olivia sighed. "I suppose I can't stop you from going with him, anymore than you could convince me not to join the Met?"

"Of course not. You got your stubbornness from me, remember?" Thicks said.

"Then watch over him, Lea," Olivia demanded. "If anything happens to my father, I *will* hunt you down."

I didn't doubt she would. With such devotion, what a formidable foe she'd be.

Second Chance
David D. Levine

I closed my eyes. The technician smeared my eyelids with a cold gel that smelled of disinfectant, then gently pressed the last set of metal electrodes in place. "All right now, Mister Eades," she said, "it'll just be a moment more."

And then I was falling.

I gasped and jerked spasmodically. But a foul sticky fluid filled my mouth and nose, and my arms and legs met resistance—something hard and cold encased me on all sides. Coughing, choking, retching, I pounded my fists against the smooth unyielding surface. I couldn't see a thing.

Oh Lord Jesus, I prayed, let me wake from this nightmare. But no dream had ever gripped me with such visceral intensity—trapped, blind, suffocating, tumbling headlong from some unknown height and moments from smashing against the ground—for so long. Still coughing, I brought my knees up to my chest and shoved my feet against the encasing walls, but my legs felt wrong... frail and thin and weak.

Then the lid sprang open of its own accord, sending me tumbling out into the bright chill air. Blinded by the sudden light, barely able to force my eyes open against the coughing spasms that wracked my chest, I thrashed desperately to catch myself on something, anything.

But I was not falling.

My gut and my ears told me I was plummeting uncontrollably through space. My eyes told me I was drifting away, gently rotating, from a man-sized lozenge of white plastic—a vivification capsule. It lay open like a clam. The inner surface glistened with a gray, viscous fluid. A moment later I bumped into a stack of boxes bungee'd to the far wall of the room.

The capsule was fastened to the wall of a small pie-wedge-shaped room. It was one of seven such capsules; the others were dry and empty. Most of the rest of the space was filled with bundles of clothing, boxes, and canisters. I knew this room—or a training version of it. But the version I'd known had not been crammed with unused equipment, and I had never experienced it without gravity.

I was in space. Aboard *Cassiopeia*. For real.

No. This couldn't be. The first scan was only supposed to be a backup. Maybe this was some kind of test.

Another fit of hacking, retching coughs made me curl around my aching abdomen, hacking out gout after gout of hot gray mucus from my mouth and nose onto my bare legs. Some of it stuck there, the gray of it looking sickly pale against my dark brown skin. Most floated away in loose obscene gobbets. I tasted phlegm and salt.

I was naked.

I shuddered in the chill air and clutched my legs against my chest—and stopped, amazed. No flabby belly intervened. No aching knees, no creaky hips. I was thin and lithe, with skin as smooth and unmarked as a baby's brown bottom. I inspected my left thumb—the old scar that had cut across the knuckle and permanently marked the nail, souvenir of a broken beaker in a high-school chemistry class, was gone.

No. Not gone.

Had never been there.

My heart raced, and I struggled to control my breathing. I squeezed my eyes shut. Oh, dear Jesus. This was no test.

I wasn't me.

I was a clone. A copy of my body, grown by machines and implanted with a copy of my mind.

Shivers ran through my torso, tendrils of steam drifting lazily away from me in the cold still air, as I tried to get a handle on the situation. I was on *Cassiopeia*, that much was certain, but clearly something had gone very, very wrong. I was supposed to be sedated for the difficult process of rebirth. There was supposed to be someone here to help me. And my memories were supposed to include two and a half years of intensive astronaut training, not just six months.

I twisted in the air, groping for a bungee cord, but misjudged my reach and scraped my hand on the rough plastic panel joint next to it. My body was all wrong—too thin, too long, the skin as delicate as a newborn's; my hands and feet wouldn't go where I wanted. My heart pounded and I took slow, deep breaths to calm myself. On the second try I managed to hook a finger through the cord and pull myself to the cluttered wall. I clung there, panting, reveling in the small triumph.

The many small compartments that lined the walls behind the stacked boxes and cans all bore tidy labels—square machine-produced letters fabricated right into the plastic—and I soon found a towel and wiped the gray slime off myself. One of the bundles gave up a white coverall, rough and over-large. I had never before realized how much I depended on gravity in putting on a pair of pants, but eventually I managed to dress myself and find slippers for my feet. Thank you, Jesus.

The door, a plain plastic panel closed with a simple latch, led to a habitation bay: four doors opening onto a circular space about three meters across and two high, smelling of fresh plastic. I couldn't tell which of *Cassie*'s five modules I was in. All five hab bays were identical, with a food prep area and a big wall screen—currently displaying a shimmering grid of colored squares that meant nothing to me—and a circular port in the "ceiling" leading to the adjacent work bay. I pushed off from the wall, caught myself awkwardly on the padded rail that rimmed the port, and pulled myself through.

The work bay was a large cylinder, eight meters in diameter and thirty long, divided into work stations by open-weave plastic partitions. The open central way extended from the hab bay port I'd just come out of, which we called the "bottom," to the systems bay port at the "top." At the waist of the cylinder two other ports led to the work bays of the adjacent modules.

Everything I could see was made of fresh gray or black plastic. Gray plastic bulkheads reeked of solvents. Black foam pads on corners and edges showed no wear. Taut gray fabric panels stretched crisp and pristine. Each of the ship's five modules had been boosted all the way from Earth, at great energy cost, as a densely-packed bundle of metal parts, electronics, and complex mechanisms. The ship then self-assembled here at Tau Ceti, fabricating its plastic parts from local hydrocarbons, and color was an unnecessary luxury. The only relief from the monochromatic came from the false colors of scientific displays glowing on some of the monitors. And there were no windows; transparency was difficult to fabricate. The only views outside were from the airlocks at either end of the cylinder.

This place was my home—my whole world—for the rest of this life. Which might be short.

Movement caught my eye: a teenaged white girl, just pulling her head from an open maintenance panel. Tall and waif-thin, with pale, pale skin and a short brush of red-blonde hair, she wore white coveralls just like mine, equally poorly fitting on her gamine frame. Who was this girl and what was she doing on board *Cassie*?

As soon as she saw me, she gasped, and paled still further. "Chaz?" she said, nearly choking on my name, and when I heard her voice I suddenly realized who she was.

Kyra. Kyra McCullough.

The last time I'd seen her she'd been a sturdy matron of fifty-one who wore her thick gray hair in a braid.

For a moment we just gaped at each other, hanging blinking in the air. Kyra was supposed to have awakened on mission day three, same as me, but the way she moved showed that she was already acclimated to free-fall. Something very wrong was happening here.

"Yeah, it's me," I said. My voice sounded strange—too high, too thin. "I... I just vived. It was... rough. No sedatives. And my memories... Kyra, I don't remember a single thing after initial scan."

"Oh, Chaz..." her eyes glistened, but she didn't say anything more.

"What day is it?"

"Uh... day ten."

"And I'm the only one who... overslept?"

She swallowed. "Yes."

So they'd all been awake for a week or more without me. "Did anyone else have any... memory problems?"

"No. Everyone's clear, right up to final scan." She stopped, blinked. "Well, except you. I... Chaz, I'm so sorry... we were... we were going to..."

"Why wasn't anyone there to help me through vivification?" I was starting to get peeved. "You could at least have handed me a darn towel."

"I... I'm sorry. You weren't supposed to w... uh, to wake up by yourself."

"And who the *heck* decided to vive me with outdated memories?" I spat.

The initial synaptic recordings that had been placed on board along with our cell samples were only a last-ditch backup; they were not supposed to be used unless *Cassiopeia* failed to receive *any* of the scans transmitted from Earth during the two years after launch. And from what Kyra had said, that hadn't happened. I gave up a lot to join the first crewed expedition to another star, but I still had the Constitutional right to control the destiny of my consciousness, and I had *not* consented to be vived with outdated and untrained memories unless there were absolutely no alternative.

"Chaz...." She swallowed. "We... we didn't..."

She paused again, seeming to gather herself. She still hadn't moved from the spot she'd been working when I entered the work bay.

"Chaz, you... you died."

"I... died." Repeating the word didn't make it any more comprehensible. It was as though my ears could parse the sound, but my brain couldn't attach any meaning to it.

"You died. Almost two years ago... I mean, two years before final scan. Just a week before scan number two. You were hit by a car in a crosswalk. The driver was on skip. We all went to your funeral. Tien sang 'Rising to the Light,' it was so beautiful, and the Director said that you..." She seemed to hear what she was saying and cut herself off. "Oh, God...." She wiped her nose on her sleeve. "I'm so sorry, Chaz, I'm such an idiot..."

I realized I had let go of the rail and was floating stupidly in the middle of the port. It must be a mistake. I couldn't be dead.

But I could be. Most likely we all were.

If *Cassie* had reached Tau Ceti on the original schedule, my last Earthbound memories were over eighty years old: forty years of boost from the drive lasers in Earth orbit, thirty years coasting, two years of repeated aerobraking maneuvers in the target system's three Neptune-sized gas giants, and ten or twenty years with *Cassie*'s automated systems gathering raw materials and assembling habitations, equipment... and crew. If Kyra were still alive back home, she'd be at least a hundred and forty.

She might be. But I wasn't. This... this copy of me, was the only one.

For a moment I wondered why I hadn't simply been replaced when I died. But *Cassie* was scheduled to launch—no, *had* launched—just days after first scan, with those initial scans and our cell samples on board. After that point, the crew roster was irrevocably fixed.

I must have cheered as the boosters had thundered into the Florida sky. Not knowing I'd be dead in less than three months. Or that my clone would be vived eighty years later with no memory of the event. Trying to make sense of the mixture of future and past made my head hurt.

"Well," I managed at last. My eyes were dry, but I felt brittle and hollow inside, as though I were a mockup of myself built from papier-mâché and chicken wire. Why should I be reacting this way to the news that a body I once occupied had died over eighty years ago? *I* was alive, thank Jesus. And I was on the greatest scientific expedition in human history.

An expedition from which I would never return.

God was everywhere in the Universe, I knew, and before I'd even sent in my application I'd consulted with my pastor and satisfied myself that my clone's soul would be welcomed in Heaven at the end of its mission to Tau Ceti. But now that *I* was the clone, faced with the reality of my own original's death, I wondered anew. How could I be certain that God would not consider this mission a form of extended, technologically-assisted suicide?

I blinked and saw that Kyra was still floating in the same spot. It was as though she feared death might be contagious. "Can I get you something?" she asked. "Something to drink?"

"Yeah. Yeah, that might be a good idea."

She slipped through the port to the habitation bay below, neatly avoiding any contact with me, and came back with a cold squeeze-bulb of tomato juice. "I was hoping for a gin and tonic," I said.

She gave me an apologetic grin. "You know the drill. No solid food for three days, no alcohol for a week." Which reminded me all over again that my body was brand new—this throat had never before swallowed anything, and no food or drink had ever before landed in this stomach.

I had thought I was prepared for this. I was learning that I wasn't. I put my head in my hands... and was startled to feel springy curls instead of the bald pate I remembered.

While I sipped my juice, mind racing, Kyra got on the intercom. "Tench tench," she said, her voice echoing from speakers throughout the ship, "Chaz is awake. I repeat, Chaz is awake. We're in Epsilon work bay."

Tench tench? What was that supposed to mean?

As each of the other crew members floated into the bay, their reactions to me varied. Tien said "oh, Chaz..." and bit her lip, eyes glistening. Bobb gave me a hug, which was very much like him—but it seemed distant, as though he were somehow not really touching me at all. Matt shook my hand and said "Welcome to *Cassie*, mate." Nuru just inclined her head in solemn greeting.

Mari was the last to arrive, and she didn't meet my eye.

As for my reactions to them... only the seriousness of the situation kept me from giggling, because the seven of us looked like the junior high school science club. Bobb, a bear of a man back on Earth, was now a tall gawky white guy with just a few wisps of black fuzz on his cheeks. Matt, an avid rock climber and bicyclist, lean and tanned with sinew flexing beneath his tattoos, was now scrawny and pale. Tien had always been elfin, but her Asian elegance had vanished under the same shapeless white coverall and brush-cut hair as the rest of us. Everyone was at least a head taller than I remembered them, the legacy of being grown in zero gravity. None of us would ever be able to stand up in a full gee.

Of course we didn't expect to ever return to Earth, or to live long enough for the long-term effects of life in free fall to catch up with us, which was why the designers hadn't bothered making the ship big enough to spin for artificial gravity. It had seemed like a reasonable decision when I'd been making it for my clone, but now that it was *me* up here, all frail and attenuated, I questioned the judgment of my previous self.

Nuru was the least changed of us, I thought at first: even floating in free fall she carried herself with the same grave dignity as before, and the deep brown eyes in that mahogany face, even darker than mine, had lost none of their wisdom. But then I realized how lithe and straight and smooth her body had become, all the infirmities of age cast aside.

And then there was Mari. My eyes kept drifting back to her, wondering what it was about her that made her look *so* different. She had the same lush black hair and dark expressive eyes, the same fine olive-brown complexion I'd always longed to touch. Maybe she'd lost more weight than some of the others...

No. More than just weight.

Mari was now male.

The realization was like biting into a ripe peach and finding it rotten inside. I knew that there were such things as transsexuals, but I'd never met one before... or so I'd thought. The idea that a person might want to change something so God-given, so fundamental, about themselves was disconcerting enough in the abstract, but seeing such a transformation in someone I'd known—and even been attracted to—was profoundly disquieting.

Before I could really come to grips with Mari, or whatever her-his name was now, Nuru clapped her hands twice. It was her usual way of calling a meeting to order. "Welcome back, Chaz," she said, and everyone murmured assent. "As good as it is to see you again, I'm sorry it must be under such sad and unexpected circumstances for you. We had planned to delay your vival until we were better prepared to accommodate your psychological needs." She looked around at her crew, dark eyes lingering on each face in turn. "I don't know why you were vived just now. Bobb, would you please investigate?"

"Monit monit," Bobb said.

I frowned. What did "monit monit" mean?

They were all looking at me. Except Mari. I shook off the question. "Thank you," I said, to Nuru and to the group as a whole. "Though I can't say I'm happy to learn of my own death, or to find myself on board with incomplete training, I'm excited to be a part of this historic mission. I hope that you will try to keep my... limitations in mind, and I promise to use as much caution and common sense as I can. But if you see me about to open the airlock thinking it's the bathroom, please don't hesitate to correct me."

No one laughed.

"So," I continued, trying to pretend my failed joke hadn't been intended to be funny, "what have I missed?"

In some ways I hadn't missed much. Nuru, the mission commander, had vived ten days ago, the others following at intervals over the next three days. So far they had checked and inventoried all of *Cassie*'s systems and performed an initial analysis on the fourteen years of data she'd gathered while building up her systems and crew.

In addition to the three gas giants we'd known about, named Voltaire, Molière, and Balzac by the French scientists who'd discovered them, the Tau Ceti system held at least three terrestrial planets, which we'd christened Achebe, Shakespeare, and Tolstoy. Unfortunately, Tolstoy was a slushy iceball and the other two tiny, airless rocks—all three subject to constant bombardment from the system's thick disk of planetesimals. Not very hospitable. But that same thick traffic of ice and rock fragments might have hidden other planets from *Cassiopeia's* instruments, so the search went on.

All of that information was fascinating, but not entirely unexpected. On the other hand, *Cassie* herself had sprung a couple of unpleasant surprises.

For one thing, the ship was only three-fifths complete. Alpha module hadn't made the rendezvous—lost somewhere in the vacant light-years between Earth and here. Also lost was Delta, which had made it all the way to Tau Ceti only to burn up in the first aerobraking maneuver. So instead of the planned pentagonal bundle of five cylinders, *Cassiopeia* was a shallow V, with Gamma module between Beta and Epsilon. Fortunately, three modules provided sufficient resources and space for our purposes; the mission had been designed to succeed with as little as one module, but it would have been tight quarters.

The other surprise was that we had no communications from Earth. *Cassie* had not received any data at all from back home for over thirty-three years.

"What?" I shouted as soon as Nuru dropped that bombshell. "No *Earth?*"

Nuru raised one long brown finger. "Ojer ojer. Don't leap to conclusions."

All three of *Cassiopeia's* surviving modules, she explained, had suffered failures in their long-range receivers during the long trip here: Beta during year eight, Epsilon in year twenty-one, and Gamma in year forty-seven. In each module's database, the signals were clear and strong right up to the end of the data, then cut off suddenly—all frequencies simultaneously, both natural and artificial. No disaster, natural or human-made, could have had such an effect; the problem had to be on our end.

"That's what comes of having everything built by the low bidder," Bobb said.

Dear Jesus, protect us from any other malfunction. "But if we can't send our data back home, what's the point of the mission?"

Nuru shook her head. "I didn't say we couldn't communicate *to* Earth. We know from the probe satellites that our long-range transmitters are putting out a good strong signal, and we have a solid navigational fix on Sol, so we can be sure our transmissions will be received. I've asked Bobb to prioritize this problem lower than some other tasks. We can wait a week or two to find out what happened back home while we were in transit."

"Not that it really matters to us anyway," Matt said.

I could see his point, but I couldn't agree. Any news from Earth was purely academic to us, since we'd never be returning, but I did want to know what we'd missed in the eighty years since we'd launched. And we had to establish two-way communications eventually, or we'd lose the insights of Earth's finest scientists into our findings... and we'd never know if we'd made a difference. Even a twenty-four-year wait for our data to crawl Earthward at lightspeed and the acknowledgement to return was better than nothing.

Assuming we survived that long. Amazing as it was that we had made it this far with ship and crew largely intact, we couldn't know how long it might be before the unknown hazards of an unexplored planetary system did us in. Even though we had our whole lives here ahead of us, and *Cassie* was designed to last at least thirty years, the mission planners had drilled into us again and again that we had to move quickly—to get as much data shipped off to Earth as possible, as quickly as possible. *Cassie* had started the job, transmitting her raw data as soon as she'd arrived, but we could add our analysis and direct the instruments to research the most interesting findings more deeply.

Assuming our transmissions were reaching Earth at all. "I'd like to look into the communications problem," I said. Though Bobb was the primary ship systems specialist and my specialty was terrestrial planetology, each of us performed multiple functions and I was secondary on ship systems. "Two pairs of eyes are better than one."

"I'd rather have you doing science," Nuru replied, her dark eyes level. "Now that you're here, I'd appreciate your insights into some questions of Achebe's crustal evolution."

I inclined my head in acknowledgement. I couldn't deny that science had to take precedence over ship systems—unless crew safety was at stake, of course.

#

Mari, our life sciences specialist and the closest thing we had to a doctor, gave me a check-up as soon as the initial meeting was over. "Breathe in," she said, listening to her stethoscope and not meeting my eye.

I inhaled as requested, watching her face. Now that I saw her... him... without make-up, without décolletage—for that matter, without breasts—I saw how blocky the planes of the face were, how thick the jaw and wrists. How had I ever considered her attractive? "So," I said on the exhale, "what do I call you now?"

She-he didn't look up. "Mari."

"No... I mean... what pronoun do I use?"

"She." Mari turned me brusquely in the air and rapped on my back with two fingers. I noticed she was still avoiding looking me in the face. "Breathe in again." I did as she asked, and then bent and stretched and presented various body parts as requested.

I tried to think of Mari as "she," really I did, but I found it impossible to ignore the very male body that was so disturbingly close to me. And when she put on the rubber gloves and asked me to turn around for a prostate check... "No way!" I said, holding up my hands.

Mari turned away from me, seeming to gather herself, then turned back. "Look, Chaz, I know how uncomfortable this makes you, but you'll just have to deal with it. I'm female where it counts... up here." She tapped her forehead. "Always have been, always will be." Her words began to gain speed and vehemence. "I've lived as a woman since I was sixteen, and I didn't get the surgery until I was thirty-five. Just having a *penis*"—she spat the word— "didn't make me male then, and it doesn't now!"

"Hey, cool down!" I sputtered. "I need a chance to... to get used to the new you. Maybe we could, you know, talk it over."

Mari threw up her arms, her face livid with anger. "You and I already hashed this whole thing out once, back on Earth, and you were a real shit about it! I don't see any reason I should have to go through the same painful process again for your sake."

"But that wasn't *me*! And I don't see any reason I should have to suffer for the mistakes of that previous person."

"Then who should? Me? *Again?* No thanks." And she kicked off from the med station and disappeared into the work bay below.

I didn't follow.

#

A couple of days later I was in Beta work bay, peering into a stereoscopic viewer at a pair of images from Achebe. This planet was similar to Mars, but a little smaller and a little farther from its star, which with Tau Ceti's lower luminance meant it was substantially colder. It also showed little sign of naturally occurring radioactivity. That lack of energy should have made Achebe solid rock almost all the way to its core... yet there were signs of recent tectonic activity. Either we'd misinterpreted those signs, or the theories of planetary evolution would need to be revised. Which was, after all, why we were here.

It sure would be nice to know for sure that the data we were gathering was being successfully transmitted. Bobb was working on the communications issue but he kept running into problem after problem—hardware failures, software glitches, database snafus—and could frequently be heard cursing the subcontractor responsible for the long-range receiver. These problems made the idea that the communications failure was entirely on our end seem more and more likely, even as they made it harder to debug. I shook my head and returned my attention to planetology.

At the moment I was looking at a surface feature that looked like a huge, ancient impact crater pulled into two separate half-circles by the motion of two plates of Achebe's crust—something never seen on any body so small and cold in Sol system. I was hoping that a stereo view would help convince me I was really seeing evidence of tectonic motion, and not just a pair of semicircular rilles that happened to look like the halves of one battered crater. But the two images in the stereoscope had been taken too far apart, and the attempt just gave me a headache.

I pushed away the stereoscope and called up an orbital chart on the monitor. *Cassie* was in an elliptical solar orbit at an angle to the plane of the ecliptic, an orbit that avoided most of the system's dense and dangerous cloud of planetesimals while still taking us in naked-eye observational range of many of the system's most interesting bodies every fifteen years or so. At the moment we were almost 800 light-seconds away from Achebe, and getting farther away every day, but two of the dozens of probe satellites that *Cassiopeia* had scattered throughout the system over the last fourteen years were in orbit around it. And, according to the chart, one of them was in almost exactly the right place. I used my stylus to direct it to take a high-resolution stereo pair in IR and visible light, then moved onto another phase of the analysis while waiting for my images to arrive.

Ten minutes later I got something, but it wasn't what I'd expected. Tien shot out of the port from Gamma work bay, diving right at me and looking like she was ready to spit nails. "What were you *thinking?*" she said, jerking to a halt with one hand on a panel edge.

"What?"

"You just turned Sat Fourteen around to point at the damn planet. I was in the middle of a system-wide solar wind analysis that needed simultaneous data from all the sats. I'm going to have to set up the whole thing again! You've cost me *days* of work!"

So that had been the meaning of that cryptic confirmation message. Focused on my task, I'd just tapped OK as I did on so many other such messages. "I... I'm sorry. I didn't know..."

"Why the *hell* didn't you check the chromo first?"

"The what?" The word was vaguely familiar, but with all the new concepts the crew had thrown at me in the last few days I couldn't keep them all straight.

"The fucking *chromo!*" She pulled herself in front of me and keyed my monitor to a new display. Hundreds of tiny colored squares filled the screen, shimmering and shifting about like the crowd at a soccer game. She pointed at a wide band of light teal that spread across the lower part of the screen, with one orange square vibrating in the middle of it. "See? There's Sat Fourteen, right in the middle of my pattern."

"I... I see, but I don't understand. I've never seen this display before."

"You... you've... *ooh!*" She squeezed her eyes shut and shook her head with an inarticulate noise of irritation. "Kay kay. Hue is topic, luminance is importance, saturation is relevance. Proximity indicates correlation, of course. Jitter is freshness, jump is urgency. Use the help if you get lost." She pointed to a tiny question mark in one corner. "If you have any questions, ask Bobb. But until you can learn how to avoid stepping on other people's work, I'd suggest you leave the damn sats alone! Now if you'll excuse me, I have a solar wind analysis to set up. Again!"

And she dove through the port back to Gamma.

After Tien left, I just hung there for a moment, clutching my stylus and clenching my teeth. How *dare* she just barge in, rip me a new one, bury me under incomprehensible jargon, and storm out? It wasn't my fault I'd died. I hadn't asked to be vived without proper training. I was trying as hard as I could to catch up, and I'd asked the crew to cut me some slack. If this was the consideration I got... well, then, to heck with her.

On the other hand, I *had* messed up. I should have realized that a satellite was a shared resource, and found out how to check that no one else was using it. I should have read and understood the confirmation message before tapping OK. But I hadn't, and now I'd made an enemy.

I considered following Tien and asking her forgiveness, but the vehemence with which she'd departed made me think that it might be better to wait a while, until she calmed down. In the meantime, I decided to learn about this "chromo" thing so I didn't make any more stupid mistakes.

I stared at the jittering, dancing array of squares for a while longer, feeling foolish and angry with myself, then tapped the question mark—the only thing Tien had mentioned that made any sense at all.

A chromo, it turned out, was a shared-source software tool for visualization of dynamic information. The *Cassiopeia* crew hadn't started using them until some time after my last memory. But, according to the local history log, once they'd started the team had gotten into the tool in a big way, and used it to coordinate all their activities. Several members of the team—including, most disquietingly, myself—had even developed new software features and contributed them to the chromo-using community. The satellite information chromo Tien had showed me was just one of a dozen in the ship's computers.

I could see how useful chromos could be—the information density of that twitchy screen was enormous. I could also see that, unless you had started from the beginning and learned the system bit by bit as it grew in complexity, the learning curve would be extremely steep.

There was a tutorial. I started in on it.

#

We had one meal a day together, in Gamma habitation bay; we called it "dinner" although it was breakfast for some, a midnight snack for others. This was our time to share findings as well as food.

Tien had put some amazingly beautiful photographs of Balzac's ring system up on the big monitor. As the slide show advanced, she pointed out the delicate structure of the G ring, peculiar waves in the H ring, a shimmering rainbow of ice crystals in the B ring. Balzac's rings were even bigger than Saturn's, relative to the size of their primary, and their peculiarities hinted at answers to longstanding questions about the formation and maintenance of Saturn's rings—answers that would never have been forthcoming from study of only a single solar system—and raised more questions, even more intriguing than the answers. Ideas and speculations ricocheted around the habitation bay like lasers, with Nuru finishing Kyra's sentences and Mari pointing out interesting implications of Tien's latest theory.

At one point Matt's hand brushed against Tien's, and a significant look passed between them. I wondered if they were sleeping together.

Sex was permitted by the mission profile. All the women were on birth control, of course, implanted before vival. We'd been offered sex-drive suppressants as well, but after reviewing the side effects we'd agreed as a group that no matter how young and lithe our cloned bodies might be, our minds were those of mature adults and we could deal with the close quarters without chemical assistance. It was another decision that had seemed to make sense when I was making it for my clone.

Despite the lively technical discussion, Kyra was looking sad and pensive. "I wonder what Mkebe Osarenogowu would think of all this?" she asked, naming one of the most prominent astrophysicists back home... or at least, one who had been prominent at the time we'd left. He was almost certainly dead by now.

"Or *anyone* on Earth," Tien added, reminding us all that we still had not re-established contact. Faces fell all around the table.

Bobb looked both sheepish and angry. "I'm sorry, guys," he said, shaking his head. "I've been giving the problem as much attention as I can, but every time I think I'm getting close to a solution it seems that something else breaks."

Nuru broke the melancholy silence that followed by taking the remote and advancing to the next image. "What's that feature there?" she asked Tien, pointing out a thread-thin wavy ring in the otherwise-empty gap between D and E rings. Tien started to explain, getting more and more excited about the possibilities, but Kyra had a different theory, and soon a lively scientific debate erupted.

Tien waved her spring roll at the monitor to emphasize some point. Kyra grabbed at the remote to zoom in on the gap, but Matt was more interested in another part of the image and refused to hand it over. The two of them mock-tussled briefly over the remote, until Matt neatly slipped it out of Kyra's grasp and flipped it behind his back to Nuru. But Mari snagged the remote from the air, and used it to back up to a previous image she'd wanted to examine in more detail. "Otcha otcha!" said Bobb, and everyone laughed.

Everyone but me. I found their doubled slang pointless and childish. Usually I could puzzle it out—"otcha otcha" was "gotcha", just as "kay kay" was "okay" and "ojer ojer" was "hold your horses"—but it didn't seem worth the effort. I sighed to myself and took another swallow of my tomato soup. It was too salty. When it was my turn to cook I'd show them how much better it could be with less salt and more herbs.

And then I noticed what I was thinking. "Them." How had this happened? When did I start thinking of my crewmates as "them"?

It had been so different six months ago... six months ago in my memories, that is; six months before first scan, which turned out to be my last. That was when the crew had taken its first meal together, right after the press conference where our selection had been announced to the world. The President had been there, and representatives of all the other countries participating in the project, and we were all in our finest formal clothing, but even as the tuxedoed waiters brought out the fish course on chilled china with the White House seal we couldn't help peering at each other and grinning our fool heads off.

We'd made it!

That dinner was the culmination of a selection process that had taken almost three years. This was the first crew of astronauts ever to be selected entirely on the basis of experience and intellect rather than physical fitness, and tens of thousands of scientists worldwide who'd never before considered themselves astronaut material had applied. The chosen seven who'd emerged from that process ranged in age from forty-eight to eighty-three, and many were fat or frail, but that didn't matter—after two and a half years of intensive training together, we would return to our previous lives, sending copies of our memories and skills to Tau Ceti in fresh young bodies.

On that evening the seven of us might as well have been one person. Despite our different ages, backgrounds, and races, we were all intensely committed to science, showed great mental agility and world-class expertise in two or more fields, and were prepared to commit the next two and a half years of our lives to the *Cassiopeia* mission. Not to mention we'd all survived the same gantlet of tests, interviews, and simulations. As each of us faced the same questions from the reporters and politicians, we gave similar modest answers, but we saw in each other's eyes the same triumphant gleam. And when, after the formalities had concluded, we withdrew to our hotel, we stayed up talking and laughing until nearly dawn, too amazed at our good fortune to sleep. The next day we'd flown to Dallas to begin our training.

It had all started out so well. But the rest of the crew had been through two more years of training than I had... two years to build up skills and tools and slang that tied them together into a single functioning unit. A unit that didn't include me.

Fine. It wasn't my fault, and it wasn't really their fault either. I would just have to make the best of it—to try to fit in as best I could.

#

I continued to study the planet Achebe, delving into the mystery of its tectonic activity. New satellite photos—this time properly scheduled via the chromo—confirmed that the thing I'd thought was an ancient crater torn apart by crustal drift really was what it seemed to be. But scans for radioactivity turned up negative, and there were no nearby large bodies to produce heat by tidal squeezing. So what was the source of the energy that kept the mantle fluid enough for the tectonic movement I'd seen?

I stretched in the air and stuck my stylus back in its holder. Maybe a short break would refresh my mind. I shoved myself away from my work station, turned in the air, and grabbed a strut to propel myself to the habitation bay.

I floated through the habitation bay's central space and into the airlock in the "floor," swinging the hatch shut behind me as required by protocol. Being just one door away from vacuum made it all feel more real, somehow; it put me more in touch with the fact that I was really in space.

But that wasn't the main reason I liked it here.

The window in the center of the outer hatch was round, twenty centimeters in diameter—I could easily span it with one hand—and already slightly scratched and smeared with fingerprints. And the view was nothing special, to be honest... spectacular ringed Balzac was farther from our current location than Saturn was from Earth at closest approach, the other planets even further away. In fact, all I could see through the window was a few bright dots, and those only if I pressed my face to the window and shielded my eyes with my hands. I didn't know which of those dots were planets; I hadn't tried to correlate the view with the orbital charts. But the sun whose rays warmed my skin through that window was not the Sun—it was Tau Ceti.

I was one of only seven human beings ever to bathe in the light of another star.

I floated there for a while, the window's plastic cold against my forehead, soaking in that alien sunlight. But then my reverie was interrupted by a muffled curse. It was followed by another curse, this one loud enough to be clearly audible through the plastic of the inner airlock door.

Curious, I returned to the habitation bay, where I saw light leaking around the door to Matt's room. That door was also the source of a continuing muttering and scuffling sound. "Are you okay in there?" I called.

Matt's voice was curiously muffled. "Actually, I'd appreciate it if you'd give me a hand..."

I'd never been in Matt's personal space before. The walls were bright with photographs of Matt and his wife, and various other trim, muscular people, on mountains, rock walls, trails, and beaches. He must have used his entire paper allowance for the first month on them. Matt himself floated awkwardly in one corner, holding his left bicep firmly with his right hand.

The hand was wet with blood. Small drops of blood floated all around it... blood, and something else. Something black.

"Can you snag me that bottle there?" he said, gesturing with his chin. He was clutching some kind of instrument between his teeth.

I grabbed the indicated bottle from where it floated near the air vent—the place where all dropped items accumulated—and tossed it to Matt. He caught it with his bloody hand and squirted clear liquid onto his bicep, drawing in his breath with a hiss as he did so. A sharp tang of alcohol hit my nostrils.

As Matt daubed away the alcohol with a fabric wipe, I saw that the injured bicep bore the outline of a four-leafed clover, cut into the skin and oozing blood. The whole area was stained black with ink.

"A *tattoo*?" I said. "You can't be serious."

"What does it look like?" he replied, and squirted more alcohol onto the cut.

"But..." I'd never understood why anyone would get a tattoo at all, never mind doing it to himself with a sharpened pair of tweezers. "I don't get it. There's nobody here to impress."

He inspected the damaged area with a hand mirror, then started rolling a fabric gauze bandage around his arm. "I didn't do it to impress anyone. I did it for me. Tear me off some of that tape, would you?" I did as he asked, handing him strips of tape one at a time. "Every tat I had, back on Earth, commemorated a significant experience in my life. This one is to remind me how lucky I am to be here. And to remind me who I am." He patted a plastic covering sheet onto the bandage; a little blood was already seeping through the fabric.

"And who are you?"

Matt looked me right in the eye. "I'm me. Me, here, now. *Not* the man who had three red and gold koi put on his left bicep in Kauai when he was twenty-three. That man was an astrophysicist, and he probably died at the bottom of some crevasse on Earth forty years ago. But the man with a lucky clover on his bicep is a fucking *astronaut*. This tat helps me remember which of those men I am."

Matt's intensity was almost scary. "You're taking your own death a lot better than I did."

"Well, for me it's just theoretical. No one here went to my funeral."

I looked down. "Unlike me."

"Buck up, mate. You've got a whole new life to screw up."

I had to grin at that. "Thanks."

#

I used the remote to move the pointer on the big monitor. "So here's Anansi crater, the feature that first gave me the clue. You can see how the two halves appear to have been pulled apart by tectonic activity. But Achebe's too small and cold to be tectonically active. So what's up?"

Mari didn't look up from her omelet. She had barely had a word for me since the day I'd been vived. Tien, too, had been very distant ever since I'd spoiled her solar wind experiment. But the others looked on with varying levels of interest. I'd been keeping to myself for the last week, thrashing out the details on my theory, and they wanted to know what I'd come up with.

I swallowed, then continued. "I'd like you to note how badly hammered the crater is by later impacts. It looks like it's a million years old. But when I did a gravitic scan for mascons, I found what I think is the original impact body just a few kilometers below the surface. That, and a seismic ring analysis, lead me to conclude that this crater is less than ten thousand years old. Achebe gets a *lot* of impacts."

My heart, already pounding hard, picked up the pace even further. I'd always been nervous about public speaking, never more so than when introducing a new idea, and in this case I was venturing into entirely new theoretical territory. I put up a slide full of statistics and formulae.

"We don't yet know exactly how many megatons of rock and ice land on Achebe every year. But based on Matt's preliminary orbital analyses of the planetesimal disk, I've estimated the average impact frequency and the impacting objects' mass and velocity." I switched to the next slide, which showed a graph of estimated temperature overlaid with an annotated cross-section of the planet. "Based on these estimates, the total energy added from infall is between ten to the twenty-first and ten to the twenty-third joules per year." Another slide crammed with data. "That might be just enough to keep the magma layer below the crust liquid, accounting for the otherwise unexplainable crustal movement."

No one said anything. They were all just looking at me.

This wasn't the reaction I'd expected. I'd investigated an extremely interesting anomaly and devised a radical new theory to explain it. I'd hoped for acclaim, but had been prepared for an argument. I got... silence.

I managed a wavery grin. "Any questions?"

After another interminable pause, Kyra spoke. "That's an excellent confirmation of Pederson and Wu. But do you have anything new to add?"

I felt blindsided. "I'm sorry?"

"Pederson and Wu. From Washington University. They published after... after you died, but surely you did a literature search?"

"I... I did, yes, of course I did, but it didn't turn up those names." I stared from face to face, in hopes that someone would rescue me from this appalling situation. But Tien just looked exasperated, Bobb refused to meet my eyes, and Nuru was slowly shaking her head. I fumbled with the remote, keyed in a search. "Peterson?"

"Pe*d*erson," said Kyra. "With a D as in dog."

There it was, right at the top of the first page of results. *Dynamic analysis of particulate interaction with prolate spheroids*, from the *American Journal of Topology*. It was dated over a year after my last Earth memory. "This is pure mathematics," I said. "It doesn't have any relevant keywords." No wonder it hadn't turned up in my searches.

"That's what Pederson and Wu thought," said Tien. "But the planetology community realized that this thesis, applied to meteorite impacts on Saturn's moons, could explain why Enceladus is so smooth."

I scrolled through the results, increasingly frantic. There were several references to the Pederson and Wu paper, but they were all in the pure math realm. "There's no sign of that connection in the database." I felt my voice trying to crack, but clutched the remote and kept it under control.

Nuru spoke up. "This was all happening right before final scan. We all knew about it, but it's possible that none of the papers on the planetology connection were actually published before the database was put to bed." She gave an apologetic little smile. "I think there was a poster session at the ASPS conference."

"Poster sessions don't appear in the conference proceedings..." I began, but it was hopeless. I'd blown it. I should have dug deeper into the literature, should have asked someone else to look at my conclusions, shouldn't have been so eager to believe I'd discovered something completely new.

I didn't finish my sentence. I left the remote hanging in the air, left my lunch untouched, left everyone behind me. I needed to be alone for a while.

No one followed.

#

I pushed myself through the air, not really looking where I was going, glancing painfully off of panels and struts. Eventually I found myself in the airlock off of Epsilon habitation bay, near my personal space. I closed and dogged the inner hatch, then curled up into a ball, clutching my knees. I drifted, trembling.

I could see now that I had never really fit in with the rest of the *Cassiopeia* crew. They were all from academic or government service backgrounds; I was the only one who'd come from industry. I'd put myself through college as a welder, then worked in the space development sector for years before going back for my doctorate at age thirty-one; they were mostly from privileged backgrounds and had been in one branch or another of space science for their entire careers. I was the only black person other than Nuru—and she was the commander, which set her apart. I was the only regular churchgoer in the bunch.

Oh, sure, we had all bonded at first. But from here I could see the cracks that had already been developing in that bond between me and the rest of them by the time of first scan. The two years they'd worked together without me had only deepened those cracks.

I wiped my nose on my sleeve. Okay, so I didn't fit in. What the heck was I going to do about it?

I might be out of sync on the technologies. I might be out of date on the science. I might be completely out of step with the rest of the crew. But I still had all the real-world skills that had earned me my position as secondary on ship systems: diagnostic, debugging, and repair skills independent of any specific technology.

Even if my relationship with the crew was beyond repair, at least I could fix anything broken in the ship itself. And there was one thing that I already knew was broken: the communication link from Earth.

The malfunction, whatever it was, had not stopped us from continuing our mission. With dozens of sats sending in petabytes of data every day from a whole new solar system, every one of us had more than enough fascinating work to do that the absence of news from Earth was something we could sometimes forget for days at a time. But I'd browsed through the forty-seven years of data we *did* have, and it just made me more curious about what had happened after that.

"Who cares?" Matt said when I brought up the issue during a coffee break one day. "It's just old news, and completely irrelevant to us. Look at this." He pulled up a page of headlines on the big screen. "Is this 'Goruba Jost' a video star, a politician, or a beach resort? What are 'greeblies' and why are the 'woffers' so upset about them? And this is from just twenty years after we left! The newer stuff is even less comprehensible. Why are you worrying about trivia from Earth when there's more than a lifetime of fascinating science to do right here?"

Knowing I'd never convince him, I mumbled some excuse and turned away. But he hadn't changed my mind either... I'd already followed the lives of my nieces and nephews as far as I could, and I wanted to know more about them, their children and grandchildren, the places I'd lived...

Nuru kept reminding us that our primary mission was to gather as much data as possible and send it back as quickly as possible. Only when we had completed the initial system survey and our situation seemed stable, she said, would we have time to spend on distractions like catching up with eighty years of scientific progress back home. But I'd done the best I could toward our primary mission and I'd gotten nowhere with it. Here at least was something I knew I could *do*.

#

I'd poked at the problem a few times in the two weeks I'd been awake, but hadn't even been able to determine the cause. Now I threw myself into the investigation full time.

I started with basic hardware diagnostics. I was certain that Bobb would already have run those, but I wanted to establish a firm baseline. And in only a few hours of work, I did determine that the communications hardware was operating properly—at least to the extent it was able to check itself.

But a hardware diagnostic was just the first step—like making sure a non-functioning device was actually plugged in and booted up. The next phase would dig deeper, isolating each component and testing its inputs and outputs separate from the system. I wrote myself a checklist and set to work.

Days went by, then weeks. Each time I thought I'd found the source of the problem, it seemed that something else nearby would fail, requiring me to fix that before I could proceed. With nothing to report, other than that I was spending almost all my time on a side project that Nuru had explicitly told me not to do, I spent less and less time in the common area at dinner, just dashing in, grabbing a bite, and dashing out; finally I stopped attending completely. I spent hours at a time with my head buried in access panels, or staring at technical readouts. Sometimes I went for days without speaking to anyone.

Nobody seemed to be missing me much. Mari, Tien, and even Bobb—who'd become extremely distant, for no reason I could discern—were probably quietly relieved that I wasn't doing anything to mess up their science or rile up their emotions. Nuru had always given her people a pretty free rein, and probably assumed I was going into more depth on Achebe's crust; she didn't pester me for a status report. And Kyra and Matt were busy enough with their own work that they might not even have noticed I wasn't interacting with them as much as I used to. Or else they, too, were relieved at it.

But no matter how hard I worked, how little sleep I got, how many other malfunctions I worked around, the answer was always the same: Nothing. Nothing. Nothing. It was an engineer's nightmare—all the pieces worked, but the whole didn't. The big dish was able to receive signals from our probe satellites, the signal was properly amplified, the amplified signal could be decoded, the decoded signal could be stored. That was under test conditions. But when I put all the pieces together and pointed the dish at Earth? Nothing.

Naturally, I began to worry that it was Earth, not the dish, that was at fault. But with all three modules showing the same sudden cut-off of both natural and artificial signals at different times, that seemed unlikely. A global multiple thermonuclear detonation would have ended with a burst of radio noise; a meteor strike would have been followed by the calls of the survivors, for at least a few hours. And when I reviewed the news channels for the weeks and months before the final recorded transmission in year forty-seven, there was no hint of concern about a disaster of global proportions. I couldn't imagine anything big enough to take out an entire planet that could strike without any warning at all.

The problem *had* to be on our end.

But then, after another fruitless day—another day of trying to solve a problem that, from all I could tell, didn't actually exist—I awoke from three hours of sleep with a key realization. Stark naked, I logged into the database from the screen in my room.

Cassiopeia's five modules had all been built from the same designs at the same time by the same contractors. It wasn't completely astonishing that a subsystem had failed in the same way on all three surviving modules. But I hadn't seen that kind of triple failure in any other subsystem. For that matter, I hadn't seen even one other failure big enough to take out an entire critical subsystem on even one module, and the long-range receiver was certainly a critical subsystem.

I'd inspected all the pieces and they were all working. The only thing that could have caused the same failure in all three modules was a systemic integration or design problem, but I couldn't imagine how a problem that widespread could leave no other symptoms.

So I looked to see if there were any other differences in the three databases that might tell me what had gone wrong. But I soon discovered that *Cassie*'s merged database didn't record the source of each individual record—I had no way to tell whether any given piece of data had been recorded by Beta, Gamma, Epsilon, or a mix of the three. There was a field for that information, but it was inexplicably blank in every relevant record. And when I went to check the original, separate databases...

They weren't there.

I ground my teeth in frustration. *Cassiopeia* had capacity for at least thirty years of data—there was absolutely no reason to have deleted those databases after the merge, no matter how redundant they may have seemed. But they weren't in the primary store, they weren't in the backup, they weren't in the archive, and they weren't in the redundant array.

And we sure as heck didn't have any off-site backups.

I floated, staring at the screen, feeling the sweat cooling on my flat belly and worrying at the things I wasn't seeing. The missing data indicated a serious problem—I wasn't yet sure if it was software, hardware, or human error. The word "sabotage" tickled at the back of my head, but I brushed it away. No need to be paranoid. Yet.

I threw on a coverall and headed off to Bobb's room, in Gamma module.

We didn't all keep the same schedule, but there was a rough consensus ship's "day" and "night," and this was the deepest part of the night. Most of the lights were off, and I drifted past static monitors and stowed equipment that loomed like reefs in a darkened ocean. My sleep-deprived brain saw movement in corners where no movement should be.

I paused at Bobb's door. No light was visible behind it, and I heard a faint rumbling snore. I asked myself if this problem was really urgent enough to justify waking him.

But just as I raised my hand to knock, a raucous klaxon sounded throughout the ship. At the same moment the emergency lights slammed on, blinding me with harsh flat whiteness.

Impact alarm.

I spun in place, blinking in the sudden light and momentarily disoriented. Where was the nearest brace point? The nearest vacuum shelter? The nearest hull repair kit? Before I could regain my bearings, a hammer blow of sound punched my ears, followed by a harsh, high-pitched whistle.

That wasn't good.

Bobb's door burst open, seemingly silent against the whistle of air and the klaxon's repeated blasts, and Bobb tumbled out, struggling into his coverall.

Matt followed him out, buck naked and holding his coverall in one hand.

As I hung slack-jawed at this development, Bobb zipped up his coverall and moved to a wall panel, where he stilled the klaxon. In the ear-ringing silence that followed, the whistling hiss of escaping air was very loud. Bobb cocked his head, listening, then kicked off from the airlock door and shot through the port into the work bay above. Matt and I followed.

The hiss was coming from behind a monitor at the gamma ray spectroscopy station. The monitor itself was black, its screen cracked in a jagged Y, and there was an acrid smell. I popped open the access panel at the base of the station and flipped circuit breakers—a fire now would only make things worse. As I worked, I prayed hard, over and over: "Lord Jesus preserve us, Lord Jesus preserve us..."

Bobb and Matt, meanwhile, were trying to remove the monitor from the wall, so they could repair the hull breach behind it. But though Bobb strained at the wrench handle, it wouldn't budge. "We'll have to saw it loose."

"Too slow," said Matt, and pulled a heavy prybar from the tool box. The tool's momentum made his free-fall movements awkward, but he tucked his legs into the work station's restraint and smashed the prybar repeatedly against the broken monitor's casing. But the casing was made of the same tough plastic as the hull, and apart from sending a few additional glass fragments sailing into the air, this had no effect.

By now Nuru and Mari had appeared, from their rooms in Gamma hab, and Bobb had briefly explained the situation to them. "You're just wasting time with that," Nuru said to Matt. "We've already lost almost fifty pascals of pressure. I want you and Chaz to prep for EVA."

Matt and I exchanged a glance of deep concern. But Nuru was right, as usual—it was beginning to look as though we might not be able to even see the hull breach, never mind repair it, from inside any time soon.

We pulled the emergency air barrier across the port between Gamma work and habitation bays as we passed through it. The barrier's translucent plastic bellied taut as soon as it was sealed, pointing out the seriousness of the leak. Then, after crossing the habitation bay and entering the airlock, we closed and dogged the inner airlock door behind us. The latches snicked into place with disturbing finality.

I called up the decompression checklist on the airlock's little monitor. It had one hundred and ninety-seven steps and, even under emergency conditions, took a minimum of two hours and twenty minutes. While Matt unshipped the lock's two exercise bicycles, I pulled two oxygen masks from their sterile wrappers.

As I inserted the oxygen hose connectors into the socket on the wall, I was uncomfortably reminded of the situation I'd encountered just before the impact alarm. Matt and Bobb had both been in Bobb's room. In the middle of the night. With the lights off. Naked.

What had they been doing in there?

I had some idea—I wasn't naïve. But the very thought made me queasy.

I shook the image out of my head and fastened one of the masks over my nose and mouth, then handed the other mask to Matt. Once he'd donned his mask, I programmed the airlock for EVA stepdown, then fitted my feet into the bike's pedals and began to pump.

It seemed insane that, with the ship losing air and an emergency spacewalk on the agenda, the first thing we had to do was work up a sweat. But our EVA suits were run at a fraction of the ship's air pressure—it made it possible for them to be much lighter and more flexible—and if we subjected ourselves to that lower pressure too quickly we'd get the bends. Nitrogen bubbles expanding in our bloodstreams could cause severe pain, neurological disorders, and even death. So we had to get all the nitrogen out of our blood before decompressing, and the fastest way to do that was to exercise vigorously while breathing pure oxygen.

We pedaled together for a few minutes in silence, side by side, the masks' straps waving around our faces like kelp in the sea as we strained at the pedals. We'd alternate pedaling and resting for the next half-hour, while the airlock ramped slowly down to suit pressure. Then we'd help each other don our suits.

As I mentally reviewed the suit-up process, I became keenly aware of how intimate it was. The liquid-cooled undergarment had to be smoothed over each limb, with no wrinkling or bunching at the armpits or crotch. Fastening the lower torso unit involved a very close embrace around the waist and hips. And fitting the urine collector...

I thought back to one of the last psych interviews I'd endured before the final selection was announced. "We're a little concerned about some of your sensitivity scores," the young white psychologist had said. Two cameras and a large one-way mirror peered over his shoulders. "You show a forty-three percent tendency to homophobia."

"I was raised in a pretty traditional family," I'd replied carefully, knowing that my selection for the Tau Ceti mission was on the line and that any attempt to BS a professional psychologist would only make things worse. "I won't deny that my parents taught me there are absolutes of right and wrong, especially when it comes to sexual behavior. But at the same time they taught me to respect everyone, no matter what their lifestyle or beliefs. Check my record and talk with my colleagues. I think you'll find that, whatever my personal opinions, I've worked cordially with people of all orientations and gender expressions."

"We have already done so, or you and I wouldn't be having this conversation. But some of your prospective crewmates are faggots and dykes." He was a professional; he spoke the words without any trace of emotional content. I was being tested. "You will be trapped in a small spacecraft with them for the rest of your life. How does this make you feel?"

I swallowed, tried to slow my heart rate. "I'm... conflicted. My father would have me hate the sin and love the sinner. But I know there's no room for any kind of hatred on board *Cassiopeia*. And I know that Jesus said nothing about homosexuality." I sat forward in my chair. "What He did say was that there are no greater Commandments than these: 'love thy God with all thy heart' and 'love thy neighbor as thyself.'" My hands clenched together under the table. "I try every day to express that love. Sometimes it's hard. But we're all God's children, so I keep trying."

The psychologist hadn't even blinked. But I must have convinced someone, because the issue had never been raised again.

Suddenly, without preamble, Matt spoke. "I'm sorry you had to see that," he said, his voice ringing hollow in the oxygen mask. "Me and Bobb, I mean. I know how much it upsets you."

It wasn't the first time I'd been surprised by another member of the crew seeming to read my mind. "Am I that transparent?"

Matt shrugged, but said nothing. His facial expression was obscured by the mask.

"I mean..." I said, after a long uncomfortable moment of silence, then trailed off, not sure what I did mean. I tried again: "I mean... aren't you *married?*"

"That was someone else. A man with a goldfish tattooed on his arm." He indicated the shamrock tattoo, still angry red around the edges, with his chin. "This whole expedition is a new adventure... a new life. What better time to try something different?"

My mouth must have gaped open at that, because the mask lost its seal and started whistling around the edges, reminding me of the air leak we were going outside to patch. I closed my mouth and the whistling stopped. "I can't believe anyone could be so flippant about something so serious."

"Why does everything have to be *serious* with you, Chaz? Can't you just accept a little fun as something worthwhile in itself?"

Fun? I noticed I was pedaling harder, as though I were trying to get away. I brought my speed back down with an effort. Love thy neighbor as thyself. "I'm sorry. It's just... it's not..."

"Not what? Natural? Neither is wearing clothes. Not to mention cloning, synaptic recording, and interstellar travel." He shook his head. "Look, neither of us is going to get pregnant, there are no sexually-transmitted diseases in this entire solar system, and no one's cheating on their spouse... the old 'until death do us part' clause has been invoked. The worst that could happen is that someone gets hurt emotionally. And that could happen even without the sex. So where's the harm?"

"But... *Bobb?*"

"Why not? He's a real sweetheart. And, to tell you the truth, I felt a little sorry for him. How'd *you* like to be the only gay man for twelve light years?"

"Bobb?" But even as I said it, I knew it was true.

"Gay as a happy day. I still can't believe you never twigged to it."

Desperate for something to take my mind off this conversation, I reached out and flipped the wall monitor from the EVA checklist to an air pressure graph for Gamma work bay. Still falling steadily. At this rate we had about five hours before we'd have to seal off and abandon that bay. Given that it was the central point of our truncated ship—everything connected to everything else through that bay—losing it would be a major disaster. "We need to discuss strategy for the repair. We'll only get one shot at it."

For the next hour we talked through the agenda and procedures for our upcoming spacewalk, while we alternated pedaling and resting and the air pressure in the lock slowly dropped. Every minute or so I had to swallow to make my ears pop.

Our biggest problem was the swarm of asteroid fragments traveling with the ship in orbit around Tau Ceti. For the last couple of decades, *Cassiopeia* had been intercepting asteroids whenever they came near its path. Those whose spectrum indicated useful materials, such as water, oxygen, or the carbonaceous chondrites that could be processed into plastic, were captured and mined by *Cassie*'s fabricators, and the unusable rock and metal ores discarded—smelting the metal was beyond the ship's capabilities. But it's difficult and expensive to throw anything away in space—unless we wanted to fit each piece of trash rock with an engine, it would move in the same orbit as *Cassie* until our next course change. So anyone on EVA ran the risk of cracking open his helmet on a heavy, jagged rock.

Given the current configuration of the swarm, visible on the same radar that had sounded the warning for the meteoroid that had hit us, I proposed that we leave the thruster packs in the airlock and go handhold-to-handhold across the hull. But Matt gestured at the air pressure graph, rubbing his shoulder with the other hand. "We don't have enough time. The last time I did something like this in the tank, it took me over an hour to crawl half-way down the ship. No, we have to take the thrusters... we'll just keep a sharp eye out for flying rocks." He rubbed his shoulder again.

I switched the monitor to the radar display. "We'll have to take the long way around the ship, then..."

But Matt interrupted me with a sharp indrawn breath. He winced, clutching his shoulder... and then his eyes went wide and his pedaling faltered.

"What's wrong?"

"My shoulder hurts!"

We both knew what that meant. Joint pain was one of the symptoms of decompression sickness. "It can't be the bends. We're breathing pure oxygen at"—I switched the monitor back to the airlock status display—"almost half an atmosphere."

But Matt wasn't looking at the monitor, or at me. He was staring over my shoulder, at the point where the hoses from our masks attached to the wall. "Son of a bitch!" He stopped pedaling, ripped the mask off his face, and punched the big red **EMRG REPRESS** button.

"What the heck are you doing?" I shouted over the roar of inrushing air.

"Look at the valve!"

I looked where he was pointing, at the valve that controlled the flow of oxygen to our masks.

It was set to MIX. We weren't breathing pure oxygen, we were breathing the usual mix of oxygen and nitrogen. And we had been for the last hour and a half, with the pressure dropping and the nitrogen seething in our bloodstreams.

"Oh shit." I had missed one of the hundred and ninety-seven steps in the EVA checklist. No, two of them—I'd failed to switch the valve to OXY, and then I'd failed to check the valve setting. "I... I'm sorry. I don't know how I missed..."

"I know exactly how you missed it," Matt said. The rush of air was rapidly fading as the lock pressure came up to standard, his anger rising with it. "You were too busy worrying about who was putting whose cock where."

"I never..." But no... I couldn't deny it. I'd been distracted, and it could have killed both of us. I shut up, started again. "You should put your mask back on." Pure oxygen was standard treatment for the bends.

Matt never took his eye off of me as he re-fitted his mask and ostentatiously switched the valve from MIX to OXY. I immediately tasted the difference in my own mask—the pure oxygen was rich and invigorating, with a slight iron tang. How could I have failed to notice its absence? Matt rubbed his shoulder again, his face taut. He moved to the wall and keyed the intercom. "Tench tench," he said, his voice echoing dully from beyond the inner hatch. "We've had a malf in Gamma hab lock and we're both suffering possible stage 1 DCS. Have repressurized. Situation stable. Please advise."

A moment later Nuru's voice came back. "Oppy oppy, Matt. Stay where you are, and keep the pressure up. I'll have Kyra and Mari prep for EVA from Gamma sys lock."

"Oppy oppy," Matt acknowledged, then cut the connection. He stared at the intercom for a long moment, then shouted "Damnit!" and slammed his palm against the wall. The whole airlock thrummed and he rotated slowly as he rebounded from the force of the blow.

"I'm sorry," I said again, though it didn't help anything.

"You're sorry." He didn't even look at me. He just swam back to the monitor and programmed the lock to raise the pressure to an atmosphere and a half.

"Kyra and Mari..."

"They're not going to make it in time." Now he did look at me, and I wished he hadn't. "By the time they get out there they'll have only half an hour—an hour, tops—to find the hole and patch it. We'll have to evacuate Gamma work bay." The vacuum that would ruin all the organics and volatiles in the bay—almost one-third of the ship—couldn't have been any harder or colder than his face just then. "You've screwed us all."

"I didn't do it on purpose."

Matt's eyes were icy above the mask. "You shouldn't even be here."

"What the heck's *that* supposed to mean?"

He started to respond, then cut himself off, waving a hand in front of his face. "No. Never mind. I shouldn't have said anything."

"What did you mean by that?" I demanded.

"Never. Mind." Our eyes locked for a long cold moment.

In the end I was the one who had to look away. I'd screwed up; he had every right to be upset.

We stewed in silence for half an hour, floating in enforced idleness—any exertion could make the bends worse—and watching the work bay pressure graph fall, slowly and steadily. At least I wasn't in any pain.

"How's the shoulder?" I asked at last, unable to stand the silence any longer.

Matt flexed and stretched it. "Better," he admitted. "I think I'll be okay." The silence wore on.

"Matt..."

He looked at me.

"You told them it was a malf. You didn't say it was me who messed up." I swallowed, to relieve the pressure in my ears. "Thank you."

Matt sighed. "I didn't want to make your life any more hellish than it already is." Then he turned in the air so he could look me square in the eye. "Listen, Charlie," he said. It was the first time anyone in the crew had called me "Charlie" since the first day of training, when Kyra had noticed that everyone but Bob and I had four-letter names and we changed them for solidarity. "I shouldn't tell you this..."

Just then the intercom burst into life. "Tench tench," came Nuru's voice, breathy with exertion and excitement. "Leak is stabilized. I repeat, leak is stabilized. Kyra and Mari, abort emergency prebreathe protocol; I still need you to go outside to complete the repairs, but no sense rushing things. Matt and Chaz, report status."

Matt keyed the microphone. "DCS symptoms resolved, situation stable. We will continue at one point five atmospheres for four hours."

"Oppy oppy."

Matt blew out a breath in relief, then keyed the mike again. "How'd you fix the leak?"

"Bobb managed to unbolt the whole damn section from the hull. There's crap floating all over, but we found the hole and patched it."

"Thank you, Jesus," I said.

#

Everything was set aside for the next couple of days as we finished cleaning up from the meteoroid strike. Kyra and Mari completed their spacewalk without incident, welding a patch onto the hull to complete Bobb's temporary repair of the fingertip-sized hole. The rock that had made it had been smaller than a grain of sand, and had evaporated on impact. Meanwhile, the rest of us labored to put all the equipment back the way it had been before the strike.

I couldn't get Matt to admit what he'd been about to say. Whatever it was, though, I was convinced it was tied into whatever was making me such a pariah.

And I *was* a pariah. I wasn't certain whether it had gotten worse, or whether I was just noticing it more, or whether I was becoming increasingly paranoid, but it was clear to me now that everyone was giving me a wide berth. Conversations stopped when I drifted near. People refused to meet my eyes, or—even worse—I looked up from my work and discovered they were silently watching me. I wondered if Matt had quietly spread the word about my error in the airlock, but that didn't seem like him.

It couldn't be racism... could it? But no, even Nuru was avoiding meeting my eyes.

Whatever the cause, there seemed to be little I could do about it other than to be as unobtrusive as possible. Whenever I considered confronting Nuru or Mari about the crew's behavior, I balked—surely complaining about the situation would make it even worse. So once the ship had returned to normal, I retreated to the communications problem I'd been working on before the impact.

My database searches led nowhere. The merged data just stopped forty-seven years after launch; the three original databases were simply gone, with no clue as to what had happened to them. When I asked Bobb to look into the situation, as I'd been about to do at the moment of the meteoroid strike, he begged off—too busy with recovery and maintenance operations. No one else had Bobb's expertise in ship systems, and in any case they were all even less willing to give me any of their time than he was.

At least Bobb had offered an excuse. Mari simply waved me away whenever I tried to talk with her.

I spent a lot of time alone. The airlock was less appealing than it had been, so I started taking extra shifts in the greenhouse, the rotating transparent tube full of plants that turned our waste products into food and oxygen. No one liked working there, necessary though it was to our continued existence, because it stank of sewage and the CO_2-heavy air led to lethargy and headaches. But I learned to cope, because it was better than the looks I got in the work and habitation bays.

It was while I was in the greenhouse, pinching back the soybeans, that I realized I was going about the communications problem all wrong.

At a certain point in the plants' life cycle, it was necessary to pinch off the growing stem end to encourage them to put more of their energy into beans rather than leaves and tendrils, a painstaking and tedious job because of the crowded conditions. I was ducking my head back and forth as I reached through the tangled vines, trying to see if I'd missed any wayward sprouts, when the shifting image reminded me of something I should have known all along.

Humans had been using multiple small radio receivers to achieve the effect of a single giant dish—a technique known as "long-baseline interferometry"—for almost a century. It was really just an extended version of the way that two eyes can give a better picture of a three-dimensional object than just one, and the farther apart the eyes the more pronounced the 3-D effect.

We already had a flock of satellites spread across Tau Ceti system. Though their radio dishes were smaller than the big dish on *Cassiopeia*, if I pointed two or more of them at Earth and combined the signals together I might be able to pick Earth's signal from the Sun's background noise. And the information I gained from the exercise might be helpful in figuring out what was broken in *Cassie*'s receivers.

Over the next few days I researched interferometric techniques, found a useful set of subroutines in the ship's software library, and reserved time on five satellites. I was being extremely cautious—I didn't want to antagonize anyone with my use of satellite or computer resources.

When my reserved time arrived, the five satellites swiveled themselves to focus on Earth and kept up this scrutiny for a full eight hours. Post-processing took another two hours. During this time I floated among the tomatoes and zucchinis in the greenhouse, trying to distract myself with pruning and pollinating but actually accomplishing little more than plant-assisted nail-chewing. When my watch chimed, I rushed eagerly to Delta work bay, where the monitor revealed...

Nothing.

The interpolated data of the five satellites did not show any signal from Earth at all.

I checked and rechecked my procedures, verified that I was using the subroutines properly, made sure that the data was not corrupt. Everything seemed nominal. But when I checked the timestamps on the data, I discovered that the satellites' realtime clocks were not properly synchronized; they varied from each other by as much as an hour and a half.

Accurate timestamps were critical to interferometry. The data was useless. And with the satellites scattered all over the system, as much as seven light-hours away, it might not be possible to synchronize them now.

Maybe there was a way. But even as I looked into the problem, my frustration grew. Bad enough that no one on the ship would talk to me, now even the machines were being uncooperative...

"Are you almost finished with the main processor array?"

I looked up from the monitor. It was Mari, floating with one foot hooked into a restraint and her arms folded across her flat chest. She'd grown her hair out, but it didn't make her look any more like a woman. Even thinking of her as "she" made my head hurt.

"I didn't want to say anything," she continued, "but your reservation ran out over three hours ago."

"This is important," I said. My teeth clenched on the words.

"Well, the rest of us have important data to process too..."

"And why is *your* important data always more important than *my* important data?" Matt and Nuru, working at their own stations at the other end of the work bay, turned at the sound of my voice. "I've tried hard. I've been cooperative. I've learned your procedures, followed your rules, listened to your stupid-oopid doubled slang for months now, and all I've gotten in return is the silent treatment!" The anger and frustration I'd been building up for weeks came pouring out. "What about *me?*"

Mari was backpedaling away, clumsily beating the air with her hands as she tried to get away from my tirade.

"I didn't mean to die! I didn't ask to be vived without training! All I wanted was a little patience, a little compassion... but you... *all* of you!" I swiveled in place, taking in Nuru and Matt—and Bobb and Kyra, who had just arrived as well, drawn from adjacent modules by my shouting—with a broad sweep of my arm. "You've all treated me like... like dirt, and I'm tired of it!"

"Chaz..." Nuru began, but I cut her off.

"No more explanations," I said. "No more recriminations. I just want a little..." I was choking up. "... A little respect..."

They were all staring at me. I couldn't blame them—I was ranting, self-centered, over-emotional...

Oh dear Jesus. They'd never take me seriously now.

I opened my mouth to explain... but I could barely breathe past the swollen lump that had appeared where my tonsils used to be.

Eyes stinging, I struggled out of the restraint at my work station and launched myself past a startled Mari and Bobb... up to the systems bay and through the lock there into the greenhouse.

I floated among the peas and peppers, curled in a ball and shaking with pent-up tears that would not come. The air here was foul and heavy. My life stank like sewage.

Once I had thought that being selected for the *Cassiopeia* crew was the greatest thing that could ever happen to me. How had it come to this?

A long time later, I heard the lock from Delta open. "Chaz?" Matt's voice. I didn't even grunt. The greenhouse wasn't that big; if he really wanted to find me, he'd find me.

Eventually a shadow fell across me. "I'm sorry, Chaz."

"You didn't do anything," I said to my knees. "I got frustrated and lost my temper."

"No. I did do something. To you. We all did."

That got me to uncurl and look at him, though my vision was blurred. Tears don't fall in zero gee. I waited.

Matt hooked an elbow around a nearby structural element. He started to speak, hesitated. Tried again.

"You died just a week before scan number two—almost six months after your last scan. You know that, right?"

I just looked at him.

"Haven't you wondered what happened during those six months?"

I considered the question. "No more than any of the rest of the two years I don't remember."

He turned away from me, spoke to the transparent plastic of the wall. "Chaz, this is going to hurt you. But you deserve to know."

"Okay, let me hear it." I wasn't really ready to hear any bad news, but this was the first time in months anyone had even started to talk straight to me and I wasn't going to let the opportunity slip by.

Matt sighed. "Okay." A long pause, then he turned back and looked straight into my eyes. "Not long after the first scan, you and Mari started dating."

"Mari." Oh, Jesus.

"Yeah. You didn't know. About her, um, personal history."

"No. I didn't. Were we... intimate?"

"Alas, yes. And when you found out... well, it was pretty traumatic, for both of you. You were..." A rueful little smile came to his eyes. "Well, Chaz, frankly, you were a real shit about it. Railing up and down about how you'd been deceived, how filthy you felt. You told me that when you came home that day you stood in a scalding hot shower and scrubbed yourself raw for over two hours."

If Mari had had sex with me without revealing she was really a he... oh, dear Jesus. No amount of love-thy-neighbor could have gotten me to accept that kind of dishonesty. I felt nauseous just thinking about it, and it hadn't even happened to me. Not in this body, anyway.

"After that, it got really ugly. You refused to be in the same room with her. And when Bobb got tired of you going on and on about it—basically, how awful it was to have sex with another man—he told you about himself, and that made the situation even worse. The mission planners had to halt the training while we all went through counseling together. I think you wanted out just as much as we wanted you out, but *Cassie* had already launched, with all our cell samples on board—we *had* to learn how to work together."

My mouth was dry. I worked up some spit and swallowed. "Did it... did it work?"

Matt thought about that for a minute. "I think it was starting to. But then you got hit in that crosswalk." He turned away from me again. "To be honest, once we got over the initial shock, we were... relieved. Until we realized we would *still* have to work with you when we got to Tau Ceti."

I had nothing to say. The silence stretched out between us.

Matt turned his head to me, but his body still faced away. "Chaz... you have to imagine how it was for us. After two years of training, we were more than a family, we were a *unit*. A finely honed machine with no extraneous parts. And every day we knew that we were going to wake up on *Cassiopeia* and have to deal with... you. Touchy, rigid, unforgiving, homophobic. With all kinds of bad history with Mari and Bobb, and to a lesser extent with all of us. And completely untrained—"

"I'm not 'completely untrained.' We crammed in a lot of training in the first six months. They wouldn't have launched with those initial scans unless they thought we knew enough to complete the mission."

Matt shook his head slowly. "We all thought that at the time. But after two more years of training we could see how naïve we'd been." He held out his hands in an appeal for understanding. "Imagine you're a senior in college. And you know that when you graduate you're going to have to go into business with... no, *marry*, your freshman roommate. Who hasn't changed a bit. Still a freshman. Still as ignorant, immature, and annoying as he was back then, while you've turned from a high school kid into a functioning adult. But you can't get out of the deal."

"You could have given me a chance..."

Matt closed his eyes, shook his head hard. "You hurt too many people, too badly. We voted not to vive you."

I blinked, trying to assimilate what he'd said. They'd voted. Not to vive. Me.

Matt opened his eyes. "We had to meet in secret. The mission planners would never have agreed. But it was unanimous."

They'd voted not to vive me. Unanimously. "How..."

"It wasn't hard. You were in the third group. Once Bobb was awake, he just jiggered the software so you wouldn't wake up."

That wasn't what I had been about to ask. I'd been starting to say "how could you?" But... I could see how. And why. I imagined what I might have done if Matt or Bobb had turned out to be a rabid white supremacist. I might have voted the same way.

Matt was still talking. "But we didn't want to... uh, to dispose of... you. Your body. We just left it in the capsule. Too uncomfortable to think about, I think. And we were busy."

Another long silence. This time I broke it. "So... why did you change your minds?"

Matt sighed, deep and long. "See, that's the thing. We didn't."

"You... didn't?"

"Nope. When you woke up, it was a surprise to everyone... or at least, everyone *said* it was a surprise. Bobb swears it wasn't a hardware or a software glitch. So, on top of the stress of having you around, we've all been trying to figure out what... or *who*... made it happen." The wry little smile returned. "Under the circumstances, I'd actually say we treated you comparatively well."

My mind was awash. Too much to take in. "Why are you *telling* me all this?" My voice cracked as I said it.

He blew out his cheeks. "Damn good question. Maybe I thought we weren't being fair to you. Maybe I just got tired of the strain of keeping secrets." He shrugged, spread his hands. The light of Tau Ceti, shining through the vines and leaves, dappled his shoulders. "Anyway. There it is, and here you are, and here we all are. So what are we going to do about it?"

"Matt... it wasn't *me*. *I* didn't do any of those things. I didn't even know they'd happened."

He paused, considering, rubbing his cloverleaf tattoo. "That's as may be. But even so, *we* still have all that bad blood with *you*. And you might do the same things again."

"But I *haven't*! And I *won't*!"

He fixed me with a hard stare, like the one he'd given me in the airlock when I messed up with the oxygen. "Not in the same way. But you've still been cruel to Mari, and to Bobb. And me."

I curled up again, hugging my legs to my chest, leaves crinkling against my back. "I'm sorry," I said to my knees. It seemed painfully inadequate, but it was all I had to offer. "At least... at least now I know. I can try to change."

There was a long silence. "Yes," Matt said at last. "You can try."

I raised my head and saw that he was reaching out a hand to grasp my shoulder. But when he saw I was looking, he drew it back.

"I'm sorry," I said again.

Without a word he turned and made his way back to the ship. I heard the lock close behind him.

#

After that conversation, I cried. A lot. And I prayed, and cried some more.

Eventually I came out of the greenhouse. But I found I couldn't meet anyone's eyes. Every time I met Mari or Bobb, in the kitchen or while passing from one module to the next, as soon as I opened my mouth to speak my throat tightened up and forced me to silence. How could I ask their forgiveness when I didn't even have first-hand knowledge of what I had done to hurt them? Indeed, could I truly be forgiven for acts I myself had not committed?

And even though I had not hurt any of the others as badly, to talk with them was just as impossible. It was a difference of degree, but not of kind.

So I kept to myself. And I continued to pray for guidance.

And I kept working, on mission science as well as the lack of communication with Earth. Because I had always found that engaging my intellect in a scientific or technical problem was the best way to free up my soul for deep contemplation, and there were so many questions that still needed investigation, no matter how badly messed up my personal situation was.

Thus it was that I came to knock on Matt's door, four days later.

"Sup sup?"

"Matt, it's me. I need to talk to you."

A moment later, Matt opened the door. He wore only a towel tied around his hips. "That's a change."

I swallowed past the lump in my throat. "Please."

Matt's eyes never left mine as he moved to one side, silently pulling the door open for me.

"I've been looking some more into the question of Achebe's crustal temperature. Balzac and Voltaire have moons that are also warmer than expected, and I'm beginning to wonder if they might be hospitable to life."

"I'll help if you like, but that's really Mari's specialty."

"I know." I swallowed again. "I... I can't talk with her."

"So you want me to be your intermediary? I'm sorry, I can't—"

"No," I interrupted. "I need your help in... changing my attitude."

Matt looked a question at me.

"I want a tattoo."

He blew out his cheeks and pulled his bare legs up under himself. "I see. You want to mark yourself as a new man." He gestured at his cloverleaf. "Like me."

"Yes. But... um, where would it hurt the least?"

He grinned at that. "Someplace with plenty of meat between the skin and the bone. Bicep is good, or buttock. Depends on whether you want to show it off or not."

"Bicep. I want people to see it."

"And have you thought about what kind of image you want?"

"I have. I want a lamb." The lamb of God, but I didn't say that. "To represent new life, a new start."

Unfortunately, neither Matt nor I had any artistic talent, and I twitched away from the pain a couple of times. So the lamb came out looking more like a rain cloud—a lumpy blob with four jerky lines coming down from it—crudely sketched in blood and ink. But I knew what it meant.

It still took me a couple of days to steel myself to face Mari. I floated at the bottom of Epsilon work bay, watching her as she jotted notes on one monitor while staring intently at another. Finally I squeezed my still-bandaged arm—the pain reminded me that whether or not I was the person who had done those hurtful things, I was not the man I had been; I was born anew, with a chance to begin again. I kicked off the bulkhead and drifted up behind Mari.

She noticed me immediately; her body language told me that. But she refused to acknowledge my presence, continuing to work, her back turned to me.

Her hair had grown long and loose and curly, the way it had been back on Earth. From here I could imagine everything else was as it had been as well. I could understand the attraction my earlier self had felt.

I waited. Though I wanted desperately to leave, to avoid confrontation, to not think about what this person had under her coverall, to keep pretending we were not all trapped in a tin can together for the rest of our lives... I waited.

Finally she stabbed her stylus back in its holder. Without turning, she said "Well?"

I had to clear my throat before I could speak. "I would like your help."

Now she did spin to face me, and her dark eyes were hard. But as soon as she saw the bandage on my arm they softened a little. "You're hurt."

I waved dismissively at the bandage. "It's nothing. No, I need your help on a scientific problem."

She cocked her head—not making any promises, but willing to listen.

I told her how I'd done infrared observations of the moons of the three gas giant planets, trying to confirm my analysis of Achebe, and had found several moons whose surface temperatures were unexpectedly high even after applying the Pederson/Wu equations. Voltaire's moons Cunegonde and Paquette were close to their primary, and tidal squeezing might be enough to explain the difference. But Balzac's fourth moon, Bianchon, was much warmer—more than warm enough for liquid water, in fact—though Balzac itself orbited barely within Tau Ceti's habitable zone and any water on its moons should have been frozen solid for most of its year.

"Have you looked for greenhouse gases in Bianchon's atmosphere?"

I had, and the results were most intriguing, but I wanted her opinion... and I needed to work on my humility. "Well, I'm not sure I know how. Could you give me a hand with the spectrographic analysis?"

Mari scooted to one side, allowing me to fit my legs into the other restraint at her work station, and called up the spectrograph control software on the monitor. "Where's your data?"

I learned a lot from watching her work—she guided the software with delicacy and finesse, teasing and cajoling meaning from the raw data many times faster than I'd been able to. "Huh," she said as the graphs built up on the screen. "That's odd..."

"What?"

"Greenhouse gases, all right. Carbon dioxide, methane, and... looks like... oxygen?" Her eyes widened at that last.

As I'd thought. I was pleased to have my analysis confirmed, and also to be working side-by-side with Mari on the question. It was a start, anyway.

We worked together for hours. I was familiar with the data, because I'd collected it; she knew what it meant, and how to use the tools. But as we worked I realized her understanding of the ship's computer systems was shallow—expert though she was in her specialist software, she made almost no use of automation or datastreaming. So, as we went on, she learned from me even as I was learning from her. And together we discovered that Bianchon was a very interesting place.

There were what Mari called "anomalous indications of biological activity." Might be life, might be something else, but *something* was generating oxygen there. The atmosphere might even be breathable—cold and thin, but capable of sustaining human life. Perhaps.

Too bad we didn't have any way of landing there. Adding a lander to the mission, never mind the gene banks and other colonization equipment some had insisted should be included, would have raised the weight of each module above what the boost lasers could push to Tau Ceti. But we could drop one of the atmospheric drones. The nearest satellite with drone capability was orbiting Balzac and could be in position in a couple of weeks. We told it to make all deliberate speed.

While we were waiting for that data, the question remained open: where was the oxygen coming from?

The problem drew Mari and I together. We built on each other's ideas, shot theories back and forth, argued over the meaning of the data. But though we had probably exchanged more words in a matter of hours than we had in the whole rest of the time we'd been at Tau Ceti, we were still uncomfortable with each other—emotionally reserved, overly sensitive to each other's personal space, shying away from any kind of physical contact. And when we realized just how long we'd been working without sleep, we went to our rooms with only a very formal good-night. Still, it was a start.

#

Over the next few days, between sessions with Mari on the anomalous composition of Bianchon's atmosphere, I continued to tackle the lack of communication from Earth. But all the dead ends I'd run into before were still dead. I tried a couple of techniques to resynchronize the satellites' clocks, or compensate for the lack of synchronization, but no matter what I did the result was the same: nothing.

Finally, after much introspection and prayer, I asked Bobb for help. He was in Gamma systems bay, cleaning the air filters—a messy chore he happily abandoned to help me.

"Have you tried a Fourier analysis on the data from one satellite?" he asked.

"Uh..."

Talking with Bobb was much harder than I'd expected it to be... harder even than with Mari. Maybe it was because he was so much bigger than me. Some part of my brain kept wondering what I would do if he tried to jump me. I kept reminding myself that this fear was ridiculous, but it was deeply ingrained. Love thy neighbor, I reminded myself.

"I don't think there's enough signal there for that to be worthwhile," I said at last.

"Maybe not. But it's still worth a try." He wiped his grimy hands on a towel and headed down to the work bay.

Once we set up the Fourier transform, it took only a few minutes to run. The result, as I'd feared, was inconclusive—natural radio noise from the Sun was the dominant factor in the signal, and any artificial signal from Earth was drowned out even after processing. We really needed to combine the signals from several satellites to augment the resolving power of their little radio dishes, but without a solid timestamp on the data that wasn't possible.

Bobb's face grew thoughtful. "What about a natural timestamp?"

I understood immediately. "I don't know if there are any pulsars in the data." But if there was one, we might be able to use its regular radio pulses as a natural clock to line up the signals from the different satellites.

"Only one way to tell..."

We signed up for the big dish on *Cassiopeia*—although I considered the whole system suspect, it had the potential to give us a quick positive—and pointed it toward Earth, then set up routines to troll the data for a faint regular pulse in the appropriate frequency range.

In some ways, doing the work with Bobb was more comfortable than working with Mari. We had similar skill sets, so it was more cooperative than mutually instructive. But the fact that I'd seen Bobb and Matt together was like a constant background noise.

Every time I found myself wondering where those hands, that mouth, had been, I reminded myself that it was wrong to think of him as "a homosexual." He was more than what he did in bed. He was a whole human being—and a fine human being, far more tolerant of me than I'd been of him. As we worked, he displayed no discomfort or awkwardness from my earlier self's mistreatment of him.

I felt like a heel.

Bobb's brow furrowed, then his eyebrows shot up. "Hey! Got one!"

"Let me see."

He swiveled his monitor so we could both see it. "There." The graph showed a nice periodic pulse at 260 MHz, not very powerful but extremely crisp and regular.

Extremely crisp. I'd never seen a natural signal with such a constrained pulse width. "Wait a minute. What's the period?"

"A little under a second." He tapped with his stylus on the controls. "Point eight two seconds, to be precise."

"Wait, wait..." A memory nagged at me. Each of *Cassie's* five modules broadcast a module beacon—a powerful omnidirectional ping at 215 MHz, which they used to locate each other on arrival at Tau Ceti. "If it's 215 megahertz, blueshifted to 260..." I turned the monitor toward myself and popped up a calculator window, which told me that the source was approaching at nineteen percent of lightspeed. A very familiar number. And subtracting the same blueshift from the signal's 0.82-second period yielded an original period of... exactly one second. "Look at this. One second period. 215 megahertz. Nineteen percent of lightspeed. Does that mean anything to you?"

Bobb's eyes widened and his mouth broke into a huge grin that echoed my own. "The module beacon."

We looked at each other. "It's *Alpha!*" I shouted.

Bobb and I grabbed each other in an enormous hug, laughing and pounding each other on the back. The return of the lost module meant more metals... more instruments... more living space! We scooted off in opposite directions to share the happy news with the rest of the crew.

I didn't realize until I was talking with Matt that I'd embraced Bobb without fear. I smiled to myself at that.

#

The grainy image on the big monitor showed why Alpha was so late. One of the four sails that was supposed to catch the light from the boost lasers, then drop off for coast phase, was still attached—bent and twisted into a crumpled C shape. The sail had probably jammed on initial deployment, and had cut the module's thrust during boost phase by twenty percent or more. There was some concern that the jammed sail could cause problems during the first aerobraking maneuver, as Alpha slammed into Molière's atmosphere at interstellar speed. But simulations showed that it would most likely come off as the module's aerobraking ballute inflated, and if it didn't do that it would probably simply burn away early in the maneuver.

Everyone chattered excitedly over the personal possessions the module held. My own two hundred and seventy grams was mostly devoted to a pocket

Bible that had been my grandfather's—I remembered thinking of alpha and omega as I placed it in the bin labeled ALPHA. But then my breath caught in my throat as I remembered something else that was on board the wayward module—a full set of crew tissue samples and memory scans. Left to its own devices, Alpha was fully capable of reconstituting the entire crew by itself.

Of course, that wouldn't happen. We had already transmitted the rendezvous code, and when Alpha joined us after two years of deceleration it would be unoccupied. But if the situation had been reversed, if it had been Alpha that had arrived on time and the other modules delayed, it would have been Alpha's cells and scans that would have created... me. Or someone like me.

Would that person have had as tough a time of it as I had? Probably he would not have been vived at all. I still didn't know why *I* had been.

Which made me realize that Alpha carried one other thing of interest.

A full set of data from boost and coast phase. And possibly the answer to the missing signal from Earth.

#

Nuru's eyes flicked back and forth between two monitors filled with figures. "Yes?" she said without looking up.

"You've locked me out of the big dish."

She glanced up at me, then returned her gaze to the monitors. "I have."

I waited for an explanation. When I didn't get one, I said "I need it to retrieve Alpha's coast-phase data."

Nuru paused, then closed her eyes and steepled her long brown fingers in front of her nose. "That's exactly why I placed that hold."

"Oh?"

Now she did look at me. Her dark, liquid eyes held mine with firm intensity. "Chaz, you've been spending far too much time on this side project. We are here for science, not engineering."

"What good is science if we can't send our results back?"

"Transmission's working fine. You've said so yourself. And as far as our *basic scientific mission* goes"—she emphasized the words with an index finger driven hard into the palm of her other hand—"we won't need to receive anything from Earth for almost twenty-four years. Plenty of time to fix the receiver. Assuming we live that long."

I was momentarily taken aback, but then I recovered: "If there have been any relevant advances in basic science since we launched, they'll be beaming them in our direction right now. We don't want to be spending our precious time out here reinventing the wheel."

She didn't blink. "Zac zac. This environment is dangerous—we have no idea how much time we have. So I want you to focus your attention *on the mission*. Do I make myself clear?"

I felt my heart beating in my throat as Nuru and I stared at each other for a long moment. "Perfectly clear," I said.

She returned her gaze to her screens, dismissing me.

#

I swallowed and licked my lips before speaking. Bobb and I were alone in his quarters, which made me nervous for many reasons. But what I had to say could not be overheard. "Something very peculiar is going on."

Bobb just looked at me, questioning.

I swallowed again. "Look... I know you guys voted not to vive me."

He dropped his eyes from mine. "Yeah. I... I thought you might find out eventually. I'm sorry." He looked up. "They did it for my sake. And Mari's. I... I wasn't happy about it, but it would have seemed... ungrateful not to go along."

"I'm sorry too. For the way I treated you. The first me."

Bobb's lips pursed. Contemplative or angry, maybe a little of both. Then he sighed and shook his head. "Water under the bridge, Chaz. You would have gotten over it eventually, if... if you hadn't died."

"Well, I'm back now. And I'm trying. To get over it."

"I can tell."

We floated there for a while, each with our own thoughts. "But that's not the only thing," I said eventually. "Nuru's put a lock on my access to the big dish. She says I'm spending too much time trying to re-establish communication with Earth, and she wants me working on science."

"Well, it's our main mission."

"But there's an... undercurrent. I think she wants to keep me from getting ahold of Alpha's data."

"Why?" His expression reflected my own bafflement. We were all scientists, and free access to information was fundamental to scientific progress.

"I don't know. But that only makes me more determined to get it."

"So you want me to get it for you."

"Yes. But be subtle about it."

He looked to one side, considering. "I could relay the communication through several satellites. Bury it in other data streams."

"Exactly. I mean, zac zac."

Bobb grinned. "Now you're getting it."

#

I focused my visible attentions on science, specifically the composition of Bianchon's atmosphere. I swapped my primary work station with Kyra so that Mari and I could work more closely together, with Mari looking into the chemical activity while I focused on a high-level planetological survey of the moon. We hadn't originally planned to go into such detail on the gas giants' moons until later in the mission, but the presence of oxygen made Bianchon a lot more interesting. As Mari and I spent more and more time together, I realized I was starting to look on her differently. Not as a woman, exactly, but as a human being rather than some kind of aberration.

I also started taking dinner with the crew again. At first I ate quietly at the back of the group—in the team but not of it—but as the days went on I began to offer my opinions, then to engage in discussion and debate. After a week and a half the interactions started to feel natural, and I found that I could even disagree with people without feeling as though I was balancing on a razor's edge.

But during what was supposed to be my sleep period, I analyzed the data that was trickling in from Alpha. The wayward module was so far away, and moving so fast, that the bandwidth the satellites could achieve with their little dish antennas was pathetic. I was frustrated as the puzzle built up, slowly, piece by piece, but I knew Bobb was doing the best he could to move the data quickly without attracting attention. I was tremendously impressed with his feats of digital legerdemain, and I told him so.

One night, as I was peering with gritty eyes at a graph comparing the growing set of Alpha's coast-phase data with the merged data from *Cassie*, I was startled by a tap at my door. "Chaz, are you awake?" came a low voice. "It's Nuru."

Heart pounding, I powered the screen down and opened the door. "I'm awake," I said, blinking in the light from the habitation bay outside. "I haven't been sleeping well."

Nuru cut the sleeves off of all her coveralls, and when she wasn't working she wore a shawl over her bare shoulders. It was her way of marking personal from work time. With the light from behind her shining through the thin fabric, patterned in vivid stripes and squares of autumn colors, I could imagine her as some high priestess or village shaman, looking over the veldt at sunset.

"Chaz... I wanted to say that I'm sorry I came down so hard on you."

I didn't have anything to say to that. Anxiety, anger, sadness, and suspicion tightened around my throat and kept the words inside.

"It's just..." she continued, then paused. "It's just that you didn't seem to be accepting any more subtle direction."

"I know you don't want me looking into the communication problem. But it's important."

"I understand. But..." Her voice was more hesitant than I could ever recall having heard. "...but you mustn't. Please don't try any more."

I waited to see if she would say anything more. When she didn't, I asked "Why?"

She shook her head. "I can't say. I wish I could." She looked deep into my eyes, and I could not withdraw from her gaze. "I'm sorry, Chaz. But I want you to know that this is for everyone's good. I... I do respect your judgment. And you'll have to respect mine."

She turned and left, leaving me shaking my head in bafflement.

#

Puzzled though I was, I meant to do as Nuru asked... leave off my nocturnal investigations, at least for a time. But when I powered the screen up again, just to close down my work before I went to sleep, it chimed and displayed something that made my breath catch in my throat.

The data from Alpha had been arriving in apparently random order, determined by its physical location in storage rather than chronologically. I'd been waiting for weeks to see what I saw on the monitor now: a purple rectangle, representing a block of Alpha data that didn't correspond to anything already in *Cassie*'s database.

To my surprise, it wasn't coast-phase data from after the cutoff. It was in a completely different part of the database, one with which I wasn't familiar.

I bit my lip, but after a brief battle with my conscience, curiosity won out. I tapped the purple rectangle with my stylus.

The data turned out to be in the medical/lifesystem section.

Specifically, the crew reconstruction and vival instructions for Charles Eades. Me.

Here was hard evidence that my vival instructions had been deliberately wiped from the system. Which only confirmed what Matt had told me. Though the news was a twist of the knife in my gut, it wasn't a surprise.

But then I noticed something that *was* a surprise, and told me the situation was more complicated than it had at first appeared. Immediately adjacent to the purple area of new data from Alpha, I saw a thin red stripe indicating data that was present in both databases, but slightly different. There was no reason I could think of for this.

I looked more closely. The Alpha data was a straightforward prologue to the following code. The *Cassiopeia* data replaced one instruction in that prologue with a jump to another section of the database.

I followed the jump.

It led to a completely separate datastore, in a different hive—temporary mission data, not instructions that had been loaded preflight.

The linked data turned out to be identical to the new data from Alpha, but with a more recent timestamp. About eighty years more recent.

I stared hard at the screen, rubbing absently at the hot rough tissue of my new tattoo. It itched almost as much as my brain.

Matt had said the crew had voted not to vive me. But then I'd been vived anyway, and no one knew how this had happened.

Here was the answer. Someone, probably Bobb, had deleted the data, but later someone else had restored it from backup. And whoever had restored the data had put it in an obscure temporary datastore so the reinstatement wouldn't be noticed. The link to the restored data was extremely subtle—the only reason I'd spotted it was that I had an unmodified copy of the original data to compare it with.

I drummed my fingers on my chin. The user ID on the data in the temporary store was some random number, not any of us—whoever had restored the data had concealed their identity. But I could check the system audit log. It was a write-only record of all significant system activities, intended to be impossible to evade or to modify after the fact. We had mostly ignored it in our training; the only reason it was present in *Cassie*'s systems at all was a general requirement for all government software.

The audit log told me that the restore had been performed using a temporary ID to obscure the user's true identity. But that ID had been created only a few seconds before it was used, and the creator's name was clear in the log.

Nuru.

I shook my head. It made no sense. Matt had said the vote not to vive me had been unanimous. As our commander, if she'd disagreed with the decision she wouldn't have allowed it to go forward. Why would she then sneak back and undo it?

While I was digesting that information, trying to decide what to do about what I'd learned, another chime came from the monitor, and another purple rectangle appeared. This one was where I'd expected the first one to be: in the coast-phase data, a couple of months after the data cutoff in *Cassie*'s database.

I tapped the rectangle with my stylus. If nothing else, I thought, it would be a distraction from the painful news about who had vived me.

I was quickly proved wrong.

#

I worked the latch and entered without waiting for a response. There were no locks anywhere in *Cassie*.

Nuru poked her head out of her sleep sack, blinking in the light from the habitation bay outside. "What the hell?"

"698463 Teitelmann," I said.

Sleep immediately fled from her eyes. "Close the door."

I shut the door behind me. A sliver of light fell across Nuru's face. I wanted to cry like a baby, to have her take me in her arms and tell me everything would be all right. I wanted to slap her hard and scream with rage. I wanted her to pray with me, to help me to understand that all of this somehow fit into God's plans. Torn in so many different directions, I said nothing. I just looked at her, breathing hard.

"Have you told anyone?" she asked at last.

"Not yet. But I will. It's not fair to keep them in the dark."

She closed her eyes and buried her face in her hands. "How did you find out?" she mumbled.

"Bobb helped me download the coast-phase data from Alpha. It was all there."

"You disobeyed my orders."

"Yes."

I waited. Eventually she raised her eyes to me. They shimmered with moisture. "Can you forgive me?"

It was a hard question. "I think... I think I can understand why you erased the news. I might be able to forgive you for that. But why... why did you vive me? Knowing what you knew?" My throat was choked with unshed tears—tears of rage or anguish or both. "How could you wake me up... to *this*? When you could have just left me in peace forever?"

Nuru's face was a mask of grief. "I'm sorry, Chaz. I'm so, so sorry. But I didn't want to be *alone*."

I didn't understand. "But you weren't alone..."

"I couldn't bear knowing that the only face like mine in the universe was the one in the mirror."

I looked into her dark, dark eyes, shining with tears, the yellowish whites and the smooth mahogany skin. So much like mine. And I reached out and took her into my arms.

We shuddered together, racked with silent sobs.

The jumbled, fragmentary video and audio from Alpha's data played over and over behind my eyelids. *...asteroid 698463 Teitelmann's orbit intersects...*

impact in as little as eight months... entire nuclear arsenal lacks sufficient... mission to Teitelmann does not seem to have... millions rioting... last few places in the shelters... a world prays... devastation even greater than... we are the dinosaurs... and then the silence, oh Jesus, the silence that went on and on...

Eventually Nuru dried her eyes on my shoulder, and it all came spilling out—how she'd deleted the data, putting the cut-off at different times in the three modules to make it look like a hardware problem. How she'd kept the news of Earth's demise to herself, and focused the crew on its original scientific mission to keep us all from falling into despair. How she'd continually sabotaged Bobb's and my efforts to find the source of the problem. I was amazed she'd been able to retain her own sanity under that pressure, never mind the technical and psychological challenge of keeping her bright and curious crew from learning the truth, and I said so. "I'm not so sure I did retain my sanity," she said.

"At least you won't have to hold it all inside now..."

"No." She gripped my shoulders, her long strong fingers biting hard into my flesh. "We can't let them know, Chaz. Matt, maybe, but the others... they wouldn't be able to go on. Trust me in this."

"This secrecy is poisonous. They deserve to know."

"They deserve *purpose.*"

"Even if it means lying to them for the rest of their lives? Lie upon lie, coverup over coverup, year after year, with nothing better to hope for than that we'll all get killed by an oxygen leak or something before they find out the truth?"

Nuru hung her head. "I can't take hope away from them."

"Then don't!" Even as I spoke, pieces of a plan were coming together in my head. "Give them a *new* hope." I outlined my idea, sketchy and conditional though it was. She raised objections—sound ones—but, driven by desperation, I came up with answers. "It might not work. We might all die in the process. But it's better than floating around in a tin can, gathering data with no audience and writing papers no one will ever read."

"We don't have the genetic diversity for a viable colony..."

"I know." I closed my eyes hard, squeezing back the tears for a moment before I could continue. "But isn't one or two generations better than nothing? And if there *is* anyone alive back home, maybe the information in our databases can benefit them." The mission planners had provided us with entire libraries and museums, to support basic research and as a hedge against boredom. "We owe it to them to preserve it as long as possible—until they can dig themselves out. No matter how long that might be."

Nuru was silent for a long time. Finally she said "Kay kay. But I need you to let me break it to them."

#

We gathered in Gamma hab bay. I'd watched Nuru as she'd approached each crew member, letting each one know how critical this meeting was: a simple statement to Bobb, a light joke to Matt, a long held glance with Mari. Suddenly I understood in my bones just why Nuru was the commander and how she'd managed to hold us together as a crew as well as she had.

Nuru clapped her hands for attention. But once she had it, she floated in silence for a long time, gathering herself. "This is hard," she said, and another silence followed. Moisture glistened in the corners of her eyes.

"I've lied to you," she said at last. "I've lied to you all, at many times and in many different ways. Sometimes that's part of the commander's job. But now it has to stop." She closed her eyes, took a breath. "First: I was the one who vived Chaz."

The crew's reaction was like a released breath. Matt jerked his head back in astonishment; Bobb nodded to himself; Mari stared sullenly at me. No one spoke.

"My reasons were selfish," Nuru continued, "and my deception... unpardonable. But this wrong also undid a greater wrong." She looked around. "We are all guilty of a gross injustice. We tried, convicted, and *executed* Chaz, in absentia, for a crime he did not commit."

Tien looked dubious. "Executed?"

"We voted to deprive him of his life—his second life, this life we all share now—before it even began." She waved one long brown hand at me. "*This* Chaz, this second Chaz, did no harm to any of us. He has no memory of the hateful things the first Chaz said and did. And even that first Chaz... I believe he, too, was wronged. Deceived." She looked at Mari. Mari looked back, for a moment, then averted her eyes. "We might all, in time, have learned to forgive each other. But we were all cheated of the opportunity." Now she looked at me. "After your death, our feelings toward you crystallized—frozen at the most terrible moment of our relationship. Chaz, can you forgive us for remembering you at your worst, and forgetting the good things we shared?"

I swallowed past the hard constriction in my throat. What I really wanted was vindication... acknowledgement that I'd been treated unfairly for crimes that I hadn't committed, or at the very least an apology. I wanted to see the tables turned, to be the one to gloat smugly while they turned their eyes away and admitted they'd been wrong. But what was needed right now was for me to turn the other cheek.

"Yes," I managed at last. "I... I forgive you."

"And the rest of you—Mari, Bobb, everyone—can you forgive Chaz, this Chaz, for his ignorance, his errors, his anger?" Most of them nodded, but Mari still did not meet her eyes. "Would any of us have done any better, if *we* had arrived here unprepared for our mission and ostracized for the sins of our earlier selves?"

"You remember how he was," Mari whispered to her chest. "Hurtful. Cruel. Unforgiving."

I pushed off the wall, floated close to her. "That was someone else," I said, so softly that she had to look up. "He's dead now... eighty years dead. Let him go." Please God, let her give me this chance.

She didn't speak for a while, just looked at me. I couldn't read her expression. "I'll never forgive him," she said at last. "And you... you look just like him. But I'll try."

"That's all anyone can ask."

I held out my hand to her, and after a moment she took it and squeezed it.

Nuru broke the moment by clearing her throat. "There is another thing. Even harder." We all looked at her, and though I knew what was coming my heart still pounded in my throat. "The communication problem with Earth... is not on our end." A deathly silence settled over the crew. "Earth... Earth was struck by a meteor, forty-seven years after we left. There hasn't been any signal since then." She raised her hands against the gasps and curses. "There may be survivors. But they aren't in any position to contact us. *Yet.*" She pointed at me. "Chaz has figured out a way for us to survive until they can."

Everyone looked at me. I swallowed. "It isn't going to be easy..."

#

When the noise and movement finally stopped, it took me some minutes to decide whether or not we'd survived. It had been a bad landing. We hadn't expected a good one, but the sheer brutal pummeling we'd taken was still a shock. One of my shoulder straps had pulled loose; the other had bitten so deeply into my collarbone I knew I'd be bruised for weeks. "Is everyone okay?" I asked.

A chorus of groans answered, but no one seemed to be seriously hurt. I offered up a brief prayer of thanks.

Then I tried to sit up, and let out a groan myself. Even a tenth of a gee was more than my abdominal muscles were ready for. Mari had been right—I should have been doing more crunches. I rolled over onto my side and used my arms to force myself to a sitting position.

All through *Spirit*, the others were doing the same. Tien was already on her feet, wobbly but vertical.

Walking. A new concept for us.

At least she could do it. We hadn't been completely certain that bodies that had never walked would be able to manage the skill, even when directed by minds with years of walking experience.

Eventually I struggled upright. The appalling effort it required was cruelly mocked by my balloon-like low-gravity gait. My sinuses felt as though they were full of lead shot.

Nuru's arm fell heavily across my shoulders, and we both nearly collapsed from the weight. But when we got stable again I saw she was grinning like the sun. "We made it," she gasped.

"We made it," I concurred, and I found I was smiling the same crazy smile.

Supporting each other, we shuffled to the airlock—the one that had been Epsilon sys lock before we'd torched it off and joined it to the growing assemblage of hardware that we called *Spirit*. There we found, to our surprise, that we were already breathing Bianchon's atmosphere. The crude welded seam joining the lock to the hull had parted from the stress of the landing.

It was a chilling reminder that our margin of safety had been almost nonexistent. But one good landing was all we'd needed.

The lock's doors were warped and distorted, and it took both Bobb and Matt to force them open with a raucous screech. We all ducked through and stepped outside.

Spirit lay on a long gentle slope of gray rock, scattered with rough stones ranging from boulder to fingertip size. Overhead Balzac's ringed and banded form loomed huge, and the tiny red disk of Tau Ceti was just rising behind a fog bank downslope. The white fabric of the parasail, which lay on the ground for hundreds of meters along the scrape marks of the lander's final descent, flapped desultorily in the wind.

Wind.

There was *wind* here.

The air was thin and cold and very dry—even here at sea level it was barely dense enough to sustain life—but there was so *much* of it. And it smelled... clean. No plastic solvents, no leakage from the greenhouses, no unwashed bodies. I opened my mouth and drank in the air like fresh cold water, shuffling in a circle and marveling at the openness of it all.

The rock-littered gray slope extended up, and up, and up—out to a horizon closer than Earth's, but hundreds of times more distant than anything I'd seen in this lifetime. It hurt to focus that far away. I trusted my eyes would learn to cope. And in the other direction, lost in fog...

"Listen," said Kyra, breaking into the excited babble of conversation. We listened.

Yes. There it was, coming from downslope. Surf. The low rumbling hush of waves on a shore.

The sound of the ocean that covered the whole equatorial region of this moon. An ocean teeming with microscopic life, devouring each other and excreting the oxygen we needed to breathe. In an atmosphere whose density was maintained by an improbably high level of outgassing from the planet's core.

Surely this highly-unlikely alien biosystem was a gift from God. Humbled, I lowered myself to the ground and said another prayer of thanks.

Nuru watched over me while I prayed. "You might want to hold some of that gratefulness back," she said when I was done. She waved a hand, indicating the cold lifeless rock all around.

Indeed, this rocky slope looked pretty inhospitable, and the cold was already beginning to bite through my foam-insulated parka. But after eight years of planning and building and testing and improvising we all knew it was our best alternative. No one had seriously suggested that hanging around in orbit, waiting to get clobbered by a passing meteoroid or suffer a blowout or lifesystem failure, was a viable long-term solution.

"We'll make this place into a home," I said. "It'll be a lot of work, but we'll do it."

Bobb was peering into a handheld monitor. "Lander nine's just over that ridge," he said, pointing. All the pieces of *Cassiopeia* that we thought would be useful on the surface—including the greenhouses, the bioprocessors, and the materials fabricators—had been sent down ahead of us, to test and refine the ablative atmospheric entry shielding and the parasails. Some of the landers had failed, and some were a long walk away, but there was more than enough nearby to get started. Only Alpha module, which hadn't completed assembling itself, remained in orbit to act as our weather satellite and meteoroid warning system. "Lander seven's about two kilometers beyond it. Three's that way, about six kilometers."

"There'll be time for that later," said Mari. "I'm going for a swim." And she burst into a clumsy, loping run, headed downslope.

"You're crazy, girl!" I shouted, and she slapped me on the ass with a raucous laugh as she passed. "Those alien microbes will eat you alive!"

"If they're going to do that," she called out over her shoulder, "I'd rather find out sooner than later!"

"Oodle oodle!" I called back, meaning "good luck."

Nuru and I leaned on each other, watching her go. "We'd better haul in that parasail before it blows away," Nuru said to me after a while. "Start setting it up as a tent." Her arm was warm across my shoulders. I'd forgotten how much taller she was than me.

"In a minute," I said. "I'm enjoying the view."

We stood side by side, watching the sun rise over our new home.

Iron Shoes
J. Kathleen Cheney

Imogen Hawkes noticed the minute hand of the clock on Hammersly's desk. It was spinning, a sure sign that her emotions had gotten out of control. In her mind she heard her mother reminding her that she must *always* remain calm. She took a sip of tea as she tried to comply with that inner voice.

"I do realize this is quite upsetting for you," William Hammersly said in a soothing tone. A handsome man in his forties with dark hair that showed gray at the temples, he sat in the leather chair across from hers, his chiseled features wearing a well-practiced expression of distant benevolence. He reached over, lifted a folder from his elegant mahogany desk, and thumbed through the contents. "Unfortunately, there is no record of any agreement that you might have had with the bank. I'm afraid either the note will need to be brought up to date on the 7th of August, or the Trust will be forced to begin foreclosure proceedings."

Imogen regarded him over the edge of her teacup. Her agreement with Mr. Solomon at the First National Bank had been a verbal one, but the banker's promise clearly hadn't been enough to stop Solomon from selling her mortgage to the Adirondack Trust, putting her under Hammersly's thumb. "How much is it in arrears?"

"At this time, about nine thousand dollars." His tone sounded sympathetic.

When she set down the tea cup, it clattered in the saucer, but she managed to keep her voice steady. "I'll have the money by the 7th."

Hammersly leaned forward and daringly laid a hand over hers. Even through her glove, she could feel the warmth of his fingers. Her own were icy. "I hope you'll remember that you can always come to me," he said. "As a neighbor, Mrs. Hawkes, and, I trust, as a friend."

She glanced down at the fingers covering hers on the arm of the chair. "That won't be necessary, Mr. Hammersly."

"I do hold you in great regard, Mrs. Hawkes," he said. "My offer is still open to you, should you find yourself in dire straits. Please remember that. You know that I have always..."

He continued speaking, but Imogen only half-listened. In the four years since her husband Henry's death, Hammersly had made several attempts to court her. Only twenty-two then, Imogen had been preoccupied with preserving the farm, not with finding another husband. She still wasn't eager to marry, not if it meant handing over the farm she'd worked so had to save into some man's control. Her lack of interest had only seemed to pique his, but she didn't believe for a moment that he'd fallen in love with her. While she could be described as 'striking', she was certainly not beautiful. Her coloring was at fault; her dark eyes and brows combined with hair the color of cream kept her from being fashionable. And it didn't help that Henry had always wanted her to wear pink, saddling her with a wardrobe full of dresses and suits she disliked. The pink silk walking suit she currently wore—a few years out of fashion, but still serviceable—didn't flatter her at all. No, Hammersly's interest in her couldn't be personal. He must have some other objective altogether. Sighing inwardly, she forced her attention back to him.

"...is the sport of kings, not queens, my dear," Hammersly was saying.

Imogen ground her teeth together. She glanced down at his expensive hand-made oxfords and noticed one of the laces coming untied. Things tended to fall apart when she was upset—literally, not figuratively. Alarmed, she slid her fingers out from under his and grasped the silk cords of her handbag. It would be wiser for her to get out of the building before anything else came undone. "Thank you for your time, Mr. Hammersly."

Smiling genially, he rose with her and escorted her to his office door. She set her gloved hand on the brass knob and was mortified when the latch came loose in her fingers. A screw fell to the floor, and then the remainder of the handle clattered onto the marble outside the door. In the lobby, people turned to stare.

Imogen gathered calm about herself. She handed the door latch to a nonplussed Hammersly and walked out of the temple-like edifice with her head held high.

She stopped outside on the sidewalk next to the tall clock. A buggy rattled by on Broadway past where she'd left her own, and then another, the mid-morning traffic lighter than normal. Mrs. Crowden bustled along the sidewalk without a word. The old woman threw an odd look at Imogen, but crossed Broadway and stepped into the drugstore on the opposite corner, casting one last glance back at her before letting the door close behind her. Imogen spotted Hammersly's black automobile parked on Church Street. His driver, a sallow-faced young man with dark hair and pale eyes, leaned against the vehicle, watching her as she stood by the clock, trying to decide what to do.

Disbelief and anger kept her fixed there. The agreement between herself and the bank allowed half-payments on the farm's mortgage. She had never been late, not once. It wasn't in her nature to go back on a bargain. She simply couldn't. It scandalized her that Mr. Solomon had. Without doubt, Hammersly had something to do with that betrayal. He must love having her under his thumb like this.

The warm July wind swirled around her and tugged at the straw hat precariously pinned in her hair. She glanced up and spotted the tall clock's minute hand moving far too fast. The hand slipped off the center post and fell to lie on the inside of the glass bezel. Imogen shook her head, annoyed with herself for being so out of control.

Mother Hawkes, she decided, would know what to do.

Imogen turned her buggy onto Broadway and headed north. The recent rain kept the dust down, but there were muddy spots everywhere. She'd dragged the lace hem of her skirt through one as she'd unhitched the buggy. She briefly hoped it stained, giving her an excuse to get rid of the suit, and then wryly reflected that she couldn't afford to replace it now anyway.

She passed by the Waverly Hotel and headed up North Broadway. Graceful homes lined the street in varying styles. Henry had chosen to build an Italianate villa for his mother there after he'd married his first wife back in the late 80s. A moderately sized home painted in a light blue, Mother Hawkes' house lacked the gingerbread trim that the house out on the farm had, which made Imogen like it all the more.

By the time she'd tied off the buggy and stepped up onto the porch, Imogen had lost the edge of her anger. Her mood had settled to a level of *annoyed* disbelief. In her mother-in-law's tasteful front sitting room, Imogen described her morning's travails as Mother Hawkes patiently listened.

"...and then Mr. Hammersly repeated his earlier offer," Imogen finished.

Her mother-in-law, an energetic woman on the far side of sixty, frowned down into her tea. "He offered to marry you? Again?"

"As a way out of the debt, of course." Imogen set down her saucer, holding to the appearance of calm like a lifeline. "He told me he knew how it must be hard for me to manage a stable alone. Then he patted my hand and reminded me that racing is the sport of kings, not queens. That was when I got up and left."

Mother Hawkes shook her head. Her family had been in horseracing for three generations. While her son Henry had run the farm for most of the previous two decades, Mother Hawkes had run things herself for just as long before that, and far more profitably. If Henry had listened to his mother more often, Imogen wouldn't be in the wretched position she was now. Knowing that, Imogen had made a point of seeking out her mother-in-law's business advice more and more frequently over the last four years.

"I hope you gave him your coldest shoulder, girl," Mother Hawkes said. "You're good at that."

She had a reputation for coldness, Imogen knew, and had since childhood. "I did my best."

"Hammersly's always wanted my family's land, although I didn't think he'd go to this length to get it. And now there's that silly practice track—he's lusting over that for his own horses, no doubt." Mother Hawkes glanced up at Imogen and added, "Not to say he doesn't want you, too, girl."

It *was* the land Hammersly was after, Imogen had no doubt of that. Marriage was simply his way of getting the lowest price. "It doesn't matter why Hammersly offered, I've no intention of marrying the man. I'll simply have to come up with the money."

Mother Hawkes nodded approvingly. "Good girl. How much?"

Imogen took a deep breath and said, "About nine thousand dollars. I have until the 7th to pay or the Trust will begin foreclosure proceedings."

Mother Hawkes frowned down into her tea-cup. "And unfortunately, all my ready funds are tied up in steel right now." She rose and began pacing the sitting room, her burgundy silk skirts rustling as she passed. "I would like to strangle Mr. Solomon. I won't, of course, but I do wonder what leverage Hammersly used to make Solomon hand over your mortgage. Hmmm. I know a couple of the Trust's board members. They might be interested to know how Hammersly's using his position there to his own advantage."

Her mother-in-law had a great many friends, a trick Imogen had never managed. She had too much to hide. "It doesn't matter. It's just over two weeks. Hammersly has the upper hand so, for now, I only have one hope."

Mother Hawkes sat down heavily as if her sixty-odd years had suddenly caught up with her. "Your horse has to win the Special Stakes."

Imogen nodded. She'd been struggling to build a decent stable out of the mess Henry had left behind. This year after paying her bills, she'd put up every cent left over as stakes for the Special. It would be her first race as the farm's owner, but she'd never dreamed so much would ride on the outcome. "The purse would be at least fifteen thousand dollars. There are nine stables running."

"Sanford has entered, hasn't he? He's got a very good two-year-old, I hear. And McCarran does as well."

"I have faith in my trainer," Imogen said. "If Paddy can't get Blue Streak up to speed by the race, I'll eat my handbag." Paddy O'Donnell had been training horses at Hawk's Folly Farm all of Imogen's life. She couldn't imagine anyone who knew horses better than him.

Mother Hawkes gave her a thoughtful look. "Give me your cup."

Imogen handed it over. Her mother-in-law had a gift for reading the leaves, and Imogen hadn't known her to be wrong yet.

Mother Hawkes stared into the teacup, her arched white brows drawn together. She turned it this way and that, and pronounced, "There's a whirlwind coming, girl, although I can't say whether it will bring good or ill. Be on the watch for it." She looked up at Imogen then. "How you handle it will determine the outcome."

Imogen pressed her lips together. Her own mother would have cautioned her to ignore foolish prophecies. She would have said that Mother Hawkes' prediction was vague, and could be interpreted in many ways. But something about her mother-in-law's words rang true.

"I'll keep my eyes open," Imogen promised.

The drive back to the farm helped calm her, the regular clopping of the horse's hooves soothing her frazzled nerves.

Hawk's Folly lay just over the rise, and when the buggy crested the hill, Imogen stopped to take it in. Despite the fact that Henry had willed the farm to *her*, Imogen had never truly felt she owned it.

The Victorian house had been built by Henry for his *first* wife, Bella, a hot-house beauty who'd filled the place with frills and lace and dainty figurines. The house's pink siding needed attention, Imogen noticed. It hadn't been painted since '01, a couple of months before Henry had died. Yet another thing that would have to wait now. The green-roofed stables were in perfect order, though.

To the east of the stables lay the practice track, the cause of her current woes. Henry had mortgaged the entire property to pay for the thing's construction. A full mile, the track had all the trappings of the one at Saratoga save its grandstand and the fancy new judges' stand. A hedge of cedars surrounded it, meant to hide the neat white posts and fine dirt from prying eyes.

Henry had had grand ideas, but he'd been hampered by both a complete inability to recognize a good horse and an unwillingness to listen to any advice, whether it came from his trainer, his mother, or his wife. It had taken Imogen a couple of years to accumulate decent breeding stock once she'd gotten rid of his questionable acquisitions. The current two-year-olds were her first crop, and the Saratoga meet would be their maiden outing.

Barely visible from the rise was the old tenant's cottage at the far end of Hawk's Folly. When Imogen's mother had come over from England with an infant daughter, a 'recently dead' husband, and a single retainer escorting her for the sake of propriety, Mother Hawkes had taken them in and let the mother and daughter live in the cottage. She'd hired Paddy to work in the stables. As a child, Imogen had played there. She would help out with the horses whenever she could escape her mother's tight grasp. Her mother had other designs, wanting Imogen to be as proper and lady-like as herself. The fourth daughter of an earl, her mother took her consequence seriously.

When her mother died, it had been Mother Hawkes who suggested to Henry that, since he'd been a widower for a couple of years, he could do far worse than to marry the girl from the old cottage. Imogen had always been grateful for his offer, even if she hadn't loved him. Eighteen and suddenly alone in the world, she hadn't had any place to go, no family that she knew, and no experience at making a living for herself.

And after Henry's death it had all fallen on her, every inch of the land, its history and its people. Now with it threatened, she could feel ties binding her there. Not just to the people who worked for her, but the farm itself. It was hers, and she didn't intend to let it go.

The day was flying by, she realized. Determined not to waste it, Imogen snapped the reins and the horse trotted down the rise. Once she'd pulled the buggy into the stable yard, one of the hands rushed up to take the reins. Imogen climbed down, grabbed the package of supplies Paddy had requested from the store, and tossed it over by the main stable door for him. She cast a glance in the direction of the stalls but decided to change out of her town clothes first, so she headed up to the wide porch of the house and inside.

Her bedroom was on the second floor with windows overlooking the green roof of the stable and the yard. Tired of living in the shadow of Henry's first wife, Imogen had repainted the room in a sunny yellow, sold the accumulation of knick-knacks, and purchased new bedding and a rug suited to her own taste—one of the few extravagances she'd allowed herself.

She glanced out her windows and saw Paddy stalking toward the house, so she dashed into the dressing area between the two upstairs bedrooms to change. She stripped off her stained walking suit and pulled on a riding skirt in heavy brown twill and a fresh cream-colored blouse—working clothes, and far more suited to her taste. Then she headed down to find out what Paddy needed.

"They're forgeries," Paddy said as soon as she made it down to the sitting room. When annoyed, his accent took on the thick brogue of the old country, but Imogen could usually follow it.

She peered at the sheaf of papers he held up for her to inspect. *The new stallion*, she realized, her heart sinking. After seeing the horse's listing for auction in Boston, she'd bid on him sight unseen. His racing record alone should have made him valuable, and she'd been quite surprised when she won him. With the other news she'd gotten this morning, she didn't want to hear her gamble hadn't paid off. "Are you certain?"

Paddy ran a hand through his gray hair and settled his tweed cap atop again. "As sure as the day is long, girl."

"They raced him under these papers, Paddy."

"Someone in Boston turned a blind eye, then, something the fine gents in Saratoga aren't going to do."

Imogen sighed. She grabbed one of Henry's old barn coats off the rack near the door. "Well, I suppose I should go take a look at the fellow. I paid enough to have him shipped here. Please tell me he has good points that outweigh his spurious pedigree. Can he be used for training, at least? A riding horse?"

Paddy held the door open for her, his expression guarded. "I think it's best you see him yourself, girl."

They walked together down the path toward the stables, Paddy clucking his tongue over their new acquisition all the while. A life-long pessimist, Paddy never failed to see the dark cloud under the silver lining. But he was probably right. If he thought the stud she'd purchased sight-unseen wasn't any good, then they probably had an expensive new gelding, not even suitable to be a riding horse.

Imogen unpinned her braided hair as they walked. It had a coarse texture—like a horse's mane, her mother had always pointed out. A few white-blonde strands blew across her eyes, escaping confinement. She tucked them back behind her ears as Paddy led the way through the stable. The air smelled of horse and manure, hay and dust, all scents that seemed welcoming and safe to Imogen. The stables were large, the French style with two rows of stalls facing each other across a center aisle. The old stud, Dalmation—the only one of Henry's studs she and Paddy deemed worth keeping—had his stall down at the far end, away from the yearlings and colts. The newcomer waited a couple of stalls over.

She looked over the door at the creature. A dark chestnut with neat compact lines, he looked exactly like the sketch published in the auctioneer's newsletter: five years old, deep chest, well-formed legs and haunches, clear eyes. About fifteen hands, he wasn't a large horse, but his racing record—she did know that to be accurate, at least—indicated he had heart. He'd had only one second place finish among dozens of wins.

The horse stood in the far corner of the stall, his entire body quivering.

"What's wrong with him?" Imogen asked.

"Not any normal sickness," Paddy said.

She glanced over her shoulder at him, surprised by his hesitant tone. "What have you tried?"

His eyes drifted toward his boots. "Nothing to try, girl. The beast has the shakes."

Imogen turned her attention back to the horse in the stall. That must be why no one else outbid her. They'd been at the auction and *seen* this display. "He certainly won enough races. The pedigree might be faked, but his track record isn't."

"That horse is trouble, girl," Paddy said flatly. "We should ship 'im back."

"We don't have the money for that now." She hadn't told him about Hammersly, thinking one catastrophe per morning all he needed. She lifted the wooden latch on the stall door. Paddy knew better than to protest—no horse would ever hurt her. Horses always knew, somehow, that she shared a bit of common blood. When she stepped closer, the horse's head came up and his eyes focused on her. She held out a gloved hand to let him get the smell of her.

The horse's nostrils quivered. He took a step forward and set his forehead against her sternum. Surprised by the gesture, Imogen scratched under his forelock. Then she stepped back to get a better look at him. "He's docile enough."

She laid one hand against the creature's neck and felt the shudders flowing through his body. When she pulled back to look at his teeth, she noticed that the halter's ring had worn a raw spot into his cheek. She found another at the top of the chinstrap as well, where that ring rubbed. A third reddened spot lay under the buckle of the headstall.

He wasn't a horse.

Imogen stared at the creature, amazed that he'd ended up in her stable. Of all the things that her mother had ever dreaded, this would be the worst—a puca, one of the Fair Folk who could wear the shape of a horse. As such, he must have even less tolerance for cold iron than Imogen herself.

She looked the stallion in the eye and unbuckled the harness, careful not to touch the metal. Even through gloves, it bothered her. Everywhere metal touched his hide, the hair had abraded away, leaving red and irritated skin.

"Shouldn't do it," Paddy said. "That beast is trouble, girl. Send him back."

She cast a glance over her shoulder at him. "You knew, didn't you?"

Paddy just shook his head.

She hung the harness over the stall door and turned back to the horse. He still quivered, which made her suspect another source for his discomfort. She leaned against his shoulder and lifted one hoof—a bar shoe, already rusting. The bar had a special tongue attached, bent upward so that it brushed the inside of his hoof on the sensitive frog. It must be torture for the creature. "Get me a rope harness, Paddy," she snapped. "I want Jack right now."

Grumbling, Paddy left.

"I'm going to have those taken off," she told the horse. "So think kindly of us here."

He nuzzled her shoulder and sighed. Paddy returned and handed a rope harness over the stall door. Imogen looked the horse in the eye, and then slid the harness up and over his muzzle. "Trust me."

The horse followed docilely when she took him over to the work area the farrier used when he visited. A gray-haired horseman who'd been at the farm nearly as long as Paddy, Jack could turn his hand to almost anything. He produced a pair of pincers and pulled off the shoes. He frowned over the odd design, but tossed them into a pile in the back with other old shoes and scrap. "Didn't know anyone used iron shoes," the wiry hand said to Paddy.

Imogen didn't comment. She took the horse back to his stall, led him inside and removed the harness. The horse lipped her sleeve, but after a moment hung his head as if too tired for even that. But the shivers had passed, so she left him there and walked with Paddy back up to the house.

"Shouldn't have done it, girl," he repeated under his breath, like a litany.

"We have troubles enough, Paddy. Don't borrow from tomorrow. It was the right thing to do, and you know it." She left him at the door and went on to the office where she could sit and stew over the investment she'd just lost. That horse would have been valuable at stud—or so she'd thought.

The house's office was one of the few places where Bella's fripperies hadn't invaded. Imogen had always liked the room. She settled at Henry's desk and tried to concentrate on the account ledgers and all that needed attention: bills for feed, bills for the kitchens, paychecks to be written out. Instead she found her eyes drawn to the far wall and the tall white bookshelves there.

Most of the books had come from the previous farmhouse, carefully packed away by Mother Hawkes herself. Imogen had borrowed many of these very same volumes as a girl. After making certain that the office door was closed, Imogen dragged over a heavy chair and climbed up onto it to retrieve a volume from the top shelf: *The Fae*, by Armstead Winston-Howell. The book was worn, its fabric cover of burgundy paisley frayed along the bottom and corners. Imogen had first read it when she was eight, although her mother would have objected strenuously if she'd known.

Eugenia Villiers Smith had told Imogen very little about her father, wanting her daughter to follow in her footsteps, not his. Imogen had grown up knowing only his name, Finn, and that he was a puca—a fairy of sorts. From him she'd gotten her cream-colored hair, dark eyes, and that tendency to make things come apart. According to the book, that was part of a puca's mischief, a talent for wrecking things.

She turned to the page in the book that addressed the puca. Only a single column, it hadn't given the eight-year-old Imogen much to build on. *The puca*, the book informed her, *is one of the Lesser Folk who can take on many shapes, most common of those being a dark horse with glowing eyes.* The book went on to describe a creature who loved to entice unsuspecting humans out for midnight rides. Most folk claimed that such rides ended with no more harm than the fright given to the rider, but in a few counties in Ireland, it was held that a puca would then try to drown his rider in the nearest lake or pond. The author, however, kindly explained that they were possibly being confused with kelpies in those instances. Imogen's mother certainly hadn't been drowned.

She read through the entry again and shook her head. The Fair Folk weren't even supposed to exist in the United States, to some extent because the ocean trapped them in Ireland. Supposedly, they couldn't cross moving water. Imogen closed the book, scowling. As a baby, she had crossed the ocean herself, although according to Paddy she'd been sick the whole way. Evidently that stallion out in the stables had somehow managed as well.

Pondering the path that must have led him to her farm, Imogen went to bed that night, her mind still in a whirl.

In the morning, she donned her aged brown riding habit and headed out to the stables to face Paddy first. When she told him about the mortgage, he said a few colorful things about Hammersly. As Paddy had never liked the man, Imogen wasn't particularly shocked by his language.

"He's always wanted to get his hands on this land," Paddy finished, and moved straight to the only solution. "I'll get Tommy up on Blue Streak, and we'll work on his times. And by the by, the fence in the west meadow washed out night before last. We need to get that fixed, girl, or we'll lose horses onto Hammersly's land."

Yet another problem, Imogen thought ruefully. It was as well she'd intended to make a tour of the fences that morning.

The dark horse nickered when he saw her emerging from the tack room with a length of rope over her shoulder, so she stopped to check on him. The irritated spots on his cheeks and under the forelock seemed to be improving, far more quickly than they would have on a normal horse.

He lipped at her ivory braid over the stall door. Imogen pulled her hair free and scowled at the creature. "Don't get any ideas."

She felt sure he could leave if he wanted to. Without iron to bind him in that form, he could simply walk away with a glamour wrapped about him to hide himself. Then again, he might not feel well enough to leave. She didn't know how long he'd worn those iron shoes, but the fact that he'd been racing in Boston for three years suggested it had been at least that long. She couldn't imagine what that had done to him.

He snorted and tossed his head, shaking out his mane.

"No, I'm not taking you anywhere," she told him. "I'm not that much of a fool."

She scratched under his forelock. Then she had the horrified thought that she shouldn't be touching him—not encouraging him in any way. He *wasn't* a horse. She climbed down off the door and walked away without looking back.

At the gate, one of the hands already had Captain saddled up for her. "Thank you, Billy," she told the young man.

Billy nodded his dark head. "Is it true, ma'am? Hammersly's trying to force us out?"

One thing she knew, the hands were all fiercely loyal to Paddy, and thus to her. "I'm afraid so. We'll weather this, Billy."

He helped her up into the sidesaddle, nodding grimly. "Yes, ma'am. Whatever we need to do."

It made Imogen feel better to have loyal workers on her side, but she was responsible for them as well. She nodded to the young man and started off on her survey of the property's fences, starting to the east of the drive and going round the entire property. She checked on the currently empty cottage and found it locked up tight as it should be. She came back up through the paddock where the yearling fillies gamboled out in the July sunshine, and finally rode through the main paddock and down the meadow to the west edge of her land.

Paddy was right about the fence. She tied Captain to a sadly leaning post and went to survey the damage. A narrow stream ran through her land there, sloping down several feet as it crossed onto Hammersly's land on its way to one of the local lakes. The fence had followed the terrain, but now four posts were missing, washed out by the stream's swelling. They would have to be completely replaced, and the posts on either side already leaned. The rails between them were down. She felt lucky none of her mares or foals had wandered through the gap and onto Hammersly's land. She'd never see them again if that happened.

She could take a couple of hands off the training schedule for a day to fix it, or hire it done, but they really couldn't afford either just now. So for the time being, she would have to make do. She unbuttoned her riding jacket and left it over one of the rails. Then she tucked her skirt up into her belt and waded back and forth across the stream—shuddering involuntarily as she did so—to fix the rope across the gap. She wished she'd thought to wear her Wellingtons, but her half-boots were ancient anyway.

Once finished, she let down her damp skirt, and turned back toward the stables just in time to see the new stallion using his teeth to tug loose the slip knot in Captain's reins. Freed, Captain simply stood and waited for her. The stallion snorted at him. Captain jumped like a startled grasshopper and took off toward the stables.

Leaving her alone with the dark horse, who turned one eye on Imogen's bedraggled form and then lifted his muzzle toward his bare back.

He'd let himself out of his stall; Imogen had no doubt of that. He'd either jumped the pasture's fence or opened that gate as well. Then he'd sent Captain packing like the lowliest servant. She could see the stable yard from the meadow, so she grabbed up her jacket and pulled it on. "It's not that far. I'll walk."

She started back and heard the horse following, his hooves squelching in the soft earth. After a moment, she felt his breath on her neck and he started lipping at her collar. She turned to fix him with a stern look. "I know what you are. I know better than to ride you."

He nickered at her and bumped her chest with his nose, but she kept her hands at her sides, resisting the urge to scratch him. "My mother made that mistake once," she said. "I know better."

He tugged at her shirt and then, with a clear 'snick' of his teeth, sheared off one of her buttons. He spat it onto the damp grass. Sighing, Imogen fished the button out and stuffed it into a pocket. She walked on, buttoning her jacket over her gaping blouse as she went and cursing her luck under her breath.

The horse followed at a distance this time.

After reviewing the farm's books, she decided they would have to fix that fence themselves. Unfortunately, if they did a poor job of it, Hammersly would know *exactly* how tight her finances were. She didn't want that.

She could sell a couple of the yearlings. That would be a last option, she decided after discussing it with Paddy. Once one started selling off stock out of season, all the other stable owners knew there were money problems. Hammersly would find out within a day if she resorted to that.

That evening, she opened her bedroom windows to let in the cooler air. She changed into her nightgown, pulled on her old apple-green housecoat, and lay down atop her covers to read for a time. Her mother had always favored improving literature and forbade the reading of novels, claiming they weakened both the mind and moral fiber. That hadn't kept Imogen from borrowing the occasional volume from Mother Hawkes. Since she hadn't had time to get to the library in town recently, Imogen had been rereading the Austen novels. She fell asleep with *Persuasion* still in her hands.

In her dreams, the horse lipped at her collar again. His lips turned to her own then, and the absurdity of that thought jolted her awake—only to see a man leaning over her in the dim light.

She drew a breath to scream, but his hand settled firmly over her mouth—strong enough to give her pause. And then she realized who he was.

A lock of dark chestnut hair fell over his forehead, and his eyes were the same shade of brown. Patches of reddened flesh marred his cheeks, and his skin was pale, as though it rarely saw sunlight; she suspected it might not have for some time. His hand lifted after a moment, and he regarded her with a raised brow.

He made an attractive man, his deep chest translating into broad shoulders and his powerful haunches into well-shaped thighs, currently on display since he had somehow entered the house still nude. She hoped no one had seen him.

He said something to her in what must be Gaelic—not a question, she guessed from his tone, just a statement. He stepped back, putting enough distance between them that she didn't feel threatened. She still didn't know how to handle him. Her mother's many rules failed to provide instructions for this situation. "Do you speak English at all?" she managed.

"Well enough," he said—with an accent that sounded much like Paddy's.

Imogen was determined not to back down in front of this creature, not inside her own house. Even so, she scooted over and got off the other side of the bed, putting it between them. She gathered up the crocheted throw draped across the curved footboard and tossed it at him. "For heaven's sakes, put that on."

He caught the bundled throw and, with an amused look on his face, wrapped it about his waist. "You know, darling, I've been standing in that stall naked for the last two days. You said nothing about your bashfulness before."

"It's not the same thing," she said, hoping to dismiss the subject.

His dark brows lifted, but he didn't answer. Instead he settled on the upholstered chair by the window. Imogen edged around the bed, and then went to the door and held it open. "Go."

"Now, darling," he said, "I only came to beg a favor. No need to make a fuss."

A favor. Imogen clenched her jaw. She should never have spoken to him at all. He would want to make a bargain, and she knew she wasn't clever enough to beat one of the Fair Folk at that. On the other hand, she really didn't have any means of throwing him out, short of summoning all the stable hands. And the presence of an unclothed man in her bedroom would be difficult to explain, even to the most loyal of employees. Imogen shut the door, but stayed there, far out of his reach. "What is your name?"

"Whirlwind," he said.

For a second her breath wouldn't come. *Mother Hawkes will find that absolutely hilarious*, Imogen thought.

She cast a glance at the window and wondered if climbing out was a viable option and then shook her head, reckoning that this must be the time when her actions would determine the outcome of whatever Mother Hawkes had foreseen. "Is that your real name?"

He shrugged. "Not my true name, of course. As real as any other."

Knowing the true name of one of the Fair Folk granted great power over them, the reason Imogen never spoke her birth name aloud. Even half-blooded as she was, it would give the speaker an advantage she didn't like to contemplate. She and her mother had always used the surname Smith instead her mother's family name—Villiers. "I understand the concept," she said.

He leaned back and put his hands behind his head as if he intended to stay. "And what is your name, darling?"

"Imogen," she told him.

His expression suggested that he didn't approve. "Imgen?"

"Im-o-gen," she said slowly. "I know what you are. I don't want you making any trouble here. We've tried to be hospitable. We have enough worries right now without your compounding them with foolishness."

He looked scandalized. "Foolishness?"

"Broken fences, leaking buckets, pregnant housemaids."

"No, never," he said, laying one hand over his heart.

"Do you mean, no, you won't cause trouble?"

His eyes narrowed.

"No, you won't cause trouble for this household," she clarified further, hoping he wouldn't take it in his head to terrorize the neighboring farms either—well, perhaps Hammersly's, a little. It would never do to say so, as asking one of the Fair Folk to do something malicious was doubly dangerous.

"Deal?" he asked.

Unfortunately her mind, once started on that track, clung to it as a matter of nature. She could no more refuse an offer to bargain than he could. She heard herself say, "What would you ask in return?"

His soft lips curved. "One night."

Imogen shut her eyes and leaned back against the closed door. He *would* keep to the word of his bargain. If she agreed with his terms, he would refrain from causing trouble, although possibly only within the strictest interpretation of her words. If she refused, he would leave, but then he might not feel any guilt over stirring mischief. That was what his kind lived for, her mother had warned.

She tried to remember if there was some special phrasing she should use to get him to obey her but, without knowing his true name, she didn't have much leverage. And being honest with herself, she admitted she didn't want him to leave. That half of herself that she'd never had the chance to know, her father's blood—the creature before her represented a window into a world her mother had always tried to keep tightly locked away from her. Imogen wanted to ask him a thousand questions, only she had nothing to bargain with. Save what he'd already asked of her.

His fingers touched her cheek, even though she hadn't heard him approach.

She hadn't made up her mind yet. She couldn't retreat through the door, so she stood there under his touch. He pressed closer, and his lips—as soft as she remembered—touched her earlobe. He wasn't much taller than she was. Imogen kept her eyes shut, trying to decide the wisest path. She probably should have shipped him back to Boston as soon as she realized what he was, but it was far too late for that now.

He kissed her, his mouth tasting of sweet hay. She pressed her hands back against the door to keep from touching his skin. She whimpered, and then felt a surge of embarrassment at her audible reaction.

"How long?" he whispered.

Her marriage hadn't left her with a desire to seek out a lover; Henry had never exhibited much interest in her, his passion saved for his horses and his memories of Bella. And Imogen wasn't the sort to jeopardize her standing in the community by indulging in affairs. It was difficult enough to garner acceptance among the local landowners without a man nominally in charge of the farm. She opened her eyes and looked into the warm brown ones so close to her own. "A long time. It's not wise for a woman in my position to become involved."

He drew back. "Is that a no?"

He didn't smell quite like a man, she noticed, but then again, he wasn't one. Her blood pounded in her ears as if it recognized that he shared her heritage, as if it recognized the likeness in him. She could tell him no and he would be bound to leave her alone, but his offer was so very tempting. Any liaison between them would be on *her* terms, under her control, and in the end he would leave with none the wiser. She licked her lips and said, "No one can know about this."

A glint appeared in his warm eyes. "*Two* nights, then,"

"What will you promise me in return?"

"I will cause no trouble for this household," he said, "and none will know I was here with you. In return for two nights."

Imogen considered that offer as his fingers slid along her braid, the pale hair simply unraveling at his touch. He lifted a hank of it to his lips and regarded her with a raised brow. "A deal," she whispered.

"A deal, then." He grinned, and added, "You should know I would never have dreamed of causing you harm, darling, not after you removed my bonds. And the fence, that was not my doing."

Imogen shook her head, disgusted with herself. She shouldn't have assumed he intended mischief, no matter what her mother had told her of his kind. But now she was bound by her word. Even half-blooded, she could no more go back on it than he could have.

His hand stroked her cheek. "I only sought you out meaning to barter work for clothes, darling, but you looked so lovely lying there. I couldn't resist trying to steal a kiss."

Imogen gazed up at him, unsure what she should do or say.

"It won't be so bad," he said, his dark eyes dancing with laughter. "You might even like me."

Imogen took a deep breath and, as she had no intention of backing down, she put her arms around his neck and kissed him.

He seemed to doze, although Imogen wasn't sure. The pinkish light of dawn stole along his pale skin and brought out reddish glints in his dark hair. She'd seen many more handsome men in her life, but he was still a pleasure to look at. He hadn't bothered to draw a glamour about himself either, which would have made it harder for a human woman to resist him. That pleased her, as if it meant he dealt truthfully with her.

His hands were still red and raw, as well as the soles of his feet. Having endured that sort of reaction herself, Imogen ached to see it. She touched a finger to his reddened palm.

He opened one dark eye. "Time to go, is it?"

"Who put those shoes on you?" she asked. "How long ago?"

He propped himself up on one elbow. "Ten years. Not a fond memory at all. Better to talk about last night. Did I not say you would like me?"

The night had been far lovelier than she'd expected. Despite looking years younger than Henry, he was likely older and more experienced in such things. She wondered briefly if he was ageless, like some of the Fair Folk were said to be, but was afraid to ask. "You did warn me," she finally admitted.

"And now I must go, more's the shame," he said. "No longer night, is it?"

None of the maids would come in, she knew. No fire to lay in the summer, and she always went down to breakfast. But tempting though it might be, it would be a mistake to give him more than the terms of their bargain. "Yes, you should go."

She thought he looked disappointed, but he dutifully pressed a kiss into her palm, and then rose naked from her bed. Then, remembering his ostensible reason for seeking her out last night, she said, "You could take some of Henry's clothes. From the dressing room, I mean."

His eyes followed her pointing finger. "Truly? I am willing to work for my keep."

"It's all right," she said, clutching the sheet to her chin as she sat up. He inclined his head and then disappeared into the dressing room.

Imogen found herself staring at the white-painted door and feeling dazed. She'd taken a lover, something she'd never intended to do. All her self-control had gone out the window when he'd come close, and for the first time she understood how her mother could have done such a thing. Her serious mother, who had traveled across an ocean with a sickly infant to start her life over, away from the censure of English society. It had cost her dearly to bear his child, but she had done so and never looked back. Imogen closed her eyes to gather her scattered thoughts.

"You're fond of pink." His voice floated out from the dressing room, laughter in it.

Imogen clutched the sheet tighter. She spotted her abandoned housecoat on the rug, dashed over and drew it on. As she tied the sash, he emerged from the dressing room wearing a pair of Henry's old trousers and what must be the most decrepit shirt he could find. The trousers were too big, but braces held them up. He set a worn pair of boots on her table and began to roll up the shirt-sleeves. He glanced at her, one brow raised.

"I don't like pink," she managed. "My husband did. I wore it to please him."

"Ah," he said.

For a moment, neither spoke. Imogen curled her bare toes in the rug. She had never been in this situation before. She had no idea what he expected her to do or say.

"So I shall go," he said. "Thank you for the clothes." He turned and walked out of her room, wrapping a glamour about himself that would likely keep others from seeing him, although it failed with her.

Once Imogen had gotten her feet moving again, she dressed in her oldest work clothes and the still damp boots she'd worn the day before. Paddy was the first to greet her when she walked down to the stables. "That damned horse was out of his stall last night."

She stopped in her tracks. "Is he there now?"

"Yes, looking innocent, he is." Paddy took off his cap to run fingers through his gray hair as Imogen tried to decide what an innocent expression looked like on a horse. "But don't be surprised if you find the fences torn down," Paddy said.

"We already had fences down," she reminded him. "We've been hospitable. There's no reason for him to cause us harm."

Paddy just shook his head, and went on to review the schedule for the day.

"We need to get the fence repaired," she said. "Can you spare any of the boys?"

"Not until after the race," Paddy said.

She'd expected that answer. "I can work on it myself."

"Not a job for a girl." Paddy knew, of course, that whenever he said that it would almost certainly goad her into action, wise or not.

"I'll see if I can get a start on salvaging what's left."

She went back to the house and grabbed her Wellingtons and a canteen full of water, then headed out to the west meadow on foot. The late July sun promised a warm day, and she was perspiring by the time she'd reached the far end of the meadow, so she tugged off her jacket and laid it over one of the steadier rails. The breeze carried the scent of the pine and larch trees that stood over on Hammersly's side of the fence to the west of the stream. As a girl, Imogen had believed those trees haunted. Even now she had her doubts about them.

She set down her canteen and plotted her morning's work. Since the rails all appeared to be salvageable, she started with those. She'd managed to drag several of the downed rails into a pile when she spotted someone walking across the meadow toward her. She squinted in the bright sunlight and then sighed.

"Don't you ever rest, darling?" he asked when he got close enough. "Me, I'd rather be in bed still, but..."

She shook her head, exasperated. "I've work to do. What are you doing here?"

He regarded her with raised brows. "You mean here on this farm? I do believe you had me brought here."

"No, I meant in this pasture," she clarified.

"Well, you did tell me no broken fences," he said. "So I came to see to this one, as I don't want you to think I've weaseled out of the terms of our bargain."

Imogen didn't think it fair to hold him to the bargain retroactively, and he hadn't caused the fence's destruction. But he had said he was willing to work, and she could use the help. She pointed out one of the rails that had fallen into the stream. "Could you help me lift that out of the way?"

Between them they carried the fallen rails to one side and stacked them neatly. When they'd set down the last of them, she wiped a gloved hand across her brow. "Do you have a name? Other than your horse name, I mean."

His eyes laughed at her. "You don't like it?"

She had no intention of calling him Whirlwind. "A name I can say without feeling foolish."

"Guaire," he said.

She tried out his name mentally and decided it suited him. It sounded Gaelic though, which meant she had no chance of being able to spell it correctly. "Thank you."

He smiled at her again and then casually asked, "So, why does Paddy hate this Hammersly fellow so much?"

She went over to get her canteen. "Was Paddy talking in front of you?"

"People will say almost anything in front of a horse, Ginny."

Imogen was tempted to say something sharp, but ground her teeth and kept the urge under control. Only her mother had ever called her *Ginny*. Not even Henry had done so. She took a sip from the canteen and then politely offered it to Guaire. And as he reached over to take it, she saw for the first time that his palm was worn bloody. She grabbed his wrist and turned his hand to survey his blistered and raw skin. "Why didn't you pick up some gloves?"

"They'll heal," he said dismissively. "There were no gloves in that wardrobe of yours, save some dainty white things that look like a lady's only far too big for your delicate hands."

No, she'd turned every last pair of Henry's useable gloves over to the stable hands, save for his dress attire. "Why didn't you pick up a pair in the stables? I'm sure they're lying about everywhere."

He shook his head and his hair fell over his eyes. "I'll not steal from your men."

Imogen bit her lip. "I'll see if I can find a pair that would fit you."

"Thank you." He nodded, wiped the blood from the canteen with his sleeve, and handed it back to her. "Hammersly?"

"His lands march with mine," she told him. "On the other side of this fence, in fact. He wants my land, and he's willing to stoop pretty low to get it."

"And how low is that?" he asked. She explained about the mortgage, at which he looked as scandalized as she'd felt. "They had a bargain with your husband, Ginny. I don't see how they could sell his word away."

"They don't have the same scruples you do." She leaned on one of the solid posts. "Hammersly has offered to pay it off if I marry him. Of course if I did so, the entire farm would become his property, so it's no real gift at all."

The more she thought about it, the more it seemed like an insult than anything else.

Guaire regarded her steadily. She didn't know what he expected her to say, so she turned back to consider the pile of rails. "I need to get the fence back up," she told him. "If any of the mares wanders through the gap to his land, I'll never get them back."

"No need to worry over that. I asked them not to," he said. "Figured you wouldn't want 'em to."

She surveyed the pasture and noted that the mares and foals were, indeed, at the far corner.

Guaire's eyes returned to the missing fence span. He gestured toward the stream bed. "The problem is the stream, not the fence. You need a deeper bed, you see. Dig it out."

"I don't have the men to do that."

"I can do it," he said. "I've nothing else to do with my days."

Imogen regarded him with a furrowed brow. "What do you want in trade?"

He shook his head. "You should not have asked, Ginny."

And she realized then he hadn't been offering a *bargain*. He'd simply offered to do the work, with no strings attached. But now he was tied to the deal; he had to make an offer. She could either accept or refuse, but there it was.

"One night," he said.

"For all that work?"

"Well worth it, in my mind," he said with a twinkle in his eye. "Well worth it."

Imogen left Guaire that afternoon with a request not to damage his hands too badly, which he seemed to take with the same lack of seriousness he brought to everything else.

"The damned horse is gone again," Paddy told her in a sour voice as he walked by with Faithful on a lead rope.

Imogen wondered if he had any idea where Guaire had been all day... and the previous night. Rather than ask him, she surveyed the two-year-old he led instead. The Special Stakes required that she list three of her two-year-olds, although Blue Streak would be the one to run. Faithful and Hawk's Cry were her two spares. "How are they doing?"

"Blue Streak shaved three seconds off his time today," Paddy said.

"I wish I'd been there to see it."

"Race day, soon," Paddy said. "If he takes the race, you'll have enough to buy that paper back, girl."

Enough to bring it up to date, at least, and pay the stakes for the next race. "That's what we have to hope for," she said. "How did Faithful do?"

Paddy shook his head and patted the two-year-old's neck. "This one just doesn't have his heart in it. We'll keep at him, but I don't know if he'll ever improve."

A shame, in her opinion, since Faithful's bloodlines were every bit as good as Blue Streak's, both colts having been sired by Dalmation out of winning mares. "Perhaps next time," she told Paddy and headed up to the house.

Imogen capped off her afternoon trek to town with a stop at the drug store. She'd arranged for a shipment of oats and a handful of fence posts, ordered the new bit Paddy requested and handed Mrs. Dougherty's list to the grocer for delivery. She'd even found a pair of gloves at the hardware store over on Caroline Street that should fit Guaire. She deserved a small extravagance.

Her heels clicked on the tile as she walked toward the case where the soaps and lotions were housed. The two clerks were near the back of the back of the store speaking with their employer's wife, so Imogen perused the neatly lettered signs in front of each stack of soap, trying to decide what fragrance she'd like to try. She'd used plain oatmeal soap for years, and thought that perhaps the time had come for a change.

She'd decided on the jasmine-scented soap and glanced up when she heard feet approaching. She was surprised to see Mrs. Menges herself come over to wait on her.

"Good afternoon, Mrs. Hawkes," the older lady said. As always, Mrs. Menges wore a stylish outfit, a light green day dress with full sleeves and ivory lace adorning the high neck. She leaned closer. "Have you heard the news?"

Not being one of Mrs. Menges' circle, Imogen usually didn't talk much with her. She was surprised to be approached now. "I don't suppose I have," she admitted.

"Well, I thought you would want to know," Mrs. Menges said. "I have it that Sanford's prime two-year-old colt split a pastern yesterday."

"Mohawk?" Imogen flinched. "How terrible. An injury like that could keep him out of racing for the rest of the season."

Mrs. Menges nodded in a conspiratorial fashion. "But good news for the other stables in the Special Stakes, isn't it?"

Imogen laid one hand over her mouth, working out how that improved her horse's chances in the race. The bell on the store's door rang, and Mrs. Menges looked past her as another customer entered the store. A flash of annoyance crossed the woman's face.

Imogen turned and too late saw that the new customer was William Hammersly. The store was too narrow for her to evade him. He strolled over to where the two of them stood, and greeted them each politely.

Imogen reminded herself that she must keep calm, and managed to return the greeting with passable civility. She wished she'd remembered that the store was directly across Broadway from the Trust building. Hammersly— or that driver of his—could have seen her enter.

Hammersly smiled at her as he stripped off his doeskin gloves—much finer things than the ones she'd bought for Guaire. He laid them on the glass of the case and glanced down at the soaps inside it. "If you need a recommendation," he said in a silky tone, "I prefer the jasmine scent."

Imogen clenched her jaw, offended that he would say such a thing in front of Mrs. Menges. But she had to keep her temper under control or risk destroying the woman's store. She turned to Mrs. Menges instead. "I'll take two of the oatmeal."

Hammersly's brows drew together in apparent vexation, which lightened her mood considerably. As Mrs. Menges started to wrap the soaps for her, he stroked his fingers over his gloves as if they were a pet animal. "Wouldn't you like to join me for supper this evening?"

"I beg your pardon?" Imogen asked.

He smiled. "You would like to join me for supper this evening, wouldn't you?"

He expected her to agree, Imogen realized. She looked over at Mrs. Menges for support and was surprised to see that lady gazing raptly at Hammersly's face.

"Of course I would," Mrs. Menges whispered.

Imogen took a step away from the counter, baffled. She'd had the definite impression when Hammersly walked in that Mrs. Menges disliked him.

Hammersly scowled briefly at that interruption and then turned his smile back on Imogen. He picked up his gloves and held them in one hand, stroking them like one would a cat. "It would be a good opportunity for us to expand the relationship between our farms. Please say you'd like to join me."

Behind him, Mrs. Menges was shaking her head as if to clear it. Imogen gave Hammersly a direct look. "You're mistaken, Mr. Hammersly. No relationship exists between our farms, and I'm not interested in discussing that possibility."

Hammersly glanced down at his gloves as if they'd done him some wrong, then jerked them back on. "Good day then, Mrs. Hawkes," he said in a brusque tone, and walked out of the shop.

"What a detestable man," Mrs. Menges said under her breath. She returned to wrapping the oatmeal soaps for Imogen as if that peculiar interlude had never happened.

Aware that something strange had just happened, Imogen decided she should definitely be on her guard around Hammersly in the future. She paid for the soaps and nestled them in her handbag with the leather work-gloves she'd bought Guaire. Somehow she doubted she would see him stroking them.

———————

Imogen ate her supper alone in her customary silence, and then studied the books for a while until she carried the lamp up to her bedroom. She unlatched the window that opened over the yard, and the cool evening air lifted the fine curtains. She caught the scent of the stables and the woods beyond. Settling at the table in her dressing room, she brushed out her hair, her mind frozen in indecision.

Not as to her actions, of course. She wouldn't turn Guaire away when he came to her. He'd dealt fairly with her so far, and she intended to uphold their bargain. She wasn't going to be a fool over him, though. Her mother had taught her that the Fair Folk had reasons beneath their reasons, layer upon layer of motivation for everything they did. She had to walk carefully around him. Even if he seemed honest, she couldn't trust that appearance of goodness to be the truth.

Imogen lay down and picked up the novel she'd abandoned the night before. She hadn't read far, though, before she dreamed of Guaire's burned hands on her skin. Imogen jerked awake—to an empty room and silence.

Imogen met with Paddy in the morning and listened as he spun out his daily monologue of chores.

He ended with an amusing observation. "And last night the horse was in his stall the whole time."

"Are you standing watch over the creature?"

"Just noticing when I walk by," he said. "Disappeared again this morning, he did."

Imogen figured she knew where Guaire had gone. "Have any of the others noticed?"

"Jack has." Paddy cast a look up and down the center aisle of the stable. "But he'll never say anything. Tommy asked me which paddock the beast was in, though."

Jack wasn't a worry. Imogen had known the old hand most of her life, and he took everything in stride. Tommy—a recently retired jockey they'd hired on last year to help exercise the racers—she didn't know as well. She hoped he wouldn't make any kind of fuss. "You could say you're putting the new stallion out at the old cottage pasture until he settles in."

Paddy shook his head. "Can't go on forever, girl. We need to do something with that horse. No telling what doom he'll bring down on us."

Imogen chewed her lower lip, wondering if Guaire could possibly be a doom. He didn't seem like one to her. "Perhaps he's lucky, Paddy. Did you consider that?"

Paddy just crossed himself and set about his day's tasks.

Imogen walked down to the west meadow, noting that the broodmares still seemed to be staying away from the break in the fence. That relieved one of her worries. She found Guaire already down by the stream, gazing down at the trench he'd begun to dig. She'd given him permission to use the farm's tools, and he had with him a long-handled shovel, the steel head well away from his feet. The stream's waters were muddied, but since it flowed from there onto Hammersly's land, Imogen decided she liked that perfectly well.

She noticed that Guaire wore the same shirt and trousers as the day before, already mud-splashed. The blood-stained spot on his sleeve had dried to an ugly brown. She handed him the gloves she'd purchased in town. "A gift."

"Thank you." He took them with a respectful nod, and then ruined it by grinning. "I said you would like me."

"If you've a need for fresh clothes, please feel free to go through the dressing room and take what you need."

He glanced down at his mud-splattered garments with a raised brow, but just shrugged.

Imogen took a breath, intending to ask why he hadn't come to her the night before, but feared it would sound overly eager. She pointed at the running water instead and asked, "Does that bother you?"

He gave the stream a calculating look. "Not much more than it bothers you, I expect."

She felt an odd irritation when she waded through it, rather like an itch she couldn't place. Then she realized the implication of his words; he must be aware of her puca blood. She lifted her eyes to his face. "How did you know?"

That seemed to surprise him. "How would I not know? I could smell it when you first held out your hand for me. And you have Finn's look about you."

She felt her blood run cold. Imogen clenched her jaw and forced down her urge to run. Her mother had *always* said she looked like her father, but it had never occurred to Imogen that someone would ever recognize her as his child, not here in America.

"You didn't think I knew." Guaire leaned on the shovel's handle, his thick brows drawn together. "You have nothing to fear from me, Ginny. I've no love for him myself, and no intention of telling him where to find you."

That implied that Guaire knew she'd been hidden from her father. "Why?"

He tilted his head. "Why what?"

"Why don't *you* like him?"

"You asked me who put those shoes on me? 'twas him."

She didn't doubt his word. "Why would he do that?"

"Over a woman, of course," Guaire said. "I don't know how he found out it was me, but he came after me, and eventually he found me."

"Were you hiding from him?"

"Aye, for sixteen years I managed, and then my own cousin betrayed me to him. For money, would you believe? Used my name to hold me until Finn came to haul me back."

Imogen blinked at him, not quite knowing how to ask the next question, but the timing sounded right. Sixteen years in hiding, ten wearing those damnable shoes, and she was twenty-six. "You fell out with him over... my mother?"

Guaire laughed. "Ah, not what you're thinking, Ginny. I was young, and foolish enough to be altruistic then. She wanted to go back to her family in England, and I took her there, 'tis all. Never laid a hand on her in an overfriendly way. Finn would have killed me outright for that. Insane jealous he was, about anything that belonged to him."

Imogen felt a profound relief. At least she hadn't taken the same lover as her mother. With creatures who didn't age like humans, that was a possibility. She had no idea how old Guaire was, and while he said he'd been young then, his definition of 'young' might not be the same as hers. Then she pieced together what he'd said. "Thank you for helping her. I'm sorry you paid such a price."

He snorted and rolled his eyes. "Finn never liked me much anyway."

"Why not?"

"I'd a human grand-dam. Makes me lower than the rest of them, you know."

"Lower?"

"Not pure-blooded. There are things I can't do, you know. Your mother told me she was worried he would treat you as badly as he did me, so she didn't want him to have you."

That Guaire was part human hadn't occurred to her before, but it did explain why another of his kind had been able to bind him. "It's fortunate then that I'm the one who purchased you."

"Ah, that was Fate, Ginny. I knew it the moment I laid an eye on you."

Imogen felt her cheeks go warm, a novel sensation. She never blushed.

When she opened the door to her bedroom that night, she saw Guaire sitting in her chair by the eastern-facing window, a book in his hands. Waiting for her, she realized, and felt a surge of nervousness. He rose when she approached and set down the book—her family Bible, the one her mother brought from England.

"Do any of the housemaids see you?" she asked.

"I don't want them to, so why would they?" He took the lamp from her and set it on the table. "I like this room best. Not fussy."

That pleased her. "I shouldn't be surprised you favor the bedroom, should I?"

"'twas not a comment on the bed, darling, or the inhabitant of it," he said. "But now that you mention it, you are the loveliest thing about this house."

Her cheeks burned. And then she managed to ask what she'd not dared out in the pasture. "Why didn't you come to me last night?"

A smile spread slowly across his face. "Missed me, did you?"

"A simple question," she said. "I would think you would want to be done with it."

"Be done with it?" He laid one hand over his heart as if wounded. "Is that how you feel about this, Ginny? As if you were mucking out the stalls? Plucking a chicken? I thought you liked me—or at least being bedded by me—last time."

She did her best to keep any reaction from her face. She suspected she'd wounded his pride, and that hadn't been her intention. "I thought more that *you* would feel that way."

He came closer and ran a finger along her cheek, then drew her braid over her shoulder. It began to unravel at his touch. "This is what I bargained for. Did you think I would have asked if I didn't want you?"

His palms still looked raw. Imogen felt a twinge of worry. "Then why did you not come last night?"

"I have to sleep sometime, darling, and so do you." He leaned forward and his lips caressed hers.

Imogen tasted oats on his breath and, for the first time in as long as she could remember, felt the urge to laugh. She stilled it, though, worried that if she gave in, she would lose control of everything.

He drew back and his eyes met hers. "Trust me."

The first night, she thought, he'd been intent on seducing her body. It hadn't been so personal. She hadn't known much of him, which made it simple—a bargain and little else. It seemed he wanted more of her this time. He wanted her trust. And she didn't know if she could give that.

He waited silently until Imogen found the courage to place her hand in his.

———

Guaire had already gone when she woke. Seeing the steep angle of the sun, Imogen jumped up and ran to check the time on the clock. She'd overslept by an hour.

She dressed in one of her better day dresses, a darker pink that almost flattered her coloring. She regarded her face in the mirror in the dressing room. With her face washed, her hair neatly braided up, and properly dressed, she didn't look much different than she had the week before. Even so, she feared something would show.

She'd been a good wife to Henry, a man twice her age when he'd married her. She'd been faithful and honored his wishes. She had even loved him, after her fashion. He hadn't expected more. It had been a marriage of convenience; he'd given her security in the hopes that she would give him a son. But just as he'd not borne an heir with his first wife, there had been no child with her, either.

Imogen had always blamed that on her cool and controlled nature. She had never warmed to anyone, not in the way of a woman after a man. Henry had been amiable, but she'd merely been a substitute for his beloved Bella. And Hammersly had never roused anything more than irritation in her. She'd known both of them far longer than Guaire, but for some reason it seemed she knew him far better. She *liked* him, perhaps more, and it frightened her to feel that way.

Annoyed with her dawdling, she grabbed up her straw hat and firmly pinned it on, determined not to let any weakness show. It didn't help that when she settled in the buggy to head into town, Guaire stepped up and sat down next to her. The stable hand didn't seem to notice him, though, so she said nothing.

"Can no one see you?" she asked as the buggy reached the end of the drive.

He'd picked an old cap from the dressing room, and wore it at exactly the same angle that Paddy wore his. "Not if I don't want them to. Most of the time. I couldn't fool you if I tried, not half-blooded as you are."

She wondered how she was going to explain all the work getting done in the meadow, but decided not to worry about that until she had to. She turned the carriage onto the road and headed toward town, mindful of the ruts left by recent rains. The trees along the way left them under dappled sunlight, which lifted her spirits for some reason.

"So, where are we going?" He sounded as if he didn't care so long as he was in her company.

"It's Sunday," she told him. "I'll go to services, and then lunch with Mother Hawkes."

"Ah, I'd not thought of that. I'd like to see the town, but you won't mind if I don't go into that church, will you?"

She'd had her entire life to accustom herself to the unusual sensations she felt when crossing holy ground. She found it surprisingly similar to crossing moving water. "I do understand."

He leaned back on the seat so that his shoulder brushed hers. "So, tell me about this town. Saratoga?"

"Saratoga Springs," she corrected, guessing that he'd heard the name spoken by one of the hands. An easy request, not too personal. She did so, telling him of the families that made up the backbone of the town and its racing history, the spas and the casinos. He listened attentively, and asked questions that proved he understood the sometimes delicate nature of a town's social structure.

They drove up Lake Avenue and through the edge of town toward where the steeple of the Presbyterian Church and the Town Hall's clock tower rose above the other buildings. When they finally neared it, Imogen found a good spot on the side of the street, jumped down from the buggy and tied the reins to a post herself. Guaire stepped down and stood watching her as a handful of churchgoers strolled past and turned onto Broadway. When she dusted off her gloves and resettled her hat, he smiled at her and said, "You look lovely, but not enough to entice me in there today."

She regarded him with doubtful eyes, trying to figure out that cryptic comment.

"Don't talk back to me," he said then, "or they'll all think you quite insane."

Which saved her from embarrassment, because she'd just been about to ask him what he meant. She turned away without even a nod and marched around the corner. She passed the Town Hall under the eyes of the large cast iron lions there, and headed up the steps into the church building. She tried to ignore that familiar prickling feeling when she stepped over the threshold, but shivered anyway.

Guaire wasn't in sight when she emerged after the service, but that didn't surprise her. She suspected he would be able to find his way back to the farm easily enough, and he had four legs to take him there if he wished so. She unhitched the buggy and drove up Broadway to Mother's Hawkes house... and found him already there, staring up at the house from the edge of the street. "How did you know this is where she lives?"

He tied the buggy to the post and helped her down. "Who?"

"Mother Hawkes," Imogen said, hoping that no one noticed her talking to the air. North Broadway didn't have too much traffic, though. "This is her house."

He cast a measuring glance up at the porch. "I followed..."

Mother Hawkes chose that moment to come out onto the porch, a regal figure in a fine blue morning suit. Imogen headed up the walk to the door, but Mother Hawkes continued to gaze past her at the buggy. She gave Imogen an odd look. "Aren't you going to invite him in? We don't want to offend him."

Imogen glanced back at Guaire, startled. "You see someone?"

Mother Hawkes set her hands on her hips. "Of course I see him, girl. I suppose he's attached himself to *you*, but I can see him well enough."

After taking a moment to make up her mind, Imogen waved for Guaire to join them. He stuffed his hands in his trouser pockets and strode up the walk to the porch, his expression guarded.

"She said she didn't want to offend you," Imogen explained.

His brows rose, but he didn't look as surprised as she expected. He held the front door open for Mother Hawkes and then followed the two of them inside.

"I'm honored to have you here," Mother Hawkes said, addressing Guaire directly.

"Madam," he said, removing his cap. "Are you the one who put the wards about the house?"

"Been some time," she said in a pleased voice, "but yes. Tell me, would they have kept the likes of you out?"

"Perhaps for a bit," he said with a twinkle in his eye. "But they're not meant for the likes of me, are they?"

"Not at all. I suspect that if one of the Folk wanted to get in, they could find a way."

Imogen listened to the discussion numbly, surprised by her mother-in-law's easy recognition—and acceptance—of one of the Fair Folk in her home.

Mother Hawkes led them toward the dining room where she and Imogen usually ate alone. She turned back to Guaire. "Now, you'll have to let the kitchen maids see you—or go hungry, that is. I expect it would be best if I told them you're visiting in town. With your accent, it would have to be Mr. O'Donnell you're here to visit. May I ask your name?"

"Guaire," he said.

"How nice it sounds." Mother Hawkes settled in her chair at the head of the table and Guaire, evidently knowing his etiquette, pushed the chair in for her. "Now, am I allowed to know how you came to be here?" she asked, and then looked at him more sharply. "Are those my son's clothes?"

Guaire paused in the midst of pushing in Imogen's chair.

Imogen wanted to close her eyes and pretend that it all made sense. "I gave them to him, Mother Hawkes."

"Tush, girl. I'm not criticizing you. I'm surprised you didn't throw them out years ago. They don't quite fit, but they'll do until he has time to have some made."

"I'm terrible hard on clothes, Madam," Guaire said. "Sometimes I have to leave them behind—can't carry clothes if you're a horse—so it's foolish for me to yearn after fine garb."

A kitchen maid came in with a tea tray but stopped when she saw Guaire. Mother Hawkes sent her packing with instructions to set another place at the table. A moment later Guaire was seated, casting a skeptical eye on the tea pot.

Mother Hawkes began ask him questions, some of which were ones Imogen hadn't dared. She supposed it was the privilege of age. She would have felt compelled to bargain for every one.

And she fretted suddenly, seeing Guaire as her mother-in-law must see him. He didn't have a jacket. His shirt sleeves were rolled up to hide the fact that they were too long. Henry's trousers were too large on him, and Imogen realized she'd never once asked if the boots fit. She had no idea if he had any socks on.

When the maid brought bowls of steaming onion soup, he eyed it with such relish that she felt ashamed that she'd not once offered him food. He had food in his stall, but that couldn't be considered the same.

Imogen watched him eat, feeling her heart sink into her stomach. After a time he cast her a questioning look. She just shook her head, not wanting to explain in front of Mother Hawkes.

"I'm sorry," she told him as he settled next to her in the buggy. "I haven't even thought about your meals, or much about your clothes, for that matter."

"I haven't asked," he said. "I haven't gone hungry."

She dared a glance at his face, hoping his lack of resentment was genuine. She didn't want him to think her inhospitable. "I mean food like that, Guaire, not oats in a stall. What am I thinking? You shouldn't be staying in a stall in the first place."

He laughed. "Ginny, I've been a horse for so long I hardly remember what this is like. I'll probably be colicky later from eating that. My belly's not used to it."

She'd never considered the ramifications of what one's stomach endured when shifting between horse-form and human-form.

"And you shouldn't be talking to me," he added. "That man over there is looking at you like you've gone mad."

Imogen followed the direction of his pointing finger and saw William Hammersly striding along the cobbles on the edge of the road toward the buggy. She groaned inwardly. She'd hoped that the previous day's meeting would have made her feelings clear. But the traffic along Broadway had slowed to a crawl, so she couldn't avoid him without making a scene.

When Hammersly set a gloved hand on the frame of the buggy, she drew to a stop, reins clenched in her fingers. "Good afternoon, Mrs. Hawkes," he said. "Are you quite well? I believe you were talking to yourself."

She turned her eyes on him, keeping her expression neutral. "I was simply discussing with myself what I need to tell my trainer when I get back to the farm, Mr. Hammersly. I assure you there's no need for concern."

He smiled up at her. "Ah, good. I saw that you've entered the Special."

Imogen wondered what he was actually after this time. That wasn't a secret. Anyone could go to the racing association and get that information. "Yes. If you'll excuse me, I need to be getting back."

The buggy stuck behind her began to try to edge around her unmoving vehicle. Imogen waved apologetically and when her head was turned, Hammersly's hand moved from the frame of the buggy. Under the edges of her skirt, she felt his fingers touch her stockinged leg, just above the top of her half-boot. Imogen froze, her jaw clenched.

"Have you considered my offer?" he asked.

The buggy swayed as Guaire jumped down, and Hammersly—possibly out of surprise—wrapped his hand around Imogen's ankle as if to steady her.

Imogen felt a warm tingling along her skin, coupled with a sensation that could only be described as yearning—surely not a natural response to a man she disliked so much. She wondered if that was what had caused Mrs. Menges to react so oddly to the man. She shook her head to dismiss the reaction and glared down Hammersly, furious. "Get your hand off me."

He regarded her with an expression caught between disbelief and irritation. His eyes narrowed, and his gloved fingers stroked her leg. "Don't you think you should reconsider my offer, Imogen?"

Guaire walked around the buggy and stood behind him, brows drawn together as if contemplating what manner of injury he intended to inflict.

And if anything inexplicable happened, Imogen realized, Hammersly would blame her. She flipped the reins over in her hand. The ends snapped toward Hammersly's face and struck his cheek with a sharp snap.

The hand around her ankle abruptly withdrew.

Imogen shook the reins, and the horse started off at a brisk walk. She didn't look back but felt relieved when Guaire caught up and heaved himself into the moving vehicle. "What were you thinking?" she asked.

He ignored her question. "Ginny, you lied to me."

"What?" She glanced around surreptitiously, but they'd gotten far enough down Broadway that the traffic had thinned. No one would notice her talking to the air. She made the turn onto Lake Road. "I never lied to you."

"You told me he wants your land," he said, folding his arms over his chest. "I'd say that's not what he's really after."

She kept her eyes on the road. "If he had to pick, he'd take the land."

"Oh, and is that why he had his hand on your leg?"

"He was trying to frighten me, Guaire. I don't frighten that easily." She snapped the reins again and the horse settled to a trot.

"And it felt like he was trying to charm you," Guaire said, "although it clearly didn't work."

"Obviously not." Imogen cast a perplexed look in his dircection. She did not count *charm* among Hammersly's personal traits. Then she realized she'd misunderstood. "Oh, you mean a charm, like magic?"

"Just so. He wants to break you," Guaire said. "You haven't buckled under, so he means to force you to his hand. I suspect that the land is secondary, darling."

She didn't answer.

"I know the sort," he said. "Men like that don't take losing well. I might..."

"Please don't do anything to him. They'll blame it on me. They'll say I've put a curse on him or something else foolish. I don't need people talking behind my back more than they already do."

"They'll think *you're* the witch? With that mother-in-law of yours?"

"No one would ever call Mother Hawkes a witch," she said sharply. "She reads tea-leaves, that's all. She is highly respected hereabouts."

"And you aren't?" he asked.

She spared him a glance out of one corner of her eye, wondering if he joked at her expense, but decided he simply couldn't see it. "Because I'm cold. And unnatural. Everyone says that behind my back."

Guaire roared with laughter. After a moment, he wiped his eyes and said, "Now that just shows they don't know you well."

She felt her cheeks warming again, that odd feeling that must be a blush. Her relationship with Guaire hadn't been like hers with other men—but then again, he wasn't a man. "Things happen when I'm upset. Things fall apart."

"Like the seat of Hammersly's trousers?" he asked. "Will he blame you when they split?"

She cast a horrified glance at him. "You didn't."

Guaire shrugged. "I might have, darling. It's second nature for us, you know, to do such things."

Imogen pressed her lips together, wishing furtively she could be there to see Hammersly's embarrassment.

"Ah, you almost smiled," Guaire said. "I'll get you to do so, yet."

She shook her head. "I didn't know," she admitted. "About Mother Hawkes, I mean."

"She has the sight," he said. "That's why she saw me. And make no mistake, she knows what you are, too."

That gave Imogen pause. If she did, Mother Hawkes had never let on. In the years of her marriage to Henry, Imogen had rarely seen his mother, as Henry kept his distance. It was only after Henry's death that Imogen had begun to cultivate her acquaintance with the woman who had, in her childhood, seemed a distant benefactress. Even so, in the course of their regular luncheons they had stuck primarily to the business of running the farm. They'd never strayed into personal matters.

It made no difference anyway, Imogen decided. Save for the apparent exception of Mothers Hawkes, few believed in the Fair Folk in this country. No one would believe that proper Imogen Hawkes had been fathered by a puca... or was sitting next to one at the moment. It wasn't reasonable, therefore it couldn't be.

Imogen looked over Paddy's list of times for Blue Streak that afternoon. They'd improved dramatically. The two-year-old had a good shot at winning now.

While Tommy walked Faithful back to the stables, Imogen watched Paddy check Blue Streak's hooves.

"Looks sound," he pronounced. He patted her kindly on the shoulder and took the horse's reins to walk him back. "I'm impressed with all the work you've done in the west meadow," he said. "I didn't think a girl could do that much in just a week."

That was, she supposed, his way of prying. Imogen fell in behind him and said, "It's almost done. I had a bit of help, as I suspect you know."

He glanced sharply at her. "Damned horse. What did you promise him, girl?"

Imogen sighed. "It's my concern, Paddy."

"Don't take chances." He crossed himself, and then added under his breath, "Like calls to like, I suppose."

They came around the edge of the stables, and in the distance Imogen could see Guaire working in the meadow. She wondered if it were only that—if she felt such a strong attraction to Guaire because he shared her inhuman blood. She stopped and watched him as Paddy walked on.

Don't take chances had always been the motto of her life. She'd been careful not to let anyone know about her mixed blood. She'd never let anyone guess at the wild strain that lay just under her veneer of civility. Guaire had simply bypassed her façade—perhaps because they had blood in common, or perhaps she had just grown so tired of guarding every word and thought that she'd used Guaire's bargains as an excuse to indulge her own wild nature.

A crack sounded to the west, sharp and clear in the unmoving air. Imogen glanced toward the wood, but a scream drew her eyes back to the stable yard. Blue Streak reared up and, with a sickening lurch, tumbled toward the ground. And Paddy, still clutching the reins, fell beneath him.

Blue Streak rolled over Paddy's prone body and back. Paddy cried out, and Imogen raced to where he lay. As Blue Streak thrashed, trying to get to his feet, Imogen grabbed Paddy's jacket and hauled him away from the horse. He yowled as she did so, and she saw his leg turn in a wrong manner.

Tommy darted out and grabbed Blue Streak's reins but the horse now lay on the ground, blowing heavily.

"We need a doctor," Imogen yelled at him. "Take Captain. Go, now!"

Tommy dropped the lax reins and dashed for the stables.

Guaire skidded to a stop before them, cast a worried glance at Imogen and then dropped to his knees at the horse's side. "The shot came from the woods."

She glanced over at him, and then back to a clenched-jawed Paddy. "Can you hold on for a few minutes?"

"See to the horse, girl" he ground out.

Imogen stripped off her jacket and laid it under Paddy's head, and then went to where Guaire knelt. A bullet hole in the horse's side leaked dark blood. Blue Streak continued to blow, his breath coming hard with the strain.

"He's got it bad," Guaire said softly, "in the gut."

Imogen glanced over her shoulder at the distant woods, a prickling feeling reminding her that her back was exposed now. "I'll go get a rifle," was all she said.

Guaire leaned down and whispered into Blue Streak's ear. After a moment the strained breathing eased and the horse's eyes drifted halfway closed. Guaire sat back on his haunches. "Do it before the poor fellow wakes. I can't keep him asleep for long."

Imogen ran to the house and unlocked the gun cabinet. Her skin burned when she touched the rifle's barrel, even though her hands were gloved. She grabbed a handful of bullets and ran back out to the stable yard. Guaire was speaking softly to Blue Streak, some fey magic of his keeping the other horse quiescent. When she stood over them, loading the rifle, Guaire rose and cast a worried glance at her. He opened his mouth, but then apparently thought better of whatever he meant to say.

Imogen sighted down the barrel and fired. The shot echoed through the stable yard, sending horses in the meadow shying away from the fence.

Paddy lay with one arm over his eyes, sobbing. It was then that Imogen saw all the others standing about: the two remaining stable hands near the doors; the maids and the cook huddled together in front of the house, one of the girls weeping into her apron; Tommy riding out to the road on Captain, bareback.

And Imogen wondered if they all knew that their hope of survival lay dead there. Surely they knew. The rifle fell from her burning fingers.

She went to kneel by Paddy's side. "Your leg's broke, Paddy."

He sniffed and wiped his sleeve across his face. "Don't you think I know that, girl?" He took a breath and then groaned in pain. "Think I might have cracked a rib or two as well."

Guaire emerged from the stable with an armload of blankets. Billy and Jack both started in surprise, but jumped when he ordered them to help him. After a few minutes, the three had laid out the blankets and, under Guaire's direction, they transferred Paddy onto them with a minimum of groaning. They carried Paddy into the house and laid him down on the first-floor guest room bed.

"Jack, go cover the body," Imogen said, her voice steady. She had to keep everyone calm. "I don't want it disturbed until the police get here." *Which, on a Sunday, could be hours and hours*, she reckoned. And it wasn't going to do much good, as she doubted they'd ever find anyone to charge. She turned back to the old stable hand as he headed toward the door. "And keep your head down, just in case."

Paddy's eyes narrowed, and she realized he was looking at Guaire. In fact, they'd *all* seen Guaire. She gestured to Billy. "I want you to saddle up and go to the police station. Tell them that someone tried to kill my trainer."

The young man's mouth fell open. "But they..."

"They're not going to come for a horse," she snapped, "so tell them that. Now go."

The young man bobbed his head and left Imogen alone with Paddy and Guaire. Imogen took the chance to shut the door. "Paddy, can you lie still until the doctor gets here?"

Paddy squinted up at Guaire suspiciously. "Who is this?"

Imogen rubbed her temples. "You know very well who he is, Paddy. His name is Guaire, and he's been helping me with the work down in the meadow."

"And what else has he been helping himself to?" Paddy asked, one hand pressed to his side. "You cannot trust their kind, girl."

Guaire regarded Paddy with a troubled expression. Imogen shook her head. "Paddy, you forget that his kind is partly *my kind* as well. I think we can trust him. And..."

Guaire's eyebrows rose.

Imogen drew a breath and finished, "...and Mother Hawkes likes him."

Paddy groaned. "Not much of a recommendation if you ask me."

Imogen tried to recall exactly what Mother Hawkes had said at lunch. "In fact, she introduced him as a relative of yours, Paddy."

"Nephew," Guaire said. "She told the kitchen maid I was his nephew."

"Saints preserve me." Paddy laid a hand over his eyes.

Imogen shook her head. "It'll be all over town by now, then, so that's what we'll have to stick with. Sorry, Paddy, you have a nephew now."

Guaire glanced at his new uncle and then turned his eyes back on Imogen. "The shot came from the woods on the other side of the fence, Ginny."

"That's what I thought." She bent over the bed to unlace Paddy's boot, her shaking fingers making it difficult.

"'twould be a difficult shot, the stable yard from there," Guaire said. "Makes me think the bullet was charmed, but I swear it was none of my doing."

She glanced up, startled. "Of course not."

He laid a hand atop hers, and the boot's laces unraveled themselves. "Then who charmed the bullet that killed your horse?"

Imogen slowly drew off Paddy's boot while Guaire held his ankle steady and Paddy groaned. "We'll just have to find out."

———

The doctor arrived two hours later and, after setting Paddy's thigh bone and splinting it, agreed that he had some ribs cracked at the very least. Fortunately, the ribs hadn't punctured anything, but that meant Paddy couldn't use crutches to get around. He would be captive in his bed for the foreseeable future. Since he'd been active his entire life, Imogen suspected he would make a difficult patient.

The police were slower, arriving near nightfall to survey the scene. When Guaire told them the shot came from the woods on Hammersly's land, the policeman responded that Hammersly had reported poachers in that area just the week before. Imogen kept her mouth closed, frustrated. They were simply looking for a way to get out of dealing with it. Poachers had no reason to shoot at a horse they wouldn't be able to eat.

The officers inspected Blue Streak's body, clucked their tongues over the shameful waste, and shook their heads. They promised to hunt through the trees in the morning. Imogen doubted that would happen. The evening stretched into night as the officers questioned the stable hands and the maids, and Imogen stood watching it all, feeling like her self-control was all that held the farm together. It was nearly midnight when the police left and everyone headed to their beds.

Once in her own bedroom, Imogen tugged off her gloves. Her left palm and trigger finger were red and swollen, marks left by contact with the gun's cold steel. It ached, but wasn't blistered. She stripped off her jacket and shirt, unlaced her boots and took off her stockings.

She couldn't recall when she'd had a day so terrible, not since Henry had died. For a time she simply sat in the chair in front of the dark window, too numb to move. She considered the rarely touched bottle of Port on the bureau, but decided that wouldn't help. It wouldn't solve her problems. With Blue Streak gone, her chance of winning enough money to buy out the mortgage had fled. Hammersly had won, and she would have to pay.

For the first time in her life, she thought about simply running away. Her dutiful feelings about the mortgage lacked the urgency of a bargain because she'd never signed those papers herself. It was Henry's bargain, not hers— but as his widow, the *law* considered her liable for his words. But she didn't intend to give up the farm, not now that she'd worked so hard to rebuild the stables, not after all the work Paddy had done, and Jack and Billy and Tommy. They had all worked hard to get Hawk's Folly back into the racing game. She couldn't give up, or give in.

After a while she decided she'd been staring at the dark windows long enough. She rose, turned down the lamp and curled up on her bed. Her mind still whirled too fast for sleep.

She didn't know how much later it was that she heard her door open. She felt the bed tilt as Guaire came to lie behind her. *His promised third night,* she thought dully.

He didn't move to kiss her, though, just wrapped an arm about her and laid there with her in the silence. He smelled of oats and hay and horse, comforting smells.

"I don't mean to cheat you," she told him, "but this is not the best night."

His hand brushed the back of her neck. She felt him sliding the pins from her hair, his gift easing them from her coarse locks. "You need only lie here with me," he said. "I bargained for a night with you, Ginny. No more is required."

She turned over to look at him but could hardly see his features in the dimness. He reached past her, and she heard the clatter of her hairpins hitting the surface of the nightstand. Then he pulled her close so that her face pressed against his shirt. "Go to sleep," he said softly. "Imogen Amelia Villiers Hawkes, go to sleep."

And she slept.

"Wake up," a voice said in Imogen's ear.

Imogen blinked, her eyes dazzled by the brilliant light of dawn streaming in the eastern windows. She lay facing them with her head pillowed on Guaire's arm. And then she recalled what he'd done to her. No one since her mother had done that. "You used my true name on me," she said, turning toward him. "I can't believe you did that."

"I wasn't sure it would work." His voice held no apology. "But I couldn't think of any way I could get you to sleep. Well, not quickly, at least."

She scowled at him. "It's unfair."

He raised one brow. "I do what I must, Ginny."

She closed her eyes, reckoning his motivation, but couldn't find any reason for him to use that power over her—not beyond helping her. She *wouldn't* have been able to sleep. And things did seem clearer now. Everything seemed much clearer. "How did you know my name?"

He chuckled. "I knew your mother's family name. 'tis certainly not Smith, as it says in your book. But your middle name, Amelia, was in there, and your married name I knew already."

A simple bit of detective work and he'd had her under his control. She'd seen him reading her Bible that second time he'd come to her, so he must have known her name since that night, but refrained from using it until now. "You're very clever."

"That I am. But since 'tis dawn, I must go." He didn't move.

He'd more or less finished his work on the fence by the stream, and she'd given him three nights, which meant all bargains between them were paid. But he didn't seem inclined to run away at the moment.

Imogen opened her eyes and considered him. His dark hair was mussed, and his clothes wrinkled. He needed a shave, although she suspected a beard might not look bad on him, even if not in fashion. "I need you to stay."

"Did you not once tell me the maids would notice if you stayed abed too long?"

"That's not what I meant, Guaire." She sat up. "You told the mares not to cross over the broken spot in the fence, didn't you?"

"Yes."

"Do you know much about racing?"

The corners of his eyes crinkled with his smile. "I spent the last ten years in racing stables, darling."

"Ten? You were only in Boston for three years."

He lifted a hank of her hair and twirled it about one finger. "Finn sold me to a racing stable in Dublin. The owner raced me there three years, and then sold me to a cousin in Cork. Four years after that, that fellow sold me to a cousin in Boston. Crossing the ocean was the worst part of all. I'll not be doing that again."

A horse down in the hold of a steamer would be close to the ever-moving water, and she suspected that the stalls and floors on shipboard were made of steel and iron, not wood—a cruel thing to do to one of the Fair Folk. "They knew, didn't they? What you were?"

"Oh, yes." His smile faded. "Kept the secret in the family, they did."

Until she'd purchased him. "Why auction you off, then?"

"The last fellow died sudden, and his son didn't want the stables. Probably didn't know. Sold all the horses off without even coming out to look at them. Myself included."

He could have ended up in far worse places than her land, and she could definitely use his help now. Perhaps Guaire was right, and his presence was due to the hand of Fate. "Do you know what a trainer does?"

He tugged on her hair to draw her closer. "Of course I do."

"Can I hire you then? As my trainer? Paddy keeps excellent records, and can tell you exactly what needs doing."

"And he'll tell me exactly where I can go," Guaire said in a wry tone. "I don't think he'd like the idea."

She bit her lip. Paddy wouldn't like it, but she was the farm's owner and manager. "He's not going to be able to get the horses ready for the meet. I need a trainer, at least until the Special is over."

"What are you thinking?" Guaire asked, eyes narrowed.

"Paddy's said it a dozen times. There's nothing wrong with Faithful. His bloodlines are excellent. He's sound. He just doesn't put his heart into the race. I need you to convince him to win."

Guaire's face took on a calculating expression. Lit by the early sunlight, his brown eyes seemed to gleam. "Hammersly would be put out if Faithful won, wouldn't he?"

"Even if Faithful places, that might give me enough to bring the mortgage up to date." It would be close, but she should be able to scrape together the difference somehow.

"If I were to agree, Ginny," he said carefully, "and I can only promise I'll try—I cannot guarantee his behavior—then I would want a promise from you in return."

He'd worded it so that it wasn't a bargain, so that her nature wouldn't force her to think of it that way. Nor his, for that matter. She kept that in mind and chose her words with care. "What sort of promise?"

His eyes went serious. "I'd want your word that no matter how the horse does, you'll not be marrying that man. Not just to keep the land, Ginny. You would have to say vows. That would bind you, and I wouldn't be able to bear it."

She laid one hand against his cheek. "I have no intention of doing so. I would die first, so you should ask for something else."

He smiled up at her. "How long then do you think it will take the maids to notice?"

"Half an hour?"

He rolled his eyes. "That's all?"

"Was I the one asking?"

"Better than nothing." He got up and went to lock her door.

Imogen introduced Guaire to the stable hands, explaining him as Paddy's nephew, visiting from the old country. They seemed to accept that, so she left them in his hands with a quick prayer that they would all get along.

Blue Streak's body still lay in the stable yard, covered with a tarp. She cast a resigned glance that way, but headed for town. The knackers would come this morning to remove the body; she didn't want to be there to watch.

It always surprised Imogen how quickly gossip traveled. At the racing association's office, they knew the whole story already. The members of the association she spoke with were understanding; none of them wanted to lose one of their horses that way. For the first time in years, Imogen felt she had the sympathy of the townsfolk behind her.

The Stakes required that she have three eligible horses listed, so she scratched Blue Streak and in his place wrote down the name of one of her two-year-old fillies, Comet. Comet would absolutely *not* be racing that day. The filly was mild-tempered, but backed up at the starting barrier five times out of ten—destined to be a broodmare, no more.

When Imogen arrived at the house on North Broadway, Mother Hawkes was packing a bag. "So our Mr. O'Donnell got his leg broken, I hear," her mother-in-law said without her normal greetings. "How is he faring?"

"Paddy's doing well enough," Imogen said, "but he won't be able to get out of bed for some time. That's going to be hard on him."

Mother Hawkes waved one hand. "He'll survive. I have that old wheeled chair from when I broke my leg a century ago. We can get it out to the farm. After a couple of weeks, I mean. Let him stew for now."

Imogen watched Mother Hawkes gathering some stationery out of her desk. "Are you going somewhere?"

The elderly woman glanced back at her. "I'm coming to stay out there with you, girl. If that bastard Hammersly is willing to shoot one of your horses to get the land, he won't stop at shooting another. I need to see if I can do anything about warding the stable yard and the house."

Imogen regarded her mother-in-law blankly, not certain what surprised her more. She'd never heard Mother Hawkes utter a vulgar word before, and she'd certainly never thought of her as the sort who would set 'wards'—which must be what Guaire had inquired about at Sunday lunch. "Thank you," she said politely, probably the safest reply.

"It's not just for you, girl. My son was a fool to take out a mortgage just to put in a fancy practice track. He got you into this mess. If he'd just sold the town house instead, we'd not be in this pickle."

Mother Hawkes had lived in this house since Imogen was nine or ten. She'd always thought of this as her mother-in-law's home. "But you live here," she said. "Henry built it for you."

Mother Hawkes chuckled. "It's a building, girl. I'm fond of it, but it's not the same as the farm. Henry just didn't want me living out there with him. We didn't rub along too well."

Imogen would never have dared to say that aloud. "Yes, I recall."

The old woman scowled and surveyed the room one more time. "I think that's everything. So tell me, what will you do now?"

While Mother Hawkes gathered her bags and had one of the maids cart them down to the buggy, Imogen explained her plan to use Guaire as their trainer until the Special. They drove out toward the farm, Mother Hawkes listening patiently. "The boy's here," she said once Imogen finished, "so we might as well put his talents to use."

"I'm not certain what I should tell the hands. About the new stallion, I mean. He'll be missing."

Mother Hawkes shook her head. "Most of them won't even look in that stall, not if he doesn't want them to."

"Paddy's noticed it," Imogen said.

"But he already knew," Mother Hawkes pointed out. "Harder to fool someone who knows better, girl. Tell him to take Jack into his confidence— Jack's trustworthy, and he won't bat an eyelash. Between the two of them, they can keep the rest of the hands from asking too many questions."

Imogen felt relieved to have some solution. "I worried you might disapprove."

"Because he's one of the Fair Folk?" Mother Hawkes shook her head. "Tush, girl, all the more reason to keep him around and keep him happy. It's when they're *unhappy* that things go awry."

Imogen bit her lips. "When my emotions get out of hand, things fall apart."

Her mother-in-law chuckled. "You have a gift of unbinding, girl. I've noticed it once or twice. It can be quite amusing."

Her mother had never called it a gift, or amusing. "My mother was always afraid someone would find out what I was. Or that I would harm someone."

"Yes, your mother was rather horrified when you turned out to possess some of your father's gifts." Mother Hawkes looked Imogen in the eye. "You are what you are, girl. Smothering your gift is unnatural. You really should learn to use it. I'm certain your guest could teach you."

Imogen had no idea what a 'gift' of unbinding would be good for, but she suspected Guaire would. "If he stays, perhaps."

After changing out of her town clothes, Imogen located Guaire out at the track working with Faithful—in horse form. Hidden from prying eyes by the cypresses that surrounded the track, Faithful came tearing around the curve barely ahead of Guaire's nipping white teeth.

Imogen watched as horse-Guaire ran the length of the track. She'd never seen him run as a horse, and the name 'Whirlwind' suddenly took on new meaning. He pulled ahead of Faithful with ease—showing off, she decided, for her sake. He was incredibly fast, his stride graceful and neat. His tail streamed out behind him.

He crossed the track's finish line and slowed. Then he trotted back to where she sat on the fence, Faithful following more slowly. Horse-Guaire tossed his mane and Imogen slipped off the fence to scratch under his forelock. "How could you give that up," she asked, "just to be human?"

He snorted and went after one of her jacket's buttons.

Imogen shoved him away. "Stop that. I hate sewing on buttons."

He turned one brown eye on her, but didn't try it again.

"Mother Hawkes is here. She wants to talk with you."

The brown eye rolled—an odd expression for a horse, but completely Guaire.

Faithful had reached them by then. He kept his distance from the other stallion, but tried to edge in as close to Imogen as possible. He wore only a harness, so Imogen grasped the cheek strap and surveyed the two-year-old carefully, wondering if she'd find bite marks on his haunches.

Guaire trotted away from them and returned a couple of minutes later in human form, slightly out of breath. His dark hair was mussed and his quickly donned clothes disordered. He carried a lead rope in one bare hand.

"What does she want?" he asked as he fixed the lead rope to Faithful's harness.

Imogen stared at him. He'd only bothered to halfway button the shirt and his feet were bare on the soft dirt. In the hours he'd spent working down in the meadow, his skin had gotten some color in it. He looked happy, as if the morning's run was something he'd missed for too long.

He glanced up at her. "Ginny?"

"Do you miss being a horse?" she asked. "I mean, when you're not?"

He laughed. "I like to run, Ginny, but otherwise no. 'tis a boring life if you ask me, which is why I think our kind have such a reputation for mischief." He winked at her. "You would do it, too, if you'd spent a month lolling about in the same paddock."

Imogen pressed her lips together.

"Do you even know how to smile?" he asked with narrowed eyes. "I swear I've never seen you do so."

"No," she said. "I never learned."

"Not even once? Never tried it in front of your mirror to see if you looked silly?"

She did her best to ignore his raised brows. "Now at least I know why you won so many races. It's hard to believe you could do it with those shoes on."

He shuddered. "Had no choice, Ginny. I had to win."

"Was there a bargain?"

"Not actually," he said with a shrug, "but the implied one was enough."

"Implied bargain?"

"A stallion who doesn't win has no value, save as a gelding. A very strong motivation, if you ask me." He grinned at her.

"Ah, I understand." Imogen felt color rising in her cheeks, and decided she should change the subject. "Mother Hawkes wants to talk to you. About the bullet, I mean. She sent a note round to the knackers' to ask them to send it back if they... dug it out."

"Ah, we'd best go back and see what she wants to know, then." He began to lead Faithful back in the direction of the stables, but turned back, holding out a hand for her.

Imogen swallowed, wondering what everyone would think of her if they saw her hanging on his arm. And after a moment, he dropped his hand and walked on. She shook her head and bolted after him, grabbing up his hand when she reached his side. "I don't know what they'll say."

Guaire paused. "Do you care?"

"I live in this world, Guaire. I have to live by their standards."

"I'm only holding your hand, darling," he said. "It's not as if they saw me making love to you out in the west meadow. Although I'm willing, if you want to shock them, that is."

Imogen turned her eyes to the ground, not entirely certain he was teasing. She walked alongside him, trying to suppress her worries. When they entered the stable yard, Mother Hawkes stood in front of the building, her arms folded over her chest and a scowl on her face. She gazed in the direction of Hammersly's property, only sparing a glance for the two of them as they approached.

"I'll have one of the boys walk him," Imogen offered. She took Faithful's lead rope.

Guaire gave her a wry look and leaned closer to say, "Don't leave me alone with her too long; she might bewitch me. She likes me."

Imogen shook her head. "Behave. She's going to be staying up at the house in the room next to mine."

"A chaperone?" Guaire groaned and rolled his eyes. "I knew my luck wouldn't last."

Imogen led Faithful on to the stable door, feeling one corner of her mouth turn up.

———————

Mother Hawkes insisted that Guaire join them for dinner. Imogen suspected the woman had ulterior motives, but she couldn't be certain. So the three of them ate in the formal dining room with its spindly-legged chairs and lacy tablecloth. Guaire perched gingerly on his seat and regarded the china hutch and its collection of pink crystal plates and stemware with a dubious eye.

"There was someone watching from the woods today, I could feel it," Mother Hawkes said once Mary had laid out the last dish and whisked herself back to the kitchen. "I don't know how long he's been watching you, but you can be sure of one thing. He saw you holding your trainer's hand. Even if it wasn't Hammersly himself, he knows by now, and he's not the type that takes being beaten out lightly."

Imogen felt that warm feeling in her cheeks. Sometime in the last few days, she'd definitely learned to blush. Mother Hawkes didn't seem as appalled as she'd feared, though, which was a relief. "Are you certain?"

"Yes. And I should also point out that one of your bedroom windows is at an angle that someone in those woods can see into it." Mother Hawkes poked at her potato and then pronounced, "We need to burn the trees down. That will keep Hammersly from setting another of his so-called poachers there."

"We can't burn the woods," Imogen protested. Setting a fire on Hammersly's land had to be illegal.

She glanced at Guaire, who turned to her mother-in-law and said, "Madam, it would be terrible unfair to burn them. The creatures there need them to survive."

Mother Hawkes pointed her fork at him. "You could drive them out, couldn't you? Warn them away? I only intend to burn that section."

"Fire's not so easy to control," Guaire said.

"It's one of the things I am good at," Mother Hawkes returned with absolute seriousness.

"Are you hell-spawned, then?" Guaire asked with a grin.

Imogen silently wondered why, when uttered with an Irish accent, that didn't sound nearly as offensive as it would have if she'd asked it.

"Don't take me lightly, boy," Mother Hawkes said. "While I've only a touch of the old blood, I more than make up for it in training."

Imogen stared.

"Oh, stop it, girl." Her mother-in-law shook her head. "Your mother never wanted you to hear of such things. Now I generally respected her wishes but she's gone and difficult times call for desperate measures." She turned back to Guaire. "I can keep the flames to that stand of trees, I assure you, if you do your part."

Guaire looked over at Imogen, apparently waiting for her verdict. She gathered her wits and weighed the consequences. "I don't want to start a war."

"You already are at war," Mother Hawkes said, punctuating her words with stabs of her fork, in Imogen's direction this time. "He had your prize two-year-old shot. He put your prize trainer into a sick bed. I know your mother raised you to be civilized, girl, but now is the time to let your other side loose."

Imogen met Guaire's eyes. He didn't disagree. "Then we'll do what we must."

Imogen sat on the ground in the darkened stable doorway with a blanket wrapped about her, watching trees burn in the pre-dawn darkness. It was less than an acre, and she was determined not to feel too guilty about it.

Since the land rose between Hammersly's stables and the trees, the fire wouldn't be visible from his house. His stable hands likely wouldn't even realize there'd been a fire until morning. That should keep them safely out of the flames' way.

And Guaire had done what he could to chase the wildlife from the area. He'd returned a couple of hours earlier, his coat covered in burrs and a scrape across his nose. That translated into several raw scratches in his human form, but they'd already stopped bleeding. He sat next to her now, looking exhausted. "Do you think she can stop it?" he asked.

"I hope so." Imogen peered upward but the sky was clear, removing any likelihood of rain. Fortunately, the winds were blowing away from her farm. "I do hope so."

Mother Hawkes was actually on the roof, having hoisted herself up through a little-used attic access. Imogen had never been up there; she preferred to keep her feet well on the ground.

"Would you want to learn what she does?" Guaire asked.

"Would you?" Imogen asked in turn.

"No," he said. "I'm not partial to fire."

"Me either." She glanced at him. "Could you teach me to unbind things, like you did with Paddy's laces?"

"'twould not be so hard," he said. "It's natural for you."

Imogen turned her head to look at him, laying her cheek on her knees. "What would you ask in return?"

He took some time to answer. "A kiss," he finally said.

That surprised her, given his previous requests. "That's all?"

"'tis my price," he said firmly, "although like with the horse, I can't guarantee how successful you'll be."

"Of course not."

His lips touched hers, warm and tasting of oats. It was a gentle kiss. Too soon he drew back, and said, "I'll teach you, then."

In the woods, the fire suddenly began to die away as if everything that could burn had done so.

"Thank heavens," Imogen said. Her land on the near side of that makeshift fence was safer now. One of the horses snorted loudly, and Dalmation kicked the wall of his stall in half-hearted response. Imogen wondered if they were as disturbed by the fire as she was. "Do you feel a tie to the land?" she asked Guaire.

"You mean like you and your farm?" When she nodded, he said, "I don't think so. Not in the way you do. I'm tied to the trees and the creatures of the forest, enough so that I hate what she's doing right now. But I understand the reason for it, and that gives me cause to fight my nature. I'll not let him keep after you like this."

Imogen buried her face against his neck.

His arms came around her. "I feel a tie to you," he said quietly.

The fire burned out completely, not even a line of embers visible. Guaire smiled, white teeth all she could see in the darkness. "Go to your bed, darling. Dream of me."

And given that she would go alone, it was all she would do.

The tract of ruined land looked ugly, and the morning wind carried an acrid hint of burnt wood. Imogen tried not to think about it as she did her morning chores in the stable yard. She knew she looked tired, but not nearly so much so as Mother Hawkes. Her mother-in-law had come down from the rooftop looking a decade older and hadn't emerged from her bedroom yet.

Save for the scrapes running across his nose, Guaire seemed normal. He took Faithful out to the track and left the stable hands to their chores. Fortunately, the horses hadn't been too overset by the fire the previous evening. The yearlings walked to their paddocks without incident.

"Ma'am," Tommy said, pointing toward the drive. "We've got a visitor."

An automobile rattled down her driveway, kicking up dust.

Imogen groaned. The only person nearby with an automobile was Hammersly. She'd known she would have to face him at some point, but hadn't thought it would be this soon. She handed off the last yearling's lead to Tommy. "Take her on to the paddock. Check the two-year-olds for me and make certain none of the other hands leads one out."

With an angry glance in Hammersly's direction, Tommy took the rope from her and led the horse away. Hammersly's surly-looking driver got out and then opened the door for his employer to step down. Hammersly strode over to the stable doors where Imogen waited, arms folded across her chest.

"Mr. Hammersly," she said evenly. "I saw you had a fire last night."

He tapped his gloves against his thigh. "And I'd like to know who set it. It was just on the other side of your fence. Do you know?"

"Set it?" Imogen looked him squarely in the eye. "Are you certain it was set? The police told me you had a problem with poachers."

His face went still, as if he'd not prepared a statement to refute that argument. "Poachers wouldn't benefit from setting my woods alight."

"Poachers wouldn't benefit from shooting one of my racers or my trainer, either." She couldn't keep the irritation out of her voice any longer. "Is there anything else you need, Mr. Hammersly?"

Hammersly's jaw clenched, as if he were struggling with keeping his temper under control. "I would like to know if someone *here* was responsible for it."

Imogen couldn't imagine why he thought she would admit to it if someone was... and then realized that he must be expecting some charm to influence her. It must somehow be related to his ever-present gloves, she decided. They *had* affected her when he'd touched her leg a few days before, and now that she paid attention, she could sense that feeling of warmth and longing, but her irritation was far stronger. She gathered her years of self-control and regarded him with her coolest expression. "And I'd still like to know who shot my colt. You'll have to pardon me if I don't share your sorrow over the loss of some trees."

His nostrils flared. She decided he expected her to be so flustered that she would simply break down and confess. It must vex him terribly not to get what he wanted. He probably wasn't accustomed to it.

"Is there anything else, Mr. Hammersly?" she asked.

"Did you set the fire on my land?"

Imogen didn't even bother to answer that time.

Hammersly cast an accusing glance back at his driver.

"Nice gloves," Guaire said from behind her then. "Is there anything I can help with, Mrs. Hawkes?"

Imogen didn't look at him, although she wanted to throw her arms around his neck in relief. "Mr. O'Donnell, I believe Mr. Hammersly is leaving now."

"And who is this?" Hammersly surveyed Guaire pointedly and then turned back to Imogen. "Are you still hiring Irish? How quaint of you."

Imogen ground her teeth together. Hammersly had picked the wrong target if he meant to make *Guaire* angry with that sort of insult. Paddy was the closest thing she'd ever had to a father. "I hire the most qualified people, Mr. Hammersly. I assure you, Mr. O'Donnell understands horses far better than any trainer you've ever met."

Hammersly slapped his gloves against his thigh, glanced down at them, and scowled.

"I believe you're done here," Imogen said again. She turned to Guaire. "Mr. O'Donnell, will you see Mr. Hammersly to his vehicle?"

"To be sure, ma'am," he said with a grin.

Imogen walked into the stable, leaving Guaire to watch Hammersly leave. The yearling stalls were empty, so she leaned back against one of the stall doors and gazed down at the tamped dirt of the center aisle while she listened for the sounds of the automobile driving away. After a moment, Guaire peeked around the corner of the stable door. "He's gone."

Imogen let loose a pent breath. "Thank heavens."

Guaire grinned. "Did you see those fancy doeskin gloves of his? They're charmed, I could feel it. Stronger than before."

Imogen pushed away from the stall door and went to join him outside in the sunshine. "I wondered."

"Don't know what they were meant to do," Guaire said, still staring at the cloud of dust left by the automobile. "But they didn't work on you, judging by his sour face."

That Hammersly had attempted to use any sort of 'charm' on her made Imogen feel a bit ill. "Was it something dangerous?"

"Depends on how a charm's used," Guaire said. "Someone can put a charm on a bullet to make it fly straight and not mean any harm. It could be used to hunt... or to shoot a neighbor's horse. Up to the person who uses them, to do good or ill."

Imogen pressed her lips together. "Well, I think it's clear his intentions are of the 'ill' sort."

Guiare stole a look at her face. "Then 'tis good you're not so easily charmed, isn't it?"

———————

Mother Hawkes had spent the whole morning setting 'wards' about the stable yard, and then did the same in the house during the afternoon. Down in the office, Imogen reviewed her mother-in-law's sketchy map. "Will these wards keep out bullets?"

"No," Mother Hawkes said, settling back in one of the older leather chairs. She seemed tired, her normal energy dissipated. "They're just look-aways."

Imogen regarded her uncertainly.

"They're like what young Mr. O'Donnell does naturally, only constructed. He's not invisible, he just urges folk to look away from him. These are meant to confuse evil intentions. Bullets should go astray, hopefully to the ground or away from the stables, but it's also possible one could end up in a horse or a person. It's an art, girl, not a science."

Imogen took that to mean that she shouldn't blame any failure on her mother-in-law. "And they'll hold until the race, at least?"

The older woman nodded. "That's less than a week. Should be fine."

Imogen wondered how safe Guaire was, out in Paddy's apartment next to the stables. She told Mother Hawkes about the gloves Guaire had commented on, but her mother-in-law didn't have much to add to Guaire's assessment. "There are people who make a living at selling charmed items. Mostly harmless, but they can be used for evil purposes as well."

"Here in Saratoga Springs?" Imogen asked.

"Not that I know of," Mother Hawkes said with a frown. "But I can think of at least one person in Albany who's in that trade. I expect Hammersly goes down to Albany with fair regularity, so it's possible he purchased something there."

"Could he have made it himself?" Imogen asked.

"Oh, no," Mother Hawkes said with a dismissive wave of her hand. "The man has no native talent whatsoever. But money, he does have that, and money can buy many things. Now that I think about it, he has always been unusually successful with ladies. I wonder..."

Her voice trailed off, leaving Imogen to merely imagine what thoughts were running around in her unusual mind. "How many people know you can do things like... the wards, and such?"

"A few," Mother Hawkes said. "Your mother knew. And Mr. O'Donnell, of course."

"Paddy knew?" Imogen sighed, feeling foolishly left out.

Mother Hawkes cast an exasperated look at her, but didn't answer that. "Your mother didn't want you to learn this kind of thing, girl. She wanted you sheltered."

"Hasn't done me much good," she said.

"No, you've ended up with me warding your house and that horse in your bed."

Imogen went still.

"Oh, don't think I didn't guess," Mother Hawkes said. "You turn pink when he's within ten feet of you."

The ribbon slipped from Imogen's hair, and her braid began to unravel. "Are you angry with me?" she whispered.

Mother Hawkes shook her head. "Imogen, it's not my place to question your... romantic attachments. You're not a child, and I certainly have no moral high-ground on which to stand. My son's been dead for years now, and he was so idiotically hell-bent on making you into a copy of his first wife that you had no breathing room. I have to admit this fellow seems far better suited to you."

"But it's your farm," Imogen whispered.

Mother Hawkes sat up and looked at her, a surprised expression on her face. "Is that how you feel?"

"It shouldn't have passed to me, should it?" Imogen asked.

Mother Hawkes frowned at her. "Why do you think I urged Henry to marry you? I've always suspected you were a kindred spirit, girl, and Patrick thinks of you as a daughter. I *wanted* you to have this farm. You're a far better inheritor for my family's land than that silly Bella would have been. Never doubt that."

Imogen bit her lips, caught between relief and the urge to cry.

Mother Hawkes sat back and stared at her for a moment. "You've been under someone else's thumb all your life. First your mother's, and then Henry's. It's time you figured out what *you* want. I'll not interfere with any choice you make."

"Thank you, Mother."

Mother Hawkes seemed to be suppressing a smile. "Although I suspect I know which way you're leaning. He's not the sort to waste time, is he?"

Imogen felt that now-familiar feeling of heat on her cheeks. "It was a bargain."

"Is it still? Or have you fallen under his spell?"

"I don't think he uses spells," Imogen said tentatively.

Mother Hawkes gave her a dry look. "I meant that figuratively, girl."

"Oh," Imogen whispered. "I suspect I have."

"I knew your mother pretty well, for all she didn't approve of me. She had no one else she could tell her story to. You do know about her and your father, don't you?"

Imogen shook her head. "She never told me much. About my father, I mean."

Her mother had explained what her father was and constantly reminded Imogen that her parentage made her reckless by nature, but she'd never truly explained her relationship with a puca in the first place, something that seemed so foreign when compared with her stern behavior.

"Her family was visiting cousins in Ireland," Mother Hawkes said, "and she found your father lurking about the stables. He took her away, but she returned two months later pregnant with you. She told me he wasn't faithful to her." Mother Hawkes shrugged. "His kind *is* born to wander, so I don't know why she expected otherwise."

"I see," Imogen said faintly.

Mother Hawkes leaned forward and patted her hand. "If he'd made her a promise, then it would have been a different thing. He would no more have been able to go back on his word than you are. But from what she told me, he never did."

Imogen knew what Mother Hawkes was digging at. "You want me to remember that Guaire will leave eventually."

"Unless you get a promise out of him, girl." Mother Hawkes tapped the desk for emphasis. "Unless you get a promise out of him."

Imogen sighed. She was never going to force Guaire into a promise that would hold him against his will. It would be cruel, and she liked him too well to do such a thing.

Imogen sat on the bench in Paddy's office that evening after dinner and stared at a length of rope. Like everything else she'd ever tried to affect *intentionally*, it resisted her urging to unravel. She scowled at it and wished harder.

"Well, that isn't working," Guaire said. He set one hand on hers and said, "Try to picture what it would look like coming undone in your mind."

She closed her eyes and concentrated. The rope had many strands, and she wasn't sure how they would come unbraided. When she said so to Guaire, he took three leather strips, knotted and braided them together and handed them to her. "Try this instead, then. Rope is complicated."

Imogen pictured the leather coming apart, much as her braid had that afternoon. When she opened her eyes, the leather hadn't moved. She sighed. "It didn't work."

Guaire laughed. "Did you think it would be easy?"

"Well, I hoped so," she admitted.

"Ah, the good things in life never are, darling." He sat down on the edge of Paddy's desk, his brows drawn together. Then he rose and shut the office door.

For a second, she thought she should protest; no telling what the hands might think if they knew the two of them were alone in Paddy's office with the door closed. Then she realized how ridiculous such a protest would be. When he settled next to her on the bench, she did her best to meet his gaze squarely.

"I think I know why it's not working for you," he said. "You have to want it to work, Ginny. You have to have a reason, like Faithful."

"I don't understand," she admitted.

"That horse needs a reason to win. You need a reason for this to work."

She gazed down at the twined leather gripped in her fingers. "I can't think of one."

He slid the back of his hand down her braid. Her hair unraveled under his touch, the ribbon that tied it off fluttering down to the floor. "I want this to come undone," he said, "because I like seeing your hair loose."

She managed not to roll her eyes.

When he touched the button at the neck of her blouse, it slid free on its own. He smiled as his fingers moved to the next button. "I like to touch your fine skin."

She tried to remain cool, but felt her cheeks heating anyway. "And the seat of Hammersly's trousers?"

His hand dropped and he grinned slyly. "Believe me, there are many things I'd have liked to do to him. Not for the same reasons, of course, but I do think he gave me cause." He touched the leather plait. "So why do you want this undone?"

Imogen turned her eyes back on the braided leather. She wanted it to work, but couldn't come up with a reason why other than that she wanted it.

When she said so to Guaire, he shook his head. "You'll have to do better than that."

She sighed and pushed her hair back with one hand. "It's just scrap leather, Guaire."

"Well, you could try something else." He took the leather from her and set his hand in hers, the buttons on his cuff turned upwards.

Imogen laid her fingers atop the cuff, wishing the buttons to come undone as hers had.

"Why?" Guaire asked. "Why would you want them undone?"

Imogen stroked the button under her finger. She had reasons, but...

But trying to use her gift was playing with fire. Her mother had always told her so.

She licked her lips, suddenly anxious. "I don't know if I should be learning to do this."

After a moment of silence, he lifted his hand to her collar and buttoned the two buttons he'd undone. "Perhaps you'd like to try again tomorrow."

Imogen retrieved her hair ribbon from the floor and braided back her hair. She didn't know why she thought she could do it. She'd been trained her entire life *not* to. "Maybe."

Guaire held the office door open for her. "Sleep well, then, darling."

Imogen didn't think she would sleep at all.

The next morning, as the sunshine slanted into the office, highlighting motes of dust in the warm air, Mother Hawkes inspected the two spent bullets the knackers had sent them. One she set back on the desk, but the other held her interest. It was flattened, as if it had lodged in bone. "This one is definitely charmed. To make it fly straight despite the wind."

Imogen rubbed her aching temples and regarded the other mangled piece of metal on her desk. The bullet she'd fired to put Blue Streak down, she assumed. "So it had to have been intentional, then."

"Did you doubt it, before?" Mother Hawkes picked a sheet of stationary from the desk and wrapped the spent bullet in it. "I'm going to take this to a friend at the racing association, if you don't mind."

Imogen shook her head. "I don't mind, but why?"

Mother Hawkes frowned and started opening desk drawers, evidently looking for an envelope. "The racing association has people whose job it is to make sure arcane methods of cheating aren't employed."

Imogen felt that odd sense that the world had turned unreal around her again, the one she'd started feeling every time her mother-in-law came out with some new and bizarre pronouncement. "They're in the top left drawer. I had no idea."

Mother Hawkes opened the drawer and drew out an envelope. "It isn't publicized. They will find this interesting, although not conclusive. We can't clearly tie this to Hammersly. Sadly, if he ever did touch it, it's been too long for any trace to remain."

"So why send it at all?"

"So they're advised that *something* is going on, girl. At least they'll know to keep an eye on him."

Which would be, Imogen decided, better than nothing.

That afternoon, Imogen sat on the practice track's fence in the warm sunshine, watching the horse fly by with Tommy clinging to the saddle. Faithful's times had improved dramatically. Jack rode a less-improved Hawk's Cry, whose times were decent, but not worthy of a winner's circle yet.

Standing next to her, Guaire held Paddy's silver pocket watch in his gloved hand. He patted her twill-covered knee and grinned. "That was two seconds less. He just beat Blue Streak's best time."

Imogen wrote that in the log. "What *did* you do to him?"

Guaire shrugged. "I told him if he couldn't beat me he wouldn't get a chance to cover one of the mares in spring."

She looked at him askance. "Did he understand that?"

"All colts understand that. So, if he couldn't beat me..."

"You'd get the mare. I see." She rolled her eyes.

"Even when I wear horse form," he said without looking up at her, "I'm never a horse. What's important is that he *believes* I'm his competition."

She gazed down at his dark hair. "When you wear human form, are you human?"

"More human than most." He smiled up at her. "Close enough, Ginny."

He patted her knee and walked out to talk to Tommy, leaving her on the fence.

Imogen watched him for a time, and then slipped off the fence and back up toward the house. She stood in front of it and eyed the wooden gingerbread trim that hung from the eaves on the porch and tried to picture how the house would look without it, something she'd done a thousand times over the last eight years. After a moment she sighed and headed inside.

She wandered down to her office. She could almost hear her mother's voice reminding her to keep her emotions in control, always in control. She hadn't done well lately, and she had no one to blame but herself. Her bargain with Guaire had been the beginning of it, just as her mother's relationship with Finn had been the cause of her downfall.

She wasn't certain what Guaire meant—what he was close enough to human *for*. Her mother had once told her that children between humans and the Fair Folk were rare, but Imogen was living proof that such children did exist, as was Guaire. As a natural consequence of her actions, she could be carrying Guaire's child. She'd reckoned that when he'd first asked to bed her, but had put it from her mind until that comment of his. She wouldn't know for a while.

Her own mother had fled to another country to hide her circumstances, but she'd been from a wealthy family who'd paid her passage and supported her new life in America. Imogen wasn't prepared to go that far, nor could she. The earl hadn't included his daughter's illegitimate child in his largesse.

Imogen couldn't help thinking her mother would have been disappointed to learn that her daughter had gotten herself into the same situation.

After dinner, she pleaded tiredness as a reason to get out of her proposed 'lesson' with Guaire. He nodded and let her go, but he didn't smile.

The next morning, the mirror in her dressing room reflected a face shadowed by another sleepless night. Her eyes seemed like dark pits looking out at her, signs of her foolishness.

Rested or not, she had work to do; tomorrow was race day. She dressed, went down and checked on Paddy, and then headed out to the stables to review Guaire's plan for the day.

He was speaking with Billy when she found him. The young hand was escorting Dalmatian out to the east pasture. Guaire's eyes met hers, and a smile flitted across his face, but faded almost as quickly. He gave Billy a few further instructions and then came over to her. "I need to show you something."

He led her to Dalmatian's stall, picked up the feed bucket that sat outside the stall door and held it up for her perusal. It was full of oats, not an unusual thing.

"What am I looking at?" she asked.

"I should have said to smell it."

Imogen cast a doubtful look in his direction, but sniffed the contents of the bucket anyway. "It smells wrong."

"And it's getting worse every moment," Guaire said. "We're lucky Billy caught a whiff before any of the horses ate it."

"Where did it come from?"

"Bin in the tack room. Filled it myself a couple of days ago. It was fine, then." He set the bucket down. "I don't know what this is. Smells like oat smut, but not."

And it occurred to her that perhaps it might be like the bullet, something charmed. "Do you think someone did this? Intentionally?"

"It would have had to be someone here," he said quietly.

Imogen found Mother Hawkes playing cards with Paddy in the downstairs bedroom. He'd gotten someone to bring up the blue blanket from his apartment next to the stables, and swapped it out for the frilly pink-and-white one they'd laid him on a few days before. He caught sight of Imogen and waved for her to enter.

"Um, Mother Hawkes," she said, "can you come out and look at something for me?"

Paddy laid down his cards. "What's wrong, girl?"

"Guaire says there's something wrong with the feed. He thinks it's been tampered with. I thought perhaps you could tell me what was done."

"If the boy claims it's been tampered with," Paddy said, "then it has. He should know. He eats enough of it."

Imogen turned back to her mother-in-law. "Could you come look at it anyway? Perhaps you might be able to figure out who trifled with it. Whether it was any of the stable boys, or someone else."

Mother Hawkes gazed at her with narrowed eyes. "You want to see if anyone's alarmed by my inspection. See who acts guilty?"

"That did occur to me," Imogen admitted. "Guaire said it was done with a charm or something like that—not poison."

Paddy cast an exasperated look at her. "I was winning."

"All the more reason for me to go, Patrick." Mother Hawkes dropped her cards on the blue blanket and rose, her regal nose in the air. She whisked out of the room.

Sparing a shrug for Paddy, Imogen followed.

"I didn't know you were on a first name basis with Mr. O'Donnell," she said, and then realized the inanity of the claim, since Paddy had been trainer for Mother Hawkes when Imogen was a little girl.

Her mother-in-law just laughed. She strode down the walk to the stables, wiping her eyes as she went. "Girl, I've known Patrick *well* almost as long as you've been alive."

"What do you mean by well?" Imogen asked, pausing on the walkway.

"Scandalized you again, haven't I? Use your imagination. I'm sure you'll figure it out."

Imogen jogged after her. "Did you bring up his blankets from the stable apartment?"

Her mother-in-law nodded. "He was afraid he'd dirty the one that was there."

Imogen sighed. "I wish he would. I'm not fond of that room, but I don't feel comfortable throwing out perfectly good bedding."

It was Mother Hawkes' turn to stop. She turned to Imogen and said, "If you don't like it, get rid of it. It's your house."

"I don't want to be wasteful," Imogen said.

"Then ask if one of the servants wants it, or donate it to the Young Women's Industrial Club; I'm certain Lucy could find a use for it somewhere." She sighed and added, "I really do think you should put Bella's ghost to rest. I hate seeing you living her life."

Imogen hadn't thought of it that way before, as if Bella's spirit lingered about the house. And Mother Hawkes was right—in many ways she had been living Bella's life. Mother Hawkes went on, but Imogen stayed there for a moment, wondering how one exorcized a ghost. Then she realized that Mother Hawkes had gotten away from her and ran after her again.

In the stables, Guaire was scowling down at the suspect bin. Imogen sniffed the bucket's contents again and sneezed. Mother Hawkes glanced up at her, shook her head and returned to conferring with Guaire. After a moment, he fetched a pitchfork and used it to dig through the oats. When he lifted it out, a small bag was speared on one of the tines, its blue fabric mottled with black spots.

Mother Hawkes carefully removed it. "Well, what have we here? This looks like something that one would find among a charlatan's wares."

"Smells a mite like smut to me," Guaire repeated.

Imogen saw black spots throughout the oats now, more than there had been when she went inside.

"Definitely a nasty fungus, but not ergot, I think" Mother Hawkes said. "I must say, this is poorly done. It would have been obvious long before it actually made any of the horses ill. Very amateurish work on the charm, as well."

Imogen frowned down at the ruined contents of the bin. "Do we have any sacks in the back?"

Guaire nodded. "We'll be fine. Just have to make certain no one uses this, and clean everything out thoroughly."

Which will take up valuable time, Imogen thought.

"I'll take this." Mother Hawkes lifted the small bag by its strings like a dead rat held by its tail. "I'll change clothes and head up to town. I'll leave the cleaning to you two."

She walked out of the tack room, leaving them alone.

Imogen had watched, but none of the stable hands seemed anything other than concerned. She wanted to believe that the bag originated with Hammersly somehow, but it had to have been planted inside the bin, which meant someone in her own household had to have done it. She sighed, wishing she had the answer instead of so many questions.

"Are you all right?" Guaire asked, a narrow live between his brows.

"Too many things to worry over. I didn't sleep well."

"Why not?" He held out an empty feed bag. "Can you hold this for me?"

Imogen held the bag open while he began scooping foul-smelling oats out of the bin with a large grain scoop. "It just seems like one problem after another," she finally said.

"No, Ginny, there's only one problem. All these little things are a part of the bigger problem. It will all be over after the race, I promise."

"And then you'll be free to go," she said. "All your bargains fulfilled."

He paused, the scoop suspended above the bin, and gave her a look she didn't know how to interpret.

"My mother always said your kind are born to roam," she told him.

"Because of your father?" he asked, setting the grain scoop on the ground. "She had no promise of him, so she should not have been surprised when he strayed."

Imogen caught her lower lip between her teeth, wishing he hadn't said that.

"But her telling you that we're all the same," Guaire said softly, "is like claiming that Paddy is the same as Hammersly because they're both human. Just because your father wandered does not guarantee that you would. Nor does it mean that I would, either, for that matter." He started to shovel oats again.

"My mother always..."

"Your mother is dead, Ginny." He emptied the scoop into the bag. "She shouldn't be thinking for you."

She stared at him, surprised by the anger in his voice.

He looked annoyed with himself then, as if he regretted saying that. He scooped more oats into the bag, paused, and set the scoop down to regard her gravely. "I know I shouldn't say this, but do you know why I think your mother left him? Not because he'd taken another woman. I think she was afraid she wouldn't be able to control *you*." He ran a dusty hand through his hair, leaving a few oats strewn among the dark strands. "Your father put iron shoes on me to bind me in horse-form. Your mother put her own iron shoes on you. She wanted you to be exactly like her and never take a step outside her rules. But she's gone, Ginny, and you've chosen to keep wearing those shoes she put on you."

Tears stung in her eyes. "I have to live in this world, Guaire."

"As do I. There's no going back for me." He shook his head, and then laid his dusty hands on her shoulders. "But you don't have to do the proper thing every moment of every day. You should do what you want. People are more forgiving than you think, Ginny, and you're stronger."

She stepped back, letting the mouth of the sack fall closed. "My mother..."

When her voice trailed off, he pushed back an errant strand of cream-colored hair, his warm hand carrying the scent of musty oats. "Was she happy, Ginny?"

Imogen closed her eyes, trying to recall her mother's face, stern and calm, always calm. She didn't know how to answer him. Her mother had worried. Her mother had lectured, warning her daughter of the danger of letting her emotions rule her. Of letting down her guard and ending up in a situation like the one she'd faced.

She opened her eyes, but couldn't meet his. Instead, she stared at the bin, now almost empty. "Can you finish this?"

"Yes," he said.

She turned and walked out of the tack room.

Imogen meant to spend her morning paying feed bills, an ironic choice given the morning's troubles, but she found herself staring at the bookshelves instead.

Guaire was right. Her mother's expectations had guided her entire life, with Henry's rules added to them after her mother's death. She had always let them tell her what to do and how to act, assuming they knew what was best for her. So now she lived in a house where she only liked two of the rooms, wore clothes she hated, and never, ever said what she thought, all for fear that someone might learn what she really was. Or who she really was.

Mother Hawkes knew, though, and found her gift 'quite amusing.' Paddy thought of her as a daughter, she'd said. And Guaire? Imogen wasn't sure what he thought of her. He seemed to care for her, and despite what her mother had taught her about the Fair Folk, she didn't think he was merely trying to manipulate her.

A timid knock startled her out of her reflections. One of the kitchen maids stood at the door, wringing her apron in her hands. Fresh-faced Mary hadn't been at the farm more than a year, but Imogen's elderly cook had already suggested the girl might be trained up as an eventual replacement.

"Come on in, Mary," Imogen said. "Is something wrong?"

"They're saying that Mrs. Hawkes—the other one, I mean—found a charm bag in one of the feed bins."

"Yes," Imogen told her. "Well, it wasn't a charm bag. It made the oats in the bin go bad. Fortunately Billy caught the scent of it before it was given to any of the horses."

Mary twisted the apron so tight that Imogen doubted the wrinkles would ever come out. "Were it a cotton bag, Mrs. Hawkes? A blue one?"

"I think so, Mary."

The girl sobbed and held her sleeve to her face. Imogen went over and patted the girl's shoulder, feeling terribly awkward. She didn't have much experience comforting other women. "It's all right, Mary."

"No," the girl said with a sniff. She wiped her sleeve across her face. "It was me that put it there, missus, but I swear I didn't know it would do that."

"What *was* it supposed to do?" Imogen asked.

"I met a fellow up at Congress Park yesterday, missus. He told me it was love charm, missus, that's all."

"A love charm?"

The girl flushed prettily. "I thought it might make Billy notice me, missus."

Imogen patted the girl's shoulder again, relieved to learn they hadn't intentionally been betrayed by a member of the household. "I can think of better ways to accomplish that, Mary. Why did you put it in the oat bin? Is that where he told you to put it?"

The girl's dark brows drew together. "I was going to sneak it into the hands' bunkroom, missus, but I was there in the stable and sudden-like it hit me that if it was in the oat bin it would be around him most of the day, so I put it in there real deep. It sounds stupid now, but I remember thinking that real strong."

Imogen suspected that Mother Hawkes would find that story interesting. "Well, no harm was done, Mary. What about this fellow at the park? How did you meet him? What did he look like?"

"One of the other girls I know from the school told me that he'd made a love charm for her, so I asked her to introduce me to him. Name's Seb. Maybe twenty-five, missus, from down Albany way, he said. Dark hair, not too tall. He drives a fancy automobile for someone hereabouts, but I didn't think to ask for who."

Imogen had a very good idea about that. "I see."

The girl's eyes sank to the floor. "I didn't mean any harm, missus, honest."

"Do you think it's fair to try to trick Billy into liking you?"

Her brows drew together. "Well, no, missus."

"Then will you promise me you won't try anything like that again?"

Mary shook her head, hope surfacing in her eyes. "No, ma'am, never. I swear it."

"Then I don't think Billy needs to hear of this. I do appreciate your being honest with me, Mary. It helps a great deal."

"You're not going to let me go?"

Imogen shook her head. "Not as long as this doesn't happen again, Mary."

"Oh, thank you, missus!" The girl hid her face behind her hands and dropped a completely unnecessary curtsy. Then she fled.

Their little ploy had worked, flushing out an unwitting culprit. At least now they knew who must be behind the charmed items suddenly appearing in the area.

"What's wrong with that girl?" Mother Hawkes had come into the office, but cast a glance over her shoulder at the departing Mary.

"She's just young, Mother," Imogen said, and then relayed most of their conversation.

"Most interesting," Mother Hawkes said with narrowed eyes. "I suspected that Hammersly was getting his trinkets from someone in Albany, if you recall. I do enjoy being right."

Imogen had no doubt of that. "So what do we do?"

Mother Hawkes held up a small box, presumably containing the mystery bag from the oat bin. "I'll take this to town and turn it over. They'll find Mary's story interesting, I think."

More evidence for the racing association, Imogen reckoned. She glanced up at her mother-in-law. "Would you mind if I took it? I need to get out and be doing something."

Mother Hawkes regarded her with raised brows. "Stewing, are you? I have a package at the department store that needs picking up. Could you fetch that?"

"Of course," Imogen said, taking the small box from her mother-in-law's hand. "To whom should I give this?"

"The track steward, Thomas Brown," she said. "And make sure you tell him about young Mary's encounter."

Imogen surveyed her work clothes and decided that for a quick trip to the track, they would do. She tucked the box under her arm, grabbed up her handbag, and walked to the library door. She stopped on the threshold though, and turned back to Mother Hawkes. "Was my mother ever happy?"

Her mother-in-law frowned. "I don't know that your mother wanted to be *happy*," she said. "She wanted to be in control. She had that."

That sounded right to Imogen. "Guaire thinks she really left my father because she wanted to control me."

"She *was* overly protective," Mother Hawkes said.

Imogen sighed.

"Of course," Mother Hawkes added, "she couldn't control him, either— your father. I'd wager she thought she could, and was sorely disappointed."

Imogen couldn't imagine herself trying to control Guaire, but she could easily picture her mother wanting to control Finn. "That's why I don't want to extract a promise from Guaire. It would be the same mistake."

Mother Hawkes laughed. "I can't say that 'extract' would be the right word, in his case. You want him to stay, don't you?"

Imogen caught her lower lip between her teeth. She did want him to stay, but she wanted it to be his choice, not the matter of a bargain. "Yes."

"Well, people will gossip for a while if you marry one of your employees, but it wouldn't be unheard of," Mother Hawkes said. "Men certainly get away with it often enough these days."

Imogen blinked. *Marriage* hadn't actually occurred to her. She suspected it hadn't crossed Guaire's mind, either. She didn't even know if he believed in the institution. "I'll keep that in mind, Mother. People will..."

"Don't worry too much about what people think, girl. It's your life, not theirs."

"Yes, Mother." With that last word, she headed toward the front door, wondering what it would be like not to worry about what others thought. It was a talent she needed to cultivate.

Imogen found Thomas Brown in the avenue of white-painted stables next to the track. Mr. Brown looked rather mundane, Imogen thought, but then again she hadn't realized her mother-in-law had 'special' skills either.

They stood under the shade of the row of trees planted between the rows of stalls while one of his assistants waited out of earshot, ostensibly surveying the occupant of one of those stalls. A handful of grooms played cards over by the end of the stables. Most stalls were already full with horses recently arrived for the Saratoga meet. Imogen herself had one narrow stall rented so that her horse could stay overnight.

The track steward held up the small cotton bag by its strings much as Mother Hawkes had done. "Ah, yes," he said, "items of this particular style of poor craftsmanship have been popping up all over town recently."

When she relayed Mary's story, he nodded sagely and tucked the offensive bag back in its box. "I suspected she might be referring to Mr. Hammersly's driver," Imogen added.

"Like the courts, we have to assume innocence until guilt is proven, Mrs. Hawkes. We can't be sure that Mr. Hammersly is the one employing the items we've seen so far. He doesn't have a smidgen of talent himself, if you ask me. Nor can we know if he's actually aware that they *are* charmed, although in the case of the gloves that your mother-in-law mentioned to me, it seems likely."

Imogen chewed her lower lip and nodded. She understood his point, even if she didn't like it.

"And as our jurisdiction only includes track lands, we... hmmmm." Brown whistled sharply, and his assistant came trotting over. "Take this to my office, Emory."

The assistant grabbed the box and, after tipping his cap to Imogen, trotted off toward the office.

"As I was saying, Mrs. Hawkes," Brown said, "we'll have that stall cleaned out tomorrow morning. We'll keep an eye on that rat problem for you."

"Thank you, Mr. Brown," she said, realizing that only one thing could have caused his abrupt change of topic. She looked up and, sure enough, William Hammersly had come striding around the corner of the stable row. Imogen knew he had a couple of horses racing that weekend as well, but the timing of his arrival couldn't be a coincidence. She wondered if he was following her about town now.

Hammersly smiled genially at her when he reached them. "Mrs. Hawkes, how nice to see you. Are you still planning on running one of your horses tomorrow?"

His tone might be friendly, but she heard a mocking undertone. He didn't think she had a horse worth running any longer. "Of course I am, Mr. Hammersly."

"And with your brand new trainer," he said condescendingly. "How adventurous of you."

Imogen took a calming breath and reminded herself that she must stay under control. "We think we have a good shot."

"We'll see come Monday morning," he said—a not-so-subtle reminder about the mortgage hanging over her head.

Imogen clenched her jaw. She saw then that his favored doeskin gloves were stuffed into one of his jacket's pockets. "My trainer was admiring your gloves," she said, pointing discreetly. "Could you tell me where you got them? I'd like to purchase a pair for him, once my horse has won."

Hammersly's eyes narrowed. He cast a glance at Brown, who'd stepped back as if he didn't want to interfere in their discussion. "They were custom-made by a glover in Albany," he said quickly, and then surveyed her work clothes with a disdainful eye. "A bit too dear for your purse, I suspect."

"May I look at them anyway?" she asked. "To judge the workmanship."

That gave Hammersly pause. "Actually I need to get back to my office. I simply wanted to check on my horses. Perhaps..."

"Is there some problem with the stables?" Brown asked.

Hammersly scowled at the interruption. "Nothing that concerns you, Brown," he snapped. He turned back to Imogen with that meaningless smile of his. "I'll look forward to seeing you tomorrow, Mrs. Hawkes. Perhaps you'll join me for supper after the last race. You could look at them then... at length."

Imogen took a calming breath. All manner of improper responses ran through her mind, most dealing with what she'd really like to do with those blasted gloves. "We'll see," was all she trusted herself to say.

Hammersly bestowed one final gloating smile on her and then walked away without excusing himself, tucking the gloves more firmly into his jacket pocket as he went.

"I do believe you're correct about the source of that rat problem, Mrs. Hawkes," Brown said in a mild tone. "We'll definitely be keeping an eye on it."

"Thank you, Mr. Brown." She shook his hand and headed out for her buggy, glad not to find Hammersly lurking about. She made her way to the department store, picking up a paper-wrapped package for Mother Hawkes, and then headed home.

The drive home gave her time to think. Hammersly had apparently given up any appearance of courting her and moved on to simple threats and innuendo—a relief in a way. It was, as Mother Hawkes called it, *war*. And Imogen was ready to fight.

"So what is it?" Imogen asked when she handed the bundle over to her mother-in-law. "Mr. Hill assured me he included everything on your list. Twice."

Mother Hawkes dug a pair of scissors out of Imogen's desk drawer and snipped the twine holding the brown paper shut. She drew it back to reveal a neatly folded stack of clothing. Men's clothing, Imogen noted, a jacket and trousers, a couple of shirts, underwear and socks.

"You can't send your trainer to the track dressed in Henry's old castoffs," Mother Hawkes said, lifting the brown tweed jacket for Imogen's perusal. "Mr. O'Donnell will be representing Hawk's Folly Farm, and he needs to be properly dressed."

"Will they fit?"

"I've had a good deal of practice buying men's clothes, girl." She waved Imogen toward the library door. "Now go ask him to come in before dinner so he can try them on for me."

Imogen pressed her lips together, imagining Guaire's probable response to that statement. At least there didn't appear to be any celluloid collars or cuffs in the lot. But Mother Hawkes was right; Guaire should have something of his own. Even though he'd said he didn't think it necessary, he deserved better than another man's clothes. "I'll go relay your orders, Mother."

Imogen went, reflecting that it was high time to get rid of Henry's things. All of them.

She stopped on the porch in the afternoon sunshine and squinted up at the nearest section of the despised gingerbread trim—curlicue-laden corner brackets with a row of elaborate fretwork in between. It had to go. She wasn't certain how difficult it would be to remove all the excess ornamentation, but she suspected she would like the house—*her* house—much better once she did so.

She lifted her skirt and tucked in into the waistband and, wrapping one arm around the pillar for balance, stepped up onto to the porch rail. She reached up with her other hand and tugged at the corner bracket. The thing seemed firmly affixed.

She tried to pinpoint where the nails attached it to the post and the eaves, working out how it was all held together. And then she imagined the piece of trim working free, coming loose in her hand. She tugged again, harder this time, and had to throw both arms around the post when the bracket came loose... along with *all* the fretwork *and* the bracket from the opposite corner. The wooden bits landed on the porch with an impressive clatter.

After a stunned moment, Imogen relaxed her tight grip on the post and carefully hopped down from the rail to the porch. The entire section had fallen out. *Iron*, she recalled, looking up at the exposed nail heads. She wasn't able to pull out the nails with her gift because they were iron, but she'd managed to convince the wood to tear itself apart to slip off the nails.

Mrs. Dougherty opened the front door, her eyes wide with dismay. "What happened?"

Imogen glanced down at the broken trim, and then back up to the cook. "It was loose," she answered hesitantly. Then she squared her shoulders and said, "I pulled it down. I've decided I don't like the trim on the house, so I pulled this section down. I'll ask Jack to come by and clean this up when he has the chance."

Mrs. Dougherty inclined her head, and left Imogen there on the porch feeling rather proud of herself for a change. She pushed a couple of the pieces of broken wood out aside with her foot and headed out to find Guaire.

When Imogen reached the track, she saw the jockey she'd hired for the Special, Dave Williams, trot by on Faithful's back. Tommy rode Hawk's Cry, and a third horse cantered past, unsaddled. She watched him, wondering what the two riders must be thinking of the rider-less horse sharing the track with them.

Sitting on the track fence, Jack held Paddy's pocket watch and Guaire's slim notebook with its listing of times. He showed her the last run, five and a half furlongs in one minute and nine seconds. "Not Faithful's best, ma'am, but I think he'll put more into it tomorrow."

"I'll pray he does," she said.

The jockey trotted over when he spotted her. "He's flying, Mrs. Hawkes. I think there's a good chance."

"Exactly what I want to hear, Mr. Williams." She patted Faithful's neck, and made a furtive check for nip marks. "He looks hale."

"Are you taking him into town tonight?"

Tommy had come up, leading Hawk's Cry. "Mr. O'Donnell wants to skip morning exercises. Walk him up in the morning."

Imogen hadn't heard that plan, but reflected that she would feel better with Faithful in his own stall tonight, rather than at the track. She nodded. "So we'll see you tomorrow, Mr. Williams."

He dismounted, handed the reins over to Tommy, and doffed his cap to her. "Ma'am. Oh, if you're going to race the little fellow, I'd love a chance to ride him. He kept up and I'd swear he wasn't even trying."

Imogen pressed her lips together, tempted to smile. "I'll keep that in mind, Mr. Williams, but he's not listed in the Stud Book, so he won't be racing around here."

The jockey, who only came up to her nose—a couple of inches shorter than Tommy, even—pounded track dust out of his riding clothes. "A real shame, ma'am."

He headed toward the stables then, leaving Jack and Tommy with the two horses. Tommy patted Faithful's neck and doffed his cap before the two hands led the horses away to cool them off. Which left Imogen watching horse-Guaire as he trotted around the end of the track and back toward her.

She didn't see his clothing anywhere. He must have changed into horse form back in the stable. So she accompanied him back to the stables, one hand against his shoulder. He walked directly to his stall and lifted the wooden latch with his teeth.

"I wondered how you'd been doing that," she said. "I just figured you'd unbound it, like the rope."

He snorted and showed her his white teeth. His form glowed. A wave of heat struck her, almost like a wind coming out from his stall, and then Guaire stood there in his human form. His shirt and trousers were folded over the rails between his stall and the empty one, but he didn't seem too eager to don them. He grinned at her, nude and apparently unbothered by that fact. "I can't unbind things when I'm a horse," he answered, "but I've clever teeth."

Recalling the time he'd sheared a button off her shirt, she couldn't argue that. "Why is it warm when you change?" she asked instead.

He grabbed his second-hand trousers off the rail, shook them out, and pulled them on. "I've no idea."

Guaire looked whole now, Imogen noted, and far healthier than when he'd first come to the farm. He'd had time to heal. She was glad of that. Even if he left after the race, they'd given him that. "Is it cold when you go the other way?"

His eyebrows rose. "You'll just have to find out, won't you?"

She watched him button the shirt and followed as he walked barefoot to Paddy's tidy office. "Mother Hawkes wants you to come up to the house and try on some clothes she's bought for you. Before dinner."

Guaire groaned.

"As you'll be representing the farm," Imogen said sternly, "she means to see you properly dressed. We wouldn't send a jockey out without proper silks, you know."

"I'll come," he said in a resigned tone, and then added, "Ginny, what I said earlier, about your mother..."

"Was the truth," she finished for him. "I'm a bit of a coward, I think. It's always been easier to do what someone else wants of me than to decide what I want on my own."

He touched her cheek. "Then you're not angry with me?"

"No." She glanced down the main aisle of the stables and couldn't see anyone else. "I wanted to ask..." She took a deep breath, Guaire waiting while she got together her nerve. "I wanted to ask if you would come to my room tonight," she managed, and then flushed when she realized how desperate she'd sounded. She coughed into her hand to cover her embarrassment, and added, "Later, I mean, after the others have gone to sleep."

He tilted his head so he could meet her eyes. "Are you wanting to learn how to use your gift? Or just asking?"

"Just asking," she said. "I don't know what you would want..."

He put a finger on her lips to stop her. "Don't make this a bargain, Ginny. Just ask."

"I've already asked," she pointed out.

"And I'll not ask anything in return," he said. "Not a bargain."

"So, you're saying yes?"

He grinned. "If, and only if, I can get past your mother-in-law, darling."

Imogen felt the urge to throw her arms about his neck, but instead she just nodded politely. She took her leave, feeling an excitement she wouldn't have believed possible only two weeks before.

The new clothes fit far better than the ones he'd been wearing, and the colors suited him, the same warm browns and creams that Imogen favored herself. He didn't have the look of a fine gentleman about him, not the way Hammersly did, but Imogen didn't care. He was, in her opinion, splendid.

While Guaire went back to the stables to make certain Faithful was bedded down for the night, Imogen spent a long, long evening with Paddy and Mother Hawkes, playing an odd three-handed game of hearts—which Mother Hawkes won every time. Imogen had never been more relieved to retire to her bedroom.

After changing into her nightdress, she washed her face and waited as the sun set, curled up in the chair by the window with a book clenched in her fingers. She didn't think she managed to read a single page.

"Ginny." A gentle touch on her cheek woke her. Guaire stood over her. "Sorry I took so long, but Mrs. Hawkes is down in the stables, playing cards with Jack and Billy. They're going to stay up all night to watch over Faithful. I had to sneak around the track so they wouldn't see me."

She blinked at him blearily, and then woke enough to throw her arms about his neck as she'd wanted to earlier. With a grin, he lifted her in his arms and carried her to the bed. He laid her down against the pillows, regarding her with a look in his eyes she couldn't place. Then he sat down and started unbraiding her hair. "This is only because you want me, and I want you," he said. "Right? No bargain."

She shook her head. "Only because I want you."

His fingers went to the buttons of her nightdress. "I like hearing that, darling."

And impatient, she sat up and undid them herself. They slipped loose at her merest touch.

Imogen didn't know how much she slept that night, but when the dawn came, she felt more rested than she had in days.

Guaire slept on—at least she thought he slept. She watched him for a time, thinking that if he left her, it would hurt worse than anything she'd endured before. Her mother's death had left her alone in the world, confused and frightened. Henry's passing had burdened her with responsibilities, but she'd never grown terribly attached to him. Neither of those partings had been by choice, either. If Guaire left her, it would be because he chose to do so, and that would tear her heart out.

But he'd admitted he felt a tie to her. He'd hinted that he wasn't the sort to stray as her father had. She hoped those things meant he *wanted* to stay, even if he'd never said so.

He opened his eyes and smiled at her, lazily, as if the two of them had nothing else to do all day. He tangled his fingers into her hair, drew her down beside him and kissed her softly. Then he nuzzled her ear and whispered a name she'd never heard before—but she recognized it anyway.

Surprise made her go stiff. His true name—the name with which she could bind him eternally, the name her father had used to bind him for a decade in horse form—he'd simply *given* it to her. Imogen drew away and stared at him, her mouth open, uncertain what he meant by it.

Guaire smiled and touched a finger to her lips. "I trust you, Ginny."

It was a terrifying power he'd given her. She gathered her wits and said, "I won't betray you, Guaire."

"I know." He rose from the bed and gathered his clothes from the floor. "I'd best go down and check on that horse now. Your mother-in-law's probably put him off his feed."

By the time he'd dressed, she'd managed to untangle herself from the sheets. She kissed him, and he held her a moment longer. "Remember," he said, "you promised. Win or lose, you won't marry him."

She shook her head. "There's no chance of it. I'd let Hammersly have this place first."

Guaire slipped out the door, leaving her to bathe and dress. When Imogen came down in her dressing gown, the maids had already set out breakfast. Mother Hawkes regarded her wearily over a plate of eggs and roasted tomatoes.

"Did you stay up all night in the stables?" Imogen asked.

"I won't ask how you know that," Mother Hawkes said, "but nothing happened to the horse. That's what's important."

"Shouldn't you stay here and get some sleep today, then?"

"Absolutely not," her mother-in-law said. "I can sleep later, girl. This is more important." She sighed and pushed her eggs around on her plate with a fork. "I still don't trust that Hammersly won't try something."

"Guaire plans to walk Faithful into town. In lieu of the morning exercises."

"Excellent idea," Mother Hawkes said with a tired nod. "Keep that horse out of the public eye as much as possible."

"I don't know how to help," Imogen said. She'd never been to the races as the owner. "What do I do today?"

"Distract Hammersly when and if he comes to find you," Mother Hawkes said. "Wear that ivory and brown dress from last year, the one you look so well in, and that brown hat with the pheasant feathers. If Hammersly's looking at you, he's not near our horse."

Imogen shuddered at the thought of making polite conversation with Hammersly. Then again, if Mother Hawkes had been awake all night and still intended to go to the races today, if the stable hands had stayed up to guard the horse, if Guaire had trusted her enough to give her his true name, then she could damn well make a sacrifice. She might even smile at the man.

She would have to practice that a couple of times first.

The dress was her favorite, one of the few non-work garments she'd purchased since Henry's death. The princess lines of the ivory-colored dress showed that she'd not lost her youthful shapeliness in the last eight years, and the fine brown lace overlay on the bodice and split overskirt complimented her coloring perfectly. She looked at her reflection in the long mirror in the dressing room and, for the first time in years, felt pretty.

She surveyed the dressing room then, taking in the preponderance of pink gowns and suits and decided that as soon as she had time, they were all going to go. If the Young Women's Industrial Club could use bedding, then she suspected decent garments might be useful to them as well. She didn't care if it left her with only a couple of old riding habits and the clothes she wore to work around the farm. People in town wouldn't die if they saw her wearing the same thing day in and day out.

Pleased with her decision, she marched downstairs to talk to Paddy before she and Mother Hawkes left. He was frustrated at not being able to go to the race himself, but she promised to send back word as soon as they could. "And if you'll stay in bed," she said, sitting in the chair next to him, "I'll talk Mother Hawkes into having that wheeled chair of hers brought out here."

He was leaning back against the headboard, still wearing his nightshirt. "Good luck with that, girl," he said in a dry voice. "I've been trying for days."

Imogen pressed her lips together. "We'll see."

Mother Hawkes picked that moment to peek into the bedroom. "Are we going, girl?"

Imogen rose and, before she left, leaned down and kissed Paddy's cheek. "For luck. We would never have gotten this far without you, Paddy."

He waved her away, his cheeks a touch ruddier than usual. "Oh, go on before she starts throwing things."

Imogen hurried out of the room and ran to catch up with her mother-in-law.

Buggies crowded the entryway to the track, a few automobiles among them, making Imogen glad they'd decided it would be fastest to leave the buggy farther away under the watchful eye of a young boy eager to make a bit of money. They walked the rest of the way. The many-peaked roof of the grandstand waited on their left, and Mother Hawkes headed that direction while Imogen went in search of their horse.

The paddock area was crowded, men and horses milling about between the races. Imogen didn't see any women there and hadn't thought to ask Mother Hawkes if a female owner was allowed inside, so she stopped at the white fence and tried to spot her people among the bustling crowd. She finally saw Guaire—looking quite attractive in his new garb—talking urgently to Billy and Tommy. Tommy held Faithful's reins. Despite the fact that the horse had already been saddled, she didn't see Dave Williams anywhere. She waved and caught Guaire's eye, and he came over to the fence where she waited.

"He's not here," Guaire told her, a line appearing between his dark brows.

"Mr. Williams?" Their jockey had never missed a race yet, and Imogen couldn't believe that he would miss today's running. He'd been looking forward to it. She glanced at the stable hands, trying to decide what would be the best course of action. "Can Tommy ride him?"

Guaire surveyed the wiry former jockey. "Faithful trusts him. I don't see much alternative if Williams doesn't show up soon. I was just going to send Billy to his lodgings to check on him."

"Well then, go ahead and ask if Tommy's willing to ride. I think he's still licensed." She tried to remember what had to be done to change jockeys at the last moment. "We'll have to improvise, but I don't intend to scratch. I'd ride Faithful myself, first."

Guaire snorted, touched the brim of his cap and crossed to where the hands waited. While Imogen watched, Billy dashed away on foot.

She headed back around toward the grandstand, clutching her hat to her head and holding up her skirt slightly with her other hand. She located Mr. Brown in the office below the grandstand and explained the situation. He noted the change of jockey with a raised eyebrow. "Your streak of bad luck is unusually persistent, Mrs. Hawkes."

Imogen couldn't help but agree. "I'm afraid so, Mr. Brown."

"I'll take care of this." He dispatched a clerk off to the judge's stand. "And best of luck to you today, Mrs. Hawkes."

Imogen thanked him and headed around to one of the many stairwells on the front of the grandstand, thinking she'd probably worn off the little heels on her boots. Currently in the interval between the second and third races, the crowds milled about. Imogen climbed the steps into the grandstand with its rows of small tables and bentwood chairs. She found her mother-in-law on the upper level talking with Mrs. Sanderson, the wife of a racing association member.

"Since we missed the morning exercises," Mother Hawkes said as Imogen sat in an empty seat, "people are already muttering about a scratch."

"I suppose it will inflate our odds." Imogen explained about the missing jockey.

Mrs. Sanderson gave Imogen a concerned look. "And Williams hasn't contacted you at all? Bother. He's scheduled to ride one of our horses next Saturday."

Imogen set her handbag in her lap and untangled the ties from around her gloved wrist. "I've sent one of my hands to check at his lodgings, but I thought it unlike him."

"Most unusual," the woman agreed into her lace-edged handkerchief. "Now, you must tell me about this affair with your trainer."

Imogen looked up, hoping her expression stayed neutral. She didn't know how the woman could possibly have heard about her and Guaire. Surely Mother Hawkes hadn't told her.

"I hear that Mr. O'Donnell has a broken leg," Mrs. Sanderson prompted.

"Oh, yes," Imogen managed, and launched into a brief explanation of the incident, which garnered several startled exclamations.

"A true shame." The woman patted her on the knee, and added, "I must say, dear, you're looking lovely today."

Imogen felt her cheeks go warm, but managed to mumble her thanks. She finally extricated herself and dragged Mother Hawkes back to the lower level of the grandstand. People had already started to move in that direction, the men heading down toward the rail while most of the womenfolk remained under the grandstand's canopy. Imogen ducked under an unnecessary parasol and dodged around an overlarge hat, finally managing to find them seats with a decent view of the finish line.

She leaned to one side to see where the trainers and handlers waited. Billy stood there, evidently having returned from Mr. Williams lodgings, but she couldn't see Tommy or Guaire at all, so she turned to look at the starting line. The horses hadn't been led out yet.

That was when she discovered that William Hammersly hadn't gone to the rails with the other men. He sat down in the bentwood chair next to Imogen's, and she barely kept herself from groaning aloud. Given their encounters over the last week, she expected he'd come prepared to gloat when she lost. She ground her teeth together and reminded herself to be polite.

On the other side of her, Mother Hawkes leaned close to whisper, "Don't *do* anything to him, girl, not on track-owned land. The racing association wouldn't be pleased."

Imogen nodded. She'd managed to master the unbuttoning of buttons the day before, and the graceless removal of gingerbread trim, but not anything more. She didn't know what she *could* do to him, no matter how tempting the thought.

"Mrs. Hawkes, how nice to see you here." Hammersly nodded toward Mother Hawkes and added, "And you, as well, Mrs. Hawkes."

Imogen was determined to smile for his benefit... but couldn't bring herself to be that friendly. "Mr. Hammersly. I understand your horse didn't do as well as hoped in the second race. So sorry."

He inclined his head in acknowledgement; a sixth-place finish wasn't something to crow over. "I've been trying out a new jockey. A mistake, it seems."

Imogen suspected that jockey would be riding for someone else next week. "Well, I'm expecting good results today."

"Even with Sanford's horse out of the running, your horse will have some stiff competition from McCarran's Voorhees." Hammersly gave her a patronizing smile. "But you're only running your second choice colt, aren't you? Too bad."

Anger burned at the edges of her awareness, but Imogen didn't let it loose. "He has rather long odds, I'm afraid."

"Twenty to one, isn't it? And I understand your new trainer didn't get him here in time for morning exercises. As I said, you really shouldn't hire Irish."

Imogen resettled her feathered hat on her head, wondering into which of his body parts she might jab her hat-pin. Surely the racing association couldn't censure her for that. She turned back to him wide-eyed, and said, "He's satisfied me so far, Mr. Hammersly."

Hammersly's eyes narrowed.

Mother Hawkes choked on something. Imogen turned to her and asked, "Are you all right, Mother Hawkes?"

"Too much soda in this," the older woman gasped. She pulled a handkerchief out of her sleeve and coughed into it. After a moment she recovered her composure, waving the handkerchief in front of her face as if to cool herself. "I would have to say that the younger Mr. O'Donnell certainly knows his horses, Hammersly. No faulting him on that score."

Imogen shifted back toward him, trying to look innocent.

"He seems rough-mannered to me," Hammersly said. "Breeding does come out in the end."

Unable to hold it in any longer, Imogen asked, "Did you know my father is Irish?"

That seemed to give Hammersly pause. "Your father?"

"Well, you apparently have such a dislike for the Irish that I thought you should be warned of my provenance."

"Is your father living?" he asked. "I understood that your mother was widowed, Mrs. Hawkes."

"It provided a simpler explanation as to why he didn't accompany us to America." Imogen suddenly had the strongest feeling that Hammersly wanted to move farther away from her. Everyone knew her mother came from a wealthy family, and was the daughter of an earl—an English earl. Learning that Imogen's other parent wasn't as noble must have sadly overset Hammersly's breeding program. For the first time since he'd approached, Imogen actually *did* feel the desire to smile. She turned her eyes toward the track to hide it.

At the starting line, the jockeys were walking the horses into place under the watch of the assistant starters. Dressed in the farm's blue-and-gold silks, Tommy perched up on Faithful's back. Imogen craned her neck to view the trainers and grooms congregated at the white rail and spotted Guaire slipping through the men to find a place. His head turned her direction and, for a second, she thought he looked directly at her. Then he turned back to watch the starting line.

The horses were lined up at the webbed starting barrier. Imogen laid one gloved hand to her breast, nerves suddenly making her stomach flutter. Mother Hawkes clutched her other hand. With a cry from the starter, the barrier sprang up, and the horses leapt into action.

The crowd cheered as the horses sped toward the end of the track. At first they bunched close together, but then two began to pull ahead of the pack—McCarran's Voorhees and Faithful.

Imogen jumped to her feet as they crossed the three furlong mark. The two horses had the field, with Voorhees on the inside as they headed around the curve. But Faithful kept pace with him, coming out with his nose slightly ahead.

Imogen clutched Mother Hawkes' hands as the two horses pounded out the distance, covering four furlongs, and then the fifth. And Faithful pulled a length ahead of Voorhees, crossing the finish line in a clear victory.

"He did it!" Imogen hugged Mother Hawkes, barely able to contain her excitement.

"Get down to the winner's circle, girl," the older woman snapped, barely audible over the voices calling congratulations around them. She wiped at one eye with a handkerchief and shoved Imogen in that direction.

Imogen excused her way through the press of bodies and chairs, slowed by the women who wanted to shake her hand. Then she flew down the grandstand's steps and dashed across the dirt to the rail, holding her skirt up to keep it from the dust. She finally spotted Guaire in the white-chalked winner's circle on the side of the track, holding Faithful's cheek strap.

Evidently someone recognized her, and the men parted to let Imogen through. Her hat came unpinned from her hair, and in her rush to get to Guaire, she just let it fall. When she got to the small circle, she threw her arms about Guaire's neck. "You did it!"

"Saints preserve us," he said, borrowing Paddy's favorite swear. "You do know how to smile."

She kissed Guaire's cheek and then turned to Tommy, who still perched atop Faithful's back. She patted his knee. "Well done, Tommy."

Tommy touched the brim of his cap and grinned. "Thank you, ma'am."

The head of the racing association came over and drew her to Faithful's head to shake her hand. "Congratulations, Mrs. Hawkes. After all that's happened the last week, I'm pleased your horse came out ahead. Congratulations."

Then it was Sanford, and then McCarran, and others after that, all shaking her gloved hand and drawing her farther away from the horse. Imogen looked back, trying to spot Guaire. He waved her on and started leading Faithful toward the paddock to cool him down.

Imogen felt overwhelmed by the noise and attention. Fortunately, Mother Hawkes appeared at her elbow and began whispering instructions: whom to thank, and what to say, and where to sign. The afternoon blurred into a hazy dream.

At least they beat the sunset. Imogen checked the traces as Mother Hawkes paid the boy who'd been guarding the buggy and climbed up. She would have liked to try to find Guaire, but they had promised to get word back to Paddy.

"What were you thinking, girl?" Mother Hawkes asked once Imogen had gotten the buggy onto the road and headed back toward the farm. "You as much as admitted to that man that you're a bastard."

Imogen glanced over at her mother-in-law. "I didn't really think about it. He irritated me, Mother."

"Well, don't think that Hammersly isn't spreading rumors about your mother far and wide already. I'm all for you showing spirit, Imogen, but honestly..." She folded her arms over her chest and smiled tightly, "Although it was precious to see him looking like he'd swallowed a frog."

Imogen lifted her chin and snapped the reins. The horse broke into a trot. "I don't care. I've spent too much time worrying about Hammersly. When the bank opens on Monday, the very first thing I'm going to do is pay down the mortgage and get the Trust out of our collective hair."

Mother Hawkes shook her head. "You didn't get a chance to talk to Billy, did you?"

"Billy?"

"One of your hands. Handsome young fellow, dark hair? You sent him to go find out what happened to Williams."

"Oh." She'd completely forgotten about the missing jockey in the hubbub. "What did Billy say?"

"He found the man in his apartment with a leg broken."

Imogen gasped.

"Williams had been talking at the Blue Dove last night about how good Faithful's times were," Mother Hawkes said, "and this morning, he fell down his stairs. Suspicious, but possibly a coincidence."

Imogen drew the horse to a stop. "That's my fault, isn't it?"

"No. Of course it's not your fault. Just a further indication of how far Hammersly's willing to go, girl. I want you to keep that in mind. This business with Hammersly isn't over."

Imogen nodded. The man would still be her neighbor, even after she paid down the mortgage. "What can we do?"

"Send the young man some flowers, to start," Mother Hawkes said.

Imogen sighed and got the horse moving again. "I meant about Hammersly, Mother."

Mother Hawkes sat back. "There's nothing for you to do, other than to be watchful."

Imogen pressed her lips together. "Perhaps we shouldn't leave Faithful in town overnight."

"Your trainer is there to keep an eye on the horse. Trust him."

Imogen got a mental image of Guaire in his fine new clothes sleeping in the hay at Faithful's feet, and one corner of her mouth tugged upward. Unfortunately, it also meant she would be alone.

A rustling noise woke Imogen some time after dark. Light from the full moon streamed through the windows. She sat up in her chair and decided that the sounds were coming from the dressing room. It wouldn't be Guaire, not with him back in town. She hefted the book in her hand, decided it was better than no weapon at all, and headed toward the door of the dressing room, prepared to do battle.

When she yanked open the door, she found Mother Hawkes inside, hopping on one foot to tug on one of Henry's boots. Her mother-in-law cast a guilty glance at her. "Couldn't you have stayed asleep?"

"What are you doing, Mother?"

Mother Hawkes stamped the boot on the floor, probably waking Paddy down on the first floor below. "Well, you didn't expect me to stay here and miss all the excitement, did you?"

"I rather thought you might get some sleep." Imogen noted that the older woman had dressed in a dark habit, and went to grab up her darkest twill skirt. "So, where are we going?"

Mother Hawkes gave an exasperated sigh and threw up her hands. "Oh, very well. I suppose you'll have to come, too. But be quiet. We don't want to wake Patrick. He'll fret."

Imogen thought it was far too late for that. Half an hour later they were in the buggy, headed back toward town. Imogen felt guilty for taking a horse out to risk the roads in the dark, but there was too much at stake. At least the full moon provided some light. "Why did we go back to the farm in the first place?"

"Patrick wouldn't approve of my getting involved," Mother Hawkes said in a prim voice.

Imogen gave her a dry look, hopefully visible in the moonlight.

"And besides, I wanted Hammersly to see us driving home," Mother Hawkes added in a reasonable voice. "We passed that automobile of his near the track entrance. I want him and that little weasel of a driver of his to think we left Guaire back at the stables alone with Faithful. Too easy for him to pass up."

"Easy?"

Mother Hawkes wore a feral smile. "A chance to get a hold of your winning horse, and perhaps get rid of Guaire at the same time."

Imogen nearly dropped the reins. "What?"

"While you were running down to the winner's circle, girl, I was keeping an eye on Hammersly. You didn't even remember he was there once the race started, did you?"

Imogen grasped the reins more tightly as the buggy bounced out of a rut in the road. She searched her memory, but came up with nothing of Hammersly for that time. "Uh, no. What was he doing?"

"Watching you, girl. He expected you to be groveling by the end of that race, and judging by the look on his face, he didn't enjoy discovering that you weren't going to be. He's not the sort who likes losing."

Imogen got the horse back onto firmer ground, the roads better now that they'd reached the edge of town. "So why take it out on Guaire?"

Mother Hawkes sighed gustily and then pointed. "Don't go up to Broadway. Take East."

Imogen tugged on the reins and the buggy swung sharply onto East Avenue, a short-cut to the track. "And?"

"You kissed your trainer in front of a couple of thousand people this afternoon, girl, making it perfectly clear which man you prefer. Hammersly isn't the sort who likes to lose, and he's lost all the way around. All that's left is revenge."

Imogen snapped the reins, urging the horse to hurry. She drove the buggy right through the entry to the track and, on Mother Hawkes' instructions, stopped near the end of the stables where the horse vans usually drove in.

In the avenue of stables, the moonlight glowed over the long rows of white stalls, the trees between each row casting occasional spots of shadow. Faithful's stall was near the middle of the second row, so they slipped in that direction, using the trees to escape the notice of those grooms who'd remained behind with their charges. Imogen caught sight of Faithful's stall just as she heard a loud cry.

The stall door burst outward. A horse bolted forth with a rider clinging to his bare back. The dark horse spun, galloped to the other end of the stalls, and disappeared out the main gate.

"Was that...?" Mother Hawkes asked.

"Hammersly's driver? Yes, I believe so."

"No, I meant Mr. O'Donnell," Mother Hawkes said. "I've never seen him like that."

Before Imogen could reply, Billy climbed up on the door of the next stall over and looked down at them with startled eyes. "What happened?"

Imogen didn't know how to answer that. "What are you doing in there, Billy?"

"Got Faithful in here, ma'am," he said. "Track steward said we could use this empty stall."

Imogen cast a glance down at the stall door from which the other horse had erupted, the "Hawk's Folly Farm" tag clearly visible. "And someone thought Faithful was in this one."

Imogen saw that the stall wasn't completely empty. She peered around the open door and spotted Hammersly lying unmoving in the straw, apparently unconscious. Mother Hawkes joined her, holding up a lamp to illuminate the scene. A silvery length of rope lay next to Hammersly in the straw. Imogen bent down to pick it up, but when she reached out her hand, she felt an odd revulsion, and stepped back.

"What is that?" Imogen asked.

"Charmed to bind its wearer. Anyone would have to obey, animal or man," Mother Hawkes said. "Once they got it over his head, that is. Leave it alone, girl. Wait for the track personnel to get here."

"Exactly so, Mrs. Hawkes." Mr. Brown stood at the end of the stable block, a lantern in his hand. "We'll handle this from here."

"Mr. Hammersly appears to be injured," Imogen said, her conscience getting the better of her.

"We heard," Brown said. "Will that horse of yours return the other miscreant to us?"

Imogen cast a questioning glance at Mother Hawkes. She had no idea if Mr. Brown knew Guaire wasn't a horse. Her mother-in-law just shrugged. "I believe..."

Imogen was saved from answering by the sound of a horse snorting, followed by a cry for help. The steward dashed down the row of stalls, and Imogen followed. Beneath the trees, the horse waited for them. He reared, and his hooves came down only inches from the bedraggled figure of Hammersly's driver. Sodden and mud-covered, the young man had evidently been dragged through the track pond.

The steward carried his lantern over to get a better look, Mother Hawkes following. Imogen stayed under the eaves of the stable, uncertain whether she'd be in the way. Another man emerged from the shadows, carrying a lantern, and then a third. Imogen recognized the track supervisor, and one of the valets—employees of the racing association. They all gathered around the sodden figure slumped on the ground.

She gathered her nerve to go out there to where Guaire stood sentry over his prisoner, and something snapped about her neck.

"Be silent," Hammersly said in her ear—clearly not as incapacitated as he'd appeared. "Be still."

Imogen tried to reach the rope held about her neck. She tried to yell, to get the men's attention, or Mother Hawkes'. Nothing happened. Her hands wouldn't move; her voice didn't come.

"Walk back along the stables."

Imogen's feet followed his whispered instructions, and she divined that he must be taking her out to where his automobile waited. She walked with him past stall after stall, one of his hands on the back of her neck. Her earlier fury with the man swelled through her, but she couldn't seem to *do* anything.

"So this thing is worth what I paid for it," Hammersly said with a low chuckle. "I'm pleased that one of Sebastian's little nasty tricks actually works on you. I could make you do anything, couldn't I?"

Imogen had no idea how long it would take the others to notice she'd gone missing. The rope about her neck wasn't choking her, but Imogen could feel a binding woven throughout it that would force her compliance. Hoping the stable floor was even, she closed her eyes as she walked. In her mind she could see that rope she'd held in her hands a couple of days before. She pictured it unraveling, letting all its magic seep out as it did so...

She heard hooves behind them, and a horse snorted loudly. Hammersly jerked her around to face the opposite direction. Imogen opened her eyes, losing her concentration. Hammersly dragged her about so she was in front of him and tightened the rope around her neck. "And what is this?"

The dark horse reared up, his hooves flailing in the air.

Hammersly kept Imogen in front of him. "Now, you don't want to hurt her," he said as if he knew he faced something that understood English.

Guaire came down to four feet with a grunt. Imogen prayed that Hammersly didn't have a gun. He would surely put a bullet in Guaire if he had the chance.

"I wonder," Hammersly said, "would you trade yourself for her?"

He had to know it was Guaire. Guaire shook his mane and came a step closer, and then slowly lowered his head.

Imogen wanted to fight, but the rope held her in place as Hammersly said, "I suspect I can sell you for a fortune."

And he could, Imogen knew. Guaire had spent a decade passing from one stable to the next, earning them purses on his abused hooves. She wasn't going to let that happen to him again. She closed her eyes and gathered every scrap of anger that Hammersly had ever inspired in her and focused it on the rope that circled her neck. As if in the distance, she heard voices yelling, a horse snorting, hooves hitting the ground.

The image in her mind slipped and twisted like the rope had a life of its own. She forced it back under her control and pictured herself unraveling the rope. An inch, then two, and then the rope began to unravel faster and faster, magic bleeding away from the strands almost like steam rising off a lake.

Imogen stepped away from Hammersly, the separated strands of rope draped about her neck. His hand brushed her jacket, but she slipped out of his grasp.

She looked about her then. The track supervisor held a gun in his hand, and Mr. Brown now held another at Hammersly's side. "Well done, Mrs. Hawkes. May we have that?"

Imogen lifted the ruined rope over her head and handed it over. Brown pocketed his gun and used the separated pieces of rope to bind Hammersly's hands.

Imogen didn't spare them another glance. She crossed to Guaire's side and put her arms around his neck. He was wet, and she could smell mud on him. She felt him shudder. "Calm down," she whispered into his ear. "Please. They'll take care of him."

He snorted, but then set his muzzle against her sternum, much as he had that first day.

"Leave the buttons alone," she reminded him.

The valet and the track supervisor began walking Hammersly back toward the stables. The steward came over to Imogen. "Mrs. Hawkes, one of my men was in the stables and witnessed Mr. Sebastian Wells attempting to remove this horse from a stall rented to you, using this piece of rope. Is this horse one of *your* horses?"

"Yes," she said. "This horse is mine."

"And his name is?" Another man with a small notebook stood there, pencil poised, like a constable taking a statement.

Imogen wondered in whose records this particular episode would appear. "Whirlwind."

"He isn't a Thoroughbred," Brown noted in a quieter voice. "You are aware that you can't race him here, aren't you?"

A subtle warning, Imogen decided. "I would never dream of doing so, Mr. Brown. I do understand the association's rules."

"Very good," he said. "That will be all then, Mrs. Hawkes."

More men with lanterns had emerged from the stables, some faces Imogen recognized and others not. They followed the steward and his prisoners back into the stable.

Imogen cast a glance at Mother Hawkes. "What will they do to him?"

"He can't claim ignorance of that bit with the rope about your neck," Mother Hawkes said, "so they'll make sure he doesn't pose a threat to anyone from now on."

"Will they send him to prison?"

"The gentlemen have other methods, girl. Now, get yourself home." Mother Hawkes folded her arms over her chest. "I'm going to stay for a bit. One of them can take me to the house in town. I'll see if someone can drive you back safely."

"The buggy," Imogen reminded her. "We can't just leave the horse there."

"Oh, I'll get Billy to take care of him." Mother Hawkes waved her hand. "I'll go get one of the gentlemen to escort you home, girl."

Guaire snorted, turned so that his side was to Imogen, and moved his nose in the direction of his back.

"I think I have an escort home, Mother," Imogen said softly.

"Hmm," Mother Hawkes said. "Stay out of the water, girl."

"I think that's kelpies anyway." Imogen climbed up on a mounting block and, after a moment of wrangling with her skirt, settled astride his back. Her legs dangled down, showing more black stocking that she was comfortable with, but in the moonlight she doubted anyone would notice. She wrapped her fingers into his mane and leaned forward to press her cheek against his coat. "I haven't done this since I was a child," she whispered.

He stepped slowly toward the main gate, and then took off. Imogen clung to his neck, but by the time he'd gained the road, she knew she didn't need to. His gait was smoother than any horse she'd ridden before. She felt almost like they were flying.

They sped down the road, past the edge of town, and out along Lake Road. Imogen's hair came loose from its pins and streamed out behind her, and she laughed in the moonlight.

Too soon they came to the turn in the road and Hawk's Folly lay below them. The horse took the fence smoothly and cut through the pasture to the stable yard. When he came to a halt, Imogen slid her leg over his back and dropped to the ground beside him.

She followed him to his stall, her hair still hanging loose, and stepped back from the blast of heat that came with his change. When he'd taken human form again, she threw her arms around his neck. "Thank you." His fingers toyed with her hair. "I do like to see you smile, Ginny."

She drew back. "And where are your new clothes?"

"Back at the stable in town," he said with a grin.

"You'll need to come upstairs to get some others."

He yawned dramatically. "Oh, I was thinking I might sleep in the stall tonight. It's well past midnight already, and I've had a long day."

Imogen pressed her lips together.

"Then again 'tis a bit chilly," he said with a grin, "so if you'd not mind..."

She took his hand. "I wouldn't mind at all."

Imogen woke late Sunday morning, well past noon. Guaire had headed back into town to escort Faithful home so, after eating a light lunch, Imogen passed a couple of hours in her dressing room, separating out the clothing she hated.

After paying down the mortgage and setting aside for taxes and a savings fund, there would still be money left over—enough to enter Faithful in the Hopeful Stakes in a couple of weeks, have the exterior of the house painted, and buy a few new dresses. Shopping for those would be her reward for enduring Hammersly's presence Monday morning.

"What are you doing, girl?" Mother Hawkes said, coming into the dressing room and giving Imogen a fright.

"Getting rid of Bella's ghost," she managed, after calming herself.

Mother Hawkes nodded. "About time." She gave Imogen a searching look, then. "So, have you heard anything from town? Anyone been out there?"

Imogen set one more dress on the pile. "No. Guaire went to the track to walk Faithful home, but he hasn't gotten back yet."

Mother Hawkes nodded. "Well, the news will get here sooner or later—Hammersly isn't going to be a problem anymore, not where he went."

Imogen frowned down at the pile of unwanted dresses. "Where he went?"

"I'm assuming hell, with that man." Mother Hawkes leaned back against the wall, looking rather pleased. "The board of the Trust hauled him in to meet with them over luncheon. Their internal investigation showed that he'd been using his position to take advantage of certain customers—a breach of ethics, at the least. So they relieved him of his position with the Trust, and informed him that criminal proceedings were in process as well."

Imogen gaped at her. "Is there going to be a trial?"

"No, Hammersly evaded that by having a fit of apoplexy on the steps of the hotel and dropping dead in the street."

Imogen laid one hand over her mouth. "Did the people at the racing association do something to him?"

"Suffice to say that one should never cross them," Mother Hawkes said. "Hammersly should have known better."

"I didn't like him," Imogen whispered, "but I didn't want something like that to happen."

"You are not responsible, Imogen, in any way," Mother Hawkes said firmly. "Now, I passed the younger Mr. O'Donnell and Faithful on the way back from town, almost at the fence. They should be here by now. Maybe you should go down and see that winning colt of yours. Take him a carrot, perhaps."

And Mother Hawkes swept out of the dressing room, leaving shocked silence in her wake. Imogen took a deep breath, and then another, and resolved to take care of her only remaining worry.

In the stable, she gave Faithful the carrot he very much deserved, but didn't find Guaire anywhere. She did find Tommy, however, compiling a list of inventory in the tack room. "Looking to see what needs to be replaced?"

He grinned. "Yes, ma'am. Oh, and Mr. O'Donnell's gone out to look at that fence."

She didn't ask how he knew she was looking for Guaire. "I'll go talk to him then."

"Want me to saddle up Captain, ma'am?"

"No, it's not that far. I can walk."

She hitched up her skirt and began the trek down the west meadow toward that burned tract of land. Guaire waited there, scowling at the fence. Shoots of grass and delicate vines had already begun to grow among the felled trunks of blackened trees. The acrid scent of the ashes was gone, replaced by the freshness of the stream and the damp earth. The breeze plucked at Guaire's dark hair and worn shirt, making him look a bit disheveled, but Imogen preferred the sight of him over any man she'd ever met. "Are you planning to jump the fence?" she asked, only half joking.

"This won't last," he said, turning to face her with a serious look on his face. "If there's a bit of money left over, we might use it to fix this up properly. It needs to be done before the spring rains come, by someone who can handle nails."

"That's a long way off," she said, reflecting how novel it was to have spare money to plan with. "But the Hopeful Stakes is coming up in two weeks. We need to prepare for that. Could you get Faithful ready to run six furlongs? The purse would be a good one."

He came over to where she waited, brushing dirt from the knees of his trousers. "We can start training at that distance, if you want."

She took a shaky breath and asked, "Were you thinking of staying until spring?"

His expression seemed hesitant. "That depends, darling. You said you wanted me to stay at least until the race was over. What did you mean by *at least*?"

Imogen stared at him, realizing then that he was more nervous than she.

He didn't know if she wanted him to stay—she had never given him permission to do so.

She'd always assumed he had the upper hand in their relationship, more experience in the world and more control over his life. But she'd been wrong all along. He had no family in America, no safe haven. In worldly terms, he had nothing to offer her. He hadn't even possessed a stitch of clothing when he'd arrived at her farm.

She recalled the worried expression he'd worn when he'd spoken to her about her relationship with her mother, one that seemed now to say he'd feared being sent away. He'd done so anyway, though, risking her ire and his only shelter to tell her something she'd needed to hear.

Imogen met his worried eyes. "Guaire, I release you from any obligation to this farm or to me. You owe me nothing."

His brows drew together, but he didn't say anything.

"You asked what I meant by *at least*," she said then. "I meant you're welcome to come and go here as you please until the day you die. I'd like you to consider this your home."

A smile spread across his face like the sun coming out on a cloudy day. "I've not had a home in nearly thirty years," he said. "I'll not leave, Ginny, not unless you ask me to."

She felt a giddy sense of relief. "Oh, heavens, I'm glad to hear that."

He came closer. "You know, I've read the words in Paddy's book, and I'm fair certain I'd be able to say them without my tongue turning to ash in my mouth."

Imogen regarded him with a furrowed brow. "The words?"

"Ah," he said. "You know, to have and to hold, from this day forward, and all that. I'm sure I can say those vows."

Imogen touched his sleeve. "They would bind you, Guaire. Are you not afraid of that?"

"With you? No." He leaned close to kiss her, then, but was interrupted by the faint sound of cheering.

Imogen drew back, and then glanced toward the stable yard where she saw the hands congregated at the fence, apparently watching them. Guaire must not have been hiding them from view. She felt her cheeks flush. "Oh, dear."

Guaire just laughed and offered his hand, and together they started back toward the stables. "So," he said in a musing tone, "what would you offer me for training your horse?"

"One night?" Imogen offered, and then amended it. "One night for each day you stay."

"A deal, then?" he said. "Although I can't promise no one will know."

"A deal, then." And since she had no intention of backing down, Imogen put her arms around his neck and kissed him. The hands could think whatever they wanted.

Breinigsville, PA USA
17 May 2010
238077BV00001B/2/P